The critics on

'A great romp .

'Gibson's eye for comedy is keen, especially her satirical take on the thorny "coming out to the parents" debate' *Gay Times*

'Gibson has written a series of unputdownable thrillers . . . [she has] cornered the market in tooth-and-claw business practice salted with romance . . . The important thing is the story, and this just keeps rocketing on from climax to farcical climax' *Books Ireland*

'Gibson has a rare insight into what it's like to be caught in matrimonial misery' *Ireland on Sunday*

'In a tale of deception, confusion and danger Maggie Gibson draws on her own experience of growing up, marriage and divorce to create a comical story that leaves you wanting more'
Birmingham Post

'For anyone who wants a light-hearted, comical read, this novel will be a joy' *South London Press*

Maggie Gibson lives in the west of Ireland with her dog.

Also by Maggie Gibson

Deadly Serious
The Longest Fraud
Grace, the Hooker, the Hardman and the Kid
The Flight of Lucy Spoon
Alice Little and the Big Girl's Blouse

First Holy Chameleon

Maggie Gibson

ORION

An Orion paperback

First published in Great Britain
by Victor Gollancz in 2000
This paperback edition published in 2001
by Orion Books Ltd,
Orion House, 5 Upper St Martin's Lane,
London WC2H 9EA

A CIP catalogue record for this book
is available from the British Library.

ISBN: 0 57540 323 3

Typeset at The Spartan Press Ltd,
Lymington, Hants
Printed in Great Britain by
Clays Ltd, St Ives plc

For Jesse

With thanks to Katy Egan, Damien Carley, Martine Egan, Jesse Carley, Christine Kidney, Maggie Haughton and George Capel

Chapter One

'I think you're overreacting, Mizz Ryan.'

He was a pompous bastard, and Cash Ryan hated pompous bastards. Tall, with patrician features and the regulation dark three-piece suit, he stood beside his car, a shiny, new, low-slung, pseudo sports jobby with metallic paint. A regular mid-life-crisis-mobile. He peered at her over his glasses, which had slid halfway down the bridge of his nose.

'And what would you know about my life that would enable you to be the judge of that?' Cash's dander was up.

Pompous Bastard gave her a patronising smile, well, more of a sneer really. 'Mizz Ryan, as you are well aware, Donovan Development purchased this property at public auction over six months ago. I think, under the circumstances, Mr Donovan has been more than reasonable. You've had ample time to relocate your little project.'

'You know we can't afford anywhere else.' Cash was hoping to appeal to his better nature. Vain hope.

Pompous Bastard shuffled his papers. 'You have until next Tuesday, the end of the month, to remove all your belongings.'

'Or?'

Weary sigh. '*Or* they will be removed. Please, Mizz Ryan, don't make this any more difficult than it already is.'

'I'm not making it difficult. Niall bloody Donovan's the one who's making it difficult. The Theatre Workshop's a public amenity, for God's sake. You can't just close us down.'

'And Donovan Development intend to build housing here. Twenty families will live on this site, Mizz Ryan. Twenty families. Surely housing is more important than an amateur theatre school in this day and age?'

'Twenty apartments? You're building twenty bloody apartments here?'

Cash was flabbergasted. Twenty apartments at around two hundred and eighty grand a throw hardly qualified in her book as *housing*. Housing implied *public* housing, not the luxury end of the market.

There was no doubt about it, Templebar was going to the dogs. Since the early nineties, when the developers had moved in, rents had gone sky high. The spin that Templebar was full of trendy Bohemian arty types was a crock. All the Bohemian types were moving out because of the spiralling rents, to be replaced by upmarket galleries, restaurants and high-cost apartments.

What would happen to the Workshop now?

Cash Ryan couldn't take credit for the Strolling Players Theatre Workshop. That credit went to a formidable woman by the name of Verity Gregory.

Miss Gregory, a woman of good family and charitable by nature, at the age of fifty had founded the Strolling Players Theatre Workshop in an old grain store owned by her family, in Templebar, in 1958. The history of the Gregory family brewing business stretched well back into the seventeen hundreds, preceding Arthur Guinness by at least twenty years.

As an actress, despite her enthusiasm, Verity was no better than average. She did, however, have a substantial trust fund, so put it to good use by founding the

Workshop. The idea behind it was to give children, for a nominal fee, all day Saturdays and on Tuesday evenings, training in all the skills of speech, stagecraft, dance and drama.

Many of the great and the good of Ireland's Thespian community had had their first smell of the greasepaint in Miss Gregory's academy, as had Cash Ryan. She, and a number of her peers, repaid Miss Gregory by giving the Saturday and Tuesday evening drama and dance classes when otherwise unemployed.

Verity Gregory had succumbed to cancer the previous January at the age of ninety, and the executors of her estate had put her entire property portfolio up for auction not long afterwards.

Cash was surprised that Miss Gregory hadn't made provision for the Workshop as she had promised all those involved that she would make sure that it would carry on after her death.

It was said that Verity Gregory had died intestate. Cash found that hard to believe, too. Dotty though Miss Gregory had been, where money was concerned she was sharp as a needle. But the sad fact remained that no will was produced. And an even sadder fact was that the Strolling Players Theatre Workshop was homeless.

As was Cash.

Three years before, after vandals had broken in and trashed the place, Miss Gregory had suggested that Cash should move into the top floor to act as a sort of unpaid caretaker. This had suited Cash fine, as work had been thin on the ground at the time. It was only ever meant to be a temporary arrangement but, three years on, Cash Ryan was still enjoying the benefits of a rent-free loft in the centre of Dublin. At least she was until Pompous Bastard put his spoke in.

Pompous Bastard unlocked his car and crammed

himself behind the wheel. Cash stood on the pavement and stared down at him. For someone who looked so ridiculous, it was ironic that he should have the last laugh, so to speak.

'One week, Mizz Ryan,' he said, before gunning the engine and screeching away on the wet cobbles.

It was raining but Cash didn't care. She stood and watched as PB turned the corner into Fleet Street.

It had not been a good couple of weeks for Catherine Ann Ryan, thirty-one, resting actress and spinster of this parish. Her big break had fizzled out like a damp squib.

Maurice Foley, her agent, had been certain, despite the fact that she had been contracted for only six episodes, that her character, Fifi Mulligan (the cynical hooker whose hard exterior concealed beneath it a heart of gold), would become a regular in the Dublin-based TV soap, *Liffey Town*. And it would have. Cash played a blinder, but circumstances beyond her control came to bear.

Jimmy Hatton, the actor playing Fifi's pimp, had a disagreement with the producers and was written out.

When Cash heard this through the grapevine she wasn't unduly worried. Fifi had plenty of mileage left in her, with or without her brutish pimp.

Then she read her lines. Every soap actor's nightmare. The dreaded word 'dies' glared at her at the bottom of the last page of her thinner-than-usual script.

Fifi, it transpired, was to be a victim of Jimmy's falling-out with management. She was to be brutally murdered by the mild-mannered schoolteacher, Sean, acting completely out of character due to a brain tumour. She hadn't even made it to the ad break.

'Those are the fractures, kid.' (Maurice continually made these little plays on words. He thought they were

4

amusing.) He softened the blow. 'But you never know what's round the next corner.'

'How true. Who would have thought, as well as having the thrill of being dumped by the national TV station, I'd be evicted, too.'

She moaned about it to Mort that afternoon. Mort Higgins was the sole proprietor of M&J Investigations. The 'J' of the company name belonged to his estranged wife, Janet.

Mort, an ex-Garda sergeant, had resigned from the force six years before, on health grounds (alcoholism), and after a spell of drying out he went into business for himself. Mort worked mainly alone, but employed off-duty cops on a freelance basis when the workload demanded.

Cash worked for him, also on a part-time basis, taking care of the secretarial work. It was a convenient arrangement all round. It allowed Cash to take any acting work, voice-overs, and so on that came along, and, as Mort didn't need a permanent secretary, it saved him having to put up with a never-ending line of uninterested temps.

'I don't know where the hell I'm going to live. Everywhere's so expensive now,' Cash whinged.

'Why can't you move in with Simon?' Mort asked.

Simon Moore was Cash's partner of three years. He was also an actor, and was at present out of the country filming a biblical TV mini-series in the Gobi desert, playing Judas Iscariot. He had been away for the past two months and, due to the remoteness of the location, she had heard little from him.

'He sublet his place when he went away,' Cash said forlornly. 'He's supposed to be moving in with me when he comes back.'

'You could always go home.'

Cash gave Mort a withering look.

'Why not? Your mother'd be only too pleased to have you.'

Cash's reluctance to run home in her present predicament was nothing to do with whether or not her mother would put out the welcoming mat – it was more to do with the fact that she held the strong conviction that anyone over twenty-five who lived at home was a sa-a-ad person.

She was also well aware that spending more than six consecutive hours in her mother's company would lead to homicide – or, more accurately, matricide.

This wasn't due to any lack of love she felt for her mother. In theory she loved her mother dearly. It was down to the two things that annoyed her most about Yvonne Ryan. Everything she said, and everything she did.

It was a two-way street.

Yvonne was acutely embarrassed and disappointed that Cash hadn't been more successful in her chosen profession. Famous even. In her youth, Yvonne's aspirations had leaned towards the theatre. In the beginning, when Cash had showed an interest in drama, Yvonne had hoped to fulfil those aspirations vicariously, but sadly Cash wasn't obliging in the fame department. Yvonne had had a rush of hope when her middle daughter landed a part in *Liffey Town*, only to have it dashed with Fifi's last on-screen gasp.

Cash hadn't had the courage to warn her mother about the demise of Fifi. Like everything else, including the problem of the grain-store sale, she hoped if she ignored the problem it would go away. Her only saving grace in her mother's eyes was Simon. It gave her heart that her middle daughter wasn't a complete failure. At least she had a man.

Mort's phone rang before he could offer any better suggestions, so Cash left him to it, and got on with transcribing the Dictaphone tapes that were lying on her in-tray.

When Cash had first started working for Mort she had been fascinated by the stuff on the dictation tapes. Illicit affairs, companies checking up on prospective executive employees, insider theft, bogus personal injury claims – a current trend was career-women checking into the background of prospective husbands. But now she hardly took any notice, and tapped out the information on her word processor, without even taking it in.

It took her most of the afternoon to catch up with the backlog, and by the end of the day she had typed up case notes and made hard-copy files for three cases Mort was currently working on. She also took care of half a dozen letters.

Just as she was putting her coat on to leave, the outer door of the office opened and a smartly dressed middle-aged woman walked in. Cash thought she looked familiar, but couldn't place her. The woman smiled uncertainly. She looked embarrassed to be there, and kept glancing over her shoulder as if afraid that someone was following her.

'Can I help you?' Cash asked.

The woman gave her a nervous smile. 'I'm here to see Mr Higgins. I have an appointment.'

Another philandering husband?

The inner office door opened at that point and Mort stuck his head out. 'Mrs Porter?'

Cash had it. She was Eileen Porter. Cash had been in the same class as her daughter Holly in the Loretto College on St Stephen's Green. They'd been quite friendly and only lost touch when Holly went on to study medicine at UCG.

The woman nodded. 'Mr Higgins?'

Mort opened his office door wide. 'Please, don't be nervous, come in.' Then to Cash he mouthed the word 'coffee' and raised his eyebrows in a question. Cash nodded and filled the kettle. Mort and Mrs Porter disappeared into the inner office.

After she had brought in the coffee, Cash finished work for the day and went home, leaving Mort and Eileen Porter discussing whatever problem it was that Eileen had brought along.

She was tempted to stop in at the Palace for some strong drink to lift her spirits, but in the end couldn't be bothered. There were bound to be people there she knew, and she didn't feel like being sociable. Instead she went straight on home to Templebar and veg'd out on the sofa, watching TV, eating chocolate and generally ignoring her problems in the hope that they would go away.

Chapter Two

Due to a strike by the maintenance men, the lift was still out of order. Sister Jude sighed. It had been six weeks now and repeated calls to Dublin Corporation had proved futile.

Phrases such as 'out of our hands' and 'beyond our control' and 'if it were only up to me' were no consolation. The fact remained that a number of less mobile residents had been marooned in their homes since the second lift had broken down four weeks previously. It was all too bad.

She rearranged the shopping carriers so that the thin plastic handles cut a little less into the palms of her hands and headed for the stairs, mentally girding her loins for the climb.

By the time she reached the fifth floor her breathing was laboured. She stopped and put down her bags, giving herself time to catch her breath.

At the age of fifty-one, Sister Jude was becoming increasingly irritated by her body and the way it failed to co-operate with her these days. She had never had any problem with the stairs before this. In fact, the twice-daily climb over the past six weeks should have resulted in an improved state of fitness, not the opposite. Maybe I'm just tired, she thought. Maybe that's it.

She sighed impatiently, picked up her bags and offered it up for the holy souls. It occurred to her, as she stood back against the wall to avoid three kids who were tearing down the stairs full pelt, that maybe there was no such thing as a holy soul any more. Had purgatory been abolished at the same time as limbo? On second thoughts, what did it matter anyway?

A voice bellowed down the stairs. 'Get back up here, ye little fuckers!'

Sister Jude continued to climb.

'I said get back here, ye little bastards, or I'll beat the shite outta ye . . . Oh . . . sorry, Sister.'

'Don't worry about it, Mrs McKenna.'

On the eighth landing, Sister Jude sagged with relief and gratefully covered the last couple of metres to her door. The flat was in darkness. The girls weren't back yet.

She unpacked the shopping and filled the kettle. That's what she needed. A caffeine shot. That would liven her up.

Those not personally acquainted with Sister Jude would have difficulty in putting an age on her, but they would be in no doubt of her calling. She was tall, but carried the extra half-stone that middle age had slapped on her hips well. Statuesque some might describe her, if she didn't look so dowdy. But, then, nuns were hardly expected to be fashionable.

She wore her grey hair straight and short, and usually favoured the same navy polyester trousers or pleated skirt, with a white polo-neck and navy cardigan or V-necked sweater. Her only adornment was a chunky silver cross on the long chair she always wore around her neck.

Hard to imagine that she was once a child of the sixties. Had done the sex, drugs and rock and roll thing. Had slept with Brian Jones. She had never been a holy Joe. A cruel twist of fate had given her a late vocation.

The kettle boiled and she made a pot of strong coffee, one of her few indulgences – along with one secret pack of Benson & Hedges a week – and sat down at the kitchen table.

She *was* tired. Weary. Not surprising. Since Omagh she'd been having the dreams again and she was sleeping badly because of it. Almost afraid to close her eyes. After twenty-five years the images were as vivid as ever. Broken bodies, torn limbs. Scorched air, burning flesh. And the screaming. The moaning.

Unconsciously she rubbed her arm where the shrapnel had torn a small chunk of flesh away from the bone. The flesh had healed long ago. She had thought she was over it until Omagh had brought it all back.

She heard the front door open and a moment later Sandra strolled into the kitchen.

'What's for the tea?'

'I'm fine, thanks, Sandra. And how was your day?'

Sandra leaned against the door frame. 'Okay, I s'pose. Except for tha' spa Mr Moran. He hasn't a clue, wha'?'

Sandra was thirteen going on thirty. She had been placed in Sister Jude's care by the Eastern Health Board. It was felt that, as Sandra had repeatedly absconded from children's homes, a less structured place of care was preferable. After a difficult and traumatic start, it seemed to be working out.

Sister Jude had been caring for troubled youngsters for the past eight years. It had started by accident when she took in one of her pupils, Paula, who had turned up on her doorstep one night soaking wet and distressed, having been badly beaten by her stepfather and thrown out into the street in her nightdress.

Paula had stayed three years. Others followed. Some more successfully than others.

At the present time, as well as Sandra, she had the

care of Tiffany, fourteen, and seven and a half months pregnant as the result of sexual abuse by her uncle.

Of the two, Sandra was the easier. Although she could be sullen and at times cheeky, at heart she was a good-natured kid.

Tiffany, on the other hand, was unpredictable and prone to temper tantrums. Not surprising under the circumstances. Allowances had to be made to a degree. Time would tell.

Sister Jude tried as far as it was possible to run a domestic democracy. She felt it was good training for the youngsters, all of whom had come from dysfunctional backgrounds and had no understanding of any alternative way of solving problems other than by means of confrontation and violence.

Sometimes, when there would be an incident, she wondered if she was kidding herself that she could make a difference. But on balance she'd had more successes than failures. She felt, on her better days, that she *had* made a difference. On her not-so-better days she just hoped so.

Sandra slumped down at the table. She was a lumpy ungainly girl, prone to greasy hair and spots. 'Where's Tiff?'

'She had an appointment with her social worker.' Sister Jude refilled her coffee mug. 'She should be back soon. Have you homework to finish?'

Sandra nodded. 'A bit. I can do it tomorra.'

Sister Jude smiled. 'Don't forget my essay. It's supposed to be in by Monday. Why don't you go and get started while I get the tea ready, then you'll be free for the day tomorrow?'

Sandra gave an exaggerated sigh and heaved herself up from the table. It was all show, of course. She was exceptionally gifted at English, despite coming from a family whose vocabulary barely included anything other than the most basic of Anglo-Saxon expletives. 'Can I watch *Home an' Away*?'

'I'll call you when it's time.'

By seven-thirty, when *Coronation Street* came on and Tiffany still hadn't put in an appearance, Sister Jude began to get anxious.

'Chill ou', Sister.' Sandra tried to make light of it. 'She'll be back. Where else has she t' go?'

'Did she say anything to you? Did she say she had plans?'

Sandra shrugged. 'Dunno.'

The next moment the door flew open and Tiffany breezed in. Sister Jude's first instinct was to demand an explanation. She opened her mouth to speak, but something stopped her. Later, on reflection, she realised it was the look of utter joy on the young girl's face. She was glowing.

'Sorry I'm late. I met these really cool people. Is there any tea left?'

Chapter Three

'Well, it could be worse,' Billie said into her drink.

'How? I've lost the best frigging job I've had in ages and I'm about to be homeless.'

'At least you went out in a blaze of glory . . . It's not every day a girl gets battered to death and lives to tell the tale . . . heh-heh-heh.'

Cash signalled to the barman for a refill. 'Very droll. Excuse me if I'm not busting my sides.'

'Aw, chill out, Cash. You'll get somethin' else. Somethin' better. Yer big break's probably round the next corner. Maybe the TV commercial'll do the trick next week.'

'Now you sound like Maurice.'

They were sitting in Pravda drinking shots of vodka. Cash was trying her hardest to get drunk. Oblivion seemed like the only solution, but her brain wasn't paying attention. Eight shots in quick succession and she was still as sober as a judge.

Billie had a theory. Something to do with mood. Something to do with chemicals in the brain counteracting the effects of the alcohol. Cash had never listened properly, but it occurred to her as she sat, rock solid, on her bar stool, that perhaps there was something in it after all. She knocked back another vodka, to test the theory further.

Billie held up four fingers to the barman, indicating

she wanted four more shots. It was getting near to closing time.

'I hope my mother's forgotten about it. I don't think I can handle her disappointment again *this* Sunday. Jesus! You'd think it was my fault.'

Billie was astonished. Cash usually limited her visits home to once a month, on the basis that it took her that long to calm down enough to be able to communicate with her mother without fear of losing her rag. To Billie's knowledge, Cash had made the pilgrimage only the previous Sunday. 'You're goin' home?'

'Only for lunch . . . It's Justine's birthday. I don't suppose you'd like to come along?'

Billie cocked an eyebrow. 'Do I *look* like a feckin' masochist?'

The barman lined up the shots on the bar. They knocked them back. Cash's second went down the wrong way and she took a fit of coughing. Billie thumped her on the back and the barman gave her a pitying look and slid a jug of water over to her.

They sat in silence for a while, then Billie said, 'So aren't you goin' to ask me how I got on?' She wasn't in as good a shape as Cash and was lolling over the bar now. It was the last shot that had done the damage.

'How you got on?' It took a couple of moments for the words to register. 'Oh, yes . . . Sorry. How did it go?'

Billie shrugged. 'Okay, I suppose. Maurice's lettin' me know.'

Billy ran her hands through her hair, resting her elbows on the bar. She was peering, unfocused, at her reflection in the mirror on the wall behind the bar. The fatal last shot had plummeted her mood towards maudlin. 'What d'you see when you look at me?' she asked.

Cash grinned. 'I see Billie Trueman . . . No . . . I see a thin Heather Small.'

'No, you don't. You see a friggin' loser.'

Tears were running down Billie's cheeks now. It wasn't like her, she was usually so upbeat. In her determined quest for oblivion, it had slipped Cash's mind that excessive amounts of vodka always made Billie depressed.

Billie climbed unsteadily down off her bar stool. 'I have t' pee.'

Cash made a move to accompany her, but Billie shook her head and waved her arms about with the exaggerated movements of the very drunk. She watched her friend weaving an unsteady path towards the toilets. Though totally twisted, Billie managed to display the consummate grace of a dancer as she manoeuvred her way through the crowd.

She was a stunning-looking woman. Tall, slender and exotic. The product of a Jamaican father and an Irish mother. Billie's baggy combats, trainers and a tatty sweatshirt didn't inhibit heads from turning.

Cash ordered another round.

Billy returned a few minutes later looking less grey in the face. She slid back on to her stool. 'Nothing like a good barf to make you feel better,' she said.

'You okay?' Cash asked, concerned.

'Gettin' there. D'you fancy a take-away?'

'Not till we've had another round.'

They stopped at Beshoff's for chips and walked down O'Connell Street eating them out of the bag. Billie had sobered up a bit and was quite steady on her feet by the time they finished the chips. She was also in a better humour.

It was something Cash envied Billie for. However down she was, it was never for long. She seemed capable of shaking her demons off on demand. But, then, she'd had lots of practice with demons.

Town was still busy even though it was well past closing time. Rat-arsed stag-parties and more normal human beings, hanging around trying to make up their minds what to do next.

Billie's bus went from O'Connell Street so Cash waited with her at the bus stop.

'What are you goin' to do for a place to stay?' Billie asked as they joined the queue. 'You're not considerin' home, are you?'

'Do I *look* like a masochist?'

That raised a laugh from Billie. 'If the cap fits.'

'Piss off. I'll look for somewhere . . . anywhere.'

'Well, the thing is,' Billie said, 'you could always crash on my couch if yer really stuck.'

'Great. Are you sure?'

'It'd only be temporary, till you find somewheres else. The place is cramped at the best of times,' Billie cautioned.

Relief. It was a reprieve from the most awful scenario of moving back home. 'Of course. Only temporary,' Cash agreed.

Billie's bus, a number eleven, turned up at that point, followed closely by two others – isn't it always the way? – so Cash waved her off and headed back to the loft, still as sober as a judge. Rats!

The only flaw in Billie's theory about the effects of alcohol on certain chemicals in the brain was that, although Cash had been unable to enjoy the effects of any alcohol-induced buzz/euphoria/oblivion, her liver remained unaware of the theory, and she awoke the next morning – Saturday – with the mother of all hangovers.

She crawled out of bed and staggered to the loo where

17

she proceeded to spend a pleasant half-hour of dry-retching over the toilet bowl, moaning, 'Never again, never again.' (It is a well-documented fact amongst her contemporaries that Cash Ryan is physically incapable of vomiting.)

Feeling no better, she splashed her face with water and peered at herself in the mirror through bloodshot eyes.

Two Solpadine and a couple of litres of Volvic followed, and by the time Billie arrived at ten o'clock she felt slightly better.

Billie was sickeningly cheerful. She plonked a huge bag of chocolate croissants and an industrial-sized bar of Dairy Milk on the table and took off her coat. She was wearing her dance gear underneath. 'Any coffee goin'?' (Billie had had the foresight to do the water and Solpadine thing before she went to bed the previous night.)

Cash made vague gestures towards the cooker.

Billie made coffee and tucked into the croissants. 'Aren't you havin' any?'

Cash winced. 'Do you have to be so fucking cheerful?'

'Come on. Chocolate's good for a hangover. The best. It releases endorphins or serotonin or somethin' in the brain . . . trust me.' She broke off a slab of Dairy Milk and proffered it.

Cash took the chocolate. 'Is this another of your theories?'

'No, it's a fact. I've done experiments.' Billie took another chomp of croissant, then gave a wicked smile. 'Oh, by the way. Maurice called me on me mobile. He got me the feckin' cruise.'

'The cruise?'

'Yeah. I tried out yesterday, remember? And while

you're freezin' your arse off at Christmas, I'll be sunnin' meself in the Caribbean. What d'you think?'

'I hate you.'

Billie grinned. 'Bein' as you're about t' be feckin' homeless, shouldn't you be packin' your stuff?'

Cash attempted to nod, but only managed one as her brain rattled round the inside of her skull. 'Piss off. Plenty of time,' she croaked, then coughed in a manner that a docker on sixty a day would be proud of.

The first notes of Wham ('Wake me up before you go go') wafted up from the floor below. Billie looked at her watch. 'Shit! I've to give me class.'

She gathered her coat and bag in her arms and, croissant clamped between her teeth, hurried down stairs to her twenty-four would-be dancers between the ages of six and sixteen.

Cash half-heartedly chewed a croissant – in the name of science – and crawled back into bed.

She was woken three hours later by a clatter. Bleary-eyed, she sat up in bed. Two men, one with a tape measure and a clipboard, were standing in a huddle by the window, muttering together.

'Who the hell are you?' she demanded, though in her present state, hair on end, peering out from under a duvet, her statement lacked any semblance of authority.

The two men spun round to face her.

'Oh, God! I'm so sorry,' said one. 'I didn't think anyone was here.'

Cash couldn't see their faces as they were standing with their backs to the light. She wrapped the duvet more closely around herself, conscious of her tatty grey T-shirt, and climbed out of bed.

'What the hell are you doing here?' She could think of nothing more original.

'I'm so sorry to disturb you,' the taller of the two men

said. He held out his hand. 'Niall Donovan. We understood there was nobody here.'

Cash ignored his hand – anyway, she wasn't in a position to let go of the duvet. Her brain was still befuddled. Then the name clicked. 'You're Niall Donovan? You're the bastard that's throwing us out into the street?'

He looked embarrassed. 'I wouldn't put it quite like that.'

'How else would you fucking put it?' Cash snarled. 'As of next Tuesday . . .' It was at that point that she recognised Pompous Bastard '. . . according to your tame Rottweiler here, all our stuff's going to be thrown out into the street. I think it's outrageous.' She stood trying, against the odds, to retain some dignity.

Niall Donovan was younger than Pompous Bastard. Cash reckoned he was in his late thirties. He was tall and well built, casually dressed in black trousers and oatmeal collarless linen shirt with a black suede jacket. PB had made no gesture towards Saturday and wore the same three-piece suit he'd had on two days before.

PB said, 'Mizz Ryan, you've had more than six months' notice. I think you'd have to agree that that's ample time to find alternative accommodation.'

'Have you any idea what a place like this would cost?' Cash snapped. A rather foolish statement under the circumstances, seeing as Donovan had probably paid a small fortune for the very floorboards on which Cash was now standing. She wanted to bite her tongue as soon as the words were out of her mouth.

'Quite so, Mizz Ryan,' PB said smugly.

She needed time to think. She looked down at the floor, desperately seeking inspiration. It didn't help. All she saw was her toe sticking out through a hole in her sock. She edged it under the duvet.

Donovan cleared his throat. 'Look, sorry to disturb you. We'll come back next week.' He headed for the stairs.

PB hung back. 'Tuesday, Mizz Ryan. Don't forget.'

As if.

Chapter Four

On Sunday morning, Cash made a feeble attempt to start packing her belongings into cartons. She had never been one for hoarding. Not one for possessions of any kind, mainly because she'd never had enough regular disposable income to accumulate stuff.

She found a few CDs and bits and pieces belonging to Simon and packed them into a separate carton, which she placed on top of the large cabin trunk containing most of his clothes. He'd left his things with her believing it would simplify matters when he returned home. He was supposed to be moving in. It had made sense. It avoided the cost of storage in some damp warehouse. Now she'd have to think of somewhere else to store it.

After the last class of the day before, a gang of the late Miss Gregory's helpers, she and Billie amongst them, had emptied the floors below and carted the contents off to storage until a new home could be found for the project. Maybe she'd slip Simon's things in with the Strolling Players stuff.

Cash knew representations had been made to the Dublin City Council, the Gregory Family Trust and the Arts Council, amongst others, on behalf of the Strolling Players, but so far without any positive result. It was fortunate that not everyone involved in the Strolling Players Theatre Workshop was as much of an ostrich as was Cash.

She gave up on the packing and took a shower.

As she stood under the hot stream of water with her eyes closed, she thought about Simon. She hadn't heard from him in weeks. Surely they had phones in the Gobi desert. On second thoughts maybe not. She could have done with his help right now in finding a new place to live. She knew there was no way she could afford anywhere decent on her own.

It was a sad fact that at the age of thirty-one she had never known the luxury of a regular income. Still, that was the acting profession for you. She'd gone into it with her eyes at least half-open.

Cash rinsed the shampoo out of her hair and rubbed in the conditioner, combing out the tangles with her fingers, and her thoughts moved on to her mother.

She still yearned desperately for Yvonne's approval. That was another sa-a-d fact. Cash truly believed that until she either married well, got a long-running part in *EastEnders*, won an Oscar or saw sense and used her English degree to earn a living, she would never measure up in her mother's disappointed eyes, her only saving grace at the moment being Simon.

Yvonne loved Simon to death and harboured hopes that he would be her son-in-law. He had charmed her into submission after her initial coolness – due to him being an actor – and he flirted mercilessly with her to the point where she'd giggle like a schoolgirl, batting her eyelashes at him and simpering, 'Oh, you're terrible,' and 'If I were only twenty years younger . . .' to which Simon would make some comment to the effect that she looked like a twenty-year-old. More giggling and blushing from Yvonne.

The plan that he should move in with Cash on his return from the film shoot had raised Yvonne's hopes considerably. And wasn't he doing well? A TV mini-series with Sam Neil and Sean Bean. My son-in-law the *famous* actor.

Cash heard her mother clattering pans in the kitchen when her father let her in. He gave her a hug and cast his eyes towards the back of the house. 'In one of her moods,' he said, before retreating back to the drawing room with the *Sunday Times* sport supplement.

Cash's father, Leo, had long ago been browbeaten into submission by Yvonne. Now he opted for the quiet life and went along with whatever she wanted to do, keeping a low profile the rest of the time. He was an accountant by profession, and Cash feared for his sanity once he reached retirement age, which wasn't that far away. His only haven of peace was the golf course.

When she was younger, she used to wonder if he was afraid of Yvonne. The jury was still out on that one. But for someone so tiny – she was only four feet eleven in her stockinged feet – Yvonne Ryan could be a fearsome woman.

Cash and her elder sister Joanne, although a good head and shoulders taller than their mother from their early teens, were terrified of her at times. Not that she ever raised a hand to them. Her looks of disapproval, her caustic sarcasm and her air of abject dejection were as painful as any wallop from a stout stick. Yvonne had made the act of heroic martyrdom into an art form.

Sometimes – but only from an approval point of view – Cash wished she could be more like Joanne. Joanne had done the right thing. She was happily married to Rodney McAndrew, a barrister, and had studied law, but had never practised. She had married Rodney straight from college. Apart from looking after him, she also did a bit of voluntary work. For no discernible medical reason Joanne and Rodney had failed to have a

24

family. They had discussed the fertility treatment option with Joanne's gynaecologist, but Rodney wasn't keen on account of the risk of multiple pregnancy and the harm it might do to Joanne. Three unsuccessful IVF treatments had proved both problematic and demoralising. It was a cause of great unhappiness for the two of them and at the moment they were in the throes of a debate on the merits of foreign as opposed to domestic adoption. Cash loved her sister but didn't much like Rodney. She found him condescending and self-important.

In the kitchen Yvonne was stirring the gravy in the roasting tin with gusto. Her eyebrows were crinkled up into a frown.

'Hi.' Cash kissed her mother on the cheek.

Yvonne continued to stir. Without looking up, she said, 'You'll have to talk to your sister.'

Cash inwardly heaved a sigh of relief – obviously she was not the cause of Yvonne's ill temper. 'About?'

'About college. Justine's taken it into her head that she doesn't want to go. She talking about working on a kibbutz. Did you ever hear of anything so ridiculous? And her with the points for medicine.'

Cash briefly considered bringing to her mother's attention the fact that she was hardly the one to lecture her younger sister on the merits of a college education, but thought better of it. Now was not the time for splitting hairs. 'I'll talk to her,' she promised.

She knew there would be no need. There was no danger that Justine would miss out on the Israel trip. Justine knew exactly how to deal with her parents. She was a youngest child. The one who gets away with murder.

Cash helped the birthday girl to set the dining table. Justine had poured her mother a large glass of sherry just after Cash's arrival and Yvonne's clattering had died down somewhat, which was a good sign. In the privacy of the dining room, Cash told Justine about her impending eviction.

'Don't tell Mother,' Justine warned. As if. 'She still hasn't got over you being fired from *Liffey Town*.'

'I wasn't fired. I was written out.' Cash knew she was splitting hairs despite her earlier resolution. 'It wasn't my fault.' In her present state of mind it took her a moment to realise that her kid sister was winding her up.

'You know she'll expect you to move back home?'

This time Justine was serious, and Cash was well aware that the pressure would come not only from her mother. It was inconceivable that her father would be able to face the thought of living alone with Yvonne after Justine's departure for sunnier climes. She couldn't blame him. She saw him as a long-suffering Mr Bennett to Yvonne's neurotic Mrs Bennett. Poor Leo.

Mrs Bennett walked in at that point, carrying a serving dish full of broccoli. 'Bring in the potatoes, Cash, there's a good girl.'

The sherry had done its job.

Joanne and Rodney arrived as Leo was carving the joint. Rodney was waffling on to Leo about the euro, and Yvonne was regaling Joanne, yet again, with her I-was-*so*-sick-during-my-pregnancy stories, as if it would make her feel better about being unable to conceive herself.

Everything was going smoothly until Rodney put his spoke in. 'I believe Niall Donovan bought your building, Cash. When do you have to move out?'

Cash almost choked on a roast potato.

Justine's quick thinking saved the situation. 'Did I hear you say you had a TV commercial next week, Cash?'

Yvonne's attention was averted. 'A TV commercial? What for?'

'A feminine hygiene product,' Cash said.

Yvonne, flustered that such items should be mentioned at the dinner table, and in mixed company to boot, spluttered, 'Anyone for more turnip?'

'What's a feminine hygiene product, for God's sake?' Rodney boomed, never one for subtlety.

Joanne shot her red-faced mother a glance. Yvonne had never experienced anything as gross as a period. Yvonne only ever had a discreet visit from her *friend*.

'It's a sanitary pad, Rodney,' Justine piped up. 'With wings.'

'Wings?'

Joanne elbowed Rodney in the ribs. 'Leave it, Rodney.'

Rodney was having none of it. 'But what does she mean, *wings*? Is that a euphemism?'

'Surely you've seen the ads on TV where the woman jumps out of a plane?' Justine sneered.

Rodney claimed that he hardly ever watched television. Only BBC2 for the documentaries and the wildlife programmes, maybe RTE's *Prime Time* at a pinch. 'So the wings are on the plane?' He wasn't giving up.

Justine gave a wicked grin. 'You're going to be the face of Invisopads, aren't you, Cash? On every TV screen, bus shelter and hoarding in the country. Isn't that amazing, Mother? Cash Ryan, the national face of sanitary protection. She'll be famous.'

That wasn't quite what Yvonne had had in mind. 'Bus shelters . . . hoardings . . . a feminine hygiene product.' What would the ladies at the bridge club make of that?

'Anyone for coffee?' Leo asked.

Rodney was still waffling on about wings as Joanne and Cash cleared the dishes and Justine loaded the

27

dishwasher. Yvonne had disappeared upstairs, so Cash took advantage of the opportunity to flee. She said hasty goodbyes.

From the dining room she heard Rodney. 'But that's an idiotic scenario. Why would a woman with her period jump out of a plane, for God's sake?'

'Just being married to you would do it for me,' Cash muttered as she made her way down the hall towards the front door. '*Without* the parachute.'

She made good her escape.

Chapter Five

Sister Jude couldn't get over the change in Tiffany. Over the past three days she had been in flying form. No tantrums, no depression. Had it not been for the fact that she was so determined to have a healthy baby and was fanatical about everything she ingested, Sister Jude would have considered the possibility that she might be on amphetamines. But that was not an option. Tiffany desperately wanted her baby, despite the traumatic circumstances surrounding its conception. She had vehemently refused to even consider an English termination. Sister Jude was relieved. Although she was against abortion as such, she – unlike the church hierarchy – respected a woman's right to choose. Anyway, all things considered, it would be hypocritical.

Half of her thanked God that Tiffany seemed so happy, but deep down she was worried. Afraid that maybe the girl was developing some sort of mental problem, such as manic depression for instance.

She was familiar with manic depression. Her father had been a sufferer. High as a kite for three days, then down in the depths of despair for months on end.

She herself had also known depression. After the bomb she had retreated inside herself. No such thing as counselling in those days. No one had heard of post-traumatic stress. After the flesh wounds had healed you were expected to get on with it.

What did they know? When referring to her father, her mother would mouth the word 'depressed' to her neighbours on the Derry estate, jerking her head towards the house where she knew her husband would be sitting by the fire, staring into space. Then she would cast her eyes up to the heavens.

What did they know?

She remembered reading somewhere that conditions such as manic depression could be triggered by pregnancy.

She asked Sandra her opinion in a roundabout way.

'Tiffany's in good humour.'

'Yeah.'

'Have you any idea why, so all of a sudden?'

Sandra looked up from her teen magazine. 'Dunno. Bu' I'm not complainin'.'

Blood out of a stone. Good as she was to them, Sister Jude was still the enemy.

She tried a more direct approach. 'Did she say anything about these new friends of hers?'

Sandra's nose was back in her magazine. She shook her head. 'Nothin much. I think they're a Bible-thumpin' crowd. Dunno.'

'You mean like Jehovah's Witnesses?'

Sandra was getting grumpy now. 'I dunno, Sister. Why don't you ask her?'

'Why didn't I think of that?'

The irony was lost on Sandra.

Chapter Six

Bullied by Billie, Cash packed the rest of her things into cartons early the following morning. Billie had borrowed a battered Ford Transit van for the purpose of the move, so Cash took the opportunity to ferry Simon's trunk along to the storage warehouse. That done, she delivered the rest of her things to Billie's flat, then her friend drove her back into town and dropped her off at M&J Investigations.

Mort was glad to see her because the answering-machine was on the blink and he had to go out. As there was no typing up to do, she set about tidying out her desk and checking the stationery supplies.

Eileen Porter phoned after lunch. She sounded in a bit of a panic. 'Is Mr Higgins in?' she asked. 'I really need to see him.'

Cash explained that Mort was out, but due back at four o'clock or thereabouts. 'Why don't you come into the office?'

When Cash explained that she had no way of contacting Mort – he'd left his mobile on her desk – Mrs Porter agreed to call into the office at the allotted time.

At five to four Eileen walked in. Her face was grey, and she looked generally wretched, prompting Cash to ask if she was feeling ill. Mort was not yet back so Cash sat her down and made her a strong cup of coffee.

Eileen's hand shook as she picked up the cup, splashing more coffee in the saucer than made it to her mouth.

'Are you sure you're all right?' Cash was concerned. She wasn't the best at handling sick people, and Mrs Porter looked close to a seizure.

That was when Eileen broke down in tears. 'No. No, I'm not. I'm out of my mind with worry,' she gasped between sobs. 'I don't know what I'm going to do.'

'What is it? What's the problem?' Cash handed her a box of tissues.

Eileen blew her nose and wiped her eyes. Cash didn't like to tell her that her mascara had smudged where she'd rubbed it, giving her the appearance of a panda. 'It's my daughter.'

'Holly?'

Eileen stared at her. 'You know Holly?'

Cash explained how she knew Holly and Eileen looked dumbfounded. 'You were a Loretto girl?' This irritated Cash. She didn't think she looked that down at heel.

Eileen dabbed her eyes again. 'It's my younger girl, Daisy.' At the mention of Daisy's name, Eileen dissolved into tears again.

Mort walked into the office at this point, much to Cash's relief. Eileen was equally glad to see Mort and leapt to her feet. 'Mr Higgins! Did you find her?'

Mort placed his hand on Eileen arm's and gently guided her towards the inner office. 'We need to talk,' he said cryptically, and led her inside.

Cash was dying of curiosity. She couldn't remember Daisy. She strained her ears, listening for any morsels of conversation seeping through the connecting door, but only heard the indistinct rumble of Mort's voice, followed by the high-pitched staccato of Eileen. She still sounded in a state. After ten minutes, she seemed to calm down, and a further five minutes later Mort led her from his office.

She still had her panda eyes, but neither Mort nor Cash made reference to the fact.

'Leave it with me, Mrs Porter. I'll be in touch before Wednesday.' He had to reassure her several times before she finally left.

'What's the story?' Cash was never one to beat around the bush.

'Daughter's fucked off with some cult,' Mort said. 'Can you wait till the guy comes to fix the answering-machine? I've to go out again.' He handed her Mrs Porter's file.

Cash handed Mort his mobile phone. 'No problem.'

It was after seven by the time Cash made it out to Drumcondra, but she didn't mind. Mort was a good and accommodating boss.

Billie was out teaching an aerobics class when she arrived, so Cash tidied her belongings away as best she could, mainly behind the couch, then lit the fire.

The flat consisted of one minuscule bedroom, a tiny kitchenette the size of a small wardrobe, a shower/toilet and a sitting room. The sitting room was cluttered with an oversized couch and two matching armchairs, a mahogany sideboard, a nineteen-fifties spindly-legged coffee table, a drop-leaf Formica kitchen table, two folding chairs, a leather pouffe and a TV.

Every available surface was covered with Billie's collection of kitsch religious memorabilia. Amongst Cash's favourites there was a two-foot high statue of Pope JPII, with motorised right arm. Three fingers and the thumb had broken off, leaving only the middle digit, so, instead of continual blessings, it appeared that His Holiness was giving the world the finger.

Another favoured piece was a battery-operated plastic luminous statue of the Virgin Mary with a halo of tiny coloured bulbs that blinked on and off. The statue stood on a golden plastic plinth which cunningly concealed a little drawer in which to secrete rosary beads. The collection also contained a number of garishly painted or luminous patron saints, and crucifixes of varying sizes.

Billie's latest acquisition was a picture of the head of the crucified Christ with eyes that appeared to be either open or shut depending on the angle of viewing.

Cash switched on the television and caught the end of *Coronation Street*. Vera and Jack were in the wars again. Nothing new there. Then she zapped to RTE One and half-heartedly watched *Liffey Town*.

She found it hard to concentrate, however, because of the picture of the crucified Christ, which was hanging directly above the TV. She realised that if she held her head at a certain angle and moved it very slightly to the left and to the right, the face of Christ winked at her. It was disconcerting to say the least, and caused her to miss the crucial part of the plot where Sean, the mild-mannered schoolteacher with the brain tumour who had murdered Fifi, kidnapped a nurse at knifepoint. Before the ad break he'd been lying in an irreversible coma in Liffey Town hospital.

Billie arrived at eight-thirty in the company of Mort.

'Found him loiterin' on the doorstep,' she said.

As Cash was making coffee, Mort apologised. 'I hope you don't mind me coming round so late, but I was wondering if you could do me a favour?'

Cash handed him his coffee. 'Such as?'

Mort sat down by the fire. 'You know Eileen Porter's case?' Cash nodded. 'Well, as I told you, the daughter's legged it with this cult, and I was wondering if you'd

34

mind checking them out. They've got a drop-in centre on Marlborough Street.'

'What d'you mean by check them out?' Cash was dubious.

Mort shrugged. 'Just get a feel for the place. See what they say to the punters. That kind of thing.'

'Okay, but I'm busy tomorrow.' Mort looked puzzled. 'The shoot?'

Mort took a slurp of his coffee. 'Oh, yes. I'd forgotten about that. How about tomorrow night – they're open till late – or maybe Wednesday? I can't go myself, I went down there for a peek this evening, and by the looks of the set-up I'd stick out like a privy on a lawn.'

'So, basically, all you want me to do is go in, have a look around, talk to a few people and report back to you?'

'That's about the size of it, Cash. No sweat.'

'I'm free. I could do that,' Billie offered. 'I could check it out for you.'

Mort shrugged. 'Well, if it's no bother.'

'I've nothin' else on. Why not?'

'Cheers, Billie. So what kind of cult is it, Mort?' Cash asked.

'The drop-in centre looks innocent enough. I'm not even sure it's a cult at all. I've only the mother's word for that. She reckons they've brainwashed her daughter. Anyway, I don't want to go steaming in there making an eejitt of myself till I've more facts.'

'Great. It's fixed, then. I'll get back to you,' Billie said.

'Good girl yourself.' Mort heaved himself out of the overstuffed chair. His parting words were, 'I'll make it worth your while.'

Cash had an early start the following morning. The shoot was in a leisure centre out in Clontarf, and involved a trampoline, a treadmill and other sundry exercise equipment. Katy, the copywriter, explained the concept as 'modern career-woman living life to the full'.

'The client's trying to attract a wider age range for the product,' she said. 'They wanted an older woman, so we picked you.'

The director decided to do the trampoline shot first, so Cash put on a ghastly pink leotard with pale turquoise tights and pink runners. The hairdresser tied her hair up in a ponytail, securing it with a pink squidgy.

'I know you look dated,' the art director moaned under his breath. 'We wanted you in a black Nike sports bra and cycle shorts, but the client has a thing for pink and turquoise. They're their corporate colours.' Dated career-woman living life to the full?

The director instructed Cash to jump up and down a couple of times on the trampoline to gain some momentum – this was the only time in her entire life that Cash was glad that she was deficient in the boob department – then to jump as high as she could, flinging her arms in the air, while at the same time kicking her heels up to her butt, all the time smiling into the camera.

The shoot took several takes. Cash had difficulty executing all the elements of the manoeuvre simultaneously. The hardest of which was to get the smile right.

After seven takes, she heard the director murmur, 'I want her to fucking smile, not to look as if she's about to have a bloody root canal done. How hard can it be?'

The next shot was in the locker room. This time Cash had to change into a snugly fitting pink sweatsuit. She was directed to bend down from the waist, keeping her legs straight, with her back to the camera. Then she had to swing her sports bag over her shoulder, straighten up and look into the camera lens while delivering the line,

'They're so invisible . . .' pause '. . . I forget I have one on.'

After nearly concussing herself a couple of times with the sports bag, she managed the line without any further problems, but the client wasn't happy with the shot and insisted on ten more takes.

The client, Cyril Bumm – really! – a portly, elderly man in a shiny navy suit, watched her with glazed eyes, through milk-bottle-thick glasses. He was red-faced and sweating profusely throughout. In the end the director called a halt, mainly on health grounds to prevent Cyril from suffering a stroke or, alternatively, being arrested for grievous bodily odour.

Cyril took a shine to Cash. He invited her to lunch but, remembering the director's crack about root-canal work, she claimed a prior dental appointment, much to Mr Bumm's sorrow.

She phoned Maurice to see if he had any more work lined up for her.

'How's the shoot?' he asked.

'Very . . .' Cash searched for a word. 'Very pink.'

Maurice gave her details of two auditions. One was for a small part in a play at the Peacock, an experimental piece based on the Scottish play – he referred to it as the Hibernian saga – the other for the part of the hooker-with-a-heart-of-gold in a forthcoming Channel 4 series called *Slappers*.

'I told you the *Liffey Town* gig'd lead to something bigger.' Maurice could be obnoxious when he was right. He crowed for another couple of minutes before promising to drop the piece for the Channel 4 audition round to Mort's office.

After lunch they did a shot of Cash on the treadmill – in the lovely pink leotard – and a shot of her using the peck deck. The final shot – though the opening scene of

37

the ad – was of her getting out of a pink Fiesta and running up the steps of the leisure centre, talking into a pink mobile phone, this time wearing a pink skirt suit, with a turquoise blouse underneath, and pink high-heeled shoes. Thankfully the director drew the line at turquoise tights.

There were no further complications – apart from her walking slap bang into the plate-glass door she wrongly assumed was open – and in the end the director seemed pleased with her work. She successfully evaded Cyril Bumm, seen loitering with intent near the exit, and got a lift back into town with Katy, the copywriter.

She stopped off on O'Connell Street for a McChicken sandwich and fries, with a coffee, then jumped on a number eleven bus and headed back to Drumcondra.

Chapter Seven

Billie walked up and down Marlborough Street, trying
to pluck up the courage to go in. Although to outward
appearances she was a gregarious character, by nature
she was shy. As a mixed-race kid brought up in a
predominantly white society, she'd often been the victim
of schoolyard bullies, so her outgoing, in-yer-face
persona was a defence mechanism.

Do unto others before they do unto you.

The bullying was the chief reason that her mother had
insisted she join the Strolling Players. She felt it would
give her daughter confidence.

That end was achieved only to a small degree, but in
the process Billie discovered that she had a talent for
dance.

She had been born into a loving and happy home.
Her father, Winston, a Jamaican jazz musician, had
met and married Molly Hogan in London in the late
sixties. In 1972, shortly before Billie was born, they
had come to Ireland, and had moved in with Molly's
grandmother in a small house in Ringsend. Winston
had taken up employment in the Jacob's biscuit factory
but had still played jazz on weekends. He had died of
cancer in the mid-nineties. Billie had one brother,
Marvin, twenty-four, and a sister, Regina, who was
twenty.

'Feel the fear and do it anyway. Feel the fear and do it

anyway.' Billie repeated her mantra, eyes tight shut. She took a deep breath and pushed the door open.

The place looked cheerful and inviting. Half a dozen round tables with four chairs apiece. A counter with boxes of KitKats and Club biscuits, a big basket of Cellophane-covered muffins, another with sundry filled rolls and a steaming urn for tea and coffee. A shelf ran along one wall, on which lay bundles of leaflets and books.

A young man was sitting at a table, filling in some sort of form. He looked like a student. A group of three, two men in their early twenties and a woman of around thirty, stood near the counter, talking in hushed voices. In the background Elvis was singing gospel songs.

Billie stood inside the door, not sure what to do next. Mort had said, 'Get a feel for the place.' What did that mean?

The student looked up at the group by the counter. 'I've . . . em . . . I've finished.'

One of the group detached himself, bounded over to the table and sat down. 'Smashing.' He spoke with an English accent. He took the form and looked at it.

The woman caught Billie's eye. 'Hi. I'm Cora. How are *you*?' She walked towards Billie, her hand outstretched, with a warm open smile on her face. 'Can I get you coffee?' She had a velvety American accent.

'Um . . .'

Cora pulled a chair out from a table. 'Hey, why don't you sit awhile?'

Billie sat down.

Cora went over to the counter and poured two cups of coffee. 'Black or white? Why, what's your name?'

'Eh . . . White, please. My name's Billie.'

'Billie. That's a pretty name.' Cora placed the two

cups on the table and sat opposite Billie. 'Where're you from?'

'Dublin. I'm a Dub.'

Cora registered surprise. 'Wow. I'd never've guessed. You look so exotic.'

'My dad was Jamaican.'

Cora slid her hand across the table and placed it on top of Billie's. 'I sense he's passed away.'

Billie was embarrassed, not sure how to react.

'My dad passed away a while back. I miss him. I guess you miss your dad, too.'

'Yeah.'

Cora squeezed her hand. 'I guess you're mad at him. I was mad as hell with my dad for leaving me.'

It hadn't occurred to Billie to be angry with her father. Why would it? He hadn't gone voluntarily. Billie decided to play along. 'Yeah. He left me ma with ten of us to look after.'

More empathy. 'That must've been tough on your mom. On all of you.' More hand-squeezing.

'S'pose so.' Billie looked around the room. 'What is this place? What d'you do here?'

Cora gave her another warm smile. 'We're here to listen. If folks have problems and no one to share them with, we're always here.' She looked deep into Billie's eyes. 'I sense you have problems, Billie. I feel you want to reach out, but you're afraid.'

'Um . . .'

'Don't worry. In your own time. We're here for you, for as long as it takes.'

Flustered, Billie looked away and took a drink of her coffee. 'Um . . . What else d'you do? I mean, are you a religious . . . um . . .' she was going to say 'cult' but reconsidered '. . . a religious group?'

Cora nodded. 'In a way. We're Christians, and we live

41

by the Christian ethos, but primarily we're a personal improvement group. We run courses and seminars. You know, yoga, meditation, self-awareness, that kind of thing.'

'Oh.'

'What do *you* do, Billie?' More eye contact.

'I'm, um . . . I'm a dancer.'

'Wow, I thought so. You look like a dancer. You know? Graceful.'

Billie flushed. 'Well . . . um . . .'

Cora looked past Billie. 'Hey, Curt, come here and meet Billie. She's a dancer.'

Curt sat down. 'Hi, Billie. Good to meet you.' He had an easy smile, the same soft accent as Cora and the most even white teeth Billie had ever seen.

'Billie lost her dad, Curt, and she's mad as hell. I was telling her how mad I was with my dad after he left us.'

Curt grabbed Billie's free hand. 'It's okay to be mad, Billie. It's okay.'

Billie was drowning in a treacly mass of empathy and sympathy. 'Er . . .'

'I was telling Billie that we're here for her any time she needs us, Curt.'

'Absolutely,' Curt said. 'Whenever you need us.'

Billie pulled herself together. 'So . . . eh . . . about these courses.'

Curt, her new best buddy, leaned closer. 'Right. What do you want to know, Billie?'

'Eh . . . Well . . . I dunno.'

'Hey,' Cora said, as if inspired. 'Why don't you do our personality test? It'll give us some idea what kind of course would be useful for *you*. It's for free. There's no charge.'

'Personality test?'

Curt, who had leapt up from the table, placed a printed sheet and a ballpoint pen in front of her. 'It's multiple choice. Give it a go, Billie. What have you to lose?'

Billie picked up the ballpoint. She shrugged. 'Well . . . okay.'

Joanne McAndrew was so excited she could hardly contain herself. 'But, Rodney, I need you here *now*. I have to talk to you,' she said firmly. 'It's important.'

Rodney had been hoping for a quiet drink in the Law Library but, recognising that certain tone in his wife's voice, he gave in. Sometimes he feared that Joanne had the potential to surpass Yvonne in the intimidation stakes. It was a daunting concept.

He was therefore surprised to find her in a terrific mood. As he opened the front door she rushed out to meet him and flung her arms around his neck. 'Darling! Wonderful news.'

For some months now, Joanne and Rodney had been making serious efforts on the adoption front. Although their preference was for an Irish adoption, statistics showed that the chances of getting an Irish baby were far slimmer than those of foreign adoptions. Guatemala was an option, as was China, and they had made preliminary enquiries.

They had learned that a home study had to be done. Joanne had been horrified by stories of intrusive social workers and red tape, but Rodney had explained that the authorities had to ensure the best interests of the children. 'Anyway,' he'd pontificated, 'what could they possibly find wrong with us?' This had mollified Joanne somewhat, so she had gritted her teeth, telling herself that it would all be worth it in the end.

Joanne poured her husband a large gin and tonic and

sat on the arm of his chair. 'I contacted that agency today – you know, the one Frank told you about?' Rodney nodded. 'Well, they said there's every chance that we could have a baby in a couple of months if we can get the paperwork sorted out.'

'A couple of months? But I thought we'd have to get on a list. I thought we'd have to wait a couple of years for a baby.' Rodney was convinced she'd got it wrong. 'What's the catch? Are you sure you heard them right?'

'There's no catch, Rodders. And, better still, they said it'll be an Irish baby.'

Now Rodney was certain she'd misunderstood. Joanne, sensing his scepticism, cut him off. 'No, really. Mrs Haffner told me.'

'Mrs Haffner?'

'The woman I spoke to from the agency.' Joanne was getting irritated now. 'You're not listening to me, Rodney.'

'I am, I am, it's just a surprise. I was just prepared for the whole business to take a lot longer, that's all. So tell me exactly what this Mrs Haffner said.'

Joanne took his hand in hers. 'It's all down to money, Rodders. Like anything else. If we pay to have this private home study thing done, that alone will cut a year to eighteen months off the maximum waiting time.' Joanne was bubbling with excitement. 'By February, Rodders, we could have a child of our very own.' Joanne flung her arms around his neck.

'February.' The excitement was getting to Rodney now. A son. Rodney Finton McAndrew, Jr. Joanne was still talking but he'd stopped listening. Straight away his mind was on the practicalities. Better get his name down for Glenstall Abbey. Blackrock College, too, in case Joanne balks at boarding. Already he was planning

44

which sports young Rodney would excel at – his preference was for rugby, a real man's game – and which university he should attend – follow in his old man's footsteps and go for Trinity.

'Rodney!'

'Sorry, what did you say, my love?'

'I said I've arranged a meeting with Mrs Haffner tomorrow, at three, if that's all right.'

'Sooner the better,' Rodney said, smiling into the distance. In his mind, already young Rodney was scoring a try for Ireland.

'Apparently I'm livid with my dad for dyin', "but it's okay to be mad, Billie".' She affected an American accent.

'So what were they like?' Mort took a piece of chewing gum and offered the packet in turn to the two women. They were sitting in Billie's flat by a roaring fire.

Billie took a piece of gum. 'Bit overpowerin'. I felt a bit of a spa because I'd nothin' to whinge about so I, em . . . I went a bit over the top.'

Cash frowned. 'How over the top?'

'Told them a load of bollocks. They got me to fill in this personality test yokey, and I told them I was a recoverin' alcoholic and that I used to be on the game.'

'I suppose that could qualify as over the top,' Cash remarked.

Billie smirked. 'When Cora read it, she gave me these.' She delved into her pocket and dug out a few leaflets. 'Accordin' to her, I need to raise my self-esteem. Like I needed her to bleedin' tell me that. An' anyway, she reckons I should do one of these courses.'

Mort took the leaflets and handed them on to Cash as soon as he had scanned them. They all bore the heading

45

'The Better Way Institute' and gave information about various self-improvement courses, such as 'Know Yourself, Love Yourself', 'The Past Is Not Your Fault' and 'Meditate Your Way to Higher Self-Esteem'.

'I picked this up, too.' Billie handed him a thin glossy brochure, entitled 'About The Better Way Institute'.

Mort frowned. 'So what did you make of them? D'you think they're a cult?'

Billie thought about it. 'Dunno. Even though they were a bit, you know, full on, I can't say I felt pressured. They were all for me goin' away to think about it. They weren't tryin' to get money outta me or tryin' to brainwash me to join them or anythin'.'

'Early days yet,' Mort commented as he handed Billie a tattered twenty-pound note.

Cash was reading the glossy brochure. 'It says here that they've a headquarters in Enniskerry.'

Mort looked up from the 'Meditate Your Way to Higher Self-Esteem' leaflet. 'Maybe I'll check it out.'

'Did Daisy turn up yet?' Cash asked as she saw Mort to the door.

'No sign. The mother's still convinced she's been spirited away by this crowd.' He held up the brochure. 'She went to the cops but, hey, the girl's an adult, she's twenty-five. You know the score. Even if she is with them, what the hell can we do about it if it's her choice?'

Cash nodded. 'Not your problem, Mort. Mrs Porter's paying you to find her, that's all . . . isn't it?'

Mort grimaced. 'She broached the subject of kidnapping, but I talked her out of it. That's heavy shit.'

'Well, make sure she pays her bill before she brings it up again.'

'You bet. See you tomorrow, Cash.'

'See you, Mort.'

When she returned to the sitting room Billie was reading the leaflets. Cash said, 'And *are* you going to meditate yourself to higher self-esteem, Billie?'

Billie blushed, then guffawed. 'No bleedin' chance.'

Chapter Eight

The girl, Cora, was very helpful and pleasant. She remembered Tiffany and, yes, said she'd been in quite regularly since the previous week.

When Sister Jude enquired further, Cora explained that she had left early the previous day so didn't know if Tiffany had dropped in then, but went away to check it out with her colleague, a fresh-faced young man of twenty or so. The young man, Curt, informed the nun that Tiffany *had* dropped in the previous afternoon.

'But you haven't seen her today?'

Curt shook his head. 'Not today, ma'am. Is there a problem?'

On the face of it, Tiffany absconding was not an unusual occurrence. In her first month with Sister Jude she had gone walkabout on four occasions, but in the last six weeks, as her pregnancy had progressed, Tiffany appeared to have settled down.

'She didn't come home last night. I wonder, can you remember what time she left?'

Curt rubbed his chin. 'I'd say around eight, eight-thirty.'

Sister Jude sighed. 'I see. And I don't suppose she gave you any indication of where she might be going?'

'She said something about staying with a friend.'

'A friend?'

'Yes, ma'am.' He paused. 'I'm sorry. She wasn't any

more specific.' He paused again. 'Oh, she did have a small bag of stuff with her.'

As far as Sister Jude was aware, Tiffany didn't have any friends. She was a loner. A common characteristic amongst abused children. Tiffany's social worker had learned, after much gentle coaxing, that the uncle had been abusing her since the age of six. The problem was compounded by the fact that Tiffany's mother, who was still in denial, had refused to believe her daughter when she had eventually approached her for help.

'Did she seem upset to you?'

Curt shook his head emphatically. 'No, ma'am. The young lady's made a lot of progress since her first visit. She's fine. She dealing with her issues.'

'Excuse me for sounding dim, but how do you know? What exactly do you do here?'

Curt smiled. 'We're the Better Way Institute, ma'am. This is the drop-in centre. We're here to listen to folk's problems and offer help where we can.' He handed her a brochure. 'Young Tiffany is a lovely young lady. Tell me, ma'am, is she a relative of yours?'

'She's in my care.'

'Right. And you are?'

'I'm Sister Jude. I take care of Tiffany on behalf of the Eastern Health Board. Why do you ask?'

'Well, ma'am, it's just Tiffany didn't mention you. She told us she was on her own.'

Something about his tone angered Sister Jude. 'And you didn't think it strange that a fourteen-year-old girl in her obvious condition would be living on her own?'

Curt smiled at her condescendingly and shrugged his shoulders. 'Wake up and smell the coffee, ma'am. There are *too many* kids of her age living on the streets, or hadn't you noticed?'

She couldn't argue with that. She wondered whether

Curt was really the cause of her annoyance, or was it the let-down that Tiffany had lied about being on her own?

Curt put his hand on her arm. 'Look, ma'am. Tiffany told me she was staying with a friend. She'd no cause to say that if it wasn't true. I'm sure she'll be back home pretty soon.'

She glanced at her watch. It was five-twenty. Rush hour. Pointless trying to get a bus before six-thirty. 'Do you mind if I stay a while, in case she comes in?'

'No problem, ma'am. Would you like coffee or tea, or a snack maybe?'

Sister Jude settled for tea and a chocolate muffin. It was a whim she regretted with embarrassment when Curt refused to take any payment. She settled herself at a table and waited.

She was hoping to avoid Garda involvement just yet. In her heart she was afraid that the Health Board, because of the advanced state of the pregnancy and her record of absconding, might take Tiffany into a secure unit for, as they would view it, her own safety. Sister Jude felt that this would be a retrograde step. As far as she was concerned, Tiffany needed to be in a stable environment, with one-to-one care. She hoped that the dilemma would be resolved by Tiffany coming home of her own accord as she had on the previous occasions.

Cora was sitting at an adjacent table with a distraught-looking woman of about forty. Cora was leaning towards her and had hold of the woman's hands. She was talking earnestly in a low voice. The woman kept nodding. Bored, Sister Jude tried to eavesdrop on the conversation, but without success. After a while the woman said something and Cora smiled and patted the back of her hand before leaving her seat and returning moments later with a printed sheet and a ballpoint pen.

The woman gave Cora a weak smile and commenced to read the form.

Time hung heavily. After a while Sister Jude stood up to stretch her legs and took a turn about the room. She picked up a couple of leaflets and returned to her table.

Curt and Cora were standing by the coffee counter talking together, watching the woman filling in her form. Sister Jude sensed, from time to time, that they were watching her. The door opened and a young man walked in. He had the look of a student about him. Both Cora and Curt gave him dazzling smiles. Curt strode towards him with his hand outstretched. 'Glad you could make it, Sean.' They shook hands vigorously.

Sean said, 'I was thinking about what you said yesterday and I've decided I'd like to do it.'

'Wonderful, wonderful,' Curt enthused. 'Let's talk some.' Sister Jude watched as he put a protective arm around Sean's shoulder and led him towards the table at the back of the room.

Cora was now sitting beside the woman, helping her to fill in the form.

Sister Jude flicked through the leaflets. 'Know Yourself, Love Yourself.' If only it were that easy. 'Meditate Your Way to Higher Self-Esteem.' That was a, hmm, possible. 'The Past Is Not Your Fault.' Sweeping statement was her first reaction to that one. She opened up the leaflet. It listed a course of six seminars at twenty-five pounds a throw.

The CD that had been playing in the background suddenly finished and a hush fell on the room. Both Cora and Curt stopped talking. Cora got up and went behind the counter. A moment later the first bars of 'A Perfect Day' filled the void.

Sister Jude glanced at her watch again. Six-ten. She was sitting facing the door in case Tiffany should come in. She didn't want to risk her fleeing before she had a chance to talk to her.

Idly, to pass the time until her bus, she flicked through the brochure, 'About The Better Way Institute'. It was a well-put-together glossy piece about the institute. There were colour photos of a large mansion in Enniskerry where residential seminars were held. Bumph about the altruistic aims of the institute.

Sister Jude scanned the page, then turned the brochure over to read the back.

Suddenly her heart began to thud in her chest and her head swam. She blinked a couple of times to clear her vision. There was no mistake even though it was over twenty-five years since she'd laid an eye on him. There he was in living colour, a head and shoulders shot, smiling up at her.

Rory Keogh.

Chapter Nine

Cash brought a comatose Billie a mug of coffee before she left for work, and got a grunt in response. She'd have given anything for a lie-in. It didn't lighten her mood at all when she had to stand at the bus stop in the rain for twenty minutes watching full buses flying past before one eventually stopped.

Mort wasn't in evidence when she finally made it into the office, but there was a Dictaphone tape for transcription in her tray. There was also a note from Mort telling her to go ahead and order any stationery that was necessary, and a cheque for lodgement in the bank. Another caffeine fix was essential to kick-start her brain, so she put the kettle on.

As she was drinking her coffee, she made a list of the stationery supplies, then rang Norseman Direct. That done, she settled down at the computer to type up the tape.

There wasn't a lot. Just a letter and receipt for the cheque received from Mrs Nuttall, for whom Mort had been gathering evidence of her estranged husband's financial affairs for use in her upcoming divorce hearing, and Eileen Porter's file which contained a few sketchy details about Daisy. Cash typed it up, then printed out hard copies. Mrs Nuttall's letter and receipt she signed on Mort's behalf, before putting it in her bag ready for the post, and Eileen Porter's material she placed in a folder ready to file away.

By now it was eleven o'clock. As it was too early for lunch she made herself another coffee and sat down to study the audition piece for *Slappers*. The script described her character as Mona, a cynical Irish hooker, hard on the outside, but with a heart of gold. Nothing new there.

Eileen Porter rang ten minutes later, looking for Mort. When Cash explained that he was out, Eileen, sounding as agitated as ever, made her promise to get Mort to contact her as soon as he came in. 'It's imperative,' she stressed, more than once.

Mort rang soon after.

'Eileen Porter's looking for you.'

She heard Mort sigh at the other end of the line. 'Shit! I was trying to avoid her till I had some news.'

'To use her words, it's imperative you call her. Where are you, by the way?'

'I'm in a pub in Stepaside.'

Cash could hear pub noises in the background. 'All right for some,' she quipped.

'It's business, and I'm on the red lemonade, before you ask. I dropped in for a sandwich. I'm on the way out to Enniskerry to check out this Better Way crowd.'

'Well, I'd call yer woman first, if I were you.' Cash didn't fancy making excuses to Eileen all afternoon. 'I don't think I could deal with another highly strung woman so soon after a visit home.'

Mort laughed at this and promised faithfully to call Eileen.

As she was putting her coat on to go to lunch she heard footsteps in the hall outside. She groaned inwardly. Please, please, don't be the dreaded Eileen P., she silently prayed. The footsteps stopped outside the office. There was a tap on the door before it opened, and Simon stuck his head in.

She was stunned and thrilled. Her flagging spirits lifted immediately. 'Sy!' She ran across the room and flung herself at him.

He looked different – thinner and very tanned – and his hair had been bleached white-blond by the sun. He gave her a gentle hug.

'How come you're back so early? I wasn't expecting you for another fortnight.'

He looked tense. 'Um . . . there was a change in the schedule and as all my scenes were done I decided to come home.'

'Deadly! We should go out to celebrate.' Cash was in the mood for a party now. She wanted to hear all his news. To hear all about the film shoot. 'I'll put the answering-machine on and take the rest of the day off.'

'Well, the thing is, Cash . . . We need to talk . . .' He looked sheepish.

Sure, they needed to talk. There was lots to talk about. The shoot, her audition, finding a new place together, Sean Bean. But there was plenty of time for that. Why wasn't he dragging her off to bed? There was loads of time for talk. Right now, Cash wanted his body. Then it hit her. The emphasis Simon had put on the word 'need'. We *need* to talk.

Oh, God! He's met someone else. She stepped away from him.

He couldn't meet her eyes.

'There's someone else, isn't there?' Her voice came out in a croak.

Simon shrugged. 'In a manner of speaking.'

Cash felt her hackles rise. The least he owed her was to be straight. 'What do you mean, in a manner of speaking? Either you're with someone else or you're not . . . What's the story?' She was glad that she was too angry for tears. She wouldn't want to satisfy him with tears.

'I'm sorry, Cash. I thought long and hard while I was in the desert. What with the filming and all, well . . . I guess I began to see life differently and . . .'

'Get to the fucking point, Simon.' Snarl.

Simon gave a heavy sigh and walked over to the window. He stood with his back to her, hands in pockets, staring out into the street below.

The point? It was clear to Cash. Judas had obviously been shagging Mary fucking Magdalene in the desert.

After a minute he said, 'I didn't want it to be like this, Cash. I care about you a lot. I never meant to hurt you.'

She sat down on the edge of the desk. 'Why is it when people say that they always *do* hurt you?'

Simon turned around to face her. 'I'm sorry.'

There was a strained silence.

'So, is it anyone I know?' she asked, a lot more calmly than she felt. She wanted to rip his ears off.

He shrugged. 'Well, yes. It is someone you know.' He paused. 'It's Jesus.'

'Jesus!' It was meant as an expletive, not a question.

'Yes, Jesus. Out there in that harsh desert, I realised that I want to dedicate my life to Him. I've decided to join the Cistercians. I'm going to become a monk.'

Cash's jaw hit the floor seconds before the other shoe.

Mrs Haffner, who was of medium height, with short blondish hair and a rosy complexion, ushered Joanne and Rodney into her office. It was bright and cheerful, furnished with a squashy cream sofa, a couple of matching armchairs and a coffee-table at one end. Next to the sofa stood a low table on which there was a phone. There was an oval beech table with four chairs over by the window. A few Miró prints were dotted round the walls, and on the polished wood floor there was a colourful rug with an abstract design that tied in with the prints. A small table near the window housed a computer. It was the only indication that the room was an office.

'Please take a seat. Make yourselves comfortable.' She indicated the sofa. She sat herself in one of the armchairs, which were arranged immediately opposite the sofa.

Joanne sat. Rodney hesitated. He hated conducting business from sofas. He liked to negotiate from a height, preferably while standing. Joanne tugged at his sleeve. He gave in and sat.

'Can I get you coffee?' Mrs Haffner enquired as she shuffled through a small pile of papers which she had placed in a neat pile on the coffee-table in front of her.

Rodney shook his head. 'No thank you. Perhaps we could get started.'

Mrs Haffner looked up from her papers. 'Of course.'

Joanne cleared her throat. 'When I spoke to you on the phone yesterday you were saying that you could get us an Irish baby?'

'That's correct, Mrs McAndrew. We have contacts with other agencies abroad and there is a strong possibility.'

'Abroad?' Rodney was confused.

Mrs Haffner smiled. 'The mother in question is an Irish national living in Morocco. She's anxious that her child be adopted by an Irish Catholic couple.'

'How old is the baby? Is it a boy or a girl?' Joanne asked, excitedly.

Mrs Haffner gave a little chuckle. 'Well, the baby isn't due for another six weeks, but I'm told scans indicate that it's a boy.'

Joanne gripped Rodney's arm and an excited gasp

escaped. Rodney caught sight of his reflection in a mirror on the opposite wall and realised that he was grinning idiotically.

He cleared his throat and rearranged his face. 'So what's the procedure?'

'Well, as I explained to your wife, we can get the home study under way immediately. That should take only a matter of about three weeks. The whole business is made easier, of course, because as the mother is an Irish national, the child will automatically qualify, and matters at this end will be a lot less complicated than conventional foreign adoptions. After we have the home study documents, we send all the papers off to Morocco, where we have a very reliable associate who will, shall we say, oil the wheels of bureaucracy . . .' Rodney was staring at her blankly. Mrs Haffner leaned forward in her chair. 'Things can move very slowly in Morocco, Mr McAndrew. Over the years we've discovered ways to speed them up a little. Trust me, we know what we're doing.'

'You mean you bribe people?' Rodney was blunt as ever.

Mrs Haffner looked affronted. 'I wouldn't put it like that, Mr McAndrew. The word "bribe" suggests under-handedness. We just give certain parties incentives to expedite matters. Of course, if you're not comfortable with that . . .'

Joanne gave Rodney a dig in the ribs. 'We're fine with that, Mrs Haffner. Whatever it takes.'

Rodney wasn't happy. 'But why doesn't the girl come back to Ireland to have her baby? Surely it would be easier for her. Safer?'

Mrs Haffner sighed. 'My thoughts entirely, Mr McAndrew. And a lot less costly, too, but the girl has her reasons – something to do with the father, I understand. The bottom line is she doesn't want to return to Ireland. She intends to stay put in Morocco. But . . .' she shrugged '. . . ours is not to reason why. In a way you're very lucky. There aren't that many Irish babies available for adoption, and age-profile-wise, you're rather pushing the edge of the envelope as it is. Any further delay and you could miss the boat entirely.'

'She's right, Rodney. We've no time to waste.' Joanne was anxious.

'Just think, Mr McAndrew, if all goes well, by the end of the year you could have a son.'

Rodney's misgivings were overruled by mental images of Rodney Finton McAndrew, Jr, tearing down the wing in a green jersey with a number eleven on his back.

'Well, it could be worse,' Billie said, staring into her drink. 'At least he isn't shaggin' someone else.'

They were back in Pravda, though not on the vodka shots.

'That makes me feel much fucking better, Billie. Three years with me and he opts for the celibate life.'

Billie ignored the sarcasm. 'Is he goin' to be a priest or just a monk?'

'He said he was joining the Cistercians so I suppose that means he'll be a monk. Why?'

'I was thinkin' of your ma,' Billie said.

Cash groaned. Another disappointment for Yvonne. Another dream dashed on the rocks of her daughter's ineptitude.

She could see where Billie was coming from, though. Maybe Yvonne would be placated a little if she thought that Simon was joining the priesthood, that he had a vocation. Cash knew this would present her mother with a terrible dilemma. On the one hand her daughter had mucked it up as far as marriage was concerned (and her not getting any younger); on the other, with the fall in vocations, how could she, as a good Catholic, a member of the parish council, begrudge the bishop a new shepherd for the flock?

'Right. I'll tell her he's going to be a priest. I'll phone her.'

They sat in silence for a while, Cash thinking about the various ways she could break the news to Yvonne, without it seeming like it was her fault that her boyfriend, the man Yvonne thought of almost as a son, had suddenly chosen the celibate life.

But really, she had to ask herself, how could she be angry with him? As Billie had so accurately put it, it wasn't as if he was shagging someone else. It wasn't as if he'd been cheating on her.

But half of her *was* angry with him. She'd played by the rules. She hadn't cheated on him, even though she'd had the chance. It worried her that she hadn't missed him more. Oh, she had from time to time, but not in a tears-into-the-pillow way. Maybe she and Simon had just been drifting, going nowhere.

Maybe it was all for the best.

Billie took another sip of her drink. 'Three.'

'What?' Cash had lost her.

'Three things. Bad luck comes in threes. First you got sacked from *Liffey Town*, then you were thrown outta the flat, now yer man's dumped you for the Great Director in the sky.'

Cash brightened up. Like most of the acting profession, she was monumentally superstitious.

Maybe Simon dumping her *was* for the best. Maybe he'd done her a favour and completed the cycle. As she knocked back the last of her vodka and tonic, she signalled to the barman for another round. Perhaps there was cause for celebration after all.

Surprisingly, Billie was thinking about the Better Way Institute. Although she had more or less rubbished them to Cash and Mort, the concept of gaining higher self-esteem appealed. She was aware that the lack of it was holding her back. She sometimes envied Cash her confidence. With her it wasn't bluff. She had the ability to shrug off rejection as just someone else's opinion, which had no bearing on her talent as an actress. Billie, on the other hand, found rejection hard, and took each failed audition as a personal reflection on her ability. It would shatter her confidence for at least two or three days. Maurice was always encouraging but, then, he was her agent. Agents are supposed to be encouraging.

Although Cora and Curt were a touch earnest, she did feel that they had been genuinely sympathetic to her problems, even though, unknown to them, they were completely manufactured. She half regretted that she hadn't been more honest. Perhaps it was time to be positive.

Cash raised her glass. 'Here's to the future.'

Yeah, Billie thought, raising her glass and clinking it against her friend's. 'Here's to the future.'

In another part of the city, Sister Jude, too, was staring into the bottom of a glass, but in her case it was soluble aspirin. She'd had a nagging headache all day.

She rolled her head slowly from side to side, trying to ease the tension in her neck. She knew it was down to stress.

Uncharacteristically, she had phoned the school and reported herself sick. It was a lie, and she seldom told lies, but needs must.

She had spent the best part of the day searching the city for Tiffany, but to no avail. Eventually, at dusk, she admitted defeat and, with a huge sense of failure, informed Tiffany's social worker that she was missing. The social worker said she would inform the Gardai.

When Sister Jude had confided in Sandra that morning about her plans to take a sick day to look for Tiffany, Sandra had been all for taking the day off and helping her. Sister Jude said she'd rather she didn't. Lying was bad, she explained. She hated doing it but this was an exceptional case and she was sure God would understand.

Sandra pointed out that if they both were looking, they'd cover twice as much ground and, as far as *she* was aware, God likes a tryer.

'Anyways,' she said, 'if we're both off sick it'll be more believable, an' there's a bug goin' round right now that gives yeh the runs. They'll think that's it.'

Reluctantly Sister Jude agreed, mainly because she was relying on Sandra as a co-conspirator, but also because what Sandra said made sense. She was also touched and pleased that the teenager would bother to look for Tiffany at all.

Sandra was in bed now, tired out. Sister Jude suspected she was as upset about Tiffany leaving as she was. In some small way it was a victory of sorts. Supercool, don't-give-a-shit-about-anyone Sandra was worrying about someone else. Being well and truly streetwise, however, particularly where disturbed teenagers were concerned, Sister Jude didn't acknowledge the fact.

She stood up and stretched her back, then after a moment's hesitation rooted in the back of the cupboard for the half-bottle of whiskey she kept for medicinal purposes. She poured herself a good measure, sat back down at the table and lit a cigarette.

'Sorry, Lord,' she said aloud, as she blew a stream of smoke towards the ceiling, 'the flesh is weak at the moment. It needs a little help.'

Tiffany's departure wasn't the only thing on her mind. The Better Way leaflet was lying on the tabletop in front of her.

The sight of Rory's image the evening before had given her as much of a jolt as if she'd been wired up to the mains. Dr Rory Keogh, Ph.D.

Ph.D. in what? Mayhem?

He looked older, of course, but that was to be expected – it had been over twenty-five years. Twenty-five years, eleven months and two days, to be exact. She was in no doubt of that.

She had last seen him on the morning of the bombing.

Chapter Ten

Cash left for work earlier the following morning, got a bus straight away and arrived at the office forty minutes too soon (as is usually the way). She considered stopping off for a double cappuccino, but her conscience got the better of her. Mort was forever turning a blind eye when she was late in, so she hurried past the tantalising aroma wafting from the coffee-shop.

She could see through the glass panel of the outer office door that the lights were still on. That wasn't like Mort. She wondered if he'd been working all night. She got out her keys, but found that the door was unlocked. She pushed it open.

The light in Mort's office was also on. Maybe he's fallen asleep, she thought as she draped her coat over the back of her chair and picked up the mail. Mostly window envelopes, a couple of brown ones with harps.

A large Norseman Direct box sat on top of her desk next to the computer. She tried to move it but it was too heavy. She left it where it was, deciding to make herself, and Mort, a pot of coffee instead.

That was one of the perks of working for Mort. He was fanatical about drinking only fresh ground coffee, none of that instant muck for him. She filled the kettle and, as she spooned the fresh grounds into the cafetière, yelled, 'Come on, Mort, wakey-wakey.'

He made no reply. Cash took out the china mugs –

another prerequisite for a good cup of coffee in the gospel according to Mort – 'Come on, Mort. Coffee-time.'

He was sitting in his swivel chair behind his desk, but as the chair was pointing away from her towards the window she couldn't see his face, only the top of his head lolling to one side.

'Wakey-wakey,' she called again as she strode around his desk and reached over to open the roller blind. There was no response so she turned round to give him a nudge.

His eyes were wide open and his lower jaw gaped on to his chest. In his right hand, which was hanging limply by his side, a small gun dangled, held only his index finger. There was a neat hole in his right temple. A whiskey bottle, three-quarters empty, and a glass sat on the desktop.

Cash was rooted to the spot. Her eyes took in the scene but it took a moment for her brain to compute the information. Mort was very obviously dead. She gave a startled gasp and let go of the blind's cord. The blind shot upwards with a wallop and continued to rotate, whap, whap, whap, whap.

It was still revolving on the roller as she backed away from the room, her eyes never leaving Mort. With shaking hands she punched the '9' button on her phone three times.

She waited in the outer office for the gardai to arrive. They took less than ten minutes to answer the call. Two uniformed gardai from Pearse Street arrived first, followed a few minutes later by a detective.

Fifteen minutes later Cash was still in a state of shock. One of the uniformed gardai encouraged her to sit down and poured her a cup of coffee. She was shivering. The detective and the other uniform had disappeared into Mort's office and closed the door.

'Your boss?' the garda asked, indicating the inner office. Cash nodded. 'Bad business, suicide.'

Cash hadn't acknowledged the concept of suicide, even though, on the face of it, Mort's death could be nothing else. It bothered her to hear the garda declare it so positively.

'Depressed, was he?'

'Sorry?'

'Your boss.'

'No.' She shook her head emphatically.

'Poor bastard. Looks like he had to drink the best part of the bottle to get the courage.'

'Mort doesn't . . . didn't drink. He was an alcoholic.'

The garda shook his head sympathetically. 'Bad business, suicide.'

The outer door opened and a man and a woman in white overalls walked in. She was carrying a case, he was holding a large cardboard carton and had a camera slung around his neck. The uniformed garda indicated the inner office with a nod. The pair nodded in reply and went through.

'Technical team,' he explained. 'Forensics.'

The situation was unreal. She couldn't come to terms with the fact that Mort was actually dead, even though she'd seen him with her own eyes.

Port Mort. He'd been good to her, and she felt he'd been as fond of her as she'd been of him. He'd always shown an interest in her career in a paternal sort of way, encouraging her at every hand's turn. Always come up with fighting talk when she'd failed auditions. 'Their loss.' 'It was a shite part anyway.' Or 'You're worth more than that.' No one had been prouder, with the exception perhaps of Yvonne, when she'd landed the part in *Liffey Town*. Now he was dead.

The detective came out of the inner office, carefully

closing the door behind himself. He looked short for a garda, but it was an optical illusion caused by his general bulk. He wore a brown leather bomber jacket that had seen better days, jeans and a suitably grave expression.

'I'm Detective Sergeant Dan Doyle, Miss Ryan. I'm sorry for your loss.'

Cash thought that was a nice thing for him to say. It wasn't as if she was a relative. 'Thank you. I still can't believe it.'

'Do you feel up to answering a few questions?'

Cash nodded. 'Okay.'

He pulled a chair over to her desk and sat down opposite her. 'Do you know if Mr Higgins was depressed about anything?'

Cash shrugged. 'Such as?'

'Well, money troubles. Business worries, anything like that?'

'Not that I can think of. Business wasn't exactly booming, but it was steady, and I think he was okay for money. I only banked a biggish cheque for him yesterday.'

'Right.' He looked down at the desktop as if trying to think of a way to phrase his next question. 'And how long had he been back on the booze?'

'I didn't know he was. I'm sure I'd have noticed.' She felt suddenly guilty. She should have sensed that something had been worrying him. Why hadn't he talked to her about it? She'd always unburdened herself to him. Why hadn't he talked to her about whatever it was? What thing could be so awful that he hadn't felt able to mention it?

Detective Doyle cleared his throat. 'He was a good man.'

'You knew him?'

The garda nodded. 'We were in Templemore together. Then worked out in Walkinstown for a while.' He smiled at the memory. 'He was a great crack. One of the best.'

There was comfort in hearing good words said about her friend.

'Did you know he owned a gun?'

Cash shook her head. 'No, I've never seen it before.'

'I see.' He sat staring at the desktop. 'You didn't find a letter, I suppose? There's usually a letter or a note of some sort in these, well, these sorts of cases.'

'A letter? No.'

'Right. No letter.' He wrote something in his notebook. The outer door opened and another detective bustled in. He was about the same age as Doyle but was smartly dressed. Doyle stood up.

'Is what I heard true, Dan?' the detective asked Doyle.

Doyle nodded. ''Fraid so, Jack. Bad business.' They walked together into Mort's office.

The uniformed garda was still standing by the wall, examining his fingernails.

Cash cleared her throat to catch his attention. 'Excuse me.' He looked up. 'Do you think I should call Mort's wife?'

'It wouldn't be a bad idea,' he replied.

She looked up the number and dialled. Janet answered on the tenth ring. She sounded breathless. Cash wasn't too sure what to say. She had never been in the position of breaking news this bad to anyone before. 'Em . . . Janet? It's Cash. Cash Ryan, from Mort's office?'

'Oh.' She sounded surprised. 'Hello, Cash. You just caught me. I was on my way out to work. What can I do for you?'

'Well, um . . . The thing is . . .' She gave up trying,

and called a spade a spade. 'Look, Mort's dead. He . . . em . . . er . . . well, he committed suicide. He shot himself in the head.' She could feel tears stinging her eyes as she said the words. In retrospect she realised it was a crummy way to break the news. What had possessed her to be so specific? There was silence at the other end of the line. 'Janet? Are you there?'

Janet sounded completely shocked. 'Shot himself?'

'It looks that way. I'm so sorry.' The tears were rolling down Cash's cheeks now. She wiped them away with the back of her hand and sniffed. 'I found him when I came in this morning.'

As businesslike as ever, Janet said, 'Thanks for calling me, Cash. Where is he?'

'He's still here. The cops haven't finished . . . well, you know? I'll find out where they're taking him and I'll let you know.'

'Thank you. It was good of you to call me, but I'll be right over.' Without further ado, Janet hung up the phone.

Cash was still holding the receiver when Detective Doyle walked out of Mort's office. As he did so, two men walked in from the hall wheeling a gurney with a body bag on top. Detective Doyle muttered something to them and they went on into the office. He looked over at Cash. 'Are you okay?'

'I just called Mort's wife. She's on her way over.'

'Janet? Oh, right. Yes. We'll need her to do the formal identification.' He was talking to himself more than Cash. 'We have to wait for the duty surgeon to pronounce him dead before we take him anywhere. But I expect they'll take him to James's for the post-mortem.' He paused, then shook his head. 'Terrible business. Terrible business.'

*

Janet Higgins had loved her husband for as long as she could remember. It was also a fact that for most of their twenty-year marriage she hadn't liked him much, but she had never stopped loving him.

This anomaly was mainly due to the drink. Mort couldn't handle his drink, or his drinking. Drink transformed him from a kind, good-humoured pussycat into a truculent and, in the end, violent bear. Janet, who had witnessed her father beating her mother, had always sworn that she would never endure domestic violence, and couldn't understand why her mother had put up with it for so long.

Then one day, ten years into her own marriage, she realised with horror that history was about to repeat itself. It started with a push. Then a shove. Then a clatter to the head.

Janet said, 'Enough.' Then she packed her bags and moved out.

It took him four more years to get his act together; to admit that he had a problem and seek professional help. He retired from the force. She encouraged him. She helped him, even bankrolling him in the company, but declined his pleas to 'give it another go'. Things were good the way they were. They were friends again. She thought he was taking responsibility for his life.

Now this.

Traffic was heavy along the Stillorgan dual carriage-way. Before leaving she'd made a quick call to the bank to say she wouldn't be in. She was non-specific about the reason. How could she be specific? Sorry I won't be in today, my estranged husband just blew his brains out.

A red light stopped her. She sat behind the wheel staring at nothing. She couldn't get her head around it. Why? He'd been okay the last time she'd seen him. He'd been solvent, sober and, as far as she could tell, content.

At the back of her mind the first inklings of guilt began to seep into her consciousness. It occurred to her that on their last meeting she had been the one in a foul humour. It had been one of those days at work and she had taken it out on Mort. Not deliberately. He had just happened to be in the wrong place at the wrong time and had got the butt end of her ill temper. He'd been nagging her about taking a winter-weekend break together at a Country House Hotel somewhere; she'd been trying to unravel someone else's cock-up in her department. In the end she'd hissed, 'Just piss off, Mort. Leave me alone.'

Her eyes filled with tears at the memory of it. He'd looked so hurt.

'No!' she said firmly. 'It wasn't my fault. I did my best.' But it wouldn't go away. It kept prodding at her. It gave her an empty ache in the pit of her stomach.

A horn beeped behind her. The light had turned to green.

Across the city, Billie was reciting her 'feel the fear' mantra. Because of the cold, damp weather, the window was all steamed up, but through a dribbly swipe in the condensation she could see the woman, Cora, chatting to a tall, middle-aged, grey-haired woman. The woman was dressed in navy and had the look of a nun. Billie waited, losing courage fast. After a few minutes the nun and Cora shook hands and the nun turned towards the door.

Billie held it open for her and they smiled at each other as they passed in the doorway.

'Billie! Good to see you.' Cora's smile was warm and genuine. 'Look, Curt, Billie's back.'

Janet and Cash sat together in the outer office. They

both held mugs of coffee, but neither of them was drinking. The same uniformed garda was standing by the wall.

It was coming up to eleven, and the duty surgeon had just arrived to examine the body. Detective Doyle had said that Cash could go long ago, but she'd chosen to stay to keep Janet company.

Cash had never met Janet before, although they had spoken from time to time on the phone. From her voice, she had imagined that Janet would be tall and blonde and beautiful. In fact, she was short, dark and unremarkable-looking.

'The last thing I said to him was, "Piss off."' Janet's voice was wavering. Cash could sense that she was trying very hard to hold it together. She was having a tough time herself. It came and went in waves.

Detective Doyle coughed. They'd been so engrossed in their own thoughts they hadn't heard him come out of Mort's office.

'Janet.' Janet looked up. 'Em . . . We've finished inside. We'll be taking him on to James's soon for the . . .' He let the sentence trail off. He couldn't say the word 'autopsy'. Cash supposed it was because he'd been a friend of Mort's. He was too close to it.

Janet nodded, understanding. Doyle coughed again. He looked uncomfortable. He stared at Cash. 'Maybe you'd like to take Janet . . . em . . . somewhere else.' He looked over his shoulder at Mort's door. 'It might be upsetting to see, well . . . until they've tidied him up.'

Cash got his drift. 'Why don't we go down to the coffee-shop, Janet?' Stupid thing to say. They were both up to their necks in coffee.

'It's okay, Dan, I'm fine.' She touched Cash's arm. 'Why don't you go on home, Cash? It was good of you to stay so long but, honestly, I'm fine. I'll drive over to

James's and wait until they're ready for me to make the identification.'

'I'll come with you. You shouldn't be on your own.' Cash bit her lip. 'It's what Mort would have wanted. He wouldn't want you to be on your own.'

That was true, to a point. Cash knew well how much Mort had cared for his wife, despite the situation, and that he wouldn't have wanted her to be alone at a time like this. Another reality was that Cash wasn't ready to let go. She wanted to see Mort again to convince herself that he was really dead, and to say goodbye.

Chapter Eleven

Yvonne met Joanne for afternoon tea in the Shelbourne. She was bursting to know what the news was. Her daughter had been very cryptic on the phone. Daughters had no right to be cryptic.

Her mind had been on nothing else all morning, and not knowing had played havoc with her badminton game. Brenda Hughes had been utterly scathing after they'd been so soundly thrashed in a game of doubles.

Even afterwards, as they sat at the juice bar cooling down, Brenda hadn't let up about it. But Yvonne wasn't listening. She was speculating to herself. Maybe Rodney's taking silk? No, Joanne wouldn't be so excited about that. Anyway, he was making a bundle from government tribunals at the moment. Maybe he was going to be appointed to the bench. God! That would be awful. Justices earned nothing. No.

Brenda was still nattering on about her backhand, and the way she'd let Sonya steal the last point.

Then it struck her. 'Maybe she's pregnant.'

'What?' Brenda's mouth gaped for a second, then she recovered. 'Don't be silly. She's no ovaries.'

'No what?'

'Sonya had her ovaries . . .' Brenda realised she was yelling, so she lowered her voice to what she considered to be a conspiratorial level, which in her case was about the volume of your average disco. 'She had it all taken away. Sonya's no womb.'

'Sonya? I'm not talking about Sonya. I'm talking about my Joanne.'

'Your Joanne's pregnant?'

'I don't know.'

The conversation continued in that vein for several minutes, before Brenda lost interest and, swearing Yvonne to secrecy, digressed about Sonya's husband James who, word had it, was carrying on with someone-or-other she had never heard of, who was twenty years younger than himself.

Yvonne had more important things on her mind and Brenda's prattle was annoying her big time. 'Well, now the whole bloody club knows, Brenda!'

Brenda took umbrage. 'Well, if you want to be like that.' She gathered up her bag and flounced off. Yvonne let her go. Flouncing off was a fairly regular occurrence with Brenda and Yvonne knew that she'd soon forget about it.

At ten to four she trotted into the Shelbourne, settled herself at a table near the fire and ordered afternoon tea for two. Joanne arrived at four on the dot. She was breathless and glowing. Happiness seemed to radiate out of every pore.

Pregnant! I knew it, Yvonne thought. The waiter came at that point and served their tea. Finger sandwiches, scones and jam and a few fancy little cakes, served with a pot of Darjeeling. They waited for him to leave.

'So tell me your news.' Yvonne couldn't contain herself. Joanne opened her mouth to speak, but her mother slapped a hand on her arm. 'No. Let me guess. You're pregnant. Am I right?'

Joanne's grin faltered. Why did her mother always

have to do this? Why did she always have to spoil things? Her irritation was only fleeting, though. She was too happy to let it bother her. 'Half-right,' she said. Yvonne looked confused. Joanne went on to tell her about the adoption.

'The end of January! But that's so soon!' her mother gasped. 'I thought it would take much longer than that.'

They were leaning across the table holding hands, and grinning like fools. 'Me, too. But we were put on to this new agency by a colleague of Rod's, and they've promised us an Irish baby. And guess what? It's a boy!'

'A boy? Have you put his name down for Blackrock yet, darling? Your father'll be so disappointed if you don't send him to Blackrock.'

'Give me a break, Mother. The child isn't born yet.' Joanne was half joking, half serious. Yvonne Ryan had a talent for taking charge of things, and Joanne was determined that she wouldn't hijack her baby. This baby was hers and Rodney's. Any decisions about his future would be made by them, not her mother.

Yvonne, sensing the slight edge to her daughter's voice, let it go, determining that she'd sort it out at another time. She changed tack. 'So tell me about this agency.'

'Well, we spoke to a very nice woman, a Mrs Haffner, and she assured us that there won't be any problems. She advised us to get the home study done privately, which saves months. They've a list of their own approved social workers. And any problems . . . Well, any problems . . .' she lowered her voice and leaned in closer '. . . can be eased away, if you get my drift.'

'Eased away?'

'They know the people to see, Mother. They'll pay the right people to speed things up.'

Yvonne grasped her meaning. 'Oh.' She nodded

knowingly. Her generation was no stranger to influence, to pull, be it political or otherwise. It was the order of things. And if they could afford it, why not?

Joanne chattered on excitedly about her décor plans for the nursery, about the merits or otherwise of pre-school as opposed to Montessori. Yvonne was day-dreaming about her grandson, the eminent heart surgeon.

It was well after four by the time Janet was asked to officially identify Mort. Cash waited with her and, when the time came, went in with her to view the remains.

The only other dead body she had ever seen had been her grandmother, who had appeared to be sleeping. She had had a smile on her lips. Cash had been surprised. She had always thought of her grandmother as a frightening sour old lady, of whom they had all been afraid. Somehow the sweet smile hadn't fitted. Justine had irreverently remarked that it wasn't a smile at all. The old biddy was looking smug on account of the large turnout at the funeral.

Mort looked as if he was sleeping as well. She was relieved. His face, with mouth agape, eyes staring, was still fresh in her mind. Someone had stuck a Band-Aid over the hole in his temple. To Cash, who was close to the edge, it seemed comically bizarre, as if a Band-Aid was all that was needed to fix the damage. She had to fight to kill a fit of giggles. Ashamed of herself, she didn't share her thoughts with Janet.

Janet, on the other hand, felt strangely detached. As if the man lying lifeless on the table were a total stranger, not the man she had been married to for half her lifetime. She stroked his forehead. He was cold to the touch, his skin the consistency and colour of a wax dummy.

Detective Doyle, who was standing a couple of paces behind the two women, coughed. Janet looked round and, after a pause, nodded.

'Thanks, Janet. I know this can't have been easy.' He laid his hand on her shoulder and gave it a gentle squeeze.

Janet offered to drive her home, but Cash refused, saying she'd be fine if she was dropped off in town. It was only after Janet had taken her at her word and dropped her on St Stephen's Green that Cash realised how exhausted she was. The rush-hour scrum was suddenly daunting. As luck would have it, there was only a small queue at the taxi rank so she stood in line, and when her turn came slid gratefully into the back seat.

Billie was home before her and had the fire going. She was chirpy and chatty. Cash wasn't in the mood. As Billie was launching into some story about Maurice, Cash said, 'Mort's dead.'

Billie stopped in mid-sentence.

Cash slumped in the chair by the fire, still with her coat on. 'I found him this morning. He killed himself. Downed most of a bottle of whiskey, put a gun to his head and shot himself.'

'Jesus! Are you serious?'

Cash nodded. 'I went with Janet to the morgue. She had to identify him. It didn't seem right to leave her on her own.'

'Yeah. Jesus, poor Mort. Why'd he do it?'

Cash shook her head. 'I've no idea. I still can't get my head around it. He was in good form the last time I saw him. It just goes to show.'

She could hear Billie mooching around the room as she spoke, and a moment later her friend shoved a glass of brandy into her hands.

'Here. Get that down you.'

The alcohol made her feel better. Billie pulled the sofa over to the fire and refilled Cash's glass several times. They phoned out for a pizza, and Billie uncovered her stash of chocolate. It was the time for comfort food and reminiscences. Each had stories to tell about Mort. He'd been a mate to both of them. There was a lot of 'D'you remember the time . . .' and 'What about when . . .'

Cash began to feel less bad about it until she remembered that he had taken his own life. Somehow it wouldn't have been as bad if he'd died of a heart attack or some illness, or in a road accident or something. The thought of his last moments as he sat trying to pluck up the courage to blow his brains out left her feeling desolate and useless. 'Why didn't he pick up the phone, Billie? Why didn't he talk to me? What could have been so awful that he resorted to that?'

'Dunno,' Billie replied. 'But at the end of the day, it was his choice. Who are we to say what he should or shouldn't've done?'

'I know, but all the same . . .'

The pizza arrived and they switched on the television to take their minds off Mort for a while. As the evening wore on Cash began to get a little more used to the idea that Mort was actually dead. 'I'll call Janet tomorrow and see if she wants me to help her to organise the funeral,' she told Billie. 'Mort wouldn't have wanted her to have to sort the thing out by herself.'

'You know,' Billie said after a lull in the conversation, 'if he was so bleedin' bothered about Janet, it was a feckin' selfish thing for him to do. And who the hell did he think was goin' to feckin' find him? I'd've never in a million years said Mort'd do somethin' like that.'

'Me neither,' Cash remarked sadly as she broke off another chunk of chocolate.

*

79

Across the city in a high-rise, Sister Jude was sitting alone in the kitchen smoking her second, and last, cigarette of the day. Although she hadn't said anything, the nun knew that Sandra was missing Tiffany. She was listless and grumpy. On the face of it they hadn't been that close, but the nun suspected that Sandra's feelings were similar to her own inasmuch as they both felt abandoned.

It would have been easier if Tiffany had left a good-bye note or something. But there was nothing. She had packed a small bag and gone, without even a thank you. It wasn't fair.

She suddenly felt ashamed. Why *should* the girl thank her? She had done nothing. Even the roof over their heads was courtesy of the Eastern Health Board, as was the girl's food and her clothing.

It bothered her to look at it that way. It annoyed her to think that she was acting out of some sort of desire for thanks and appreciation. If her motives for service were pure, they should be altruistic. There should be no need for thanks or recognition. This was the pact she had made with God in exchange for her life.

No better reminder than the brochure lying on the table in front of her.

She stared down at Rory Keogh's image. It struck her that even in a photograph the man had charisma. The years had been kind to him. His face was fuller, but hardly lined, apart from the crinkles around his eyes as he smiled into the camera lens. The hair was short now and receding slightly, but it was the same colour, with just a touch of grey at the temples.

After the bombing he had disappeared off the face of the earth. There had been rumours. Some said he'd gone to the States. Others said he was just lying low. Her brain replayed the scene in slow motion as it had done so many times before.

The Christmas decorations. Carol singers in the street. The woman behind the counter wishes her a happy Christmas. The walk towards the door of the newsagent's. The elderly man. He raises his hat to her. She smiles. Stands back and holds the door open for him.

'Please, after you,' he says.

'No, after you,' she insists. He reminds her of her grandfather. He walks out ahead of her. She drops the pack of cigarettes and stoops to pick it up. Smoking can damage your health. All hell breaks loose. Acrid fumes, twisted metal. She is trapped under a huge weight, winded. A tweed jacket. It is the elderly man. Smoking has saved her life. As she ducked down to pick up the cigarettes, she was shielded from the blast by the elderly man.

To her right, directly in her line of vision, there is an arm lying in the rubble. Nothing else. Just a severed arm. A woman is shouting, 'I've lost me arm. I've lost me arm.' Hysterical.

'It's over here,' she shouts. Not meant to be funny, but in the heat of the moment, the horror, the hysteria, she starts to laugh. Then the pain grips her and she passes out.

Coming to in the hospital. IV drips. Plaster. Pain. The sense of loss. She asks about the man. They are evasive, so she knows he is dead.

Sandra padded into the kitchen and over to the sink, where she filled a glass with water. 'Can't sleep.'

Sister Jude sighed. 'Me neither. I'm too wound up.'

Sandra stopped by the table. 'D'you think she's okay? Where d'you think she went?'

The nun patted the back of Sandra's hand. 'I wish I knew, Sandra. But she'll come back when she's ready. I'm sure she will.' She was sure of no such thing, but she wanted to say something to cheer Sandra up.

Streetwise Sandra had no illusions. 'No, she won't. She wouldn't've gone in the first feckin' place if she was comin' back,' she snapped. Tears of anger sprang to her eyes. 'Don't kid yourself, Sister. She's off with someone. She's not comin' back.' She turned and stomped from the room. Sister Jude let her go.

Earlier in the day, as she'd had a free period before lunch, Sister Jude had caught the bus to Marlborough Street in the hope of bumping into Tiffany.

The nice American girl at the drop-in centre told her that Tiffany hadn't been in since. She was very sympathetic, but repeated her assurance that Tiffany had been in very good spirits the last time she had been in. She was confident that Tiffany had dealt with her issues (whatever that might mean).

She reminded Sister Jude that Tiffany had told Curt that she was going to stay with a friend. They had no reason to doubt that. She'd had a bag with her. Cora explained that at the time she had been very pleased to hear that, as they were under the impression that Tiffany had been living rough.

That stung.

Her expression must have said as much because Cora offered her coffee. Sister Jude accepted, using it as an excuse to bring the conversation around to Rory. First she asked if the Better Way was a religious group. Cora explained that although they were Christians and lived by the Christian ethos, their mandate was merely to listen, to motivate and to help.

'In what way?' Sister Jude asked.

Cora smiled. 'Well, take Tiffany. She came to us disturbed, confused and feeling isolated. We talked her problems through with her. Counselled her, and pretty soon she began to view life differently. I'm sure you saw a change in her yourself.'

'Well, yes,' Sister Jude admitted. 'She did seem very . . . well . . . high.'

'If we can help only one young person to lead a happier life, that's our mission fulfilled.' Cora said.

'Right. So, who gives these seminars?' Sister Jude turned over the brochure, pointedly looking at Rory's picture.

'Oh, Tiffany didn't attend one of our seminars, we just gave her free counselling.'

'Oh, I see. That was very good of you.'

Cora smiled. 'That's what we're here for.'

'So, about the seminars. Is it this Dr Keogh who gives them?'

'Dr Rory? Yes. He's our founder, and a truly brilliant man.'

'I'm sure he is. American, is he?'

Cora picked up the brochure and looked at the photo. 'Actually, he's Irish by birth. One of your own. But he lived in the States and studied there for many years. He has a Ph.D. from Stanford.'

'Ph.D. in *what* exactly?' Sister Jude asked a touch sharply.

Cora frowned. 'Dr Keogh is a leader in the field of psychology, Sister. He is a highly qualified man. Much respected by his peers.' All the statement lacked was an 'I'll have you know' in front of it.

'I've no doubt of that, Miss, em . . . Cora.' Sister Jude smiled to take the harm out of it. 'I wonder if I might take a few of these leaflets. I care for disturbed young people on behalf of the Eastern Health Board. I'm sure, judging by the effect your counselling had on young Tiffany, you could help others in her situation.'

'Certainly.' Cora pushed her chair back and stood up. Sister Jude followed her over to the counter where Cora collected up a selection of various leaflets, slipped them inside a shiny Better Way folder and handed it to Sister Jude. 'Maybe you'd like to leave me your number, then, if we hear from Tiffany, I can call you to put your mind at ease.'

'That's very kind of you.' Sister Jude took a card from her bag and handed it to Cora. They shook hands.

As she turned to leave, Cora called after her, 'Don't worry Sister. I'm sure she's fine.'

If only I could be so sure, the nun thought.

A tall attractive black girl held the door open for her as she left.

Chapter Twelve

Cash couldn't sleep. She lay awake tossing and turning all night, but every time she closed her eyes she saw Mort's face. She experienced waves of guilt now and then. Awful gut-wrenching feelings that she had let him down, by not seeing that there was something bothering him or guessing how desperate he must have been.

The ghostly glow of the various luminous icons dotted around the room hadn't helped either. It was a hang-up she'd had since primary school. Abstract concepts of holy souls and spirits had led her to the conclusion that the glowing statue of Our Lady of Lourdes that her grandmother had always kept next to her bed was actually a tortured, trapped spirit. Since that time, irrational as it was, she subconsciously associated anything luminous with the dead.

As the first light filtered through the curtains she gave up trying to sleep, swung her legs off the side of the sofa bed and padded to the kitchen to make tea.

On her way back to bed she switched on the radio and grabbed a stray chunk of Whole Nut which had escaped consumption the previous night. She pulled the duvet around her shoulders. It was a chilly, wet morning and she could hear the swish of tyres on the road outside. Life going on. People going about their business. No point in her going in to work. Too early to call Janet.

She wrapped her hands around her mug of tea and thought of Mort.

As Ian Dempsey cut to the eight o'clock news, she dunked a lump of Whole Nut in her tea. The melted chocolate oozed over her tongue, a comforting, sensuous feeling. The newsreader prattled on about Brussels and the by-election in Cavan, and some farmer in Roscommon who had found a cure for impotence derived from distilled bulls' urine. Cash was only half listening, but she shuddered at the thought of what could have led him to that earth-shattering discovery.

Then her ears pricked up as she caught the tail end of a report concerning a hit-and-run incident that had occurred on Bath Avenue, in the early hours of the previous day.

'The woman has been identified as Eileen Porter, a fifty-eight-year-old mother of four from Foxrock. Gardai are appealing for witnesses to come forward.' The newscaster gave a couple of phone numbers before returning to the *Breakfast Show*.

At first Cash thought that it couldn't possibly be *the* Eileen Porter, the woman to whom she had been speaking not forty-eight hours before. But, then, who else? How many Eileen Porters with four children live in Foxrock? She was the right age, too. Dreadful.

It occurred to her that she should go to the funeral on account of Holly. It was probable that Justine would be there. As far as Cash could remember, the youngest Porter girl had been in her year at Loretto. She resolved to call Justine later to check out the arrangements, hoping that Eileen Porter's funeral wouldn't clash with Mort's.

Billie wandered in at that point. She was wearing what Cash always referred to as her giant Babygro, a baby blue one-piece fleecy sleepsuit with feet. She poured herself a mug of tea and climbed into bed beside Cash.

'I couldn't sleep either,' she said, helping herself to the last of the Whole Nut. 'I'll never slag me ma off again when she says she's seen every hour on the feckin' clock.'

Cash sniggered. She'd had the very same thought concerning Yvonne's anguished claims.

'What time are you callin' Janet?'

Cash looked at the clock. It was only eight-fifteen, but she guessed that Mort's widow had also experienced a sleepless night.

'May as well get it over with.' She scrabbled in her bag for her mobile. 'I heard on the news that the mother of one of my old school friends was killed in a road accident, so that's another funeral I'll have to go to.'

'Feast or famine,' Billie commented.

Cash was right in her assumption concerning Janet's inability to close an eye. She, too, had lain awake all night, though in her case guilt wasn't involved. She had long ago given up feeling guilty about Mort. He had been the architect of his own destruction as far as the drink was concerned. She knew that she had done her best. Supported him in every way she could, helping him to rebuild his life off the drink. And he'd succeeded. She was proud of him.

Had been proud of him.

That was the difficulty. However hard she searched for a reason, she could think of nothing that could be worse than the hell her husband had survived. What could be worse than waking up in the gutter? What could be worse than losing your self-respect? Your marriage, your career, everything?

The more she thought about it, the less she could

comprehend it. Mort was a survivor. Hadn't he proved that? She'd attended counselling with him. The sessions had been difficult, but productive; as useful to her as they had been to him. For the past three years they had been able to communicate in a way that they had never been capable of before. It just didn't make sense. And the gun. Where the hell did that come from? Mort hated guns.

Eight-ten. Better get up. Things to do. People to see. The funeral director for one. Dan Doyle had hinted that the autopsy wouldn't be even started until Sunday at the earliest. Then there was the coroner's court for the inquest. She tried to recall. Did the funeral have to wait until after the inquest? She couldn't remember. In some ways a delay would be all for luck. Mort had brothers in Australia and a sister in the States who'd want to come. They'd have to be told.

God! She hated being the bearer of bad news. Never knew quite what to say.

She was pondering this when the phone beside her bed rang, making her jump. It was Cash Ryan.

Janet had been grateful that Cash had chosen to keep her company the previous day. Dan Doyle had been very kind and sensitive, but she felt that Cash really cared. It was obvious that she was grieving for Mort, not merely suffering from the shock of finding him.

After an awkward minute or so of small talk, Cash said, 'About the funeral. I'll help you with the arrangements if you like. It's no trouble. Have you any idea when it will be?'

'Not really. Well into next week, I should think.' Janet explained, 'There's the autopsy and the inquest. And Mort has a couple of brothers and a sister abroad. I guess they'll want to come.'

Cash hadn't thought of that. 'Oh . . . Right . . . Well, whatever you want me to do, just say.'

'Thanks. You're very good.'

'Nonsense. Mort was a good friend to me. It's the least I can do. Anyway, I want to.' She felt her voice wavering. 'I'd really like to.' She swallowed hard to avoid breaking down and upsetting Janet.

Janet was just as wobbly. Cash heard her clear her throat and take a couple of deep breaths. After a minute she said, 'It doesn't make sense, does it?'

Cash couldn't argue with that. 'No, that's for sure.'

'No. I mean it doesn't make *sense*.' The more Janet thought about it, the less she believed that Mort would kill himself. 'I can't believe, after all Mort went through, getting sober and getting his life back on track, that he'd kill himself.'

Cash didn't know what to say. It was natural enough for Janet to be in denial about it, but was it a good idea to encourage her? She saw a straw and clutched at it. 'Well, um . . . I suppose the autopsy will clear that up.'

Janet was suddenly angry. 'All the autopsy'll establish is that he died as a result of a gunshot wound, Cash.' She was crying now. Angry with herself for being so helpless, Cash stayed silent at the other end of the line, waiting for Janet to say something else. After a while she heard Janet blowing her nose.

Cash felt so sorry for her. She wrongly assumed that Janet was burdened with guilt just as she was, even though, all things considered, if any one had been there for Mort, it had been his wife. 'Would you like me to come round to keep you company, Janet? You shouldn't be on your own right now.'

Company was the last thing Janet felt like, though she appreciated the offer. 'Thanks all the same, but I think I'd rather be on my own today,' she explained. 'I can't cry in front of anyone and I think I want to have a weep for Mort.'

Cash understood and was glad that Janet had been so up front about it. It saved all the usual rigmarole of her asking half a dozen times and Janet refusing, only to give in in the end. Janet, too, was pleased that Cash hadn't insisted.

'Would it be okay if I went in to the office to collect a few things?' Cash asked after a pause.

'Of course. There's stuff I'll have to sort out there, too. I don't suppose you could give me a hand at some stage? You're more familiar with it than me.'

Cash assured her that she would be only too happy. She was grateful to be asked for help. It made her feel less guilty about Mort if she was actively helping his widow.

After she hung up, Janet had a shower and washed her hair. It was relaxing and soothing but her mind kept going back to Mort. She could see him clearly, lying on the table with a white sheet pulled up to his chin. The hot power jet pummelled her shoulders. She circled her head to ease the tension in her neck. Then all of a sudden it hit her. Mort couldn't have taken his own life. Suddenly, despite the fact that she was grieving for Mort, despite the fact that her husband was dead, she felt her spirits lift.

After hastily wrapping a bath sheet around herself, she picked up the phone.

Chapter Thirteen

Joanne drove into town and parked her car in the Jervis Centre. Her appointment was at eleven so she planned to do a bit of shopping in Marks & Sparks, take a hasty trip around Debenhams, then she'd just have time for a quick coffee before shooting over to Marlborough Street for her meeting with Mrs Haffner at the agency.

Marks was relatively quiet, so after she had successfully located the particular kind of opaque tights that she preferred to wear from the dozens on offer, she ambled over to the children's wear section.

She was half-afraid to buy anything in case it would be tempting fate. But, then, it wasn't as if *she* were pregnant, and Mrs Haffner had assured them that both mother and unborn baby were in excellent health. What could possibly go wrong? A navy and white striped sailor suit caught her eye. It had a cute little anchor motif and a dinky hat to match. She hesitated for a micro-second, then rooted through the rail for the smallest size. 'Why not?' she said aloud.

On her way across the concourse to Debenhams she literally bumped into Cash who was mooching along with her head down and her hands in her pockets. 'God! You look awful. Who died?'

Cash looked startled for a second, until she realised that her sister was trying to be funny. 'Haven't you heard? Mort Higgins is dead. He killed himself.'

Joanne was mortified. 'Good grief, that's terrible. I'm so sorry.'

'I found him in the office when I got in to work yesterday.'

Joanne could see that her sister was traumatised. She surreptitiously squinted at her watch, estimated that she had time and took her by the arm. 'Come on, you could do with a strong cup of coffee.'

They chose a table in Bewleys. Cash declined anything to eat, but Joanne ordered a Danish. Despite her sister's gloom she was elated, but it didn't seem decent to enthuse about her news when Cash was so down. 'So . . . em . . . So when's the funeral?' she asked for want of something better to say.

'Not sure. Probably after the weekend. By the way, weren't you at school with Hazel Porter?'

'Hazel? Yes. Why?'

'You didn't hear, then. Her mother, Eileen, was killed in a hit-and-run the night before last.'

'Good God, it's a bloodbath out there.' Joanne didn't mean to be facetious, but she was in such good spirits she was having difficulty in relating to the misfortune of others. Cash's expression told her that her reaction wasn't appreciated. 'Sorry. Would you like a lift to the funeral?'

'Please.'

They chatted on for a while. Joanne was bursting to tell her about the baby, but somehow the opportunity didn't present itself and time was marching on. At ten to, she stood up and gathered her shopping bags. 'Look, I have to go. I've an appointment in ten minutes on Marlborough Street.'

Cash didn't seem too put out. 'Marlborough Street? What for?'

Joanne grinned like a Cheshire cat and sat back down. 'Well, seeing as you're asking . . .'

Breathless, Joanne hurried across O'Connell Street against the lights, dodging a taxi and cheating death. The clock above Cleary's said eleven-ten. She cut down Sackville Place and a couple of minutes later stopped outside the offices of Adoptions Home & Abroad. She peered at her reflection in the glass door and fixed her hair. The office was located on the first floor above a café. A sign on the steamy café window read DROP-IN CENTRE.

With her breathing back to normal, she pressed the buzzer, and a moment later a disembodied voice crackled over the intercom.

'Adoptions Home & Abroad. How can I help you?'

'I have an appointment with Mrs Haffner. My name is Joanne McAndrew.'

Instantly the lock released and she pushed the door open.

The receptionist showed her into Mrs Haffner's office. Mrs Haffner strode across the room, hand out-stretched, to meet her. 'Joanne, good to see you.'

'Sorry I'm a bit late. I was delayed.'

'Think nothing of it.' Mrs Haffner ushered her over to the sofa, then took her seat, as before, in one of the armchairs. She cut straight to the chase. 'Good news, Joanne. Our mother's decided to come home to Ireland to have her baby.'

'But that's wonderful.' Could the day get any better? 'What made her change her mind?'

'Your guess is as good as mine, my dear, but I suspect she realised that, compared to here, the hospitals in Morocco leave a lot to be desired.'

'So does that change the procedure much?'

'Oh, yes, indeed. Things will be a lot more straight-forward now. There is the matter of our mother's air fare, of course, and her expenses while she's over here, but I'm sure that won't be a problem for you.'

'No, not at all. How much do you need?'

Mrs Haffner pushed her glasses up her nose and shuffled through her papers. She extracted a document. 'Well, there's the home study fee, the mother's return air fare, her accommodation, hospital fees, etc. Then, of course, there's our fee.' She picked up a calculator and punched numbers in. 'That comes to £4700. Is that okay?'

'That's fine.' On their previous meeting Mrs Haffner had estimated that expenses would come to around the six thousand mark, between one thing and another. Joanne had heard of some foreign adoptions coming to as much as ten thousand pounds. Not that money was a consideration. Both she and Rodney were desperate for a child. She opened her bag and took out her cheque-book.

Billie was having a pig of a day. Recklessly she had offered to stand in for Taragh, who had an audition for the Gayety panto, and teach her jazz classes. What Taragh had omitted to mention, however, was that every student in all four classes was totally devoid of any sense of rhythm. After a baptism of fire with the first lot tripping over their own feet, she decided that perhaps drag runs were a little ambitious and simplified the routine for the second class. Even then none of them seemed capable of counting to eight in time with the music. By the final class she decided to concentrate on stretches and eliminate the routine altogether, until the would-be hoofers protested. Roll on Christmas and the Caribbean sun.

She was cheered by the thought of the seminar. After her initial reservations she had found Cora and Curt very encouraging. After just talking to them the previous day she felt better about herself. More confident. More in control. She hadn't had the courage to come clean and admit that the revelations of her previous visit had been so much bullshit, but she'd decided that it shouldn't make any difference. Self-esteem is self-esteem whichever way you look at it. And if, after the load of cobblers she'd spouted, they still thought she was worth something, then all the better.

Of course, it was early days yet. Who was to say that if a challenging situation arose she would be capable of rising to meet it? But, then, that was the purpose of the seminars. Self-help. 'You need to face your issues, Billie,' Cora had said. 'We can help you to do that. We can help you to shake off the negative thoughts and attitudes that are holding you back. You're a beautiful human being.'

She wasn't so sure about that but, hey, what did she have to lose, apart from twenty-five quid? And if it made her feel only slightly more confident it would be money well spent.

Only five minutes to go until the end of the class. 'Okay. One more time from the top.' She pushed the play button of the CD player. The first bars of 'It's Rainin' Men' boomed out of the speakers. 'Okay, guys, five, six, sev-ven eight . . .'

At last, twelve pairs of feet stomped in unison . . . at least they did for the first three beats.

Janet Higgins was fuming. Dan Doyle's attitude to her assertion that Mort had been murdered had been patronising and dismissive to say the least. The nub of her argument was the fact that Mort had been shot in the right temple. Doyle had stared at her blankly. His body language screamed, So?

'Dan, you know as well as I do, Mort was *left*-handed. And if you're left-handed you wouldn't pick up a gun in your right hand, for God's sake. Do I have to spell it out?' She was tempted to add, *you moron.*

Doyle had just nodded non-committally and sighed. 'Look, Janet. I know this is hard for you to accept, but you're forgetting Mort had taken nearly a whole bottle of whiskey. He was hardly in a rational state of mind. Anyway, why would anyone want to murder him? Where's the motive?' He wished she'd just let it go.

At this, Janet had almost guffawed. 'Are you kidding? Have you forgotten what Mort did for a living? There must be dozens of people who he's investigated who'd gladly see him dead.'

'In theory, maybe,' Doyle conceded. 'But . . .' He shrugged and left the sentence hanging. It was an unpleasant situation. It was understandable that she'd be in denial, only natural, and in his experience survivors always found suicide hardest of all to come to terms with. It would have been easier if Janet were a stranger. It was to her credit that she so obviously cared about Mort when he'd led her such a dog's life while they were together. Despite what he had said to Cash about Mort being a great crack, Doyle had never really liked him.

Janet Higgins had no intention of letting it go, even though it was obvious she was going to get no joy from Dan Doyle.

She was still seething when Cash walked into the office half an hour later. After their earlier conversation, Cash was surprised to see her there. She was under the impression that Janet was going to spend the day crying.

Janet was muttering angrily to herself, while sorting through Mort's files. Cash could only catch the odd word. 'Stupid . . . *mutter, mutter* . . . eejitts . . . *mut-*

ter, mumble. Couldn't organise . . . *mutter, mutter . . .* piss-up . . . *mumble, mumble* . . . fucking brewery.'

She didn't look up from her task. Without preamble she said, 'I need to see all Mort's current files and the stuff he worked on over the past month for starters.'

Cash was at a loss, but didn't ask for an explanation. 'Em . . . okay.' She moved over to the metal filing cabinet, and Janet stood back. Cash started to leaf through the files and Janet started to pace. 'That moron Doyle won't listen. I'll show the bastard.'

Cash continued sorting. 'Show him what?'

Janet was still pacing furiously. 'That Mort was murdered, of course!'

Cash spun around from the cabinet, whacking her elbow in the process. 'What?'

Janet was standing in the middle of the room with her feet planted apart and her hands on her hips, daring Cash to argue. Cash hadn't a notion. Humour her maybe but, in Janet's present state of mind, certainly not argue.

Janet drew breath. 'He's too fucking stupid to see what's right in front of his eyes. I knew it didn't feel right. I knew there was something iffy about it.'

She said it with such fury Cash just gaped at her, uncomprehending. Had the shock of Mort's death finally caused her to crack up? Janet ranted on. Cash hadn't a clue what she was talking about, her diatribe a mishmash of disjointed sentences. Eventually after a couple of minutes she ran out of steam.

'What makes you think Mort was murdered?' Cash asked tentatively, mentally cringing away from another outburst.

Janet suddenly felt foolish. It was rare for her to lose her composure, and she hated how undignified it made her feel. She took a couple of deep breaths and sat down at Cash's desk. Very slowly and calmly she repeated to Cash her reasons for believing that Mort had been murdered. She cited the fact that he had been left-handed and also pointed out that Mort had had a deep and abiding hatred of guns, that there was no way, if he were to kill himself, that he would ever have used a gun. In fact, he had said as much to her once while in a drunken depression. She finished off by stating, 'And I'm a hundred per cent certain that Mort wasn't back on the drink. I'd stake my life on it. I'd have known. I'd have sensed it.'

'I don't think he was back on the drink either.' Cash was glad that she wasn't the only one to doubt the notion that Mort had fallen off the wagon. 'But who d'you think murdered him?'

Janet shook her head. 'I don't know. I can only assume it has something to do with his work. The spouse of an ex-client, maybe. People can get very bitter over marriage break-ups. Especially if it costs them more than they think is fair. Mort did a lot of divorce work, didn't he?'

'A fair amount.'

'That's why I want to check the files. It might give me some possibilities to go to the cops with.'

Cash turned back to the filing cabinet and flipped through the buff folders, drawing Mr Harbinger's file out – insider theft – and placing it on top of the cabinet. 'You're really serious about this, aren't you?'

Janet nodded emphatically. 'Absolutely. The more I think about it, the more I know Mort wouldn't commit suicide. No way. He'd been to hell and back already.'

Cash located Mrs Nuttall's folder, the Leinster Insurance company file – fraudulent claim – and the Morrison file – matrimonial. As she was searching, Janet was making a pot of coffee. 'These are his most recent jobs,'

Cash said. She started on the Ps. 'There's one more. A Mrs Eileen Porter, but I can't seem to find the file.'

Janet poured the boiling water on the coffee-grounds.

Cash went back to the beginning of the P section. When she had no luck she checked the Es in case Mort had misfiled it, then the Qs, with no success.

Janet poured the coffee into two mugs. 'Any luck?'

Suddenly it hit Cash. 'Oh, God!' Her hand shot to her mouth.

Janet looked concerned. 'What?'

'Eileen Porter. Mort's client. She's dead. She was killed in a hit-and-run accident the same night as Mort. And her file's missing. It's not here.'

'Are you sure?' Janet's face was pallid and her eyes looked huge.

Cash nodded. 'I'm certain.'

Chapter Fourteen

From the doorway of the shoe shop, Sister Jude had a good view of the drop-in centre. She was glad that Marlborough Street was busy with shoppers as it made her feel less conspicuous. It was a cold evening and she stomped her feet, trying to ward off the chill that was creeping up through her limbs.

Someone had wiped the condensation from the inside of the window so she could clearly see the woman, Cora, standing near the coffee-counter, talking to Curt and another young man of about the same age. A black girl and a middle-aged woman were sitting at a table together. The black girl was studying her feet, avoiding eye contact with the others in the room. The woman was studiously examining a leaflet. As Sister Jude watched, the young man she had seen on her last visit – the student, Sean – pushed the door open and was immediately greeted by Curt. He joined Cora, Curt and the other man by the coffee-counter.

She'd been standing in the same spot for over an hour now. She had come straight from school. She was disappointed, though not greatly surprised, that Tiffany hadn't put in an appearance, but Tiffany wasn't the reason for her visit.

Sister Jude was standing in a cold shop doorway in Marlborough Street solely to see for herself if Dr Rory Keogh, Ph.D., was the same Rory Keogh she had last seen twenty-five years, eleven months and two . . . no, four days before.

Not that she was in any doubt. The picture left no room for doubt.

She held her wrist nearer to the bright light of the shop window and squinted at the time. Five-fifty. Only ten minutes to go. The leaflet had advised that the seminar 'Meditate Your Way to Higher Self-Esteem' commenced at six p.m. and that the speaker was Dr Rory Keogh, Ph.D., hence Sister Jude's vigil.

Her feet had lost all feeling now. She was tempted to go into the shop to purchase a pair of thermal insoles, but decided there wasn't time. Good call. A moment later a taxi drew up outside the drop-in centre and a man got out. He was bundled up in a heavy overcoat and scarf, with a fleecy hat pulled down over his forehead so she didn't get a good look at him. A bus drove by, shielding him from view for a moment. Sister Jude felt a wave of frustration. Then, there he was. Inside the drop-in centre. Standing talking to Cora. No hat. No scarf. Rory Keogh.

Her heart was pounding in her chest and she could hear the blood coursing through her brain. She felt suddenly faint. She staggered slightly and held on to the edge of the window.

'You okay, Sister?' a voice asked.

'I'm fine, thank you.'

Fine.

Sister Jude had first met Rory Keogh at the Stones' free concert in Hyde Park at the end of the sixties. He was from home so the accent had attracted her. They had talked. Smoked a couple of joints together and generally hung out for the rest of the weekend. He'd been with a gang of lads and they'd all had a great crack. There had been no mention of politics. No talk of the troubles back home. It was as if they were in a different world. Anyway, politics had never interested her as a girl. It was before the days of internment.

Internment had changed all that. After she returned to Derry to study for her Master's, she got caught up in it. It was unavoidable. Friends were picked up and interned, lads that she knew had nothing to do with the troubles, some for no other reason than they played Gaelic games or spoke Irish. It spread bitterness through the community. The politically disinterested suddenly became politicised. She'd be out with the best of them, banging dustbin lids, warning those who needed to be warned about approaching army patrols. But that was the limit of her involvement. It was almost like a game to her. High on rhetoric, low on action. She was playing a part.

It was on campus that she ran into Rory again. There was talk that he was a Provo, but he was never lifted. He kept a low profile. She was drawn towards him. Even back then he had charisma, could hold a person spellbound when he spoke of the cause. He wasn't one for rabble-rousing. His oratory was confined to small groups, or one to one. It was inspiring stuff. He sucked her in.

She carried guns for him from one place to another. Passed on messages. It was exciting. It turned her on. Rory turned her on. It was all part of the game.

The game had turned to grim reality the day she witnessed a soldier hit in the face by a sniper's bullet. He dropped at her feet. He was screaming. The bullet had taken his nose off and shattered his cheekbone. There was blood everywhere. She had never seen blood like it. Not for real. He only looked about nineteen. Younger than her. Only a boy. She couldn't move. Stood rooted to the spot, staring. A soldier shoved her out of the way.

He was shouting unintelligible stuff about Fenian bastards. Sirens were whooping, people running every which way.

Rory had been dismissive. He was a Brit. A member of the occupying force. A casualty of war.

'But he was only a kid,' she'd protested.

'He's a serving member of the British Army, sent here to occupy *our* country. He's expendable. Don't waste your sympathy.' Rory spoke the words with venom. She was disgusted.

After a time he convinced her to a degree, but she still couldn't get the young soldier's face out of her mind. She never found out what had ultimately happened to him. The incident had opened her eyes. She began to see Rory Keogh in a new light.

Seeing him in the flesh again brought it all back. Across the street the brave Rory was standing by the coffee-counter, talking to Cora. Then he turned and spoke to the black girl. She stood up and he shook her hand, before turning his attention to the middle-aged woman.

Sister Jude had no idea what to do next. No real idea of why she was there at all. As she watched, the group, with the exception of Cora, moved out of view through a door at the back of the room. She hesitated for a moment, then pulled her coat collar up around her throat and hurried off to find her bus.

It was decided after discussion that Cash should approach Detective Doyle about the matter of Mrs Porter and the missing file. Cash argued that, as he was of the opinion that Janet was in denial, there was a better chance he would listen to what *she* had to say.

She phoned him, but was told by the desk sergeant, after some persistence on her part, that Detective Doyle was off duty and wasn't due in again until Sunday morning for the six-till-two shift. This took the wind out of her sails. She was all fired up and raring to go. She'd rehearsed exactly what she was going to say to him, mindful of the fact that he'd already thrown Janet's murder theory into touch, so to speak.

Janet was disappointed, too. She was equally anxious to get Doyle on their side. Without him she knew there was little chance of getting to the bottom of Mort's death. Equally, she was conscious that she needed it to be a fact that Mort's death was down to murder, not the awful spectre of suicide. Even though logic told her that she had no cause to feel any guilt, it was still there at the back of her mind, gnawing away at her.

To fill the void of anticlimax Cash and Janet headed for the Palace for a drink and a more congenial atmosphere in which to review the situation. The pub was crowded with Friday evening drinkers and they had to squeeze in at the crush by the bar. But just as the barman slid their drinks across the well-worn mahogany counter, Cash spotted two girls and an older man vacating a table in the corner. She scooted over and laid claim, causing much huffing and puffing from a couple of fifty-something civil-servant types in suits, who had spotted the vacant table only nano-seconds after Cash. She draped her coat across the back of one chair and sat on the other, spreading herself out, claiming the territory. Janet came over with the drinks.

Because of the chill of the evening Cash had ordered a hot whiskey and Janet a hot port. They clutched their glasses to warm their hands. It was more for want of something to do. Although the purpose of their adjournment to the pub had been to discuss a plan of action, the truth was that they had no real plan of action if Doyle didn't buy their story. As if reading

Cash's thoughts, Janet said, 'What if Dan Doyle won't do anything?'

Cash took a swig of her hot whiskey. 'Let's not be negative,' she said. 'Surely Eileen Porter's death and the file going missing at the same time should be enough to at least make him take another look at it.'

Janet wasn't as confident. She had known Dan Doyle for as long as she'd known Mort. She was well aware that he and Mort hadn't exactly been best buddies. They had history.

Until his problems with the drink Mort had always enjoyed more success in the job than Doyle. Janet knew that there was a certain amount of resentment on Doyle's part. Which wasn't fair really. Mort had been a good cop. Methodical and meticulous. It had been down to hard work, not luck, but Dan Doyle didn't see it that way.

Janet also suspected that Doyle, despite his murmurs of support and sympathy, had been secretly pleased when Mort had messed up. She had also been uncomfortably conscious at the time she had walked out on Mort that Doyle had tried to move in on her, but she'd just played dumb and brushed it off. Doyle hadn't persisted. She wondered if the rebuff would count as another reason for resentment on his part. Because of the history, she knew that it would take hard evidence to make him change his mind. She took a sip of her drink and inhaled the fruity fumes. 'What exactly was in this file?'

Cash sighed despondently. 'Not a lot really. Just a few details about Daisy Porter.'

'I don't understand. Why would anyone want to steal it, then?'

Cash shrugged. 'Got me there. But it doesn't alter the fact that Eileen Porter was killed the same night as

Mort. It's the only link we have. Mort and the Eileen Porter case. The missing file.'

Janet frowned. 'So let's get this straight. Eileen Porter's daughter, Daisy, runs off with this cult, and the mother asks Mort to look into it?'

Cash nodded. 'That's about the size of it. Of course, I can't say for sure if they're a cult or not. Personally I think they sound like a crowd of chancers but my friend Billie checked them out and she didn't seem to think they were sinister at all. A bit *full on*, as she put it, but they didn't pressure her in any way to join or anything.'

'That doesn't mean a thing. It could be their way of building up confidence. Anyway, she might not be the type they're after. What do you know about this Daisy?'

'Nothing much. She's around twenty-five. I was at school with her older sister. They're a pretty ordinary family. Well off, but ordinary. I think Mr Porter's a dentist, but I'm not sure.'

'It's not much to persuade Doyle.'

Cash took another sip of her drink. Now that the first flush of excitement had worn off she, too, was having doubts. Not about the fact that Mort's death was murder – she, like Janet, needed to believe that – but on the face of it the connection between his murder and Eileen Porter and a missing file containing nothing in any way incriminating was tenuous to say the least.

She frowned. 'One thing worries me, though. Mort said Eileen Porter talked about snatching Daisy back. He told me he hadn't a notion of getting mixed up in kidnapping, of course, but what if she talked him into it and something went wrong?'

'Surely you don't think these cult people'd kill him on account of that? If he and the Porter woman were caught trying to snatch the daughter, surely . . . I mean, all they'd have to do was set the cops on Mort.

Daisy's an adult. They wouldn't have a leg to stand on. No, I can't see it. Mort must have discovered something bad about them. Something that made them panic. Something they wouldn't want to involve the cops in.'

'So what about Eileen Porter?'

Janet pursed her lips, exhaling through her nose. 'I don't know. If she was with Mort at the time . . .' She let the sentence hang for a moment, before adding, 'I'm just trying to think of all the possibilities so we have some ammunition when you talk to Doyle.'

Talking it through with Janet, Cash was beginning to see all the flaws in their hypothesis. 'That still doesn't explain the elaborate scene they set up with Mort in the office. Why didn't they just leave him in the road with Eileen Porter?'

Janet frowned. 'You tell me.' She sounded very down.

Cash said, 'I'm going to Eileen's funeral tomorrow. I'll talk to Holly. She's the sister I was at school with. If I can get her interested, that'll put more pressure on the cops to do something about it.' Then a thought struck her. 'Hey . . . Daisy might even be there. I could have a word with her, too.'

'Do you think she'll show up?' Janet suddenly sounded more hopeful.

Cash shrugged. 'Well, if she does, all well and good. It'll be a bonus.'

Janet drained her glass, straining the clove through her teeth. She picked it out from between her lips and dropped it back in the glass. 'Okay. And for Doyle's benefit, while you're doing that, I'll go through all Mort's files and see if there are any other candidates.'

Cash nodded. 'I'll help you after I get back.'

'Would you?' Janet sounded grateful. Cash was surprised that she'd be in any doubt.

Janet gathered her coat from the back of the chair. 'I'd

better go. Mort's brother Hubie's phoning me from Oz at seven. I don't want to miss his call.'

As Cash knocked back the rest of her now lukewarm whiskey, Janet pushed back her chair and stood up. Cash did likewise. She noticed the civil servants getting ready to pounce. Before they had a chance, three girls in bank uniforms appeared as if from nowhere and snatched the seats from under their outraged noses.

As she passed one of the civil servants she heard him muttering about how the country was going to the dogs when slips of girls were drinking in pubs.

Billie was as high as a kite. Bursting with enthusiasm. The seminar had been a great success. She felt energised by both the meditation and the talk by Dr Keogh. Suddenly anything was possible. So much so that she'd signed up on the spot for the next two sessions. There had only been the three of them – Jean, Sean and herself. Cora had said that two others were expected but they hadn't shown up. Their loss, Billie thought.

She fingered the small clear crystal that now hung from a thin chain around her neck. Dr Keogh had explained all about the power of crystals and positive energy. He had further explained that the purpose of the crystal was to serve as a conduit by which to drain negative energy from the system. He had demonstrated breathing techniques, combined with personal mantras, by which to boost the positive forces. The actual meditation had lasted for a good hour, but to Billie it had seemed like only ten minutes. She had never felt so good, or so good about herself. It was a cold, miserable evening but she didn't care.

As she turned the corner into Tara Street she saw a number three bus at the stop by the cinema. She broke into a run and reached the stop just as the last person in the queue was paying his fare. Now, there was a bit of luck. She had expected that she would have to walk out to Ringsend.

As was usual on Friday nights, Billie called out at Ringsend to see her mother. It was a weekly ritual but, unlike Cash's home visits, she looked forward to it. Marvin was usually there. He still lived at home, and Regina always made a point of calling in at some point. She was dying to tell them about the cruise and the fact that she was to be dance captain. When Maurice had broken the news she had been apprehensive of the responsibility. It involved coaching the other dancers in the choreographer's routines, but now, since this evening, and thanks to Dr Keogh, she was ready for the challenge, ready and able.

Tiffany Ring lay on her back and stared at the ceiling. She found that nowadays it was the only way she could sleep. If she had learned one lesson it was that pregnancy was an uncomfortable business. If she lay on her side her swollen boobs got in the way and the baby kicked like he was in *Riverdance*, and lying on her stomach, as was her preference, was out of the question. Then there was the indigestion. God! Was that chronic. One of the other expectant mothers at the antenatal clinic had said that indigestion was a sign that the baby had hair. Given the choice, she'd have chosen a bald baby any day.

It was strange lying there in the pitch darkness. And the silence. All her life Tiffany had been accustomed to the yellow glow of streetlights and the hum of traffic at night. She decided she liked it. Liked the peace and quiet. For now, anyway. It was a change from Sister Jude telling her what to do and Sandra whinging about her choice of music. Good to have a room to herself.

Better than home and her ma. Better than being near Uncle Barry.

She was angry now. Thinking of Uncle bloody Barry always had that effect. And her ma, blaming *her* for it. Though she had blamed herself, even after she'd been taken into care by the Eastern Health Board and they'd brought her to counselling. She felt responsible for bringing the baby into the world. Responsible for its care. It was only now, after talking to Cora, that she was beginning to see things as they really were. That it wasn't her fault. She wasn't responsible. She had a future. She was a good person.

She rubbed her stomach. The skin felt so tight she was afraid sometimes that she'd burst. Yes, pregnancy was an uncomfortable business all right. The sooner the six weeks were over and they got the baby out of there the sooner she'd be free to start over.

Chapter Fifteen

At nine o'clock on Saturday morning Joanne got a call from Mrs Haffner. It left her anxious. Mrs Haffner had been vague as to the nature of the problem, but left her in no doubt there was a hitch of some sort with the adoption. She asked if Joanne could meet her at the office on Marlborough Street, but when she explained that she had to attend a funeral, Mrs Haffner kindly offered to drive out to Dalkey. 'I'm not that far away,' she explained. 'I only live in Monkstown.'

Rodney had just left for his Saturday morning round of golf and his mobile was switched off so she couldn't reach him. Then – inspiration – she called Richard Dillon, hoping to catch Rodney's golf partner before he left. She was in luck, and Richard promised to pass on her message about a crisis at home as soon as they met up in the locker room.

Mrs Haffner arrived twenty minutes later. Joanne had heard the sound of a car engine and had gone immediately to the front door. When Mrs Haffner got out of her Range Rover, Joanne noticed that she was still wearing the same suit she had worn previously but with a different blouse. She also wore a very serious expression.

'Mrs McAndrew, Joanne,' she said by way of a greeting.

'What's the problem, Mrs Haffner?' Joanne tried to

sound light-hearted, but her stomach was in knots. She stood back, inviting Mrs Haffner in, and indicated the open door of the drawing room. Mrs Haffner led the way and perched herself on the edge of the sofa. Joanne was too wound up to sit. She hovered by the mantelpiece.

'What's happened? What's the problem? It's not the baby, is it? There's nothing wrong with the baby?' Joanne suddenly thought of the blue striped sailor's suit. Had she tempted fate after all?

Mrs Haffner smiled for the first time. 'Oh, there's nothing wrong with the baby. As far as we know, the baby's fine. It seems our mother's got herself in some trouble, and the Moroccan authorities are holding on to her passport until she pays them five thousand American dollars.'

'But how can they do that? She's an Irish national.'

'Apparently, as far as my contact can ascertain, the five thousand dollars is a fine of some sort. At the moment the girl's in jail.'

'Jail!' Joanne could only imagine what a Moroccan jail would be like. 'But what for? What did she do? Surely they can't do that. She's nearly eight months pregnant, for God's sake.'

'So far we don't know what the fine's about. My contact's getting on to the Irish consul as we speak, but our first concern must be for the baby. I'm sure you agree.'

'Of course. Of course. What can we do?'

Just then the phone rang, making the already stressed-out Joanne jump sky high. She ran to the hall.

Rodney was not happy. His Saturdays were sacrosanct. Nine-thirty, eighteen holes. Eleven-thirty, a couple in the clubhouse. One o'clock, lunch at home. In season, rugby at Lansdown Road, or maybe racing at the Curragh or wherever there was a meeting. Saturday was his day to unwind.

'What the hell's the matter?' he barked.

It was too much for Joanne. She broke down in tears. Rodney was shocked into silence. Joanne rarely turned on the waterworks and, on the rare occasions she did, he couldn't handle it. Couldn't handle anyone crying, particularly his wife. He softened his tone. 'I'm sorry, precious. What's the problem? What's happened?' He, too, was feeling panicky now.

Joanne explained as best she could between sobs, and Rodney told her to pour herself a stiff drink and that he'd be home in fifteen minutes.

An hour and two stiff brandies later, Joanne was much calmer. Mrs Haffner had left, along with a cheque for three and a half thousand pounds to cover the five thousand dollar fine and a promise to get back to them as soon as possible with news of the matter. The plan was to get the pregnant girl out of Morocco as soon as the fine was paid and her passport retrieved.

Rodney had a few misgivings at first but Mrs Haffner was very persuasive, citing the wellbeing of the unborn child as their highest priority. She also pointed out the scarcity of Irish babies and reiterated the fact that if they let the opportunity go, who was to say when another child of any nationality would be available, let alone an Irish one. At once his mental picture of Rodney Junior in his green rugby jersey evaporated with a pop. Rodney Senior took out his cheque-book.

Cash had spent the night on her own in the flat as Billie was sleeping over at home. She wished she was as keen as her friend when it came to spending time with her family.

She rose at nine and had a long hot shower. She had slept only fitfully the night before. Her mind had been racing and wouldn't settle. From time to time, as she'd tossed and turned, she'd tried to think of more pleasant things, but the picture of Mort slumped dead in his chair kept overriding all other thoughts.

She wished Billie was home. She could have done with some company other than the tacky icons. Inadvertently she had somehow hit the on switch of Pope JPII and, as there didn't appear to be any means by which to switch him off, he'd been giving her the finger all night. *Buzz, eeek, buzz, eeek.* And he was still at it.

As she was drying her hair, the tinkly sound of 'Jingle Bells' alerted her to the fact that there was an incoming call on her mobile. She slung the hairdryer on the sofa, picked up the phone and hit the 'yes' button, making a mental note to change the ring tone. She'd been meaning to do it since the New Year but hadn't got around to it. That the tune was now almost back in season again didn't occur to her.

Justine was at the other end of the line.

'Change of plan,' she said. 'Can you get a cab out here? Joanne's been held up so she won't have time to collect you. She'll pick us up together. Is that okay?'

It wasn't really okay. Going home meant talking to her mother, and in the past two weeks she'd been on overdose levels of mother-induced stress, but what could she say? After Justine hung up, she ordered a minicab and hoped that Yvonne would either be out or, if not, that she hadn't yet got wind of Simon's premature return.

Cash finished drying her hair and then dressed in a black suit, teaming it up with a charcoal grey velvet short-sleeved top, black tights and black court shoes. Her make-up only got as far as the foundation before the minicab was at the door. She asked him to wait, then went back inside and hastily daubed a coat of mascara on her eyelashes. She dropped her lipstick and it rolled under the sofa bed. She couldn't be bothered looking for it, so just slipped on Billie's long black coat, which she had offered to lend her the previous day, grabbed her bag and ran out to the taxi.

Yvonne opened the front door to her. 'Darling. So awful about poor Eileen Porter.' She looked suitably anguished, though to Cash's knowledge Yvonne had never met the deceased.

'Yes, awful.'

They walked down the hall together towards the kitchen. She knew her father would be out seeking sanctuary on the golf course, so she resigned herself to an uninterrupted half-hour of interrogation by her mother. She was glad that at least she could brag about the Channel 4 audition and, although she wasn't sure she wanted to do it, the small part in the offing at Andrews Lane.

Cash could hear Justine moving about upstairs. She wished she would get her butt down to the kitchen to lend her some moral support.

Justine had a talent for defusing awkward situations where Yvonne was concerned. Shamefaced though she was to admit it, Cash acknowledged the fact that she was still afraid of her mother.

She decided to get in first. 'I've got an audition for a Channel 4 series.'

Yvonne's head snapped round. 'Channel 4?' She sounded impressed. It was a good start.

'Yes. If it comes off, it'll be for thirteen episodes. Possibly more if the series is successful.' This was stretching the truth. Cash hadn't a clue about the life expectancy of this Irish-hooker-with-a-heart-of-gold.

She just hoped she'd prove to have more longevity than poor Fifi Mulligan.

It was a false dawn. Things went rapidly downhill after that. As Yvonne poured boiling water into the coffee-maker she suddenly said, 'Why didn't you tell me Simon was home? I saw him at a distance in town yesterday.'

'Simon who?' Cash squeaked lamely.

Yvonne was looking at her oddly. 'Your Simon, of course.' She paused, then frowned. 'What have you done? You haven't fallen out with him, have you?' The anguished look returned, this time mingled with under-lying disappointment.

'Not exactly.'

Yvonne pursed her lips and squinted at her. 'How "not exactly", exactly?'

'Um . . .'

Yvonne made a humph sound and stood with her feet planted apart and her hands on her hips. 'Listen to me, my girl. If you've fallen out with him, you'll get on the phone to him right now and kiss and make up. Do you hear me?'

'Um . . . Well, it's not as simple as that. You see . . .' Here Cash affected a cross between a cough and a sob, and covered her eyes with her hand. 'Simon has decided that he has a vocation. He's going for the priesthood.'

Yvonne looked stunned. 'The priesthood? Simon? Our Simon? Your Simon?'

Cash gave a dainty sniff. 'He's not *my* Simon any more, Mummy. He belongs to Jesus now.' The state-ment was followed by another sob. Cash wished that the Channel 4 crew were there to witness her performance.

Unexpectedly, Yvonne put her arm around her middle daughter's shoulder, then gave her a comforting squeeze. 'Poor pet. Poor, poor pet.' The subtext of the remark being, 'So sad that you can't hold on to a man.'

Cash gave one more sob – no need to overdo it – then sniffed heroically. 'I know, Mummy. But how can we begrudge him to God? If God's calling him, how can we stand in his way?'

Her mother stood back and stared at her, and for a moment Cash thought she'd blown it. Then Yvonne nodded sagely and enveloped her again in a hug. Over her mother's shoulder Cash saw Justine's gobsmacked expression as she walked down the hall and came upon the scene.

At that very moment the door-chimes bonged and Cash could see Joanne's shadow on the outer side of the glass door panel. She seized the moment to break free from her mother's vice-like embrace.

'Oh . . .' Sniff, sniff. 'Here's Joanne. Better . . .' sniff '. . . get on.' It was heroic stuff. Justine gave her another weird look, then trotted down the hall to open the door for her eldest sister.

Yvonne fussed over the coffee-maker, then poured each of them a cup of coffee, insisting that they'd need a hot drink or they'd catch their death of cold standing round a freezing cemetery.

Under her breath, Justine was heard to comment, 'No better place.'

As the three siblings stood in the kitchen, forcing down the unwanted beverage, out of the corner of her eye Cash saw Yvonne throwing pitying looks her way every couple of minutes. It was marginally less awful than bearing the brunt of her mother's martyrdom.

Ten minutes later they hit the road. Joanne had picked up a wreath on the way over and handed Justine the card and a ballpoint with which to sign it.

Justine obliged. 'What was *that* all about?' she asked

as she handed the card and pen over the back of the front seat to Cash.

'Oh, I was just trying to let mother down gently. Simon dumped me the other day, you see. He's chosen the celibate life instead of me.'

Justine guffawed. 'No, really . . . What was it?'

'I told you. Simon dumped me. He suddenly decided that he's got a vocation. I think he got stuck in character while he was playing Judas so he's joining the Cistercians. I told Mother he's going to be a priest, though. I thought she'd take it better if I said that.'

Justine was in paroxysms of hysteria by this time. Joanne hadn't made any comment. Cash looked over at her, expecting her to be equally amused, but her elder sister was staring straight ahead, knuckles white, gripping the steering-wheel. It was obvious that she wasn't listening. Cash tapped her on the shoulder. 'What's up, Jojo?'

Joanne gave a cursory look over her shoulder. 'What?'

Justine, having recovered her breath, spluttered, 'Simon's dumped Cash, Dougal. He's going for the prie—' She couldn't get any further and exploded into a fit of the giggles again.

Joanne, uninterested, sighed. 'Oh.'

Cash shot a warning glance at Justine. It was obvious that Joanne was upset about something. Cash's glare stopped her in mid-chortle. She stared at her sister for a moment, then shrugged, spreading her hands and mouthing the word, 'What?'

Cash gave her another withering look and shook her head.

Justine gave a histrionic sigh and slumped in her seat, digging her hands into her pockets. 'I was only saying, Ted.'

They concluded the journey to the church in silence.

Sandra was at band practice over in the community hall. She certainly needed it. She hadn't a note, but she was very enthusiastic. Every Saturday without fail she headed across the estate, lugging her tuba in order to effect serious injury on Elgar and Souza.

Sister Jude washed the breakfast dishes and tidied around the flat. As her charge would be going on to soccer training after the musical carnage, she had the rest of the morning and a couple of hours of the afternoon to herself. It was bliss. She sat at the table, poured herself a mug of very strong coffee and lit a cigarette.

It was rare for the nun to have time to herself, as she usually had at least two teenagers in the flat. She felt a twinge of guilt that she was enjoying the moment, when she had absolutely no idea what had become of Tiffany.

Sister Jude had been brought up on guilt. When she was a child in the fifties and early sixties, until Vatican 2, Catholic teaching had been based on the concept of guilt and penance. Understanding the concept of guilt wasn't a problem, especially after surviving the bomb, but even now, as an adult, she couldn't comprehend the notion of penance.

Pity. If she had, at least there would be some purpose in giving up her twenty cigarettes a week and the odd drop of alcohol, but somehow she couldn't reconcile the idea of penance with a loving God.

Why would a loving God require souls to walk barefoot up holy mountains? Why would he expect physical or sensory suffering and deprivation? What was the point in that? As a child she had listened to stories of the martyrs. Of pain and death. Of saints wearing hair shirts, fasting, flogging themselves and that kind of thing. As far as she was concerned, it was sick. Sick and completely pointless.

Far better to do something positive, something useful. Shuffling round the hospital wards and seeing other bomb victims clinging on to life, some horribly mutilated, she had realised that service was the only course of action open to her. That was how she could make good her promise to God.

At twenty-six she'd been old for a postulant. The oldest by a good eight years, in fact. It was hard for her. She'd had an uneasy relationship with God for a long time. She'd never been a Holy Joe but religion went with the territory. She realised that if she wanted to be a nun and pay her debt to God, by serving the poor and needy, she would have to bite the bullet and go along with it, so she kept her opinions concerning what she saw as outdated doctrine and stupid rituals to herself.

She had doubts from time to time, usually at five a.m. when the bell summoned her to morning prayers, as to why it was necessary for her to be a nun at all, when she could quite easily have gone as a volunteer to Africa or India. But, then, usually at the still times in the chapel before Mass, she would realise that there was no alternative. It had to be the full Monty. She'd promised. Lying in the rubble under the body of the old man, she'd promised God that if he let her live she'd give Him her life.

Rash promise.

Hard to live up to, particularly for one who'd rarely crossed the threshold of a church after she had left home. Ironically, towards the middle of her noviciate she began to find comfort in the familiarity of ritual and ceremony. It made her more spiritual and brought her closer to God, or at least it made their relationship less difficult.

When she first went to live out in the community, the residents hadn't been convinced, and she'd been known as the Charity Nun. It was meant to be a sneering derogatory tag. A 'what the hell would she know about real life' tag. 'And her only out of the convent.'

They were right, of course. She'd thought she'd seen it all, thought she'd known all about the deprived and the socially marginalised, but her view was only the sanitised perspective – years out of date – of a rebellious grant-aided student living in a squat in London during vacation time. How hard could that be?

It took a few years of the frustration of knowing that she was blundering in where she was neither wanted nor needed before she finally, by chance, found her niche and took in her first charge.

She was tolerated with mild amusement and a modicum of grudging respect by the residents of the sprawling council estate these days. That would do. She could live with that.

It was thanks to Sandra, who always called a spade a spade, that she was loosening up a bit now. Sandra had stated in no uncertain terms that she thought Sister Jude should have a hobby of some sort. She thought it wasn't healthy for her to be working all the time.

Sister Jude brushed it off, but Sandra wouldn't let it go.

'All work, an' no play . . .' There she got a little confused and uncertainly finished off the quotation, 'Um . . . laughs last . . . or longest or somethin'.'

Sister Jude laughed at that. Affronted, Sandra flapped her hands in frustration. 'Yeh know what I'm gettin' at. Did yeh never do nothin' else 'cept prayin' an' stuff? Was yeh always a nun?'

'No. I was a real person once, Sandra. I became a nun for other reasons.' She was mildly amused now.

As Sandra opened her mouth to demand more information, Sister Jude added, 'And I like bikes, Sandra. Motorbikes.' Sandra's mouth gaped open. 'Yes, Sandra. Bikes.'

She proceeded to tell the girl a little about her childhood in Derry and about how watching her Uncle Joe fixing up an old Triumph had given her an interest.

'What? Like me and me music?'

'Well . . . yes. In a way.'

Eventually, after more probing, goading really, Sister Jude took the girl downstairs and across the open space at the back of the flats to the lock-ups at the rear of the scruffy row of shops that served the estate. Sandra stood by in anticipation as the nun unlocked the stout padlock and swung the door open.

Under a tarpaulin, in pristine order, sat a gleaming 1968 Norton 600.

As Sister Jude inhaled deeply on the cigarette, drawing the soothing smoke down into her lungs, her eye fell on the now dog-eared brochure sitting on top of the worktop. Suddenly she felt agitated again. Agitated and angry with herself that she hadn't had the courage to go in and confront Rory the night before when she'd had the chance. She reached over and picked up the folded sheet of shiny paper. There was a crease across the middle of Rory's face. She smoothed it out with her fingernail.

She felt the bile rising up in her as she crumpled the paper into a ball and savagely threw it into the corner. It bounced off the wall and rolled under the vegetable rack.

Tears were rolling down her cheeks now and she wiped them away with the back of her hand, furious with herself for being so cowardly and lily-livered. What could he have done if she had gone in and denounced him? Denied it? What would be the point? He knew, she knew. Knew that it was he who had placed the bomb in the car. Timing it to go off so that it would result in maximum death and destruction.

'We need to make a statement,' he had said. She'd heard him but not understood. Never would have imagined that he could, so cynically, cold-bloodedly and callously, perpetrate such an obscene atrocity. Thirty-two dead. Fifteen who would have been better off if they had been, seventy-four seriously injured and over a hundred walking wounded whose mental scars would never heal.

She was overcome by the overwhelming weight of guilt. Someone had to pay. But how? It was over twenty-five years since the bomb. She had no concrete proof to present to the authorities. It would be her word against his. In all probability both governments, Irish and British, would find it an embarrassment, what with the Good Friday Agreement. An inconvenience better left to lie like a sleeping dog. Unconsciously she rubbed at the scarring on her upper arm. With an air of desperation she stared up at the ceiling and wailed, 'Please, God. Tell me what the hell to do. Help me.'

There was no reply.

Chapter Sixteen

They arrived at the church with barely five minutes to spare. Joanne was getting flustered as she couldn't see any parking spots until Cash pointed out a space a few yards down a narrow lane to the left of the church. It was a tight spot and, after several failed attempts, Joanne finally admitted defeat and abandoned the car, nose into the hedge.

She was red-faced and jittery by this time, partly due to Justine's garbled instructions – left hand down, no, no, *left* hand, sorry, I meant right – but largely due to the upset earlier that morning. She was appalled by the thought of the girl languishing in a Moroccan jail, and the effect it could have on their unborn child. Breathless from the effort of parking, she hurried to catch up with her sisters as they briskly walked towards the church.

Music played quietly in the background as they crept along the side aisle to an empty pew halfway up. In front of the altar the coffin lay covered by a huge wreath of lilies.

At the end of the front pew, Cash could see Hazel Porter. She was sitting next to a man whom she recognised as Mr Porter. She couldn't remember his first name. On his other side sat Holly. She hadn't changed at all. Cash craned her neck, but before she could get a look at the other chief mourners to see if

Daisy was present the congregation stood as the priest and servers processed up the aisle.

Cash's gaze wandered around the congregation. She spied several old school friends, some she hadn't seen for years. A couple of them smiled in recognition when she caught their eye. Generally, it was a good turnout. A lot of middle-aged couples, friends and business acquaintances of the Porters, as well as the younger contingent who, like Cash and her sisters, had come to support the girls.

As they sat again Cash caught sight of a familiar figure and her hackles immediately rose. 'What the hell's he doing here?' she hissed at Justine.

'Who?'

'Niall bloody Donovan. There in the third row.'

Justine peered at the row of mourners. Three places in, a head taller than the rest, she spied Cash's nemesis. 'He's Rose's cousin. Eileen Porter was his aunt.' After pausing for a nanosecond she added, 'Nice fellow,' and gave Cash a wicked grin.

Cash gave her sister a withering look in return as Joanne glared at them and put her finger to her lips.

After a few words, acknowledging the sad occasion and asking the congregation to pray for the family of Eileen Porter, the service commenced.

It was a simple ceremony. Just the funeral Mass. Holly did a reading, as did Hazel. Hazel looked white-faced and wretched. After the priest had spoken briefly and kindly about the deceased, making reference to the fact that she had been snatched away before her time, a girl of about nineteen made her way to the coffin and sang 'Ave Maria', unaccompanied and in Latin. She had a sweet voice, shaken only by emotion.

Justine nudged Cash. 'That's Rose.' Cash could see the family resemblance.

After communion the congregation again shuffled in a line up the aisle to sympathise with the family. Cash, Joanne and Justine joined the queue. When they reached the front of the church Cash noted that, along with the widower, only three of the four Porter girls were present. Rose was weeping openly as Cash shook her hand and murmured the usual, 'I'm so sorry for your loss.' Holly was standing stoically with her arm around her younger sister's shoulder.

It was obvious, in grief, that the faces of the people shaking their hands and sympathising weren't really registering properly, so Cash was surprised that when she took Holly's hand and offered her condolences, Holly smiled and replied, 'Thank you so much for coming, Cash.'

After they had all resumed their seats, the priest concluded by blessing the coffin and saying prayers for the soul of Eileen. As he was doing this Rose and Holly left their pew again and stood on the altar steps at the head of the coffin. The priest announced, 'Now Holly and Rose will sing their mother's favourite hymn.'

Holly grabbed Rose's hand and, after the organist played a brief introduction, Holly sang the first bars of 'Faith of our Fathers'. Rose joined in, harmonising on the 'Oh, how our hearts beat high with joy'.

After two verses and chorus, during which Rose broke down again, the priest led the coffin, which was immediately followed by the family, out of the church towards the cemetery. Most of the congregation followed in straggly groups. The cold hit them full on as they trailed up the broad path towards the site of the grave.

'Hazel looks desperate,' Joanne whispered to Cash. 'Poor thing. I wonder where the other sister is?'

They looked over towards the grave. The family and

close relatives, including Niall Donovan, were grouped around it and the priest was passing rosary beads through his fingers as he recited the prayers in a monotone. The mourners responded, mumble, mumble, mumble. Holly was once again supporting the now inconsolable Rose. Hazel was standing with her father. This time he had his arm around her.

Cash scanned the group. There was no one there who bore any resemblance to the Porter sisters. No one who could possibly be Daisy. 'Mort Higgins was looking for her. Eileen Porter thought she'd run off with a cult,' she whispered to Joanne.

'Good grief! And has she?'

'I'm not sure.'

Before she could elaborate the priest started another decade and Justine muttered, 'God! This has to be the coldest place in the bloody universe. If he doesn't get on with it we'll all freeze to death and be joining Eileen in the hereafter.'

'Shut up, Justine. Show a bit of respect,' Joanne hissed. 'Why do you have to make a skit out of everything?'

Behind her oldest sister's back, Justine gave Cash a leery look. However, after the third decade of the fourth mystery, even Joanne muttered words to the effect that the priest was making a meal of it.

At the end of the ceremony the group dispersed, some walking towards their cars, others stood in small groups chatting either to the Porters or to friends they rarely saw except for occasions such as this. Joanne trotted over to a group of school friends and started to chat. Justine was talking to two girls of her own age, so Cash was left standing on her own.

She could see Holly talking to Niall Donovan so was deterred from going over to her. She was anxious to ask her about Daisy's whereabouts but wasn't quite sure how go about it in a sensitive way. Just then Holly caught her eye and, after saying a couple of words to Donovan, left him and walked over.

'Cash.' They embraced. 'Won't you come back to the house? We've just got soup and sandwiches on the go, but it'll warm you up. You must be frozen, like the rest of us.'

'Of course.' Cash was glad of the extended window of opportunity to talk to her, especially in a setting a little more removed from the actual burial. 'How are you bearing up? It must have been an awful shock.' She could have kicked herself for being so banal, but couldn't think of anything else to say.

'You could say that. What we can't understand is what she was doing in Bath Avenue in the first place. You know her car was found with a flat tyre out near the RDS? It's baffling.'

'Yes . . . Um . . . Look, is there somewhere we could talk? I think there's some stuff you should know.' It was a blundering attempt to catch her interest, but Cash didn't want to let the opening pass.

'What do you mean? What stuff? What are you talking about?' She wasn't in any way angry or irate, just perplexed.

Cash marshalled her thoughts. 'Okay . . . um . . . I don't suppose you know, but I work . . . used to work for a private investigator, Mort Higgins, and your mother asked him to look for your sister Daisy. She thought Daisy had run off with a cult and wanted . . .'

'Run off with a cult? Oh, God! Where did she get that idea?'

'Well . . . um . . . I'm not sure it is a cult exactly, but your mother . . .'

Holly cut in again. 'Daisy didn't run off. She's just

keeping a low profile at the moment because . . .' She faltered. 'Well, she's just keeping a low profile.'

'But do you know where she is?'

Holly stared at her, her brow crinkled. 'Why? What has Daisy to do with you?' She was on the edge of annoyance.

Cash could sense this, and blundered on. 'For reasons I'll go into later, I think your mother's death might not have been an accident.'

It took a moment for the words to register. 'What are you saying? That Mummy was . . .' She couldn't say the word.

'I think your mother was murdered.'

There, she'd said it. Holly was gaping at her, a look of total disbelief on her face. Eventually, after an uncomfortable silence, she said, 'Murdered? My mother? You can't be serious.'

Cash sensed that her friend was teetering between disbelief and anger that she would make such a statement, so far without qualification. 'Look, Holly, I know this isn't really the time or the place but, believe me, I'm serious. I've reason to believe that your mother's death wasn't an accident . . .' Holly was still gaping at her. Cash placed a comforting hand on her arm. 'Is there somewhere we could talk, so that I can tell you what I know and you can make up your own mind?'

What little colour there had been in Holly's face had all but drained away. Cash was afraid that she was going to either faint or become hysterical, so she was relieved when Holly took a couple of deep breaths and pulled herself together. 'Okay. I'll see you back at the house.' She abruptly turned and headed off towards her father who was talking to the priest.

Cash was left standing alone again. Joanne was talking to a woman whom Cash half recognised and

Justine was nowhere to be seen. Joanne caught her eye and smiled, so Cash wandered over.

'Cash, you remember Alana Donovan?'

Cash nodded. 'Oh . . . yes.' Aware that she was a cousin of Holly's, it occurred to her that Alana must be Niall Donovan's sister. 'I'm so sorry about your aunt.'

Alana nodded and smiled. 'Thank you.'

Joanne and Alana talked on for another couple of minutes before saying goodbye, and Alana walked off towards a small huddle which included her brother and an elderly couple.

'Are you ready?' Joanne's eyes searched the church-yard. 'Where's Justine?'

'Aren't you going back to the house?' Cash asked.

Joanne frowned. 'I hadn't planned to, why? Do you want to?'

Cash nodded. 'I need to talk to Holly about . . .' she hesitated '. . . about Daisy.'

Justine hurried around the corner of the church at this point. She had her coat wrapped around her and looked frozen. 'Let's get out of here. I'm perished.'

'Cash wants to go back to the house.' Joanne, duty done, sounded singularly unenthusiastic.

Justine groaned. 'Aw, Cash! C'mon.'

'Just drop me off, then. I'll find my own way home.' Irritated, Cash turned on her heel and stomped off towards the car. Joanne and Justine sheepishly followed.

The Porter residence was a stoutly built double-fronted affair, *circa* late sixties. It stood, detached, in about half an acre of well-tended, mature garden. Cash remembered visiting once before for Holly's twelfth birthday party.

Joanne pulled into the kerb. 'Are you sure you'll be okay?' Guilt was setting in.

'It's only Foxrock, for God's sake,' Cash snapped. 'I

think I can find my way home from here.' She slammed the car door and headed up the drive without looking back.

The front door was open so she tentatively stepped inside. She could hear the rumble of conversation in the drawing room which opened off the hall to the left, so she went in, hoping to see Holly.

It was a large room with a bay window, wallpapered in a Laura Ashley floral print and matching border. The heavy swagged curtains were of the same design but in a contrasting colour. Very eighties. A maroon distressed leather chesterfield sat to one side of the slate fireplace, over which hung a heavy gilt framed mirror, and two matching armchairs sat on the other side. A log effect gas fire spluttered in the grate. A glass-topped coffee-table had been pushed into the bay window and several straight-backed dining chairs, appropriated from the dining room, were dotted around in vacant spaces. At the far end of the room, taking up a large amount of space near a set of French windows, stood a baby grand piano on which a cluster of family photographs were grouped.

Cash surveyed the room. It was crowded and although she vaguely recognised a lot of faces – there were about a dozen people standing around, or perched on chairs in small groups talking – she didn't really know anyone. Feeling like an interloper, she turned to go in search of Holly, only to bump into Niall Donovan.

'Can I get you a drink?' He showed no sign of recognition, which was understandable as the only time he had previously laid an eye on her, hair on end and wrapped in a duvet, she had looked more like a cross between a troll and a demented Teletubby than a human being.

'Um . . . I was looking for Holly.'

'I think she's sorting out the soup.' He looked over his shoulder towards the back of the house. 'I'd say she's in the kitchen.'

Cash fled, afraid that he might have recall at any moment. She found Holly in the kitchen, stirring a huge pot of steaming soup. A woman of about fifty or so was cutting up fruit cake and piling it on a plate. Another woman of around the same age was unpacking soup bowls out of a box and stacking them on the kitchen table.

Cash caught sight of clingfilm-wrapped trays of sandwiches on the worktop. Obviously the Porters had done the wise thing and had had the wake catered. 'Shall I unwrap these?' she asked no one in particular.

Holly turned from the cooker. 'Thanks. Maybe you could take them into the dining-room.'

She did as requested, returning to the kitchen to help with the soup bowls. On her second trip Holly said, 'Could you cut up a few of those baguettes, please, Cash?' Again Cash obliged, anxious to get the refreshments sorted out so that she could talk to Holly on her own.

Everything from that point on conspired against her. As soon as she had cut up the bread and piled it in a basket, the woman who had been cutting up the fruit cake handed her a pile of paper napkins and instructed her to wrap a soup spoon and a knife in each one. By the time she had finished that and carried them into the dining-room, Holly was nowhere to be seen.

The house was quite crowded by this time, and just as she caught sight of Holly across the hall she was collared by Nanette Hughes, an old classmate. Nanette greeted her effusively and prattled on about 'the good old days' at Loretto. Her enthusiasm was a tad over the top, Cash thought, but her view was probably influenced by the fact that she had never particularly liked Nanette or had had much to do with her. Her set, to Cash's recollection, had always thought they were a cut above the rest and had rarely deigned to even speak to the likes of Cash.

As Nanette was launching into another reminiscence, Cash caught a glimpse of Holly making her way upstairs. She left Nanette in mid-sentence. 'Sorry, have to find the loo.' And she hurried off. Nanette was left staring after her with her mouth agape, her opinion of Cash confirmed.

She caught up with her friend on the landing. Holly turned when she heard her approaching. 'I suppose we should talk.' She moved to her right and opened a bedroom door. 'We'll go in here.'

Cash followed her. A shaft of sunlight was shining through the half-closed curtains. Tiny specks of dust tumbled and tossed in the sunbeam. Holly walked over and swished the curtains apart, bathing the rest of the room with light. Laura Ashley was also predominant in the over-coordinated décor – everything from the bed linen, wallpaper and drapes to the lampshades and the guest towels thoughtfully laid out on a pine blanket chest at the end of the bed.

She stood looking down at the back garden. 'Mummy loved the garden,' she said. 'She was out there every spare minute.'

Cash moved over beside her and put her arm around her shoulder. They stood there silently surveying the garden. Two small children were chasing around, playing a game, oblivious of the occasion. The boy caught up with the girl and started stuffing leaves down the back of her coat. They could hear her shrieks of protest.

'Hazel's kids,' Holly said.

'About your mother . . .'

Holly turned from the window and sat on the end of the double bed. She nodded, then smoothed the bed cover. 'Okay. I think you'd better start from the beginning.'

Cash leaned her back against the radiator. The warmth comforted her. 'Right.' She took a deep breath, then slowly exhaled. 'The man I used to work for, Mort Higgins, well, I found him dead in the office last Tuesday. To all intents and purposes it looked as if he'd shot himself in the head . . .' she heard Holly gasp '. . . and at first I thought that was the case . . .'

Holly cut across her. 'What has this to do with Mummy?'

'Bear with me, I'm coming to that. Anyway, Janet, his widow, reckoned if he were ever to kill himself, he'd never use a gun. Mort hated guns. At first I thought it was understandable that she be in denial – I mean, we were both feeling guilty about it – but then she pointed out that Mort was shot in the right temple and Mort was *left*-handed. Why would he pick up a gun in his right hand if he was left-handed?'

Holly shrugged in a got-me-there gesture.

'Well, anyway, I still didn't fully go along with Janet's murder theory until the following afternoon when we were in the office and Janet asked me to help her check through the files of Mort's old cases. She was looking for someone with a motive to kill him. I went along with it, humouring her really, until I noticed that your mother's file was missing. Then I remembered hearing about the accident on the radio and sort of put two and two together.'

'My mother's file?'

'Yes. As I told you, she came in last week and asked Mort to find your sister Daisy. She thought that she'd run off with a cult. She was very worried and distressed about it.'

'But where did she get that idea? Daisy hadn't gone off with any cult.'

'Do you know where she is, then?'

Holly cast her eyes down and picked at an imaginary piece of lint on the bed cover. 'Like I said, Daisy's keeping a low profile at the moment.'

Cash let the ensuing silence hang, hoping that Holly would elaborate. It worked. Holly looked up. 'The truth is, Daisy's pregnant and she didn't want Mummy and Dad to know. For the past two months, since she started to show, she's been keeping out of the way. She's staying at the nursing home where she'll have the baby, and they'll take care of the adoption.'

'But why wasn't she at the funeral?'

Holly spread her hands and shrugged. 'She's eight and a half months pregnant. It's bad enough for Dad losing Mummy, without having to deal with that. It'd kill him, particularly as Daisy isn't going to keep the baby. It'd break his heart.'

'But does she know? Where does your father think she is?'

Holly looked sheepish. 'Dad thinks she's in Bosnia with Refugee Trust and can't get back.' She blushed self-consciously. Cash stared at her, aghast. 'She worked as a volunteer before in Somalia with them . . . She spoke to Dad on the phone.' She stood up and leaned her back against the radiator beside Cash, staring at the floor as if she was ashamed to look her friend in the eye.

After a pause Cash said, 'About this cult business. Mort seemed to think that she was in contact with them, though, in all honesty, I'm not sure they are actually a cult as such.' She was talking to herself more than to Holly. Holly didn't comment. Cash continued. 'And what about the missing file and your mother's death? It's all a bit coincidental, don't you think?'

'So what was in this file – did you see it?'

'I typed it up, but there wasn't really anything incriminating in it. That's what I don't understand.'

Holly sighed, then shook her head. 'What was Mummy doing in Bath Avenue?' She, too, was talking to herself. 'It's weird. She'd never leave the car and walk around at that time of night on her own. Who was she with?'

Cash had a thought. 'Another thing. Mort was a recovering alcoholic. I know he'd been dry for a few years, and there was the remains of a bottle of whiskey on his desk. The cop in charge reckons that's why he shot himself in the right temple, that he was drunk and out of his senses, but I'd have known if he was back on the drink. I'm certain he wasn't. So is Janet.'

'So what are you saying?'

'I don't know exactly. But if Mort had drink in him it wouldn't have been voluntary.'

'What did the autopsy report say?'

Cash shook her head. 'It's not happened yet. They're short-staffed at James's, apparently, so it's not being done till tomorrow.'

'Tomorrow? Then it'll probably be on my list, though they'll have done the preliminary for the time of death and so forth.'

Cash looked at her quizzically. Holly, noticing her confusion, explained. 'I'm a pathologist. I work at James's. Along with the flu epidemic, I'm the reason they're short-staffed. I'm back on duty tomorrow.'

Cash felt a rush of excitement. 'Will you let me know if you find anything strange? Anything that would even suggest foul play?'

Holly looked very uncomfortable. 'I don't know about that. I mean it wouldn't be very professional.'

'Oh, come on, Holly. Mort's death is probably tied up with your mother's. I'm sure of it. Don't you want to find out who's responsible? Find out who killed your mother?'

'Always assuming my mother *was* killed,' Holly countered.

'Please, Holly. I just have a gut feeling something's not right here. Think about it. As you said, there's no way under normal circumstances that your mother would be wandering around Bath Avenue at the dead of night with her car parked two miles away at the RDS. And then there's the stuff with Mort. The drink. The gun.' She could see that her old school friend was having an argument with herself.

After a good two minutes' silence Holly sighed. 'Well, as a professional, you know I shouldn't, but under the circumstances, I will. If your friend was murdered it does point to Mummy's death as being suspect, what with the file and all.' She paused. 'Poor Mummy.'

Then, talking to herself again, she said, 'I'll make a call and get a look at Mummy's autopsy results, see if there's anything dubious there.'

They stood with their backs to the radiator both deep in their own thoughts. After a while Holly said, 'But why? What's the motive? Why would anyone want to kill Mummy? I don't understand.'

'Me neither,' Cash admitted. 'But you have to admit that the three elements . . .' she counted off on her fingers '. . . doubts about Mort's death, along with your mother's hit-and-run on the same night, and the missing file add up to something.'

Holly nodded. 'What about this cult? Why did – what's his name? Mort?' Cash nodded. 'Why did he think Daisy was mixed up with them?'

'I don't know. But I intend to find out.'

There was a scream from the garden below and both women turned to look out of the window. The small girl was lying on the path where she had fallen. The boy was standing by with a guilty look on his face. Hazel ran into view and bent down over her daughter, helping her up, then rubbing her knee and comforting her. She said something to the boy and he hung his head.

'Have you spoken to Daisy?'

'I phoned her on Wednesday to break the news about Mummy. She was in bits.'

Cash nodded. She could only imagine.

Holly continued. 'Her doctor advised her, circumstances considered, that she shouldn't attend the funeral. He was afraid that the stress of facing Dad and the ordeal of the actual service could be detrimental. I was inclined to agree with him. Daisy's a bit hyper at the best of times.'

'Have you spoken to her since?'

Holly shook her head. 'I'll give her a call tonight.'

Two hours later Cash stood in a windswept bus shelter. It was now lashing with rain and her teeth were chattering. In the distance she saw an approaching bus. She stepped out and raised her arm to stop it. Just then a two-door Mercedes flew by, drenching her with muddy water from the large puddle of rainwater that had collected by the bus stop. As the car flashed past she recognised Nanette Hughes, oblivious to ordinary mortals, behind the wheel. The bus sped past, full. Freezing, wet and irritated, she gave the retreating car and the bus the JPII blessing.

When she got back to the flat, Billie was out. Thankfully the fire was lit and the sitting room toasty warm, so she took a long hot shower in order to defrost. Since talking to Holly she was more confused than ever. She reran the facts through her mind as she stood under the soothing stream of water. The more she thought about it the more she was convinced that both Mort's and Eileen's deaths were linked. Holly's bewilderment about her mother wandering alone around Bath Avenue at the dead of night was confirmation that there was definitely something suspect about it. But what had Daisy to do with it? She was the link after all. If Eileen hadn't come to Mort about her in the first place, they might both be still alive.

As she towelled herself dry she consoled herself with the thought that surely Detective Doyle would have to look into things now.

She tried to reach Janet but only got her answering-machine. She left a brief message, telling her that she'd spoken to Holly, then settled in front of the TV with a cup of tea and the remains of a packet of ginger nuts and watched the black and white movie on BBC2 for the remainder of the afternoon.

Billie came in some time after twelve. Cash was asleep on the sofa bed with the TV still on. She crept over and switched it off. She was disappointed. She had hoped that Cash would still be awake. She wanted to tell her about the seminar, Dr Keogh and the positive effects she was experiencing.

The second seminar, out at the institute's headquarters in Enniskerry, had left her feeling even more positive about herself than the first. Dr Keogh certainly knew what he was about. There had been eight people present at the second seminar but he'd singled her out after the session and they had talked for a long time. She felt he understood her. He had made her feel as if she were the most important person in the world and had encouraged her to talk about her beliefs and fears. They had discussed spirituality and, for the first time in her life, Billie had felt she'd been talking to someone on the same wavelength who hadn't belittled her ideas or convictions. She had scarcely believed how quickly the time had flown. Suddenly it had been past eleven. Dr Keogh had been as surprised as she and insisted on driving her home in his Land Cruiser right to her door. He was so considerate. Made her feel so special. She thought of waking her friend, but changed her mind. There would be plenty of time to talk in the morning.

Chapter Seventeen

Cash awoke at six-thirty and immediately phoned Detective Doyle at Pearse Street. True to the information the sergeant had given her, he was on duty and took her call. She asked if they could meet but was vague about the reason in case he gave her the brush-off. After some persistence on her part he reluctantly agreed to meet her in his office at eight a.m.

She arrived fifteen minutes early and had to wait in the public office for him after the desk sergeant had informed him of her arrival.

She could see by his expression as he approached her that he wasn't in a good humour. Maybe it was the early hour. She decided to use the direct approach in any case, and had rehearsed what she wanted to say on the way over.

'Miss Ryan. What's the problem?'

Bad start. He was on the defensive. 'I'm not sure, Sergeant Doyle. Is there somewhere we could talk?'

Doyle hesitated. He'd obviously been hoping that their meeting would take only a couple of minutes. Cash stood her ground. Doyle gave an irritated sigh, then walked past her and opened the door of an office and looked in. 'Okay. In here.'

Cash followed him into the room. There was a table with two chairs on either side, but Doyle didn't sit. He stood a couple of feet inside the door with his hands in his pockets. Cash walked past him and stood, leaning her back against the edge of the table.

'It's about Mort Higgins's death. I'm sure it wasn't suicide. We . . . I think he was murdered.' At this point she had planned to go into details, citing the coincidence of Eileen Porter's hit and run and the missing file, but he didn't give her the chance.

'Look, Miss Ryan – Cash – I know it's hard for you to face, but Mort *did* kill himself. And do you want to know why I'm so sure?' He didn't wait for her to reply. 'Mort was a troubled man. He'd messed up his marriage. Ruined his career. All because of the demon drink. He couldn't handle his drink.'

'But . . .'

Doyle cut across her, raising his voice to drown out her protests. 'And after he gave it up it was worse because he could see all the things he'd thrown away and couldn't get back, and he lost courage and fell off the wagon.'

'But he didn't fall . . .'

Doyle raised his hand to quieten her again. He was angry now. 'I know you thought a lot of him, and I'm sorry for your loss, but the fact remains that Mort Higgins went to his office with a gun and a bottle of whiskey for Dutch courage, and blew his brains out. End of story.'

'But Mort hated guns. And he wasn't drinking . . . And what about Mrs Porter? What about the file?' In her frustration with Doyle, her planned speech had flown out of the window. She was babbling and, worse, she knew she was babbling.

Doyle shook his head vigorously. He wasn't listening. He pulled out a chair from the table and invited Cash to sit down. She hesitated until he pulled out another and sat on the opposite side of the table.

He sighed. 'Look, Cash. Give it up. I know the fact

that Mort Higgins killed himself isn't something either you or Janet want to face, but the fact remains that's exactly what happened.'

Cash opened her mouth to protest again, without success. Doyle shook his head. 'Hard as it is to say this, you leave me no option.' He paused again. 'I take your point that Mort Higgins *did* hate guns. But he knew a hell of a lot about them. At one time he was a firearms instructor.' That was news to Cash. 'And in this case he chose his weapon carefully. He chose a .22 pistol, Cash. Do you want to know why?'

Cash just stared at him, stunned by the passion of his outburst.

Doyle continued, enunciating his words slowly and deliberately, 'He chose a .22 because, first, he knew that there was a better than average chance that you'd find him and, second, because he wanted to be sure that he did the job right.'

'I don't understand.'

Doyle, although still angry, looked at the same time sad. 'Mort was well aware that the low velocity of the .22 load would pierce his skull on the way in but, unlike a higher velocity bullet, most of its energy would be spent by the time it travelled through his brain and hit the other side. In short, Cash, Mort chose the .22 knowing that there'd be no exit wound, and that when the bullet hit the other side of his skull it'd bounce back and make so much tomato puree of his brain.' He paused again. Cash was appalled by his frankness. 'See, Cash, he knew you'd find him and he didn't want you to have to see his brains splattered around the room. He also wanted to make sure he wouldn't make a balls of it and leave himself a vegetable.'

'Okay. But why would he use his right hand? Mort was left-handed.' She was desperate now.

'He'd also just downed the guts of a bottle of whiskey.'

The shock of hearing Doyle spell out the grisly details concerning Mort's manner of death had left Cash muddled. Sensing that Doyle was about to get up and terminate the interview, she quickly dragged her mind back to the purpose of her visit. 'But what about Eileen Porter? What about the file?'

'Who's Eileen Porter?' Doyle asked.

Cash told him of her theory concerning Eileen, about the missing file and about Holly's concern and bewilderment as to the reason her mother would be walking around Dublin on her own in the small hours of the morning while her car was two miles away. He listened intently. When she had finished he stayed silent for a full minute, as if tossing the facts over in his mind. She couldn't read his expression. She found she was holding her breath and exhaled.

He sighed, pushed his chair back and stood up. Cash sensed that the interview was at an end but didn't follow suit. She remained in her seat. Doyle didn't seem sure what to do. He had his hands in his pockets and he was swaying from one foot to the other. He sighed again. It was a condescending sort of sigh this time and Cash was expecting him to send her on her way with a patronising pat on the head, but instead he said, 'I'll look into this, Miss Ryan. Thanks for bringing it to our attention.'

'You mean you believe my story? You'll do something?'

Doyle nodded. 'Of course. Leave it with me and I'll check it out.'

Cash could have kissed him except that he was so singularly unattractive to her. She'd been building herself up for an argument, with her coming off worst. Then he spoiled it.

'I still think you're wrong about Mort Higgins, though. He was a loser.'

Cash was livid. He was clearly just going through the motions. 'But what about Eileen Porter, the file?'

Doyle made a placating gesture. 'I said I'll look into it, Miss Ryan, and I will. It'll be thoroughly investigated . . .'

Cash cut across him. 'But as far as you're concerned there's nothing in it. There's no connection.'

It was a statement, not a question, but Doyle treated it as the latter. 'How would I know for sure yet? I haven't checked out the facts. I told you I'll check it out, and I will. Even though I think it'll be a waste of time and resources, I'll check it out. I'm a professional, Miss Ryan, and I resent your implication that I'd let my personal feeling cloud my judgement.'

Cash didn't believe him, but what else could she say? He'd promised to look into it so there was no point in antagonising him further on the off chance that he might actually do it, even in a perfunctory manner, and come up with something despite his best efforts at indifference. She cut her losses, mumbled half-hearted thanks and left. She could feel his eyes boring into her back as she walked towards the front door.

Billie was up and about when Cash returned to Drumcondra with the Sunday papers and some freshly baked croissants she had picked up at the convenience store. Billie took the bag of croissants out of her hand and emptied them on to a plate which she carried over to the table on which there was already a large pot of tea, butter, a carton of milk and a jar of marmalade. 'What got you up before dawn cracked?'

'I went to see Detective Sergeant Doyle – you know, the cop who was dealing with Mort's case?'

Billie was back in the kitchen, getting another cup and plate from the cupboard. 'What for?'

Cash had forgotten that Billie knew nothing about the murder/conspiracy theory. 'I think you'd better sit down,' she said.

When she had finished her story Billie was staring at her, her eyes huge, mouth slightly open. 'But why? Why would anyone kill the likes of Eileen Porter? I suppose it's not beyond the bounds of possibility for someone to take a pop at Mort, but what did yer woman ever do? I thought she was yer ordinary middle-class housewife from what you said about her.'

'She was. She was. The only link we have is the daughter, Daisy. Both Mort and Mrs Porter seemed to think that she'd run off with the Better Way crowd. You know? The chancers Mort asked you to check out?'

Billie nodded even though she didn't concur with Cash's definition of the institute.

Cash continued, 'But the sister, Holly, says no. Daisy's actually eight months pregnant and lying low because she didn't want the parents to know about it. She's in some nursing home waiting to give birth. It doesn't make sense.'

'No,' Billie agreed. It certainly didn't make sense. She was stunned by it all and couldn't believe that Dr Keogh and Cora and the rest would be mixed up in anything shady. 'Wasn't Daisy at the funeral?'

'No. They told their father that she's in Bosnia and couldn't get back. I think Holly was a bit embarrassed about that.'

'Not surprisin'. So where's this nursing home? D'you think they're involved in it?'

That possibility, strangely, hadn't occurred to Cash. She was blinkered by the initial proposition of Mort's and Eileen's notion that Daisy had run off with a cult, namely the Better Way Institute. 'It's a thought,' she said as she reached for her phone.

Janet answered after the third ring. They exchanged the minimum of pleasantries, then Cash cut to the chase. 'Could we meet? There's stuff we have to talk about that I'd rather not go into on the phone.' As she said it she felt foolish, realising that it probably sounded overly dramatic, but she was conscious that she was using a mobile phone. If Janet thought she was displaying the first stages of paranoia she made no comment, and agreed to meet at the office at one.

Next she called Holly, forgetting that she would be at work. She left a message on her machine asking her to call, then tried James's. The operator put her through to the mortuary, but the mortuary assistant informed her that Dr Porter was busy on a procedure and was unable to come to the phone.

Cash had never thought of an autopsy in terms of it being a *procedure*, but on reflection she supposed it was a tad more sensitive than saying the doctor was cutting up a stiff. She found it hard to understand why any doctor would want to be a pathologist. It seemed so unsatisfactory in terms of the Hippocratic oath and the whole notion of healing. She had said as much to Holly the previous afternoon as they'd talked together in the bedroom, though in a slightly more diplomatic way.

Holly had explained the reasons behind her choice of speciality. 'When I was in training, I found that I didn't really relate to the patients very well. Sick people irritate me, so I figured with pathology the patients couldn't answer back.'

At first Cash had thought she was serious until Holly had cracked a smile and told her the real reason was her lifelong need to know how things worked, and if they didn't work the explanation. It made a certain sort of sense. It also gave Cash hope that Holly would be equally anxious to get to the bottom of her mother's death.

Later on, Cash and Janet were back in Mort's office. Janet was leaning against the window ledge, arms folded. Cash was pacing furiously backwards and forwards across the rug.

'I can't believe that fucking eejitt calls himself a cop. What the hell does he need, for God's sake?' Relating the interview to Janet had reminded her of Doyle's patronising and dismissive attitude. She was still stinging from it.

Janet was equally angry but she said nothing, giving Cash the chance to get it out of her system.

'I think coincidence is taking it a bit far, particularly with the file missing as well. That's three things. *Three*! And so what if there wasn't much in the file? It doesn't mean to say Mort didn't find out something else, does it?'

'But I thought your friend said that Daisy had nothing to do with the Better Way people, that she was in a nursing home. If that's the case Mrs Porter's hit and run could be exactly that. It probably has nothing to do with Mort's death. And as for the missing file, who's to say Mort didn't take it home? We don't know it's actually missing at all.'

Cash was flabbergasted. 'What are you saying?' She couldn't believe that Janet would give up so easily. 'But you know Mort didn't commit . . .'

Janet held up her hand. 'I know. And I still think he was killed by someone. But as you said yourself, there wasn't anything incriminating in Eileen Porter's file, just a few details about the daughter, nothing that warranted murder, for God's sake.' She paused. 'No, it had to be something else. Something we missed in the files. I think we need to take another look at all the files.'

The fact that Janet hadn't changed her mind about the possibility of murder placated Cash somewhat, but she was still leaning heavily in the direction of Eileen being involved in some way. What was she doing, wandering around Bath Avenue at the dead of night all on her own?

Janet got up, walked over to the filing cabinet and slid open the top drawer as if to make her point. She picked out a file at random, opened the buff cover and started to read.

Reluctantly Cash gave in. 'I suppose you have a point, but in that case I think we should sort the files into most likely, less likely, etc. It'd save a lot of reading through irrelevant stuff.' She walked over, took the file from Janet's hand and read the label. 'For instance, this woman, Madge Adams, hardly had a motive to kill Mort. He traced her long-lost sister.'

'I see what you mean,' Janet said. 'Will you help me?'

'Of course.' Cash was surprised that Janet had felt the need to ask again. Then a thought struck her. 'You know, if it's nothing to do with Eileen Porter's case or any of Mort's past cases, then it could even be related to his time as a cop. Who's to say it wasn't some criminal he put away? Can you think of anyone?'

Janet shook her head. 'No. Not offhand. Anyway, if it was, why would they wait until now? Mort's been out of the force for nearly seven years.'

'Maybe they were taking an extended holiday in Mountjoy and they just got out.'

'Well, if that's the case,' Janet said despondently, 'we've no chance.' She tapped the top of the filing cabinet. 'Let's just hope that the answer's in here.'

They emptied the top drawer and placed the files on the floor in a pile, then Cash picked one off the top of the pile. 'Well, Madge Adams can go in the "no chance" pile.' She dropped the buff folder on the floor and picked up the next one. 'Just read the first paragraph, that'll give you an idea.'

Janet picked up the next folder and flipped it open. 'Another missing relative. Two down, a truckload to go.'

Sister Jude had the wind in her hair. On the pretext of taking Sandra for a spin, she was roaring along the short stretch that was the M11 between Ballybrack and Bray. It was the less direct route to Enniskerry. The more conventional way would have been to go through Dundrum and then take the R115, but she wanted the opportunity to open up the engine. The Norton needed it. She needed it. Speed had always heightened her senses. Sandra was clinging on, arms wrapped around her waist, and every now and then she gave a whoop of excitement, urging the nun to go faster. A grin she couldn't control spread across Sister Jude's face. Sandra's excitement was infectious. The feeling of freedom was overwhelmingly wonderful.

At Bray she turned right onto the R117 towards Enniskerry. After full throttle on the motorway, the bike gave the illusion of creeping along, but, in fact, the speed was still above fifty.

After a short distance she pulled to the side of the road, unzipped her leathers and took out the folded road map. She flipped up her visor and studied it, eyes searching for the pencil line she had traced to her objective. She looked around and, satisfied that she was heading in the right direction, put the map away and revved the engine.

Once again, she wasn't sure what she was doing, why she was there. It was a sort of compulsion. The same compulsion that drives a rejected lover to seek out the object of their wretchedness. She and Keogh had once been lovers, albeit briefly. Heady days. Not hard to understand how she could have been so thoroughly besotted by him. But it was all a long time ago. A lot of water . . . and blood . . . had passed under the bridge.

At the next intersection she turned right and slowed down, looking to the left and the right, searching for the house. Fifty yards on she pulled in and idled the engine.

The sign, painted in gothic script, read GLENCULLEN HOUSE NURSING HOME AND TREATMENT CENTRE. Attached to it there was a cut-out hand with the index finger pointing up the driveway. She was about to ride on when at the bottom of the sign, in much smaller lettering, she read, THE BETTER WAY INSTITUTE REGD OFFICE.

The gates were open, but the house was not in view due to a bend in the gravel drive and a thick, high screen of mature rhododendrons and other shrubs.

'Why are we stopped? What's this place?' Sandra was anxious to get back on the road.

'I don't know, Sandra. Let's take a look.'

Sister Jude revved the engine again and turned up the drive. She expected to see the house as she rounded the bend in the driveway but instead only saw another stretch of gravel with a thin ribbon of green on a small central hump leading to a further curve. She drove on, slowing to about five miles an hour. The shrubbery on either side of the gravel surface looked thick, overgrown and neglected.

As she rounded the next bend she caught sight of the house. It was large and imposing, probably late Victorian or early Edwardian by the look of it. Several cars were parked in front of the hall door, facing the house. Unlike the drive, the gardens in the immediate vicinity of the building looked well cared for and the lawn manicured. She drove right up to the house and cut the engine. The sudden silence was deafening. Winter. Not even a bird singing.

The front door was open but the way blocked by a mahogany vestibule door inset with stained-glass panels. A further cut-out hand pointed up the steps to Reception. To the left of the front door there was a brass sign fixed to the wall indicating that this was The Better Way Institute regd office.

As she was reading it, the door opened and the woman whom she had met at the drop-in centre, Cora, walked out on to the front step. She had a smile on her face, but Sister Jude read concern in her eyes.

'May I be of help?'

Sister Jude removed her helmet and tucked it under her arm. Cora showed a flicker of recognition, but it was obvious that out of context, in the leathers and helmet, she couldn't place her.

'Jump off, Sandra.'

Sandra obliged and Sister Jude swung her leg over the body of the machine, heaving it back on the parking stand. When she was done she strode over to Cora. 'Sister Jude. We met the other day at your drop-in centre?' She thrust out her hand.

Cora's face broke into a smile of recognition. 'Of course. Forgive me. I didn't recognise you.' She gave an embarrassed laugh. 'How may I help you, Sister?'

Sister Jude turned to Sandra who was standing, staring up at the house. 'This is Sandra. I'm her foster-carer. Say hello to Cora, Sandra.'

Sandra awkwardly stuck out her hand. 'H'lo.'

Cora shook the girl's hand and gave her a pleasant smile. 'Pleased to meet you, Sandra.' Then she turned her attention back to the nun.

Sister Jude was surveying the house. 'Lovely place. Do you live here?'

'Oh. Well, we actually share the main house with the nursing home. We run some of our seminars from here, and Dr Rory and some of the staff stay here sometimes. Why do you ask?' She sounded slightly edgy.

Sister Jude smiled. 'I just wondered. It would be a shame for a beautiful house like this not to be lived in . . . What is the purpose of the treatment centre? What kind of treatments do you do here?'

'Dr Keogh runs addiction programmes, psycho-therapy and a counselling service.'

'I see. And is the doctor in right now? Would it be possible to see him?' She was edging up the steps, looking over Cora's shoulder towards the slightly ajar vestibule door. 'I'd like to talk to him about the courses you run to see if any would be suitable for my troubled teenagers.'

Cora backed up as Sister Jude advanced. 'I'm afraid the doctor's away today, but if you'd like to come in, I'd be more than happy to show you around and tell you about our services.'

'Away? Oh, that's a shame.' Sister Jude hesitated, then decided to take a look anyway. She needed to breathe his air. To invade his space. To prove to herself that she wasn't afraid of him and that she could confront another demon from her past.

She smiled. 'Thank you. I . . . We'd love to have a look around . . .' She turned to the girl. 'Wouldn't we, Sandra?' She strode forward up the remaining steps. Sandra lagged behind, crash helmet hooked over her arm, annoyed that the bike ride was to be interrupted. It would be dark in an hour, and from the two previous occasions on which the nun had taken her out on the Norton she knew that once the light went Sister Jude wouldn't drive at any great speed. Her guardian's brisk instruction to come along caused her to sigh, hunch her shoulders and follow in a sulk.

Cash and Janet worked on the case files until well into the evening but didn't come up with one case serious enough to have led to the subject having a wish to exact the ultimate vengeance on Mort.

As the two women finished restacking the files in the relevant drawers, Cash said, 'Well, that leaves us with Eileen and Daisy Porter.'

'Or alternatively a recently released psychopath.'

A thought struck Cash. 'Do you know anyone in the Gardai who'd be able to narrow it down a bit? Have some handle on likely suspects?'

'Not offhand,' Janet said. She knew very few of Mort's ex-colleagues. Mort had been a man's man and they had rarely socialised together in the latter years of their marriage. With hindsight, Janet wondered if it had been Mort's way of trying to conceal the seriousness of his drink problem from her. The only cop she really knew, apart from Mort, was Dan Doyle. She felt uncomfortable with the notion of asking him a favour and being under any kind of obligation to him. But, hell, needs must. 'I could always ask Doyle.'

Cash guffawed. 'Right. I can guess what his reaction'll be.'

Janet shrugged. 'There's no one else. Anyway, I think if I asked him he'd do it for *me*.'

Cash caught the implication and raised her eyebrows.

Janet gave a self-conscious smile. 'He had a thing for me a while back after Mort and I split up.'

Cash nodded. 'Oh.'

'Nothing came of it,' Janet hastily added. 'I acted dumb, as if I'd no idea he was coming on to me. He gave up after a while.'

'What if he wanted his pound of flesh in return?'

Janet slammed the metal drawer shut with a clunk. 'Then he'll be disappointed.' After half a beat she added, 'Of course, he doesn't know that yet, so let's just see what we can get out of him.'

Janet dropped Cash home, and as she fumbled for her keys her mobile rang. It was Holly. 'We need to talk,' she said.

Chapter Eighteen

Holly was flushed and fidgety when she arrived on Cash's doorstep half an hour later. Cash brought her in and introduced her to Billie. Billie shook her hand with the formality of condolence, murmured the appropriate words and then disappeared into the kitchen area to make tea.

Holly slipped out of her coat. Cash took it from her and hung it over the back of a chair. When she turned back, Holly was sitting on the edge of the sofa, arms wrapped around her body. She looked tired and drawn. Without preamble she said, 'I did the autopsy on Mort Higgins and I think there are things that need to be looked into.'

'What does that mean? What things?'

Holly leaned conspiratorially towards Cash. 'I found puncture marks. One into the antecubital fossa, a fairly large one, and a second . . .'

Cash cut in, 'The what?'

'Sorry, that's a vein in the right arm.' She turned her arm over and touched the crook of her elbow. 'And there was a second smaller puncture on the back of his neck. Under normal circumstances I'd probably have missed the one on the neck.' She paused, collecting her thoughts. 'Tell me, do you know if Mort Higgins had blood taken recently for any reason?'

'Not as far as I know. In fact, I don't think he ever gave blood in his life.'

'It might not have been a donation, it could have been just a blood test for some reason.'

'How recently is recently?'

Holly shrugged. 'Well . . . say on the day he died?'

Cash thought for a moment, then shook her head. 'No. I'd have known because I'd have made the appointment for him. He was useless at stuff like that. Why?'

Holly frowned. 'Well, the thing is, the puncture mark on the arm was covered by a plaster. It looked to me as if someone had put a line in. It was fresh, and by the look of it I'd say whoever inserted it was a professional. A nurse or a doctor.'

Cash's stomach clenched. 'But what does that *mean*?'

Holly straightened up in her seat, at once the businesslike professional. 'I'm not sure, but let me run this by you. There was ante-mortem bruising on his upper arms which suggests someone gripped him by the arms, but there was nothing else to suggest any other violence.'

Cash was confused. 'So what are you saying?'

Holly couldn't conceal her excitement. 'I can't be sure until I get the labs and the toxicology back, but the way I see it . . . Now, I don't know why or anything, I've no idea what the motive could be, but what if your friend was grabbed and held, then someone jabs him in the neck with a hypodermic full of sedative to knock him out, then takes him back to the office, or maybe they were in there all the time? They sit him in his chair and shoot him in the head. It would explain why he was shot in the right temple. They'd hardly have known he was left-handed.'

Cash was stunned and excited. 'But what about the puncture mark on his arm?'

'Again, I'm not sure, but you say Mort wasn't back on

the drink?' Cash nodded a vigorous confirmation. 'What if, to make the whole thing look more like a suicide, they pumped the stuff into a vein?'

'What? Three quarters of a bottle?'

'Whatever. Maybe not. I don't know yet. It depends on the alcohol concentration in the blood. But don't you see? It's enough to get the cops to look at it again.' She paused again, before adding, 'He wasn't an addict, was he?'

'No. No, he never touched drugs, even when he was on the drink.'

Billie returned with a tray of tea and an open box of Jaffa cakes. 'But d'you think he was killed in the office or did they just dump him there after?' she asked.

Holly reached for a cup and helped herself to a Jaffa cake. 'Had to be killed *in situ*. The post-mortem lividity suggests he wasn't moved at all after death.'

'Right.' Billie nodded sagely. 'Lividity. That's the bruisin' on the body where the blood settled after he died, isn't it?' Holly nodded, registering surprise that she should know. 'I read a lotta crime books,' the dancer qualified.

Billie sat on the sofa next to Holly and picked up a cup of tea from the tray. 'I'm sorry t' bring this up, but what about yer ma?' Cash had wanted to ask but had been hoping that Holly would bring it up first.

Holly didn't seem at all fazed by the question. 'I phoned a friend of mine, a pathologist at Vincent's, and he faxed me the autopsy results.' She delved into her briefcase, picked out a long, curly fax and unrolled it. 'My mother died of extensive head injuries.' She gave Cash an anguished look. Cash's heart went out to her. 'She would have been unconscious from the moment of impact, thank God. She wouldn't have known what hit her.' She dropped the fax paper on to her knee and it immediately rolled up again. 'The pathologist, Kevin Mulroy, thinks, from the pattern of bruising he found on her body, that she was hit by a high off-road vehicle with bull bars. She wouldn't have stood a chance, even if she'd been found sooner . . .'

Her voice faltered and she looked up at the ceiling, biting her lip, trying to keep the tears away. Billie put an arm around her and gave her a squeeze. Cash leaned over and took her hand. After a half a minute or so Holly sniffed and shook her head. 'I'm sorry, it comes in waves.'

Cash could identify with that. 'God! This must be so hard for you.' She squeezed Holly's hand.

'I'm fine. I'm fine.' She eased her hand from Cash's grip and took another sip of tea. 'How about you? How did you get on with Detective Doyle?'

'Not very well. But your report should make him sit up and take some notice.' Holly nodded in agreement. After a pause Cash said, 'Have you spoken to Daisy since?'

Holly shook her head. 'I was going to phone her on Saturday night, but I couldn't bring myself to talk to her. I was too raw. Anyway, I don't want to upset her any further. She's enough on her plate as it is. She's feeling guilty as hell that she had to lie to Dad and that she missed the funeral, but it was her doctor's call. Like I said, he thought it would be too much for her, being so close to full term. I have to say I agree with him. Why do you ask?'

'I don't know.' She bit her lip. 'I suppose she'd have said if your mother had found her at the nursing home?'

'Of course. If Mummy had found out about the baby she'd have told Dad and there'd have been no reason for her to stay away from the funeral.'

'That's a point,' Cash conceded. 'So whatever your mother and Mort found out . . .'

'Who's to say they found out anythin'?' Billie cut in. 'How d'you know they weren't just in the wrong place at the wrong time?' Both Cash and Holly stared at her uncomprehendingly. 'What I mean is, who's t' say, in the course of lookin' for Daisy, that they didn't happen on somethin' completely unconnected, by chance?'

It was a bleak prospect. With the other two scenarios, at least they had points from which to start, always assuming Doyle did the right thing and checked out the Garda files for Janet. If Billie's surmise turned out to be the case, they'd have little hope of getting anywhere.

Cash thought about the proposition for a moment, then shook her head. 'I don't see it. If that was the case, why didn't they do the same with Mort as they did with Mrs Porter? Why go to all the trouble of making Mort's killing look like suicide?'

Billie shrugged. 'I was just speculatin'.'

Thinking of Doyle's reluctance to take on board even the possibility that Mort's death had been murder, Cash said, 'What if Doyle still won't do anything?'

Holly put her empty cup back on the tray. 'It won't be down to him. The autopsy report will go to his superintendent. I called in a favour and the lab promised that I can have the tox. and blood-work results back by tomorrow night, Tuesday at the latest. My guess is we'll find some sort of barbiturate in his blood. Enough to prove he was sedated. As it is, Doyle would have a hard time ignoring the ante-mortem bruising on his arms. That has to suggest something iffy.'

'He wasn't impressed about our theory about your mother, but he said he'd check it out. I doubt he'll break his back, though.'

'Well, if the cops start investigating Mort's death, it

stands to reason that if they follow up his last movements and so forth, they'll have to look into it.'

'Good point. So what happens now?'

Holly sighed and shrugged. 'We wait for the super to start the ball rolling. I'm not going to say a word about my mother until he starts the investigation. You can do that when they ask you about Mort's movements on the day he died.' She wearily heaved herself up off the sofa. 'I'm off. After the last few days I feel as if I could sleep for a week.' Cash walked with her towards the door. 'The trouble is, I know the moment my head hits the pillow I'll be wide awake.' She turned at the door. 'Bye, Billie. Nice meeting you.'

Billie held up her hand in reply.

They stood for a minute on the front step. It was a cold night and Holly pulled her coat collar up around her ears. 'Will you call his widow – Janet, is it? – and fill her in on the autopsy results?'

'No problem. It should cheer her up a bit. She's seeing Doyle tomorrow. She's going to try and get him to check the Garda files for criminals who might bear a grudge against Mort. Should I tell her not to mention the autopsy stuff?'

'Might be better. Apart from the fact that she's not supposed to know the results yet, he'll have no argument ready for the super. What *is* his problem, by the way?'

A freezing gust of wind rattled across the street, causing Cash to shudder. 'Hard to say. Mort used to be a cop and Doyle knew him back then. I get the impression he didn't like him much, maybe that's it. Of course, Janet said he came on to her after she and Mort split so bruised ego could possibly play a part, too.'

'Oh, the intricacies of the male ego,' Holly mused. She gave Cash a hug. 'You'd better get back inside before you catch your death. I'll call you as soon as I get the labs back.' She hurried to her car and drove off, giving a little wave as she passed.

Billie had cleared the tea things away when Cash returned to the sitting room. She was subdued, mainly because all the talk about Mort and murder and autopsies had stolen her thunder. She had been bursting to tell Cash about how good she felt, about Dr Keogh and the Self-Esteem seminars, but somehow it didn't seen appropriate now. If she admitted the truth she would have to say that she was uncomfortable even mentioning The Better Way Institute. It was obvious from her attitude that Cash thought they were, at best, some class of chancers.

She decided to keep it to herself for the moment. The results would speak for themselves.

Chapter Nineteen

Joanne was awake at the crack of dawn the following morning. The night had been endless and she had slept little. She watched the hands crawl around the clock face, counting the minutes until she could phone Mrs Haffner to check on the progress in Morocco. Eventually, at seven, despite Rodney's protests, she called Mrs Haffner at home.

She picked up on the second ring and Joanne went into a long rigmarole of apology for calling her at such an early hour and at home and so forth. Mrs Haffner cut her off. 'Think nothing of it, Joanne. That's what I'm here for. I know how concerned you are.'

'So what's the news?'

'No news as yet, what with the consulate being closed over the weekend, but my contact assures me he'll set the ball rolling as soon as they open today. In fact, with the time difference, I expect he's on to it as we speak.'

It wasn't the answer Joanne had been hoping for, but at least Mrs Haffner sounded positive. 'So how soon do you think they'll let her leave the country?'

She heard Mrs Haffner exhale at the other end of the line. 'Hard to say, but pretty soon, I'm sure. I mean, if the fine's paid, they'll have no other reason to hold her, will they?'

'No, no. Of course not.' She paused. 'But, look, if you need to . . .' She had been going to say 'bribe' but the word stuck in her throat. 'If you need to give any *incentives* to speed things up, please let me know. It won't be a problem.' She was glad that Rodney was in the shower and had missed her last statement. But anyway, she always acted on the assumption that what Rodney didn't know he wouldn't weep over.

'I'm sure that won't be necessary, but it's good to bear in mind should there by any further hitches. I'll call you as soon as I have any news, Joanne. Now, don't worry. I'm certain it will all work out in the end. Trust me.'

Mrs Haffner continued to reassure Joanne for another few seconds, then, after promising again that she would call the moment she heard from her Moroccan contact, they terminated the call, just as Rodney emerged from the *en suite* bathroom damp and wrapped in a towel.

'Did you speak to her?' He walked over to the wardrobe and selected a charcoal three-piece suit and a white Egyptian cotton shirt.

Joanne gave a cheery grin, though in reality she wanted to vomit. Stress had that effect on her. From her first contact with Mrs Haffner the previous week, nerves had caused her to be intermittently nauseous. And since Mrs Haffner had called on Saturday and informed them about the poor girl languishing in a Moroccan jail, the nausea had been almost constant. Not wanting to worry Rodney, though – he had an important case in the Supreme Court that day – she hid her true feelings. 'Yes. Everything's fine, Rodders. She's going to phone as soon as she has any news.'

'Excellent.' He held up three silk ties. 'Which one?'

Cash, too, was up with the lark. Despite her fears that she would be unable to sleep, she had, in fact, slept like the dead, and was woken only by the clang and crunch of the refuse lorry, compacting the garbage in the back of the massive truck. She peered at the clock. Seven-forty and not yet light. She was about to turn over for another hour's sleep when her phone rang. Cash got out of bed and groped for it in the dark. It was Holly.

'Did I wake you?'

'No. I had to get up to answer the phone.'

'Ha, ha. Listen. I was talking to my cousin last night and between us we came up with a couple of ideas. Do you think you could meet us some time this afternoon, preferably after four-thirty?'

'This afternoon? Well . . . um . . .' Cash remembered that she was due at the Westbury at two-thirty for the Channel 4 audition. 'Okay. How about the Westbury? I'm in town for an audition. I should be finished by that time.'

'Sounds good. Hopefully I'll have the labs back by then.'

A thought struck Cash. Tentatively she asked, 'Um . . . which cousin were you talking to?'

'Niall. My cousin Niall Donovan. You don't mind talking to him, do you? It's not a problem, is it?'

Cash groaned inwardly. 'Problem? No. Why should it be a problem?'

Holly confirmed the time and place and hung up. Fully awake, Cash made herself a cup of tea, then got back into bed with her audition piece.

After half an hour she gave up. She was having a hard time concentrating on the script as thoughts of Mort kept filtering into her mind. Holly's visit the previous night had left her even more unsettled about the whole business. If her theory was correct, the killing, and the act of trying to pass it off as suicide, was all so cold-blooded. It wasn't as if whoever had done it had done it in the heat of the moment. Not that Mort would be any less dead, but somehow the notion that someone had thought through the implications and carefully orchestrated the whole charade was unnerving and evil. What kind of person was capable of such a thing? She gave a humourless laugh as it struck her – the kind of person Mort routinely came into contact with when he was a cop.

She glanced at the clock. Eight-thirty. There was no movement yet from Billie's room so she switched off the lamp and slid down under the duvet. Maybe just another hour.

Janet had also had a restless night. Disjointed dreams which had featured Mort and Dan Doyle. Mixed-up, anxious images. At one point she'd had a strange sense of hanging over a precipice. Mort had been holding on to her hands. She had felt her grip slipping, and had awoken with a start and the sensation of falling. She had lurched bolt upright in bed, bathed in perspiration, heart beating like a jackhammer.

When her heartbeat had returned to something resembling normal, she swung her legs over the side of the bed and, elbows on her knees, rested her chin on her fisted hands. The time-switch for the boiler hadn't kicked in yet and the polished wooden floor was cold beneath her feet. The whole bedroom was cold. Janet could not sleep with the window shut, no matter how cold the weather. It was about the only thing she and Mort had agreed upon towards the end.

Leaning over and reaching to the foot of the bed, she grabbed her dressing-gown and slipped it round her shoulders. It was pointless trying to get another hour's sleep, she knew she wouldn't be able to rest. Cash's call was on her mind. She'd been shocked by the autopsy results. Even though from the start she had believed that Mort had been murdered, there was a certain obscenity in the detail. The cold-blooded way the killer had drugged Mort in order to subdue him. And, if Holly was correct in her assumption, the possibility that they had injected him with the whiskey to make it look as if he were still a pitiful alcoholic. The latter fact made her angry. She felt that, as well as his life, they had stripped away his dignity, too.

A gust of wind billowed the curtains. She looked over her shoulder towards the window. Outside, it was still dark. It occurred to her that she had forgotten to call Hubie, Mort's younger brother, the previous night as she had promised, with details of the funeral arrangements. Cash's news about the autopsy had pushed it completely from her mind. She was momentarily annoyed with herself for the oversight. Even though they hadn't been that close, she sensed that Hubie had been devastated by the news. Of course, when she had phoned him there had been no talk of murder. She wondered if he would be relieved or horrified when he was in full receipt of the facts. The funeral would be delayed again now.

She looked at her watch and calculated that it was early evening in Sydney. Better call and warn him not to book a flight just yet. As she was turning this over in her mind the radio alarm clicked on and the Spice Girls dragged her back to reality, telling her what they wanted, what they really, really wanted.

Seven thirty-five.

She dialled Hubie's number and waited. In one way she was relieved when she got his voice-mail. She wasn't sure she was up to answering his inevitable questions. After the tone, she succinctly advised him to delay his flight booking as there was a hold-up in the funeral arrangements, and asked him to pass the information on to his brother and sister as she didn't have their phone numbers. After hanging up, it crossed her mind that perhaps she had been over-economical and austere in her language. She thought about ringing back, but dismissed the idea, mainly on the grounds of moral cowardice.

Figuring that Doyle would probably be on the same shift as the previous day, and feeling utterly feeble, she phoned Pearse Street and asked for him.

After an interval she heard a click and his voice came on the line. As advised by Cash, she didn't mention Mort's autopsy results, just went straight into her theory that maybe Mort could have been a victim of some criminal with a grudge. She spoke as if it was an acknowledged fact that Mort's death had been murder, giving Doyle no chance to cut in.

'So I was wondering, would you have any ideas? Is there anyone you can think of who had it in for Mort and who may have recently been released from prison? I figure it has to be someone he'd have sent down for something serious, otherwise they'd have been out long ago.'

'It's a thought,' he said.

She was surprised that Doyle wasn't shooting the idea down out of hand. She had half expected him to do so in the knowledge that he would not yet have seen the autopsy report. Holly had to wait for the lab results before she could submit it. He was silent at the other end of the line, but she could hear him breathing.

'Are you still there?'

'Yes, yes, I'm still here. I was just trying to think of any likely candidates.'

Growing in confidence, Janet ploughed on. 'I thought you could maybe check the police files of the cases Mort worked on against the prisoners recently paroled.'

Again Doyle was silent.

'Dan?'

'Yes, I'm still here. I was thinking.' He paused. 'I'll tell you what. I'll see what I can find out and maybe we could meet for a drink this evening, or I could come to your house.'

As far as Doyle was concerned, Janet was more comfortable on neutral ground. Not much chance of him collecting his pound of flesh in a public place. 'Fine.' She feigned enthusiasm. 'How about the bar of the Montclare at, say, seven?'

'The Montclare? Okay.'

She thought she detected a tinge of disappointment. She hoped it wouldn't influence the thoroughness of his file search. 'I thought it would be quieter than a pub.'

'Seven, in the bar at the Montclare, then.'

She breathed a sigh of relief as she hung up the phone. Heading for the shower, she made a mental note to ask Cash along to the Montclare for moral support.

Maurice called Cash just before eleven to remind her about the audition and to advise her to get there early as it was a closed audition and the Channel 4 bods wouldn't want to hang around any longer than necessary.

It was the first real chance Cash had had to ask him about the series. He explained that even though it was set in the North of England, taking full advantage of the tax breaks, the producers planned to shoot the entire series in Dublin. Cash felt a twinge of disappointment. She had been hoping to get away, even for a short period. Still, on the upside, with the shoot in Dublin she'd be able to sublet Billie's flat while she was away on the Caribbean gig.

At the conclusion of his call, Maurice wished her luck in her audition with his usual 'shatter a femur' blessing.

Billie was off at a dance class so she studied her audition piece for an hour, then rummaged through her clothes, looking for something suitable to wear. She was of the opinion that dressing for the part always helped her to get into character.

After some indecision she settled on a silver fake-leather (tacky plastic) micro-mini she had bought for a *Star Trek* theme party the previous year, which she teamed up with a black crêpe camisole top which had accidentally found its way into the hot wash and was now two sizes too small. Under the skimpy top she wore her trusty Wonderbra, hiking her reluctant boobs into some semblance of a cleavage. Further rummaging unearthed another victim of the hot wash, a pink cardigan, which added a certain *je ne sais quoi* to the ensemble.

Shoes were a problem. She tried on every pair she owned but none looked right. In a moment of inspiration she remembered the pair of CFM black patent platform pumps Billie had lurking in the back of her wardrobe. Although they were a half a size too big, she knew if she stuffed the toes with cotton wool she'd get away with it. Despite the cold, she had planned to go for the bare-legged look, but closer inspection caused a change of mind due to the fact that a leg wax was way overdue. Instead, she plumped for not-too-sheer black tights.

Having settled on costume, Cash packed her make-up and the clothes in a small sports bag, planning to change in the Ladies' at the Westbury. Better not to turn up in character, they might not let her in.

Noon.

Time to eat. Stress always improved her appetite. Not that she was in any way anxious about the audition. Cash had the ability to take auditions in her stride. It was more the thought of that smart arse Niall Donovan. She wondered briefly why Holly wanted her to talk to him. Still ruminating on this, she prepared a bacon sandwich and a pot of tea, then ate it standing over the sink. It rankled that he felt he had to put his twopenny-worth in. Then, always the pragmatist, she dumped her cup in the sink, dismissed him from her mind and set off for the Westbury.

Holly had a busy morning ahead, but her mind wasn't on the job, and everything took longer than normal. Every time the phone rang she held her breath in the hope that it was Kirsty calling from the lab with Mort Higgins's results. Realistically she knew there was no chance before mid-afternoon at the earliest. No matter how Kirsty expedited the forensic tests, they took the time they took.

Every now and then a vision of her mother lying in the mortuary at Vincent's Hospital flashed into her mind. Her face had been horribly bruised and swollen. It had been she who had identified the body. She had stalled her father, hoping that the funeral directors would be able to tidy her mother up a bit, but in the end there was little they could do.

It was the first time she had seen her father cry. They had clung to one another and wept together, then he had straightened up and asked her to try to hold herself together for Rose's sake.

Rose had always been their mother's favourite. Not that she, Hazel or Daisy had ever been deprived of love or affection. Her mother had been a very demonstrative person but, Holly supposed, it was inevitable that Rose and her mother would be close. She was the youngest, the baby.

Rose had been born six weeks premature and in the

first few days it had been touch and go whether she would survive at all. She had been accustomed to hearing her mother describe Rose as her little miracle. Not only because she had survived against all the odds, but because until the sixth month of her pregnancy, and a threatened miscarriage, Eileen hadn't even been aware that she'd been pregnant.

For the past five years, Holly had dealt with death on an everyday basis, but it had never touched her before. Not like this. At the age of thirty-two she had never experienced bereavement. Her paternal grandparents had both died while she was still a toddler but she had no memory of it. This fact had never occurred to her before.

She thought of the priest's words about her mother being taken before her time. She had been fifty-eight years old. She had been healthy and strong. Statistically, she should have had at least another twenty years. It was so unfair. Doubly so as she hadn't died of any illness. And if Cash's theory was correct, not even an accident.

Although for the past three days, since Cash had first spoken to her at the funeral, she had believed that her mother had been killed deliberately, strangely it was only now for the first time that the implications fully dawned on her. Not an accident. Someone had deliberately driven into her mother, leaving her to die on the side of the road. Despite what she had said about her mother not suffering, she realised that she didn't know if that was a fact. What had she been doing on her own at that time of night on Bath Avenue? Had she been alone? Had she been afraid?

Holly felt an aching hollowness in her chest as she thought about it. She looked down at the cadaver on the table in front of her. A man of fifty, the paperwork stated, but he looked ten years older. The spark that was life had gone from him. She wondered if he had family to grieve for him. She hoped so.

'Dr Porter?'

She felt someone touch her arm, and was suddenly embarrassed as she realised that she had been staring into space.

'Are you all right, Dr Porter?' Joseph Neary, the mortuary assistant, looked concerned.

She turned her head. 'I'm fine, Joe, thanks. Fine.'

'You shouldn't be back so soon. You should've taken at least a week.'

Holly made light of it. 'And we'd have had bodies stacked up from here to the Phoenix Park.'

'No more thanks you'll get in this place,' he muttered.

'Maybe not.' She turned back to the body lying on the table. 'But these guys would still be here, waiting for me, even if I was off for the month.'

Chapter Twenty

In the ladies' toilet, Cash changed into her hooker clothes, then stood in front of the mirror to apply her make-up. Over a thick layer of foundation she brushed blusher on to her cheekbones, sucking in her cheeks and blending the colour down into the hollows. Brown eye shadow and thick black liner round the eyes. Several coats of mascara left her eyelashes looking like spiders. Taking a brown pencil, she lined her lips, then filled the outline with paler brown lipstick.

Next she started on her hair, back-combing at the roots and spraying it with hairspray to make it bigger. Finally she dug into the bottom of her bag and took out a pair of big hoop earrings. The finishing touch. She stood back and surveyed the result. Over her shoulder she noticed a woman eyeing her suspiciously.

Cash smiled at her.

The woman, without taking her eyes from Cash, edged over to the basin and washed her hands.

Cash smiled again. 'Isn't deh bleedin' rain on'y shockin'?'

The woman froze, horrified, then fled, her hands still dripping. Her reaction gave Cash a certain sense of satisfaction.

After she had packed her regular clothes into the holdall, she gave herself a final once-over and headed upstairs to the conference room the producers had hired for the audition.

Eight other actresses, most of whom Cash knew, were sitting at the back of the room, some talking quietly together, others reading the audition piece. As she entered, a youngish, red-haired woman, dressed in black combats, platform trainers and a fluffy turquoise sweater, who identified herself as Amber Tinkler, Mr Patterson's PA, took her CV and apologised for the delay. Mr Patterson's flight, it transpired, had been delayed, but she expected him within the next half-hour.

Sally-Ann George caught her eye. She smiled and beckoned to her. Cash trundled over, glad to have someone to talk to to pass the time. Sally-Ann was also a graduate of the Strolling Players, and Cash had known her for years. Because of her curly red hair and freckled complexion, at the age of twelve she'd been chosen to play Annie in the Dublin production of the show and at the time Cash had been green with envy. Sally-Ann had also done a six-month stint in *EastEnders* as Maureen, the Irish colleen with the stereotypical drunken father. She, too, had suffered a violent end, but hers had been due to the ratings war with *Coronation Street*. Today she had opted for the classy hooker look, which Cash thought was a mistake as the script obviously called for a slapper, but she kept her opinion to herself.

'Thought you might be up for this after *Liffey Town*.' She offered Cash a Polo mint, which she accepted.

'Thanks.' Cash looked around the other assembled hopefuls. Some were dressed in character, others in their normal day clothes. It occurred to her that maybe Sally-Ann wasn't dressed in character at all. 'How many parts are they casting, do you know?'

'Just the Irish hooker, as far as I know. That's what I'm up for, anyway. How about you?'

'Yeah. The hooker. I seem to be specialising in them these days.'

Sally-Ann smiled.

Cash looked at her watch. The time was two-thirty.

It was three-fifteen before Jock Patterson put in an appearance. He blustered in with a woman whom Cash recognised from a previous audition as a casting director, Maudie something – she couldn't remember her surname – and a young man in his early twenties lugging a heavy box. Amber hurried over to them and they stood together talking for a while and looking through the pile of CVs, while the young man opened up the box and, after much messing with cables, set up a video camera on a tripod.

After a further fifteen minutes, Patterson checked that the camera operator was ready, then he and Maudie sat at a table and the proceedings got under way. Sally-Ann was called first. She had learned the piece by heart and executed it well. Cash thought it was a pity that she didn't really look the part.

It was going on four-thirty before Cash was called up. She had to read the part as, between one thing and another, she hadn't managed to find the time to learn it off by heart. Amber read the part of the punter. An actress she was not, but that fact didn't deter Cash in any way. She was well used to the drill. She'd failed more auditions than most people had had hot dinners. It went with the territory.

She was pleased with her reading, and felt confident she was in with a chance. Jock Patterson thanked her courteously and said that they would let her know.

By the time she left the audition it was four-fifty. Her plan had been to shoot to the Ladies' to clean off the heavy make-up and change back into her street clothes, but that was out of the question now. She compromised and dug her overcoat, now somewhat creased, from her bag, and threw it over her slapper clothes, before hurrying down to the lobby.

It took her a moment to recognise Niall Donovan. She was thrown because her eye had been searching for Holly, but Holly was nowhere in sight. Reluctantly she walked smartly over to Donovan and stood by his chair.

He was dressed in a dark business suit with a white shirt and a silk tie with a Monet design, identical to the one she had bought for her father in the National Gallery. His long legs were stretched out in front of him and he was reading. By nature a shoe person, on closer inspection she noted that his looked Italian and very expensive.

'Sorry I'm late. The job took longer than I expected. Where's Holly?'

Donovan, who was reading some sort of report, looked up. Cash thought she caught a look of surprise on his face. He hesitated for a millisecond, then sprang to his feet. 'Cash?' His hand shot out towards her. Slightly startled by his reaction, she shook hands. 'I'm afraid Holly's been delayed, too. Won't you sit down? Can I order you a drink? Some tea or coffee maybe?'

Cash automatically started to unbutton her coat, then thought better of it. 'Um . . . Well, after the afternoon I've had, I could murder a gin and tonic.'

Donovan smiled and nodded, then signalled to a waiter. She edged past him and sat in a low armchair which was set at right angles to the chair on which he had been sitting. She sank right down into it and had difficulty keeping her coat from falling open. She noticed Donovan fleetingly look her over, then avert his eyes.

The fact that Holly wasn't there left Cash feeling awkward. She wondered if Donovan would get straight down to business, or would he make polite small talk until his cousin arrived? He didn't strike her as the type who went in for polite small talk.

'Holly shouldn't be long,' he said as he sat down. 'She had someone to see and they were delayed. It took longer than she anticipated.'

'Same here. I thought he'd never come.'

Donovan looked startled for a moment, then mouthed a silent, 'Oh.'

The waiter appeared with her gin and tonic, and placed it on the table in front of her. He placed an empty glass and a bottle of Ballygowan in front of Donovan. Cash dumped the tonic into her glass and took a long gulp. Donovan was making her edgy.

'So . . . em . . . You had, em . . . a *job* in the hotel today.'

Cash nodded. 'Yes. That's why I thought it was a good place to meet.'

Donovan nodded. 'And, em . . . have you been at it . . . ?' He blushed. 'I mean to say, em . . . have you been doing this line of work for long?'

Small talk it is, she thought. Cash couldn't make him out. The last thing she had expected was for the likes of Niall Donovan to be so wet. 'Since I was ten,' she said.

Donovan, who had his glass to his lips, spluttered and choked at her reply. When he caught his breath, he exclaimed, 'Ten? My God, that's so young. I would have thought . . . em . . . I mean, your parents . . .' He blushed again. 'I'm sorry. It's not for me to judge.'

Weirdo.

Thankfully Holly appeared at that point, looking flushed. She hurried over. 'Sorry. I hope I didn't hold you up. I imagine you've introduced yourselves.' She signalled to the waiter, then sat down in the chair opposite Cash.

178

Irritated by Donovan, Cash ignored him, leaned forward in her seat towards Holly and got straight to the point. 'Did you get the lab results back?'

Holly was rooting in her briefcase. 'Not everything. They finished the blood work, though, which is very interesting. They should have the rest by tonight so I'll pop back later to James's and finish the autopsy report for the cops.'

She paused as the waiter sidled over and she ordered a glass of Guinness, then looked at Cash and her cousin in turn, raising her eyebrows, enquiring if they wanted to order something. Both shook their heads.

When the waiter had gone, Holly spread a sheet of paper out on the low glass-topped table. 'I was right about the sedative. There was thirty milligrams of Valium in his blood – that alone was enough to render him unconscious. Mind you, we've no way of proving that it wasn't self-administered, but get this – there was over *four hundred* milligrams of alcohol in his blood.'

Cash looked at her blankly. 'What does that mean?'

'Well, bear in mind that the drink driving limit is 80 milligrams per 100 millilitres of blood. Four hundred milligrams would have left him incapable. With that amount he'd scarcely be able to pick up a gun, let alone manage to squeeze the trigger.'

'So your theory about the line in his arm . . .'

Holly nodded. 'Exactly. And it's my belief that there won't be any sign of alcohol in the stomach contents.'

Donovan cleared his throat. 'About your theory . . . The wrong place at the wrong time idea . . .'

'That was my friend Billie's idea. I don't see it myself. If that was the case, why kill Mort in the office? Why take the trouble to make it seem like suicide? Why kill your aunt at all? And lastly, why in Bath Avenue? As far as I know, Mort had no cause to go anywhere near there.'

Holly cut in, 'I know, I know. But we were looking at it from my mother's perspective. If someone was out to get Mort, surely they'd wait till he was on his own.'

Cash nodded in agreement.

Donovan took it up. 'We were talking about it last night – think about this for a minute. Assuming someone was out to get your friend Mort, for revenge or whatever reason, what if they were following him with a view to killing him and, for whatever sick reason, making it look like suicide? Okay?'

He was waiting for a response, so Cash nodded, not sure where he was heading.

'So, say my aunt had arranged to meet him. You told Holly she phoned looking for him on the day he disappeared and that he said he'd call her.' Again Cash nodded. 'What if they made an arrangement to meet, and then the bad guys come along and nab him at the same time as my aunt shows up?'

Holly earnestly cut in. 'Now they have a plan in place to kill Mort and to make it look like suicide, but my mother's a complication. Don't you see? She was the one in the wrong place at the wrong time as far as the killers were concerned.'

'So you're thinking along the same lines as Janet? The psycho with a grudge? But what about the missing file? Why would they take your mother's file?'

Holly frowned. 'I don't know. Are you sure it's missing? I mean, isn't it possible Mort just took it home or something?'

'It's always possible, but I don't think so. He had no reason to take it home – there was nothing in it.'

'So why steal it at all, then?' Donovan asked.

Cash shrugged. 'I don't know. It's just gone missing.'

The waiter came back with Holly's Guinness and placed it on the table in front of her. The three of them were silent until he moved away, then Donovan sighed and shook his head. 'We need to get things into some sort of order.' He looked directly at Cash. 'Tell me about the Wednesday. What happened? Did Mort Higgins get any other calls? Did he have any appointments?'

Cash took another gulp of her G and T and cast her mind back. Both Holly and Donovan were staring at her expectantly. 'Well . . .' she started. 'I got in late and Mort must have already been in and gone, because he'd left a tape on my desk for transcription.' She backtracked in her own mind. 'Unless, of course, he put it there the day before. I was off on the Tuesday, you see, I had a gig. I only worked part time for Mort.' She could have sworn Donovan blushed again. 'Anyway, on the Wednesday he wasn't in. I typed up the stuff he'd left, then later in the morning Mrs Porter . . .' She looked directly at Holly. 'Your mother rang. She sounded very agitated and asked for Mort. When I told her he was out she made me promise to tell him it was imperative he get in touch with her. That was the word she used, "imperative".'

Holly interjected. 'That sounds like Mother.'

Cash continued, 'Anyway, Mort called not long afterwards and I passed the message on.'

Donovan cut in, 'Where was he calling from?'

'He said he was in a pub out in Stepaside. He said he was going to check out the Better Way Institute. They have their headquarters out in Enniskerry apparently.'

'And he told you he was going to call my mother?'

Cash nodded. The memory of her plea to Mort about hysterical women flashed across her mind but she didn't share it.

'So what do you know about the Better Way people?' Donovan asked.

Cash gave a heavy sigh. 'Only what I already told Holly. They've a drop-in centre in Marlborough Street and they do self-improvement courses, that kind of thing.' As she was speaking, she leaned forward and rummaged in her bag for some of the leaflets Billie had harvested the night she'd done her research for Mort. She only found two rather dog-eared ones giving details of the 'Meditate Your Way to Higher Self-Esteem' and 'Know Yourself, Love Yourself' seminars.

'Cash's friend Billie checked them out for Mort.' Holly was addressing her cousin.

'What did she make of them?' he asked.

Cash extended her hand and rocked her wrist from side to side. 'Hard to say. She seemed quite impressed. I'm inclined to think they're probably chancers.'

'Based on what?'

Smug bastard. She handed the leaflets to Donovan. 'So see what *you* think.'

As he took them from her she noticed that he was averting his eyes again and she realised that her coat had fallen completely open. She thought about wrapping it around herself, but then decided not to. It was hot in the lobby. She sat back in her armchair as Donovan perused the leaflets, handing them over to Holly as he finished reading each one.

'They don't look particularly sinister.' He glanced over at Holly, then he turned his attention back to Cash. 'You didn't go there yourself?'

Cash shook her head. 'I didn't see the point. Billie's opinion was the same as yours.'

Donovan raised his eyebrows in surprise. 'Oh. I thought you'd have been . . .' He rubbed his chin as he searched for a word. 'I don't know . . . curious?'

Cash didn't comment. Just then Holly's mobile rang.

'Dr Porter.' She put her finger in her ear and screwed up her eyes in an effort to hear. 'Daisy! Sorry. It's too noisy in here, I'll go outside.' Leaving her briefcase, Holly hurried towards the exit.

An uneasy silence hung in the air. Donovan was studying the toe of his shoe, studiously avoiding eye contact with Cash.

Well, sod you, too, she thought. Suddenly it occurred to her why he was acting so strangely and she had to stifle a snigger. She hoped Jock Patterson had been as impressed with her portrayal of the hooker.

'What's funny?'

Cash grinned. 'Nothing.' She considered winding him up, but changed her mind. It wasn't appropriate under the circumstances. He was staring now.

'Em . . . Have we met somewhere before? Holly said you were at the funeral, but I don't remember meeting you there.'

'Maybe we met on a *professional* basis,' she said, deadpan.

Donovan's face went through half a dozen different emotions. 'Oh, no. I don't think . . . I mean, I'd have remembered. Not that I . . . em . . .'

He lapsed into a helpless silence and a light film of perspiration glistened on his forehead, but that could have been due to the heat in the lobby.

Cash had a self-satisfied grin on her face as Holly returned a few minutes later. She, too, had a smile on her lips.

'That was Daisy and she's fine, thank God.' She slumped down in her seat with an air of relief. 'I said I'd pop out to see her tomorrow.'

Donovan nodded. 'How did she sound?'

Holly shrugged. 'All things considered, she sounded

better than I expected her to be. Of course she's down because of Mummy, and I think she's feeling a bit isolated, too.'

'Stands to reason,' Donovan agreed.

Cash struggled to get out of the low chair. 'I'll call Janet and tell her about the lab results. I know she was seeing Doyle some time today.'

'Hopefully, the full post-mortem report will be on the superintendent's desk before lunch tomorrow.' As she was speaking, Holly started to gather her stuff. Cash followed suit. Donovan signalled to the waiter for the bar bill. The two women walked out together towards the lobby exit and stopped near the lifts.

'Do you fancy coming out to see Daisy with me tomorrow? Are you free?'

It hadn't crossed Cash's mind, but Holly's I-could-do-with-the-moral-support expression caused her to agree without question. Niall Donovan joined them at this point, just as Cash remarked, 'I have to change out of these clothes.' Then, looking pointedly at him, she added, 'I don't want to be picked up by the cops for soliciting.'

Holly laughed then hugged her. 'I'll call you later.'

Niall Donovan nodded a curt goodbye.

After washing her face and changing into more normal clothes, Cash left the Westbury and headed towards Grafton Street, stopping in a doorway to phone Janet. When she switched on her mobile to make the call, having switched it off whilst in the audition, she saw that she had two messages. Both were from Janet, telling her about the scheduled meeting in the Montclare and suggesting that she come along. In the second, her voice had a certain urgency. She looked up Janet's number in her diary, then dialled.

'Janet Higgins.'

'Hello, Janet, it's Cash. I got your message.'

'Great. So can you come?'

'No problem. Just one thing, though . . .' She related the information concerning Mort's blood alcohol level and the presence of the Valium. Also Holly's assertion that there would be no alcohol found in Mort's stomach contents.

Janet stayed silent at the other end of the line as Cash imparted the developments. It struck her afterwards that Janet would have been shocked by the autopsy information, and she rather regretted the fact that she hadn't done it in a more sensitive manner. Mort had been, after all, her husband, and it all sounded so cold-blooded, but she had been unable to contain her excitement.

There was a long pause.

'Are you there, Janet?'

Janet cleared her throat. 'I'm here.' Another pause. 'Doyle *has* to do something now.'

Chapter Twenty-One

She didn't mention to Sandra that she intended to take a sick day, the main reason being that as it was patently obvious that she was in no way under the weather, it would only set a bad example. Besides, she knew if Sandra got even the slightest inkling that she was going out on the bike, there would be no living with her unless she agreed to let her come, too.

Sister Jude had no intention of taking Sandra along. Not this time.

Sister Jude had a plan.

The woman, Cora, had said that Dr Rory, as she insisted on calling him – Sister Jude thought it made him sound like a character from the Muppets – would be in the institute all day on Wednesday. On impulse she had made an appointment, ostensibly to talk to him about her disturbed teenagers and the suitability of his self-esteem seminars and possibly psychotherapy.

She wondered if he would recognise her. Probably not. He thought she was dead. The body in the shattered carcass of the car had been identified as hers. Not that there had been much to identify, only a confusion of burnt-out bones and, miraculously, the intact contents of her handbag. There had been the ring, of course. She thought of her mother identifying the gold signet ring which Alice had insisted on trying on, and her heart lurched in her chest.

Whilst in the hospital and only semi-conscious, she

had heard the nurses talking amongst themselves. Brenden, though virtually blown to pieces, had still been identifiable.

'Good enough for the bastard,' had been the general consensus. After hearing that, she'd had the sense to lie low and had feigned amnesia.

It had been a long time since she had thought of Alice. Alice Flynn, whose bones were lying in the grave with *her* name on it. Poor Alice, who had begged a lift, unaware that the car had been stolen or that Brenden had been parking it in the centre of town for Rory.

She and Brenden. Both lambs to the slaughter. Brenden had insisted that she go with him for the ride. Had it been anyone else she would have been suspicious, but Brenden had had no guile. He hadn't been the brightest. Arguably not the full shilling. She wouldn't have hurt his feelings with a refusal. Rory would have been well aware of that, and the fact that Brenden had worshipped the ground that he'd walked on. It had only been as they'd stopped outside the tobacconist's shop that Brenden had let it slip that Rory had said, 'Be sure to bring Helen along for the ride.'

She had been puzzled and slightly bemused.

With hindsight she knew that if Rory had instructed Brenden to 'be sure to bring Helen along for the ride', Brenden would have made sure that he did. She wondered if the poor soul had been aware that there was a bomb in the car. She doubted it. Rory wouldn't have trusted him that far.

How was she to know that Rory had set the whole thing up that way? How was she to know that he'd timed it to a T, killing two birds with the one stone? With the one bomb. If she hadn't stopped off for the cigarettes . . . She shuddered at the memory.

It had taken her time to piece it all together. In the

aftermath of the bombing all she could focus on was the carnage and the barbarity of it. She was in shock. Numb. Terrified that they would assume that she had been in any way responsible for the obscenity, hence the convenient amnesia.

She needed time to get her head together. She was in denial. Initially, until she heard the nurse's outraged comments about Brenden, she had assumed that the bomb must have been in a different car, one parked nearby. Rory knew her opinion on the matter of bombs. She'd told him in no uncertain terms. Told him there was a better way. Violence was solving nothing, only begetting more violence. (Now, there was an irony – a Better Way.) He listened, the way he always did, arguing the point. Dialogue, he said, had got them nowhere. The Brits weren't interested in dialogue. Where was the dialogue on Bloody Sunday?

Thinking back, she realised that was the point at which he had decided that she was expendable, that she had to die. She, in her naïvety, had thought she could just walk away. His last words to her echoed round her memory. 'We have to make a statement.'

A loud rapping on the doorframe made the nun jump, and she slapped her hand to her chest.

'Sorry, Sister. Didn't mean t' startle yeh.'

Spike was brandishing a spanner. He was a big man, at least six feet six, and at the age of forty was thickening around the middle. He was as bald as a coot and his face, sallow and eroded by acne, sported bushy eyebrows and an off-kilter nose. A straggly black beard clung to his chin. His leathers were well worn and oily from working on the bike.

'It's okay, Spike. I was miles away.' She placed her hands on her knees and heaved herself into a standing position. 'What can I do for you?'

'Wanna see the Hog?' He had a gleam in his eye.

Sister Jude registered genuine surprise. 'It's finished? You got the gasket?'

'Yeah, got the gasket.' He inclined his head in a 'come on' gesture and disappeared. Sister Jude hurried after him.

Spike had a lock-up two doors down from Sister Jude's and they had become acquainted whilst working on their respective bikes.

Spike rode a vintage Triumph, the same year and model as her uncle's, and for as long as she had known him had been restoring a 1958 XLH Harley Sportster, piece by piece.

Apart from a perfunctory hello there had been little conversation for the first few months. He was naturally suspicious of her. Not many middle-aged nuns rode vintage Nortons to his knowledge and he was half expecting her to start spouting religion at him. It was the Triumph that broke the ice. From the engine note Sister Jude had been able to judge that there was something wrong with the timing and had offered advice. 'Eh . . . excuse me . . .'

Sceptical and dismissive, he had snarled at her and she'd backed off to her own space after offering an opinion. He'd cranked the music up and Iron Maiden thundered out of his lock-up, drowning out the vroom of the engine. But later on he'd put his head round the door, holding up two cans of beer. 'How come an aul' biddy like you knows about bikes, then?'

She had accepted the beer and they'd sat and talked. He'd admired the Norton and they'd been friends ever since.

Spike and a group of his friends fancied themselves as rebels without a cause. All enthusiasts, they called themselves Hell's Angels but, as far as she knew, they were harmless enough. She was an honorary member of the chapter. Her moniker, Heaven's Angel.

Sister Jude enthused over the gleaming Harley, but her mind was elsewhere. Spike was listing specifications and ratios, ccs, torque and rpms. She'd heard it all before. Biker talk. As proud as if he'd physically given birth.

Sister Jude oohed and aahed in the appropriate places, but as soon as it was decently possible to leave without causing offence, she excused herself, retreated back to her own lock-up and closed the door.

She felt sick inside. Sick with apprehension. Checking that the door was firmly bolted, she bent down and opened the trunk. She lifted out her neatly folded leathers and rummaged in the bottom. For a moment, panic gripped her as she thought that it wasn't there. But then, after further searching, she found the box. She picked it out and, closing the lid of the trunk, she sat on top and placed the box on her lap. Her heart was pounding now, faster than the rhythm of the White Snake CD that was blaring out of Spike's megawatt speakers.

She lifted the lid and took out the bundle lying inside. It was heavy in her hands. Slowly, she unwrapped it. The gun oil had left the metal dull. She wiped it with a piece of rag, then held it in her hand. It was cold to the touch. A full clip of ammunition was lying in the bottom of the box. She picked it up and, after fumbling a little, snapped it into the Uzi. Bit heavy duty, she thought as she checked to make sure that the safety catch was on, but it was all she had. Then, heart still pounding, she replaced it in the box and put it back in its hiding place.

In two days' time she feared she might need it.

Mrs Haffner poured the tea and handed the delicate

china cup to Joanne. 'Help yourself to milk and sugar, dear.'

They were sitting in her office, waiting for a call from Morocco. Joanne felt sick with apprehension. Just in case, she had brought along her cheque-book. Best to be prepared for any eventuality. Nothing was too good for *her* son. Even now, and the child not yet born, she felt he was hers . . . theirs.

'Biscuit?' Mrs Haffner proffered a plate of Bourbon Creams. Joanne detested Bourbon Creams. Couldn't imagine how anyone would eat them. They were second only in awfulness to Nice biscuits.

'No thank you, Mrs Haffner.' A pause, then she said anxiously, 'Will he be much longer?'

'You're in a hurry?'

'No. No, it's not that. I'm just . . .'

Mrs Haffner leaned across the table and put a comforting hand on her arm. 'I know. Don't worry. I'm sure we'll get the call soon. Try and relax.'

Relax? How could she relax when her unborn son was in such jeopardy? She felt a pang of guilt as she realised that the welfare of the young mother hadn't crossed her mind. Why could things never be straightforward?

The phone rang and she gasped. Mrs Haffner picked it up.

'Adoptions Home & Abroad. How may I help you?' She listened for a moment. 'I'm with someone right now. Can I call . . . ?' She furrowed her brow and shot a frustrated look at Joanne who had the urge to grab the phone from her and terminate the call. Mrs Haffner cast her eyes to the heavens. 'Yes, yes. Look, I have to go. I'm waiting for an important call. I'll get back to you as soon as I'm free.' Another pause. 'Yes, yes. I'll call you.' Then determinedly, 'Goodbye.'

She plonked the receiver back in its cradle. 'Really! Some people can't take no for an answer.'

Joanne gave a silent sigh of relief. She had been in Mrs Haffner's office for well over an hour now. The call to say that the girl had been released from her Moroccan hell-hole should have come through ages ago. What if something had gone wrong? Get a grip, she admonished herself. Think positive. In those Arab countries things moved more slowly. Everyone knew that.

Joanne took a sip of tea. It tasted stewed. She noticed Mrs Haffner surreptitiously peeking at her watch. She looked agitated. It made Joanne feel even more so. Up until that point Mrs Haffner had been positiveness personified.

'You don't think something's gone wrong, do you?'

Mrs Haffner gave her a faltering smile and very unconvincingly said, 'Not at all.'

Just then the phone rang again, giving both women a start. Mrs Haffner snatched up the receiver. 'Hello?' She screwed up her eyes in concentration. 'Can you speak up? It's a very bad line.' Joanne was holding her breath. 'I said can you . . . ? That's better.'

'Is it . . . ?'

Mrs Haffner held up her hand for silence. 'Yes. Yes.' She was almost shouting now. 'I see. Yes.' A smile spread across her face. 'That's wonderful. When?' Joanne felt her spirits lift. 'Very well. Call me when you have the flight details. And thank you.' She smiled and nodded at the receiver as if the voice at the other end could see her. 'Yes. Yes. Thanks again . . . You, too. Goodbye.' She replaced the receiver and sat smiling at Joanne. Joanne waited. The silence lengthened. The woman was certainly milking the moment for all it was worth.

Eventually the suspense was too much for Joanne.

'Well? What's happening? Is she free? Is she coming home?'

'They're coming home some time tomorrow. I'll meet the flight.'

'Is the baby okay? They're both okay, right?'

'Both fine. Now, shall we have a decent cup of tea?'

Suddenly Joanne felt like a limp rag. 'A decent cup of tea would be wonderful.'

With time to kill, and it not being worth her while to go home before her meeting with Janet and Doyle, Cash treated herself to a basket of spicy chicken wings at the Elephant and Castle.

It occurred to her that the last time she had eaten there, it had been Mort's treat in celebration of her big break in *Liffey Town*. She'd ordered the chicken wings and a beer then, too. Mort had gone for the steak sandwich and a Coke. He had been a dedicated red meat man. She smiled at the memory. Hard to believe that he was dead. Hard, too, to realise that less than a week ago he had been alive and well with no thoughts of the hereafter. Poor Mort. A wave of desolation overcame her and she had to close her eyes to prevent the tears from flooding down her face and making a show of herself. It passed quickly. Holly's words about grief coming in waves came back to her.

Now that the autopsy was over, she wondered when the funeral would be. She reminded herself to ask Janet about it and to offer help if it was needed.

After she had finished the chicken wings – enough for two, but no bother to Cash – she ordered a double espresso. It was at times like this she wished she was a smoker. She could have done with some chemical assistance right now. The caffeine hit would have to suffice.

The Elephant and Castle was filling up now. She felt conspicuous, sitting on her own with an empty coffee-cup, so she paid her bill and left. It was a chilly night. She walked briskly in the direction of Dame Street. Still only six-thirty. She was ages early for Janet. On impulse, she turned around and made her way back towards Crown Alley, then down through Merchants Arch towards the Halfpenny Bridge.

Niall Donovan's arrogant question about what she based her opinion of the Better Way Institute on was still rankling her. Across the river, she cut up Liffey Street, then right into Middle Abbey Street. The drop-in centre should still be open. She would take a look for herself, if only to prove to the conceited so-and-so that she was right about the Better Way crowd.

Through the window she could see a woman of about thirty and a young man who looked about twenty-odd. They were talking together, standing by a counter. Except for these two, the place was empty. She was reluctant to go in for this reason and hung around outside for a couple of minutes, hoping that someone else would appear, preferably a punter. After ten minutes or so it was decision time. If she didn't bite the bullet and go in now, she'd be late for her meeting with Janet and Doyle. It dawned on her, too, that it would be good if she could tell Doyle that she had been into the place.

She pushed the door open and looked around. Paul Simon was singing 'Diamonds on the soles of her shoes' in the background. Cash loved the track so she stood and listened for a moment.

'One of your favourites, too, huh?'

The woman was standing in front of her. She had a pleasant friendly smile and a soft American accent. Her hand shot out. 'Hi, I'm Cora. What's your name?'

Automatically, Cash returned the handshake. 'Hello. Em . . . my name's Cash. Cash Ryan.'

'That's a pretty name.'

They stood and listened together. When the track had finished, Cora said, 'Haven't seen you in here before. Is there anything I can help you with?'

'I'm not sure.' Panic. What to say next? 'What do you do here?' Unoriginal start.

Cora smiled again. 'We're here to help.' She gently took Cash's arm. 'Can I get you a coffee?'

At seven-fifteen, Cash emerged into Marlborough even more confused. Altruists or chancers? It was a tough call. On the face of it the woman had seemed genuine. She had explained all about the self-esteem seminars, the meditation, yoga and the counselling service, but at the same time Cash felt as if she was being gently interrogated. It made her feel uneasy. She'd never been one for baring her soul. She wondered if she'd been wise to give her proper name, then, feeling silly, dismissed the fear as paranoia.

As she stood on the pavement, trying to make sense of it, the glass door beside her opened and Joanne walked out in the company of an older woman whom Cash did not know.

'Cash! What brings you here?'

They hugged.

'I was just . . . Never mind.'

Joanne smiled at the woman. 'Mrs Haffner, I'd like you to meet my sister, Cash.' She turned to Cash. 'Cash, this is Mrs Haffner. She's the wonderful woman who's arranging our adoption.'

Mrs Haffner smiled and shook Cash's hand. 'Good to meet you, Cash.' Cash smiled politely.

'Believe me, Cash, she's a miracle-worker.'

'Oh, I wouldn't say that.' Mrs Haffner bowed her head in mock embarrassment. 'I'm only doing my job.'

They stood awkwardly in a triangle on the pavement, none of them really knowing how to take their leave. After a beat, Cash took the initiative. 'Well, lovely meeting you, but I'm almost late for an appointment.'

'Oh . . . Can I give you a lift?' Joanne was bursting to tell someone her good news.

Glad of the offer, Cash asked, 'Can you drop me at the corner of Merrion Square? I'm going to the Montclare.'

Joanne nodded. 'No problem.' She and the miracle-worker said their goodbyes. Mrs Haffner smiled a farewell to Cash and scurried off towards North Earl Street. Joanne watched her go, then linked Cash's arm in hers. 'I've so much to tell you.' They set off towards the car.

Chapter Twenty-Two

Janet was early. Much too early. She sat in the bar feeling very conspicuous and wishing she had brought the *Evening Herald* or a book or something with her to pass the time. She took a sip of her drink. She was relieved that she had managed to contact Cash eventually. Towards the end of the afternoon she had feared that she'd have to deal with Doyle on her own, and she wasn't sure she was up to it. He had too many hidden agendas.

She had been pleasantly surprised by Cash Ryan. Although she had, on occasion, spoken to her on the phone before Mort's death, it hadn't altered her preconceived notion that, in person, Mort's part-time secretary would be a flighty piece. It touched her that Cash was so obviously grieving for Mort. She appreciated the way she had offered to help, even at first when Janet knew that the girl must have thought her talk of murder the crazy ramblings of a grieving spouse still in denial.

Two blue-rinsed American matrons, one wearing a knock-off Calvin Klein sweatshirt and jog pants, the other emerald-green plaid polyester, bustled into the bar and took the table next to Janet. One was complaining loudly about the inadequacies of European plumbing, the other was carrying on an independent gripe about the price of cabs in the city.

'And the cab drivers are so *ru-ude.*'

Janet picked up her drink and moved to a table in the farthest corner of the bar. She wondered if Doyle would prove to be the professional he claimed, or if he would let an age-old grudge cloud his judgement. Her gut feeling was for the latter assumption. It left her feeling a little despondent.

The door opened and Doyle walked in. He looked around, then smiled and held up his hand in greeting as he caught sight of her. The two Americans eyed him up and down in mid-rant as he passed.

'Janet. Can I get you a drink?'

'I'll have another of these, please.' She indicated her glass. 'Hot port.'

'Hot port it is.' He turned and strode over to the bar. Janet snatched a shifty look at her watch. Cash was late. She hoped that she wouldn't be let down.

No sooner had the thought crossed her mind than the door of the bar opened again and Cash hurried in. She looked flustered. Taking a quick look around, she headed over to Janet, unwrapping a long scarf from around her neck and pulling off her gloves. She dragged out a chair and sat down, casting a jaundiced look in the direction of the Americans, who were still whinging on about the various shortcomings of the Old Country.

'Hive of activity in here.'

Janet smiled. 'I thought somewhere quiet would be better.'

'Quiet? Do you have the remote so I can turn the volume down?' She indicated the dowagers with a tilt of the head. They both laughed at the joke, weak though it was.

Doyle turned from the bar and did a double-take as he spied Janet's newly arrived companion. His expression was hard to read. He carried over Janet's hot port and bottle of Bud for himself.

'Cash. How are you? Can I get you a drink?'

If he was angry at her presence or irritated that he didn't have Janet to himself, his tone of voice didn't give any indication.

'Thanks. I'll have the same as you.'

Doyle caught the barman's eye and lifted up the bottle of Bud, indicating that he wanted another, then sat down.

'So, ladies.' He rubbed his hands together.

'How did you get on?' Janet asked. 'Did you unearth any suspects from the files?'

Doyle took a long swig from his bottle. The two women stared at him, knowing that his next words would set the tone of the meeting. He put the bottle down on the table, ignoring the beer mat. To their surprise he nodded. Cash shot a look at Janet.

'I found a few. Mort worked on some high-profile cases in his time.' He leaned over the table and lowered his voice. 'I need to check a few things out, mind you. I don't have all the information I need yet.'

'Like what?' Cash couldn't hide her surprise that he'd even bothered.

'Like I haven't traced the whereabouts of a couple of suspects. They could still be in the nick, or they may be out on parole. I won't know for certain until tomorrow.' Cash thought she detected a hint of annoyance in his tone as he spoke to her this time, but she conceded that perhaps she was prejudiced on account of his attitude at their last meeting.

Janet said, 'We have some new information.'

Doyle's eyebrows shot up. Just then the barman came over with Cash's bottle of beer. When he had gone, the detective repeated, 'New information?'

Janet nodded. 'I can't tell you how I know, but we've proof that Mort was murdered. There was unexplained bruising to his arms and . . .' Cash kicked her under the table. Janet faltered for a second but ploughed on. 'And puncture marks on his body. Somebody injected him with enough Valium to render him unconscious, and enough alcohol to knock out a horse.'

Cash was astonished. They'd agreed to say nothing about the autopsy. She kicked Janet again, but Mort's widow had no intention of shutting up. 'The pathologist's report states that the puncture mark on his arm's consistent with a IV line having been inserted.'

Doyle's face registered utter astonishment. 'Jesus! How do you know this?'

Janet leaned towards Doyle and put her hand on his arm. 'I can't tell you, Dan. You'll have to trust me on this for now. You'll see for yourself some time tomorrow. The pathologist's handing the report over to your superintendent. It explains why he was shot in the right temple. Whoever did it obviously didn't know Mort was a left-hander.'

Cash was appalled. Janet was compromising Holly for the sake of a day.

'What do you mean about the IV line? Why a line?' Doyle directed the question at Janet.

'A line into his vein. Dan, they pumped whiskey into his vein so it'd look like he was still on the drink. The pathologist reckons that there won't be any whiskey in his stomach contents.'

Doyle rested his elbow on the arm of the chair and cradled his chin in his hand. Slowly he exhaled, then shook his head. 'Jesus!'

Janet nodded. 'I know.' She was close to tears. In a way Cash could understand why she had spilled the information about the autopsy report but, still, she felt it had been unnecessary to drop Holly in it so thoroughly, particularly as when her mother's involvement with Mort came out and the subsequent suspicion concerning her death, it would be patently obvious who had leaked the information to Janet.

'This has to be investigated further.' He was shaking his head and his eyebrows were now knitted together in a frown. He looked straight at Cash. 'I'll need to get a statement from you, Cash, about his movements on Wednesday.' He rubbed his chin thoughtfully. 'And I think we'll need to look at all his case files to cover our backs if the other theory doesn't pan out.'

'We looked through the files,' Janet cut in. 'We didn't see anyone with a motive.'

'Not as far as the case in point maybe, but there maybe a name or two that could be known to the Garda for one reason or another.'

'How do you mean?' Cash couldn't see where this was leading.

Doyle took another swallow of Bud, then shrugged. 'Mort did a lot of matrimonials, right?'

Cash nodded.

'Well, your normal Joe Soap wouldn't react violently to Mort snooping into his affairs, financial and otherwise.' He smirked at the pun. 'He'd probably be pretty pissed off, you know yourself. But a hard man with a history of violence might not be so understanding, particularly on account of the fact that Mort might have put him away while he was a cop.'

'The ex-con theory?' Janet talking.

Doyle nodded. 'It's just another avenue to follow. We'll need to look at everything.' He glanced at Cash. 'When could you give me the statement?'

'I could do it now if you want.'

Doyle shook his head. 'Not here. It's not appropriate. How about you come back to Pearse Street with me now?'

'Sure.'

Janet couldn't thank Doyle enough when they were leaving. She was stunned and relieved by his change of attitude. Cash was relieved but also perplexed. It was possible that Dan Doyle was still just going through the motions, trying to turn himself into Janet's hero. Or maybe, when he'd realised that there was going to be an investigation anyway, he'd decided he'd nothing to lose by showing willing before the event, and at the same time scoring Brownie points as far as Janet was concerned. She came to the conclusion, however, that his motives didn't really matter a jot, as long as they caught Mort's killer.

They walked Janet to her car, which was parked on the south side of the square, then Doyle and Cash reclaimed his and drove to Pearse Street.

It was almost nine before she left the Garda station after giving the cop a detailed statement about Mort's movements on the Wednesday and the week leading up to it. She mentioned how distressed Eileen Porter had been when she had called, looking for Mort, and her insistence that it was *imperative* they meet. Doyle took it all down patiently and conscientiously, every now and then interjecting with a question to clarify a point.

At the end of the interview he walked Cash out of the building on to Pearse Street.

'Would you be able to meet me at Mort's office in the morning so I can go through the files?' he asked. 'I think it might be too upsetting for Janet. Anyway, I expect she has things to arrange.'

Cash nodded. 'Sure. Em . . . How long will that take,

d'you think? I'm supposed to be at an audition in the afternoon.'

'Not long. As long as you show me where everything is, I can manage by myself after that.'

Cash agreed to meet him at nine-thirty the following morning. He apologised for the fact that he couldn't give her a lift home because he had something else to see to, but Cash didn't mind. The interview room had been stiflingly stuffy and she felt like taking some air. She wrapped her scarf around her ears, turned up her coat collar and set off at a brisk pace for Drumcondra.

So immersed in her thoughts was she that before she realised it she was on Drumcondra Road coming up to the canal. She was quite hot now from the exertion. She crossed at the lights and after twenty yards turned down Fitzroy Avenue. Nearly home. She hoped that Billie would be back so she could tell her the news.

She was conscious of the sound of a car engine so, before crossing into May Street, she cast a look over her shoulder. The vehicle was coming at speed. She stopped at the kerb, waiting for it to pass, angered that it was speeding in a built-up area. A lot of Billie's neighbours were elderly and not so snappy on their feet.

The headlights were full on. Suddenly she realised that it was coming straight at her. She leapt back and threw herself into a doorway, whacking her head against the corner of the porch as she landed in a crumpled heap. The vehicle was high off the ground. It lurched on to the pavement but couldn't reach her as she crouched in terror. The bull bars were a foot away from her face, the headlights blinding her. Abruptly it reversed, then the engine revved and it accelerated down the street, swerving around the corner. Cash lay where she had fallen, heart pounding, dazed. She put her hand to her head and it came away sticky with blood. The street was silent.

Gathering her wits, she staggered to her feet and covered the last twenty yards to Billie's door at a gallop.

Chapter Twenty-Three

Doyle was there within fifteen minutes of Billie's call. Cash, still in a state of shock, blabbed her story while Billie cleaned up the graze on her forehead. The significance of the type of vehicle hadn't escaped them. Doyle, it appeared, had no idea what she was raving about until Billie pointed out that the vehicle involved in Eileen Porter's hit and run had also been an off-roader with bull bars.

'How do you know that?'

Cash winced as Billie pressed a Band-Aid over her wound. 'Check out Eileen Porter's autopsy results.'

Doyle let it pass. 'Are you sure it was deliberate?'

'Of course it was bloody deliberate. The bastard drove straight at me. He swerved on to the pavement, for God's sake.'

Doyle held up his hand in a placating gesture. 'Okay. Okay. Point taken. Did you get the registration and actual make of the vehicle?'

Cash glared at him. 'Yeah, right! I took out a pen and made a note of it while I was trying to avoid being killed.'

Doyle pursed his lips. 'It was just a thought. So I don't suppose you got a look at the driver either?'

Cash shook her head, immediately regretting the action. It felt as if her brain was loose inside her skull. This time she dispensed with the sarcasm. 'No. The headlights were shining in my eyes.'

'Pity.' Doyle made a note in his book.

Billie handed Cash a lump of soggy cotton wool soaked in Dettol. 'Here, clean the heels of your hands with this while I get some ice. You'll probably have a black eye t'morra.'

Cash groaned and took the cotton wool. 'Great. Just what I need if I get a call-back from Jock Patterson.'

'Oh, I dunno,' Billie observed dryly. 'Might make you look more the part.'

Doyle got to his feet. 'Right. I'll put in a report. And I'll get back to you as soon as I've any news on the other matter.'

Cash gaped up at him. 'Is that it?'

Doyle stared at her blankly.

'What about the maniac out there who's trying to kill me?'

'There's not a lot we can do, Cash. We've no make or registration. Not even a colour. All I can say to you is be careful out there. Watch your back.'

Cash was outraged. 'Be careful out there? Watch my back? That's it? You can't be serious.'

Doyle sighed. 'Look, Cash. I sympathise. I know you got a fright, but what can we do? We've nothing to go on.'

'But it's probably the same bastard who killed Eileen Porter. Can't you . . . ?'

Doyle cut across her. 'Yes. I appreciate that, but other than pulling in every four-wheel-drive, off-road owner in the Greater Dublin area . . .' He left the sentence unfinished. Cash could see his point.

'Well, it shows one thing,' Billie said, as she gingerly held a dishcloth full of ice to Cash's forehead.

'What?'

'Whoever did in Eileen Porter's worried about Cash.

So at the end a' the day it goes to prove that it wasn't a hit and run, doesn't it?'

Doyle didn't comment.

Billie had been all for taking Cash to A and E to get her head checked out, but Cash wasn't into sitting in a draughty hospital waiting room half the night so she settled for two Solpadine and an early night. Billie insisted on making up the sofa bed for her and, after Cash had had a healing shower, ministered to her with tea, sympathy and a large bar of Golden Crisp.

The combination of the chocolate and the Solpadine knocked her out for the count and she slept like a log.

The following morning, however, she felt as if she'd been hit by a train. Further examination revealed extensive bruising to her right shoulder and most of her right side. As she was dressing, Billie gleefully pointed out that she had a map of the Arran Islands on her bum and halfway down the back of her thigh. The eye, no doubt due to the ice pack the previous night, wasn't as bad as Billie had anticipated. Cash looked as if she had only done two rounds with Mike Tyson instead of the usual fifteen. It was swollen and there was a purple shadow underneath, but it wasn't closed.

'What are you doing today?' she asked her friend.

'Just a couple a' classes. Then I'm goin' shoppin' for some gear suitable for the Caribbean sun. How about you?' Billie handed her a mug of coffee.

'I'm going into the office first thing with Doyle so he can sort through Mort's old files, then I'm going to see Holly's sister Daisy.'

'The pregnant wan?'

Cash nodded. Big mistake.

Detective Sergeant Doyle was waiting for Cash, standing in the corridor, leaning his back against the wall. He was drinking from a polystyrene cup. As he saw her approach, he took a final gulp of the contents, then looked around for a refuse receptacle. When he saw none, he crunched the cup in his fist.

'Been waiting long?' Cash enquired as she fumbled with the keys.

'Only a couple of minutes,' he replied. 'You got here in one piece, then?'

He followed her into the office and tossed the crumpled cup in the bin. Cash walked over to the filing cabinet and slid the top drawer open. His flippant attitude had annoyed her. She wouldn't satisfy him by telling him that she'd spent ten minutes standing in the porch like a fugitive, making sure that there were no four-wheel-drive vehicles lurking up the road, or that she had waited for the lights to change from red to green to red, simply because she wouldn't cross the road in front of a black Cherokee Jeep that was revving at the crossing. Neither did she mention the pitying looks she had garnered from a couple of women on the bus as they openly stared at her bruised and swollen eye.

'Evidently,' she said tersely, then turned back to the cabinet. 'All the hard copy files are in here, filed in alphabetical order.'

Doyle walked over and ran his hand over the tops of the buff folders. They made a whirring sound as they flipped through his fingers. 'How will I know if there are any missing? Do you have any sort of directory or list of what's supposed to be here?'

Cash shook her head. 'There's no directory as such.' She turned and walked over to her desk, leaning over to click on the computer. 'But all the files and correspondence are on the hard disk. I suppose you could check through those. They're listed according to date, though.'

Doyle walked round the L-shaped desk and sat in

Cash's chair, facing the computer screen. The computer was still booting up and the Windows 95 Microsoft Internet Explorer logo flashed on to the screen as the C drive buzzed and hiccuped, loading the software.

He looked up at Cash. 'Can you access the files for me?'

Cash leaned over and double clicked the mouse on the 'Files' icon, and a list of case files appeared on the screen. 'There you are.'

Doyle nodded. Scanning down the list, he opened a file at random. He read for a couple of seconds, then cast his eye in her direction. 'What if I want to print one out?'

Cash glanced over at the filing cabinet, then she realised what he was getting at. 'Oh, you mean if you find that the hard copy's missing?' Doyle nodded. 'The printer's here.' She walked round to the long side of the L and slid open a drawer. The printer easily glided out on rollers. 'I'll load it up with paper for you.' She clicked the printer on.

'It's okay. Just show me where it is and I can manage.'

Cash pointed to the Norseman Direct box sitting on top of the desk above the printer. 'Copy paper's in there. I never got round to unpacking it.'

'Fine.'

Doyle remained sitting at the computer, scanning the files. Cash stood awkwardly by the desk. After a few moments he looked up. 'I can manage now, thanks, Cash. It's easier to read the files from the screen. You can go if you want. I'll pull the door after me.' He stared at her as if to say, The sooner you go the sooner I can get on with this.

Cash took the hint. 'If you say so. I'll be off, then.'

When Doyle didn't respond, she walked over to the door. 'Well, goodbye, then.'

Doyle nodded without looking round.

Holly arrived on the doorstep at two. 'What the hell happened to you?'

'Not a lot, apart from some psycho trying to kill me.'

Her mouth gaped open. Cash took her arm and led her inside, then, after making her a cup of tea, filled her in on the evening's events, starting with her brush with death. Holly was horrified but at the same time heartened that the incident confirmed their suspicions surrounding her mother's death.

'So what are the cops doing? Are you still in danger?'

'Huh! The cops are doing sweet damn all about it.' She mimicked Doyle's voice, rocking her head from side to side. 'We've no registration, model or even a colour. We can't pull in every four-wheel-drive owner in the Greater Dublin area.' As she was speaking she rapidly opened and closed her fingers against her thumb like a gibbering mouth. She didn't mention the paranoia of her journey in and out of the city earlier that day.

Holly could understand Doyle's point, but didn't comment. Having dispensed with her angst, Cash went on to recount the previous night's meeting with Doyle and Janet. At the end of reporting the nuts and bolts, she tentatively added, 'Um . . . And I think Janet might have dropped you in it.'

'How d'you mean?'

'She mentioned Mort's autopsy results.' Cash cringed, waiting for Holly to explode with indignation.

Instead, she turned down the corners of her mouth and gave a what-the-hell shrug. 'What can they do? Janet's the next of kin. It's not as if I was compromising a murder investigation or anything.' She gave a wicked grin. Cash was relieved. After promising not to mention it, she would have felt bad if it had caused Holly any grief.

They hit the road a few minutes later. Cash rooted out her Raybans to disguise the pugilist's eye. Holly drove and she sat back to enjoy the scenery.

It was a beautiful day, the sky as clear and as blue as summer. Apart from the obvious lack of foliage on the trees and the chill in the air, it could well have been August. They chatted for the first few minutes, then both fell silent. Cash was thinking over the events of the past week, Holly was thinking about other things. After a while Cash heard her chuckle. She turned her head.

'What's the matter?'

Holly had her eyes on the road. 'Niall thought you really *were* a hooker.'

Cash smiled to herself but opted for a display of indignation. 'The cheek of him.' But she couldn't sustain it and burst out laughing.

'You knew, didn't you? You wound him up.'

'Well, maybe just a little. He deserved it.'

'Niall. Why? He's a lamb.'

She snorted. 'A lamb is he? Is that why he threw me out into the street?'

Holly's head shot round. 'What?'

Cash backtracked. 'Well, not exactly into the street, but his company bought my building and I had to get out.'

'He gave you notice, though, didn't he? Surely he gave you notice.' Holly sounded both outraged and embarrassed.

'Um . . . well, yes.'

Eyes narrowed. 'How long?'

Cash cringed. 'Six months.'

Holly gave her a wry look, then concentrated on the traffic again. They drove on in silence. The traffic was heavy but flowing freely, and Holly managed to do a steady fifty. After a while Cash said, 'Did you put him right?'

'What?'

'Niall Donovan. Did you put him right about me?'

'I wasn't going to, but then I felt sorry for him.' She turned her head again and glanced over at Cash. 'He said that you'd told him you'd been at it since you were ten, and he was appalled.' She paused. 'Did you *really* tell him that?'

Cash sniggered, smug in the knowledge that she had exacted some sort of revenge on Donovan, however petty. 'Sort of. He asked how long I'd been in my, as he put it, line of work, so I told the truth. It's not my fault that we got our wires crossed ever so slightly.' She laughed. It was the first time she had really laughed spontaneously since the day she had found Mort sitting dead in his chair.

Holly grinned and turned his eyes back on the road. The traffic slowed and soon they were crawling along at ten miles an hour. Cash peered up ahead but couldn't see any reason for the tailback.

'Probably an accident,' Holly said as an ambulance sped past, siren whooping.

Thirty yards further on, as they crested a rise in the road, ahead of them they spied the flashing lights of a Garda traffic car and two ambulances near a jumble of twisted metal. As the distance shortened Cash could make out a Micra embedded in the back of a Hiace van. She looked away as the cop waved them past. She heard Holly mutter, 'Nasty.'

It crossed her mind that she had never been so conscious of death before.

Holly switched on the radio. Maura from Co Meath was on the line to Joe Duffy. It was a sad tale concerning her husband and how he had been leading a double life for the past twenty years, living with another woman by whom he also had a family. The situation had only come to light when the man had dropped dead in his mistress's house. Joe was sympathetic. The woman was devastated that her husband had deceived her for so long. Jacky, a farmer from Co Mayo, phoned in with a comment to the effect that if he'd been getting what he'd needed at home he wouldn't have strayed. Maura and Jacky got into a hot debate, and after a couple of minutes Joe cooled it by going to the commercial break. Holly leaned over and switched him off.

'I don't remember Daisy that well,' Cash said out of the blue.

'Why would you? She'd have been a junior when you were in sixth year.'

'True. What did she do after school?'

Holly snorted. 'Bit of everything. Daisy's quintessentially a quitter. Can't stick at anything for more than a month.'

'Oh? But I thought she was a volunteer in Somalia. Surely that isn't work for a quitter.' She turned her head in Holly's direction, but Holly had her eyes on the road.

After a long pause she said, 'Daisy was never in Somalia.'

Cash frowned. 'But I was sure you said . . .'

'I did. I did say she was in Somalia. Tell a lie for long enough and you begin to believe it.' She nodded her head towards the radio. 'Like the man with the double life they're talking about on Joe Duffy's programme.'

Cash was staring at her, uncomprehending. Holly continued, 'Daisy had a drug habit, amongst other things. She managed to hide it from Mummy and Dad, but I noticed the signs early on. She claimed she was in control, the way they do. I was always on at her, warning her, but . . .' She shrugged. 'Daisy had other ideas.'

'So what happened?'

'Well . . . Daisy has an addictive personality. Whatever she gets into, she gets well and truly into. *And* she has shit taste in men. Anyway, she hooked up with this loser, Tommo, and the next thing she's on crack cocaine.'

'Jesus!'

'Yes. Anyway, she looked so awful and spaced out, we knew Mummy and Dad were bound to notice something was up, so Hazel and I, after a lot of resistance, finally bullied her into a rehab programme. Hazel's husband, Derrick, paid for it, and we told the folks she was off in Somalia.'

'Good grief. I'd no idea.'

Holly sighed impatiently. 'Daisy's her own worst enemy, but she always seems to get someone else to pick up the pieces. It's been like that for as long as I can remember.'

'So is Derrick paying for her stay in the nursing home, too?'

'Well, you can bet your life it ain't Daisy,' Holly snapped. 'Sorry, I didn't mean to be sharp with you.'

'That's okay.'

'I mean, it's like this baby. Daisy didn't even consider the option of keeping it.'

Cash said, 'I suppose that *is* her choice to make.'

'Sure. But it's so bloody predictable. Daisy's never taken responsibility for anything in her life. She just blunders from one disaster to another and someone else picks up the pieces. Usually Hazel and me.' She was visibly angry now. Her hands were gripping the steering-wheel and unconsciously she had speeded up to around seventy.

'Um . . . shouldn't you slow down a bit, Holly? There might be speed traps on the dual carriageway.'

Holly's eyes flicked to the speedometer. 'Sorry.' She braked and the car slowed to a reasonable speed. 'Daisy just makes me hot under the collar.'

'So I see.' It occurred to Cash that Holly's anger with Daisy could be more to do with the fact that she blamed her for their mother's death, rather than her inability to take responsibility for her life. If she hadn't disappeared from the scene, their mother would never have gone to see Mort in the first place.

'Why was your mother looking for Daisy at all if you told them she was in Bosnia?'

Holly shook her head. 'I've no idea.' Suddenly she slapped her hand to her mouth. 'Shit! She went to a fund-raiser a couple of weeks back for Refugee Trust. She must have met someone there who was home from Bosnia.'

'You should have chosen somewhere more remote,' Cash said wryly. 'Like the Himalayas.'

'I wish.' She signalled right into a side road and slowed. 'It should be along here somewhere. Look out for the sign.'

'What's the name of the place?'

'It's the clinic where she did her drug rehab. The Glencullen Nursing Home and Treatment Centre.'

Twenty yards further Cash noticed a large signboard beside an open set of iron gates. She peered at it as they approached.

'This is it . . . Good grief! No wonder your mother thought Daisy had run off with the Better Way crowd. Look.' Cash indicated the notation at the bottom of the signboard.

'But I thought you said they were a crowd of chancers. What've they to do with the nursing home?'

215

'Maybe they're not such chancers.'

Holly crinkled her brow. 'Meaning?'

'Meaning after your smart-arsed cousin's comments yesterday, I thought it wouldn't do any harm to go to see them for myself, and now I'm not so sure. I talked to a woman there and she seemed pretty genuine.'

'So what are they about? What do they do?'

'Well, they do self-improvement courses, as you know, but the woman I spoke to said they do counselling and stuff. Maybe the head honcho, yer man Dr Keogh, is involved in the rehab clinic. It says on the leaflet he's a psychologist.'

Holly, still frowning, nodded. 'Right. That could be it, I suppose.' She slid the car into gear and turned into the driveway.

Chapter Twenty-Four

There was no sign of activity as they walked through the vestibule into the hall, but they could hear a one-sided conversation coming from a half-open door to the left, as if someone was talking on a phone. They stood and waited.

The hall was large and airy with doors to the right and left of the vestibule. A dark wood staircase climbed to a half-landing, then it did a ninety-degree turn to a shorter flight, which changed direction again and ultimately led to the first floor. A bulky Victorian sideboard stood at the back of the hall beside a closed door which, in more genteel times, would have led below stairs, safely separating the family from their minions.

Although the place looked more like a country house hotel rather than a nursing home-clinic, that cloying hospital disinfectant smell was very evident.

'You weren't here before when Daisy was having her treatment, then?'

Holly shook her head. 'No. I was working away in Galway. To tell you the truth, I couldn't face it. I've seen people go through it. It's not a pretty sight. Anyway, the patients on those programmes aren't allowed visitors. Can't say I was disappointed.'

The one-sided conversation came to an end and a moment later a plump nurse in a white uniform dress, which was straining at the seams, walked out of the room into the hall. She wore a starched nurse's cap and, ironically, a badge pinned to her dress above an ample bosom informed them that she was Staff Nurse Sharon Slimm. Nurse Slimm smiled as she greeted them.

'Hello. How can I help you?' She had a strong Cork accent which caused the last three words of the sentence to blur together and rise in intonation.

Holly informed her that they were there to visit Daisy Porter. A doubtful expression crossed the nurse's face for an instant until Holly qualified. 'She's not in rehab. She's pregnant. She's in the nursing home.'

Nurse Slimm smiled again then nodded her understanding, after which she directed them to the day room on the first floor. Cash, whose sense of direction was non-existent, switched off, relying on Holly to take it all in.

Holly followed Nurse Slimm's directions and Cash followed her. They climbed the staircase. The walls were lined with portraits of stern-looking Victorian ladies and gentlemen, all of whom looked constipated. At the top of the stairs they turned right and followed a corridor, turning left through a set of double doors.

'I think it's down there somewhere,' Holly said, indicating the corridor leading towards the back of the house.

From behind a few of the doors, as they passed, they could hear the muffled sounds of music.

A door opened and a nurse stepped out. She took no notice of them, except to nod a greeting. She had a kidney dish covered by a green cloth balanced on her forearm.

As she closed the door an elderly man in an electric wheelchair zoomed past them at a rate of knots, almost taking Holly's legs from under her. She staggered but regained her balance, holding on to the wall. Cash leapt out of the way.

'Mr Gardener, if you don't observe the speed limit I'll have to take away your batteries.' She turned to the two women and shook her head. 'Are you all right? He's a divvil in that bloody thing.' Then she headed down the corridor in hot pursuit.

Cash sniggered. 'At least his didn't have bull bars fitted.' Afterwards it occurred to her that perhaps it wasn't the most sensitive comment to make under the present circumstances, but if Holly took offence she didn't show it. They carried on towards their destination.

A sign suspended from the ceiling directed them down a side corridor to the day room.

The day room turned out to be a small glass conservatory tacked on to the back of the house. It was lined with vinyl-covered hospital armchairs, most pointing towards a television set.

As soon as they entered Holly made a beeline for Daisy, who was sitting by the window, listlessly leafing through a magazine. She turned her head as she heard her sister approaching and for a moment her face lit up. Cash stood back. It was the first time the two sisters had met face to face since their mother's death and she felt she should give them some space.

She could clearly see the family resemblance in Daisy's facial features. Although her face was thin to the point of gauntness, she had the same long nose and almond-shaped eyes as her siblings. Cash watched as she heaved herself out of her chair. Her belly was so large, compared to her arms and legs, that she reminded Cash of a Humpty Dumpty doll. The sisters hugged, with some difficulty, then murmured together for a couple of minutes.

As they were doing so, Cash stood near the door and looked around. The speed freak in the wheelchair had taken up position about two feet from the TV screen. As far as Cash could tell, he was watching *Open House*. He was puffing on a cigarette as he hung on Marty Wheelan's every word.

A young girl of no more than fourteen, and obviously pregnant, sidled past her into the room. She glanced at the speed freak, and at Holly and Daisy, then Cash heard her sigh. Picking up a magazine from a pile on a side table, she proceeded to waft the cigarette smoke away, before steering herself into a seat in view of the television.

'Oprah's on four.' She was talking to the speed freak. He paid her no attention. She raised her voice. 'I said Oprah's on four, yeh deaf aul' fart.' When he still made no reply she grabbed the remote control and switched channels.

This action got a reaction, but his eyes never left the screen. 'I was watching that, young lady. Turn it back.'

The girl clung on to the remote, tight-lipped. Cash lost interest in the altercation.

Holly and Daisy were sitting now, so Cash walked over and Holly introduced them.

'What happened to your face?' Daisy gasped.

Holly was horrified. 'Daisy!'

'It's okay,' Cash said. 'I suppose it does look rather gross. I was involved in an accident.'

'Oh. Are you okay?'

Cash nodded. Holly's earlier comment about Daisy being hyper fitted the picture as her hands were never still. Holly had brought along some magazines and chocolate for her. Daisy had the bag on her knee and was unconsciously but systematically shredding the plastic.

'I'm so sorry about your mother.'

Daisy gave her a weak smile. 'Poor Mummy.'

Holly, sounding overly bright and cheerful, said, 'You're blooming. What's your due date again?'

'Eleven days.' She paused. 'Can't wait.'

Holly leaned over and took hold of her sister's hand, squeezing it. 'Never mind, honey. Have courage. They've terrific pain management these days.'

'No. I mean I can't wait.' Daisy cast her eyes down to the shredded plastic on the narrow shelf that was now her lap. 'I've decided to keep the baby.'

Holly stared at her then cleared her throat. 'You're going to keep it?' There was no hiding the surprise in her voice.

Cash butted out. This was family stuff. She made every effort to be invisible.

Daisy's smile vanished. '*Him*. Not *it*. It's a *boy*. And I'm going to keep him. I'm keeping my baby.'

Holly jumped up and attempted to hug her sister, but the fact that she was now seated, and the size of the bump which was her unborn child, made the manoeuvre impossible. She compromised and put an arm around Daisy's shoulder. 'That's wonderful,' she said, but the tone of her voice didn't convince Cash.

Strangely, Holly's reaction irritated her. Even though Daisy's decision had nothing to do with her, made no difference to her life, she felt that, after Holly's tirade in the car about Daisy never taking responsibility for anything, her lack of enthusiasm was hypocritical.

Holly attempted to rescue the situation. 'No. I'm really pleased, Daisy. That's wonderful. What made you, eh, change your mind?'

Daisy shrugged. 'It's what Mummy would have wanted.'

Holly straightened up. She was angry now. 'This should be about what *you* want, Daisy. A baby's for life, not just for Christmas.'

Cash could see where Holly was coming from, and could understand why to a certain extent. The whole mess had come about because of Daisy's refusal to admit to the pregnancy in case her parents pressurised her into keeping the baby.

Daisy's face crumpled and she buried it in her hands as she started to cry. Holly looked over her head at Cash and, with lips pursed, shook her head angrily. After a moment, she relented and bent again to comfort her sister. 'I'm sorry, Daze.' She gave her a squeeze and stroked her hair. 'Don't be upset. I'm just a bit surprised. You were so adamant before about having it – *him* – adopted.'

'Things change,' Daisy mumbled through her weeping. 'Mummy dying like that made me think, that's all. I want this baby. I want to keep him. He's Mummy's grandson.'

Holly was sitting on the arm of Daisy's chair now, still with her arm around the weeping girl's shoulder. After a pause she said, 'Have you thought this properly through, Daisy? A baby's a huge responsibility, you know. How are you going to manage?'

'You okay, Daze?' The young girl was standing by Cash's chair. In her soft shoes, Cash hadn't heard her approach.

Daisy's head snapped up. 'I'm fine, thanks, Tiffany.' She sniffed, then looked pointedly at Holly. 'I just expected a bit more support from my own sister.'

Tiffany threw a warning glare at Holly. 'Don't upset her, you. It'll affect the baby. It's bad t' be upset when yer pregnant. Babies know it. It's the bad chemicals. They get through t' the baby in the womb.' She had her hands on her hips and her feet were planted apart.

Holly glared at the girl for a moment, irritated by her

interference, then capitulated, resigned. 'Sorry, Daisy. I'm there for you whatever you decide. Really.'

Daisy looked up at her sister through damp eyes. 'Thanks, Holly. I knew you'd understand.' She smiled at the young girl. 'This is my friend Tiffany. Tif, this is my sister Holly and her friend Cash.'

Tiffany nodded a terse greeting then, as she made a move to return to Oprah, threatened, 'Don't upset her again.'

They watched the girl waddle back to her seat.

'She's only fourteen,' Daisy said in a low voice. 'Her uncle was abusing her.'

'Poor kid.'

'Yes. She's lucky Dr Keogh found her. She was living on the street, you know.'

'Are you serious?'

Daisy nodded. 'Dr Keogh says it's his mission. You know, giving something back.'

Cash frowned. 'Sorry?'

'He looks after homeless pregnant girls like Tiffany. Does it for free.'

Holly was impressed, aware of how much Derrick was having to shell out for Daisy's stay. 'Really?'

'I thought he was a psychologist, not an obstetrician,' Cash said.

'He is. Mr Hanratty's the obstetrician. He comes in.'

'Oh.'

'He's very good.'

'Who? Mr Hanratty?'

'Dr Keogh.' She glanced at Holly, then lowered her voice as she leaned towards Cash. 'He treated me before, you know. I had a little problem with drugs and he helped me clean up my act.'

Cash wasn't sure how to respond so she settled for a feeble, 'Really. That's nice.'

223

Speed freak had changed the channel back to Marty. Tiffany made a grab for the remote but the speed freak of the corridors was faster and snatched it out of her reach.

'Say please.'

There was a stand-off situation for a full five seconds, then Tiffany muttered a grudging, 'Please.'

'She's tough,' Holly said. 'She seems like a survivor, despite what she's been through.'

Daisy touched Holly on the arm to recapture her attention from the girl. 'Tell me about the funeral.'

Feeling as if she shouldn't really be there while the sisters discussed such private family stuff, Cash stood up. 'Is there a cafeteria? Shall I get some tea?'

Daisy gave her vague directions to the cafeteria. Cash was grateful for the excuse to get away. 'Okay, then. Shan't be long.'

She fled.

Janet was stunned. 'Are you serious?'

'Absolutely,' Doyle replied. 'We have him in custody.'

'Already? That's . . . I don't know. That's amazing.'

'Detective work. I systematically went through Mort's files and the Garda files and came up with some names, that's all. It's down to thorough detective work.'

Janet knew he was just being modest. 'So who is he? Why did he . . . ?' She couldn't say it.

'Jacko Mulroy. Mort was largely responsible for putting him away for fifteen years. He's IRA. Remember the security van robbery in Athlone?' Janet frowned, trying to recall. 'The one where Garda Tommy McCale was shot and killed. Remember? There was a shoot-out and two security guards were seriously wounded?' Janet remembered. She hadn't seen hide nor hair of Mort for three weeks while the investigation had been ongoing.

She nodded. 'That was him. He got out five months ago. Did his full time with no remission. He's one evil, dangerous bastard.'

Doyle was sitting in Janet's kitchen. He'd called round to give her the good news in person. Janet couldn't keep still. She was pacing backwards and forwards across the kitchen, a cigarette between her fingers. She'd given up ten years before, but when Doyle had asked permission to smoke she'd bummed one of his.

'But how do you know he's the one? Have you evidence?'

Doyle sounded affronted. 'Of course. No point arresting him without evidence. We found some of Mort's personal stuff in his house. There was his driving licence and his passport.'

'But why? Why did he take them?'

'Don't know yet. He's saying nothing. But I guess when he didn't see anything in the papers he thought he was home free. Maybe he just kept them as souvenirs. We'll see.'

Doyle had made the arrest at one o'clock. The information he'd been waiting for from Portlaoise prison had come through just after ten-thirty and he'd taken it straight over to the super. Milligan had been surprised, and impressed. He'd only just received the autopsy report from James's. Doyle had explained how, after the widow had voiced her concerns, he'd made a few inquiries on his own account and checked through the Garda files. It was a matter of record that Mulroy had made serious threats to Mort Higgins at the time of his conviction. 'He's a psycho,' Doyle had pointed out to the superintendent. 'He took out another prisoner's eye just for stealing his fags.'

Milligan had nodded. He understood. Mort Higgins

and Doyle had been colleagues. He had been one of them. He used to be on the job.

Milligan organised a speedy search warrant and Doyle, Jimmy Heart and a couple of uniforms raided Mulroy's address. Doyle sent the two uniforms around to cover the back, then kicked the door in.

Mulroy was sitting at the kitchen table in his vest and a pair of manky grey sweatpants, eating a fry. He could see the uniforms through the back window so he didn't bother to make a run for it. He knew the form. Doyle slapped the warrant down on the table.

'Didn't waste much time, Mulroy. Missing Portlaoise already?'

Mulroy stared at him lazily. 'Fuck off, Doyle. I've done nothin'.'

'So where were you last Tuesday night, you little piece of shit?'

Mulroy speared a sausage with his fork and bit off a chunk. 'I was here watchin' the telly all nigh'.'

'On your own?'

He swallowed the mouthful. 'Yeah, on me own. I done nothin'. Now fuck off.'

He reached nonchalantly for his mug of tea, but Doyle swiped it off the table and it slammed into the wall, shattering and splattering the contents. Mulroy rose out of his chair and swung his fist at Doyle. He was stocky, built like a tank. Muscles bulged on his tattooed arms. The garda, expecting some reaction, had ducked out of the way, just as Heart grabbed Mulroy from behind and, twisting his arm up behind his back, forced the man's head down on to the table into his half-finished breakfast.

As Doyle let the uniforms in the back door Heart, ignoring Mulroy's tirade of curses, attempted to hand-cuff his hands behind his back, but Mulroy wasn't having any of it. He donkey-kicked the struggling garda squarely in the kneecap. Heart's legs went from under him and then there was a general free-for-all. The two uniforms landed on Mulroy, pinning him to the kitchen floor. Jimmy Heart struggled to his feet, red-faced and roaring. The uniforms had Mulroy's arms held out behind him now, effectively immobilising him. Heart attempted to give him a hefty kick in the side with his good leg, but his damaged knee couldn't take the weight. He screamed with pain and made a grab for the table to stop himself from falling. To compensate, Doyle did the honours, punching the kneeling man in the kidneys. 'That's for Mort Higgins, you IRA bastard!' Then the uniforms dragged him to his feet and Doyle cuffed his wrists.

Mulroy was still roaring and shouting, demanding to know what the fuck it was about, proclaiming in one long tirade, 'I done nothin', yeh shower a' bastards.'

'Shut the fuck up!' Doyle punched him once in the stomach for luck and he collapsed into the chair and cursed Doyle and all his progeny to hell.

Fifteen minutes later Doyle returned to the kitchen. Mulroy was still sitting in the chair, his hands cuffed in his lap. Sensing that the situation was serious, he'd adopted the standard stare-straight-ahead, say-nothing attitude.

Doyle leaned against the doorframe. 'Hey, Mulroy. Catch.'

Mulroy's hands instinctively snapped up and he caught the object that Doyle had tossed to him. 'What the fuck?'

'Where'd you get this?'

Mulroy looked down at the small leather wallet in his hands. 'Never seen it before. This is a fit-up.' He tossed it on the table. Heart, who had finished in the sitting room, limped in, smirking. 'It's a fuckin' fit-up,' Mulroy roared at him.

Heart laughed in his face.

'Yeah, yeah, yeah.' Doyle waved the passport. 'Why'd you take this, you stupid fuck?'

From then on, Mulroy maintained silence, only breaking it to demand his brief as soon as they reached Pearse Street.

Janet sat down at the table. 'I can't believe it.' She inhaled on her cigarette and blew the smoke out in a steady stream. 'I knew he wouldn't kill himself, Dan. I knew it. He'd already been to hell and back – why would he kill himself?'

Doyle placed his hand over hers. 'He was a lucky man to have you, Janet. Despite your problems you never let him down. You had faith in him to the end.'

She frowned and brushed a stray hair out of her eyes. 'You're sure this is the guy?'

Doyle nodded. 'One of them. There has to be someone else involved. Yer man couldn't have hooked Mort up to an IV line. There's more to this than meets the eye. Mort caused his crowd a lot of grief one way and another.'

Janet couldn't remember the specifics, but she recalled that when Mort had picked up Mulroy he'd stumbled across a large arms cache and bundles of currency in the house. The media spin was that Mort had smashed a major IRA cell. She reached across the table for Doyle's packet of cigarettes. 'May I?' Doyle nodded, sliding them towards her with his lighter. 'What do you think about this missing file and the hit and run? Do you think it's connected?'

Doyle shook his head. 'I don't know. I can't see how. According to Cash Ryan, there was nothing in the file, and we're not even certain it's missing at all.' He paused. 'Of course, she claims someone tried to kill her last night.'

'What?'

'On her way home after she left Pearse Street. She called me straight away. Claims an off-roader drove straight at her and tried to kill her.'

Janet was staring at him now, horrified.

He reached for the packet of cigarettes and took one himself. 'I've a feeling she could be overreacting, though. This has been a pretty stressful week for her . . . I mean, *she* found him. She must still be pretty stressed out.'

'So you think she was imagining it?'

Doyle sucked the nicotine down into his lungs, then rubbed his chin as if trying to make up his mind. He exhaled and nodded. 'Yes, I do. I can't see the two deaths being connected. Why would an IRA terrorist kill a middle-class housewife, for God's sake?'

'But what about the wrong time, wrong place theory?'

After a long pause he sighed and said, 'Look, these guys are pros. And it looks like they had a plan. The whole thing's too elaborate for them not to have had a plan. If they were after Mort and Mrs Porter showed up, my guess is that they'd just cut their losses and do it when he was on his own. Why would they want the complication? They'd have waited, don't you see? Waited until he was on his own and then grabbed him.'

Janet could see his point. She wondered if Cash would phone later. She decided to call her and arrange to meet. If she was so stressed out that she was imagining assassins at every corner, maybe the news of the arrest would calm her down a bit.

After a couple of moments, he pushed his chair back

and stood up. 'Better get back. Work to do, things to check out. He's not talking yet, but if he thinks he's going to cop for the lot, I know he'll turn. There has to be more to it than just a grudge.'

'How do you mean?'

Doyle hesitated. 'I'm not sure yet. But I'll figure it out.'

Janet saw him to the door. 'Thanks, Dan. I know you and Mort didn't always see eye to eye.'

'I just thought he was never good enough for you, that's all.' He leaned towards her and gave her a peck on the cheek. 'I'll drop over later and let you know how the interview's going.'

Chapter Twenty-Five

The call came through at four-thirty. Joanne had been in a state of high excitement since early morning. In fact, since the previous evening, she had been unable to eat or sleep with anxiety. Rodney was heartily sick of it. Not the adoption – he was still as delighted and excited by that as his wife – but it was her incessant 'what ifs' that were getting him down. Most of them totally irrational, culminating in, 'What if Mrs Haffner's friend gets mugged and robbed on his way to the prison?'

Unwisely he had countered with, 'What if the plane crashes?' He was being facetious, of course, but in her wound-up state Joanne had taken his comment at face value. It took him a good ten minutes to calm her down.

It was so unlike his wife. Joanne was usually so steadfast and sensible. Thinking it through that morning on the slow drive into the city, it made him realise for the first time just how important the baby was in Joanne's scheme of things. Indeed, in his scheme of things. True, he'd been able to provide all the trappings – the house, the cars, the holidays, the lifestyle – but sometimes it all seemed so empty and futile. There was something missing. The truth was, they both needed this baby.

Joanne meanwhile was trying to keep herself busy so that the time would pass more quickly. She had phoned Yvonne but got no reply, then straight away phoned

Mrs Haffner on her mobile to see if she had been trying to get through, even though it was only just after ten and Mrs Haffner had stated that the connecting London flight from Morocco wasn't due in until the afternoon. In between bouts of vomiting, she would pick up the phone to make sure it was still working, or phone it on her mobile to check that there wasn't a bell fault. Then, of course, she would have to call Mrs Haffner again . . .

When Mrs Haffner finally called she snatched up the receiver, expecting the worst.

'Joanne. Good news.'

Joanne had to sit down as all the strength suddenly drained from her legs. 'Mrs Haffner. Is everything all right?'

'The plane landed just twenty minutes ago, and mother and baby are doing fine.'

Joanne felt tears of relief flooding her eyes. 'Oh, thank God. Thank you, Mrs Haffner. Thank you so much. I must call Rodney with the news.'

'Now, I'm taking the girl to a private nursing home to settle her in, then she'll have a full check-up with the obstetrician and I'll phone you tonight to let you know the outcome of that.'

Anxiety gripped her again. 'You don't think there'll be a problem? She looks okay, doesn't she?'

Mrs Haffner chuckled down the phone. 'She looks marvellous. A little thin perhaps, but otherwise she's glowing. Don't be worrying yourself, my dear. Everything's under control.'

'Thank you so much, Mrs Haffner. You've been so kind.'

'Think nothing of it, dear. I'm only doing my job. Now, chin up. I'll phone you tonight.'

Joanne sat cradling the receiver in her hand long after

Mrs Haffner had said goodbye, weeping tears of relief and happiness.

It was growing dusk outside. Cash sat in the cafeteria, drinking her coffee from the pottery cup. She hated drinking coffee from plastic cups. She'd never paid any attention to it until Mort had demonstrated the difference. Of course, china would have been better than the thick white hospital issue utensil she was drinking from right now, but china wasn't on offer, and the pottery was at least one step up from polystyrene, even though the coffee wasn't up to much.

She toyed with the piece of carrot cake on her plate, but it was dry and unappealing. She wasn't sure why she had picked it up, except perhaps she wanted to give Holly and Daisy time alone to talk about the funeral. It reminded her that she hadn't asked Janet about Mort's funeral arrangements the night before as she had intended. There had been too much going on. Only a week ago, Mort and Eileen Porter had both been alive and kicking. Was it only a week? It seemed much longer.

The cafeteria was almost empty, save for a couple of tables. Nurse Slimm was sitting with a colleague two tables down, nibbling her way unenthusiastically through a plate of green salad, and a man and woman were sitting further down. The woman had her back to Cash, but she recognised the saintly Dr Keogh from his picture in the glossy brochure.

Behind the trees the sky was growing crimson. Shepherds' huts on fire again, she thought.

The noise of a chair scuffing the wooden floor dragged her from thoughts of shepherds' huts. She pushed the carrot cake to one side and took a final sip of her coffee.

She recognised Mrs Haffner straight away. 'Hello,' she said as the woman passed her table.

Selina Haffner's step faltered. 'Oh, hello.' Then she hurried on. Cash watched her leave the cafeteria, briefly wondering what she was doing there so out of context, then her train of thought made the connection between adoptions and young single homeless girls who hadn't the resources, mental or otherwise, to keep their babies. It occurred to her that the woman probably hadn't recognised her with the black eye.

She pushed her cup away and picked up her coat and bag, then went over to the counter to buy two take-away coffees and a couple of Snack biscuits for the two girls. The cafeteria woman put them in a small paper carrier.

By the time she found her way back to the day room via the scenic route, she was regretting that she hadn't left a trail of crumbs in her wake. Holly and Daisy were sitting in silence. Holly looked very stressed and tight-lipped. Daisy just looked sulky.

The day room was filling up with teenage girls in various stages of pregnancy, one of them looking even younger than Tiffany, who were sitting watching the television. Speed freak was the only man present. He was still sitting in the same spot, hogging the TV, but Tiffany had won the battle of the remote and the credits were rolling on Oprah.

As soon as Holly caught sight of Cash she jumped up and gathered her coat and bag. Cash handed Daisy the paper carrier with the two cups of coffee inside. 'Er . . . The milk and sugar's separate,' she said lamely.

'Better be off.' Holly bent down and pecked her sister on the cheek. 'Take care, Daisy. I'll see you soon.'

Daisy looked up. 'Fine.' She looked very tense.

'Goodbye, Daisy. Nice meeting you.'

Daisy flapped her hand in the air in acknowledgement, then dumped the bag of coffee on the floor beside her chair. 'Bye.' She stared out of the window, deliberately ignoring their departure.

'What's wrong with her?' Cash asked as they reached the corridor.

'She took the hump when I pointed out a few home truths.'

'Such as?'

'Such as she can't dump her baby on Hazel and me when she gets fed up to the back teeth with it. I've a job. A life. If I wanted a baby I'd have one myself.'

'Don't you think you're jumping the gun a bit? In fairness, how do you know she'll do that?'

Holly stopped dead in her tracks. 'Give me a break! Daisy couldn't even look after her bloody goldfish. The poor creature starved to death.'

'Ours died of chlorine poisoning,' Cash said. 'Joanne changed the water too often.'

'Is that supposed to be funny?'

Cash shook her head. 'No. I'm just saying that having a baby could change Daisy. So could your mother's death. You don't know. You have to give her a chance.'

'A chance? And what if she fucks up again?'

Dr Keogh strode past where they stood in the corridor. He gave them a cursory glance. Cash stayed silent until he had gone out of earshot.

'And what if she doesn't? What if it's the making of her?'

Holly's teeth were clenched and Cash could see that she was having difficulty keeping her temper under control. She recognised the symptoms. She'd often been through the same gamut of emotions when dealing with Yvonne. After about ten seconds Holly sighed deeply and touched Cash on the arm.

'You're right. I'm sorry. But with Daisy I always expect the worst.' They walked on towards the double glass doors. 'Anyway, she'll probably change her mind.'

As they marched out of the front door Cash noticed a dark blue Toyota Land Cruiser parked in a reserved bay five yards from the entrance. She stopped dead in her tracks and her heart started to thud. Holly, still complaining about Daisy, was two steps ahead. After a couple more paces she turned when she realised that Cash was no longer by her side.

'What's up?'

'Nothing. I'm overreacting.' Cash inclined her head towards the vehicle. 'It was the Land Cruiser. I'm just . . . never mind.'

Feeling stupid and embarrassed, she pulled herself together and hurried to catch up. As they drew level she saw Dr Keogh behind the wheel. Despite feeling like a complete spa, she quickened her step until she reached the safety of Holly's car, which was parked at the end of the line. Holly was still giving out about Daisy, but Cash was more intent on watching the Toyota. She kept telling herself to get a grip. Lots of people owned off-roaders, but her heart didn't slow to a normal speed until she saw the off-roader back out of its slot and speed away.

'You're not listening.' Holly's voice intruded.

'Um . . . Sorry. What were you saying?' She fastened her seat belt as her friend started the engine.

'I was . . . Never mind. I was only moaning about Daisy. It's not important enough to repeat.' She was staring now. 'That business last night really shook you up, didn't it? You look terrible.'

'Gee, thanks.'

'I'm sorry, Cash. Daisy's got me so wound up, I'd

236

forgotten.' She placed a comforting hand on her arm. 'It must have been terrifying for you.'

Cash felt her eyes filling with tears. She knew it was in direct response to seeing the vehicle with the bull bars, and the associated stress. 'I thought I was okay till I saw that bloody thing. I know I'm being stupid. It was just a gut reaction.'

'Not so stupid,' Holly remarked. 'Someone did try to run you down last night. A bit of caution's a good idea, if you ask me.'

Janet was over at Drumcondra by six-thirty. She had phoned Cash on her mobile, catching her in transit. Immediately she arrived she told them all about Doyle's arrest of the ex-IRA man and his theory about others being involved. She turned to Holly. 'By the way, he's inclined to think that your mother's death was just a coincidence.' It was almost a throw-away remark.

'Coincidence? But I thought he agreed with our wrong time, wrong place theory.' Holly was stunned.

'Well, no. He reckons that if your mother just happened along, they'd have waited for another opportunity to catch Mort on his own. He reckons they wouldn't make complications for themselves. Mort wasn't going anywhere.'

'But what about last night? Someone tried to run me down last night!' Cash was outraged. 'Does he think I'm fucking making it up? It was even the same sort of vehicle, for God's sake.'

Janet cringed. 'Well, um, he thinks you might have been overreacting.'

'Overreacting? A big fucking off-roader drives straight at me and he thinks I'm overreacting?'

Billie said, 'How did they know?'

Three heads snapped in her direction.

'How did who know what?' Cash snarled, still angry.

'How did whoever ran Mrs Porter down know you were rummaging around? Why did they try and run you down?'

'So you don't believe me either?'

'Chill out. It was a question. How did they know . . .' she counted off on her fingers '. . . one, you were lookin' into things an', two, who you are an' where you live?'

Holly was way ahead of Cash, who was still smarting from Doyle's suggestion. 'She was Mort's secretary.'

'Yeah, but how did they know she was sniffin' around?'

They were all silent for a while thinking about that.

'I think there are too many coincidences altogether,' Cash said after a while. 'First off, Holly's mother was hit by a four-wheel-drive vehicle, then out of the blue one comes straight at me and tries to do the same. Then there's the Better Way thing.'

Immediately Billie was on the defensive. 'What d'you mean? What've they to do with it? I checked them out an' they're kosher.'

Cash held up her hand for silence. 'Bear with me, okay? Holly's mother came to Mort on account of she thought Daisy had run off with a cult, namely the Better Way people – right?' There was a collective nod. 'Okay. But Daisy's actually in the Glencullen Clinic, which also happens to be the HQ of the Better Way Institute, and the head honcho of Better Way, Dr Keogh – who, incidentally, drives a Toyota Land Cruiser – was buzzing around there today.'

'Well, he would, wouldn't he, if that's their head-quarters?' Billie said. Cash gave her a weird look, not sure why she was being so defensive.

'As well as that, we know that Mort was out in

Enniskerry checking up on the Better Way Institute on the day he died, and that Holly's mother was anxious to meet him. Mort promised me he was going to phone her back on it, so I'd say, knowing how agitated your mother was . . .' she glanced at Holly '. . . Mort would have made some sort of arrangement. I'd imagine your mother would have insisted. Also, I dropped into the drop-in centre . . .'

'As you do,' Holly quipped.

'And I was talking with this woman, Cora. Now, I thought she was okay, but I did feel as if I was being gently interrogated.'

'That's just the way they are,' Billie said. 'They were like that with me. Asked me all sorts. They have t' do that t' figure what kinda help you need.'

'So what are you getting at?' Holly asked Cash.

'I'm not sure. But it was after I'd been in there that I nearly got run down. What if they *are* involved in some way and they were aware that I was Mort's secretary? They'd probably have been watching the office for all I know. Then all of a sudden I turn up at the drop-in centre. It could have made them spooky.'

'Hang on a minute,' Janet cut in. 'Aren't you forgetting something? Dan Doyle's arrested someone already. An ex-IRA guy with a grudge. Are you saying that these Better Way people are involved with the IRA?'

Cash's thinking was as confused as the rest. 'I don't know, except that that's what started this whole thing off. Holly's mother going to Mort.'

'Not necessarily,' Janet cut in. 'I think you're just trying to make it all fit. Just because Mort was checking up on these people, it doesn't logically follow that they're involved in an IRA conspiracy, for God's sake. It's a bit of a quantum leap. They're not necessarily involved at all. Dan reckons it's just a simple grudge.

239

Mort caused this Mulroy and his friends a lot of grief. Cost them a lot of money.'

Cash nodded. 'Granted. But he did say others were involved. Who's to say it isn't someone connected to these Better Way people? Just because they appear to be kosher, it doesn't mean to say someone belonging to the group couldn't be involved, unbeknown to the others.'

'And just because Mort was going to see them the day he was killed, it doesn't mean they are either.'

'So what about the other night?' Holly cut in. 'You're forgetting someone tried to run Cash down.'

The more Janet thought about it, the more she believed Dan Doyle's assertion that Cash had imagined the incident. 'Look, Cash, we're all very stressed out right now. We're not thinking straight. I think we should talk to Dan Doyle again. See what he thinks.'

'I know what he thinks,' Cash snapped. 'He thinks I'm crazy.'

'Far from it,' Janet said appeasingly. 'Look. He's the professional. He has all the facts. And he's not the only one involved in the investigation. They'll follow everything up.'

Holly touched Cash's arm. 'She's right, Cash. The cops will look at all the evidence. They'll have to investigate your statement about Mort's last movements.'

'So you think your mother's death mightn't be connected to Mort now?'

Holly sighed. 'I'm beginning to wonder, given that the cops have arrested that IRA guy. I mean, like Janet pointed out, are we just trying to fit all the pieces together when maybe they're not really connected at all?'

The meeting put Cash in bad humour. Long after Janet and Holly had left she was still chuntering on to herself about Doyle and his belief that she had imagined the incident of the previous night. Billie was quiet. It took Cash a while to notice that her flatmate wasn't her usual self either. 'Are you okay?'

Billie bit her lip. 'I'm not sure.'

'What does that mean? Are you sick?'

'I think it might've been my fault you nearly got killed last night.'

Cash just stared at her.

Billie thrashed on. 'I've been goin' to the "Meditate Your Way to Higher Self-Esteem" seminars at the institute, you see.'

Cash's eyebrows shot up to her hairline.

'Yeah, yeah. I know. But I went anyway, right?'

Cash held up the palms of her hands defensively to show that she wasn't going to argue.

'They were really good, the seminars, and afterwards I got t' talkin' to Cora and Dr Keogh, and, well, he's really nice and interestin' and he was askin' me about myself and stuff . . .'

'Billie, what are you talking about?'

'I told him how I came t' check the place out. How Mort asked me to. I mean . . .' She was wringing her hands now, really agitated. 'He was nice and interested in what I had t' say, and I didn't think in a million years they were a cult or anythin'. I didn't think there was any harm in sayin' it . . . You know . . . He's a way of drawing you out when you're talkin' to him.' She shrugged helplessly. 'D'you really think it could've been them? D'you really think they were the ones who tried t' kill you?' Her face was agonised.

Cash didn't know what to say. In one way she was pleased. At least Billie's concern showed that she for one believed her story about the off-roader. She reached over and squeezed her friend's hand.

'I don't know, Billie. But I do know that Janet and Doyle and Holly are all wrong. I *know* someone tried to run me down last night and, all things considered, I think someone at the Better Way Institute, for whatever motive, could be a strong contender.'

Chapter Twenty-Six

Sister Jude was up early, and by the time Sandra put in a sleepy appearance at eight she had already baked a brown soda loaf, put a load of washing on and finished a pile of ironing. It was nerves. She had hardly slept the previous night in anticipation of seeing Rory again. During the course of the night she had changed her mind half a dozen times, then talked herself back into it. Right now she was sick with anticipation and anxiety.

Sandra stood by the kitchen doorway in her Bart Simpson nightdress (not the best role model perhaps). She was scratching her head and looked very sleepy. But, then, Sandra was never at her best in the mornings. 'Yeh weren't bakin'?' Pure disbelief.

It wasn't an unreasonable remark. Sister Jude rarely baked, especially at the crack of dawn.

'I couldn't sleep, okay?' She was sharper than she should have been.

Sandra yawned. 'I was only askin'.'

'Hurry up and have your shower. I'll do you an egg.' She busied herself at the sink, standing with her back to the girl. 'I'm not going in with you today.'

'Why not?'

She knew she was a hopeless liar – that's why she couldn't meet Sandra's eyes. 'I've an appointment in town.'

'What kind of appointment?'

Guilty, and at the same time exasperated, she snapped, 'Just go and get ready, Sandra. You'll be late.'

Sandra made a snorting sound and stomped off to the bathroom, muttering to herself. Sister Jude felt bad taking it out on the girl. She briefly thought of following her and apologising, but an apology would lead to explanations and so to other lies. She let it go. Sandra would survive. She had survived much worse.

When the eggs were ready, she called Sandra, then sat down at the table and cut the top off hers. It was like a bullet. She had never got the hang of boiling eggs. She scooped a knob of butter and smeared it over the overcooked pale yellow yolk in the hope of making it more appetising. Little chance. It was boiled beyond redemption. Just like Rory Keogh . . . Beyond redemption.

But, then, who was she to say? She hadn't seen him in half her lifetime. Who was to say he hadn't turned his life around, paid his debt?

Sandra slouched in and slumped at the table, her body language showing her annoyance at the nun's earlier unwarranted sharpness. She peeled the top off her egg, stabbed at it with her spoon, then pushed it to one side.

'Sorry. I'm afraid they're a bit overdone. Would you like something else instead?'

'No thanks.' She reached for the toast, not giving in an inch to Sister Jude's frail attempt at reconciliation.

'Are you going to band practice tonight?'

Sandra nodded, her mouth full.

'It's just I may be quite late back. Will you be all right?'

'Yeah.' Still sullen.

'You could go to Burger King for your tea if you like.' Wheedling. She knew she was trying too hard.

Sandra relented. 'Thanks. I migh'. Is it okay if I get a

video?' She was pushing her luck now. It was school night.

'Maybe at the weekend. How about that?'

The girl nodded and, negotiations complete, stood up. 'Okay. See yeh later, Sister. Have a good day.'

Sandra was a resilient child.

'Goodbye, Sandra. Be good.' A moment later she heard the front door slam.

Time to kill. Leaving the breakfast dishes, she threw on her coat and headed for the lock-up.

By Janet's prior arrangement, she and Cash met Dan Doyle at Pearse Street Garda station at eight-thirty sharp. Each had a different agenda. Janet's was merely to get an update on the situation regarding Mulroy, but Cash was determined to steer Doyle in the direction of the Better Way Institute. Neither confided their intentions to the other, however, and the atmosphere, although not exactly frosty, wasn't that convivial either.

He was waiting for them outside, and without any ceremony ushered them up to the canteen.

'I'm glad you called,' he said. 'I didn't have a chance to get back to you last night.' He chose a table near the window and the two women sat down. 'Tea? Coffee?'

Janet got straight to the point. 'No thanks, Dan. Did you charge the Mulroy man?'

Doyle hesitated, then took the seat opposite Janet. 'No. We didn't have enough.'

'What? But I thought the man had Mort's passport and stuff. Surely . . .'

Doyle raised his hand and cut in, 'I know. I know. But that's not enough to get him on the murder charge. He sat and stared at the wall for the six hours we had him in. The usual form. A file's been sent to the DPP on the theft charge.'

Cash was outraged. 'So what happens now? You didn't just let him go, surely?'

'We had to. But it's all for the good. He said nothing, so we'll keep an eye on him and his known associates, IRA and otherwise. The pressure'll get to him eventually and he'll slip up one way or another. It's early days yet.'

'You seem very confident, Dan,' Janet said.

Doyle smiled at her. 'I am, Janet. He'll slip up, count on it.' Janet smiled back and Cash felt like a gooseberry all of a sudden. What was going on here?

'Em . . . The thing is, we were talking last night.' She nudged Janet for confirmation. 'And I know you don't think it's relevant, but did you talk to the people out at the Better Way Institute in Glencullen House? Mort *was* on his way to see them when he phoned me.'

'From the pub in Stepaside? I remember. Yes. My colleague Jimmy Heart went out there early yesterday.'

Cash was surprised. 'Oh. So you've changed your mind?'

Doyle gave her a stiff smile. 'Personally, no. But we had to check Mort's movements out. It's procedure.'

Janet gave Cash an I-told-you-so glance, which irritated her greatly.

'Anyway,' Doyle continued, 'it turns out Mort never got there, neither did Eileen Porter.'

'But they must have. Eileen Porter was meeting him there.'

'No, Cash. You don't know that. It's possible Eileen Porter met Mort all right, but her car was at the RDS. It was nowhere near Enniskerry. Mort probably came back into town. You don't even know what the Porter woman wanted to see him about. Did she actually say she wanted to see him about these people that day?'

'Well, no . . .'

'Exactly. I think you're muddying the waters here. We have a definite IRA connection with Mulroy. It sounds to me almost like an execution.' He shot a look at Janet. Her face wore a pained expression. 'Sorry, Janet.' Cash didn't miss the fact that he placed his hand over hers as he said it. Very cosy.

'Did you know that Dr Keogh has a Toyota Land Cruiser?' She was grasping at straws now.

Doyle furrowed his brow. 'So?'

Cash was getting frustrated. 'Well, don't you think there are rather a lot of coincidences here? Eileen was hit by a four-wheel-drive. I was nearly hit by one. Mort was out in Enniskerry on the day he died.' As the words were coming out of her mouth, Cash realised it sounded really feeble now, especially after Doyle's assertion that there was no proof so far that Eileen had been anywhere near Enniskerry.

Dan Doyle shook his head. 'As you ask, no, I don't. Are you sure you weren't overreacting the other night? I know you're pretty stressed at the moment and it's understandable – you, too, Janet. You've both . . .'

It was the only thing she *was* sure of right now. 'Give me a break! Janet, talk to him.'

Janet sighed. 'He does have a point, Cash. Detective Heart checked it out. They weren't out there.'

'How do you know they weren't lying?'

Doyle gave an impatient sigh. 'Give me a break, Cash. We've absolutely *no* evidence of any kind that they were there. But if anything new comes to light we'll check it out, okay? That's the best I can do.'

Cash angrily pushed her chair back and stood up. It scraped noisily on the floor. 'Fine!' She was livid. She looked pointedly down at Janet's hand, still encased in Doyle's. 'I'll leave you to it.'

As she stormed towards the door she heard Janet call after her, but she ignored her and flounced out.

Irritated and at a loose end, she dropped by Maurice Foley's office for want of something better to do. He was his usual ebullient self. He had coffee on the go, but Cash declined. Maurice's coffee was legendary for its awfulness.

'A little ornithological specimen told me that a certain producer was impressed the other day,' he said. 'Things are looking good for a call-back.'

'Really?' It was a cheering bit of news. She sat down by the desk and he looked at her for the first time.

'Jesus! What happened to your face?'

Cash had all but forgotten about her bruised forehead and swollen eye. 'I had an accident.' She gingerly touched her forehead. 'Does it look really awful?'

'Not at all,' Maurice said, very unconvincingly. 'I barely noticed it. Tell me, are you on your way to the Hibernian Saga audition?'

In all the excitement the Andrew's Lane gig had slipped her mind. Maurice sensed her reluctance. 'The director's deffo on the way up. Word has it the production's booked for the Edinburgh Festival.'

'The Edinburgh Festival?'

'Well, the fringe . . . um . . . maybe the outer fringes of the fringe, anyway. What d' you say?'

Cash wasn't in the mood. 'I don't know, Maurice. The part's only a spear-carrier, isn't it?'

'A bikini-clad bazooka warrior, to be exact. It is a speaking part.'

Cash wasn't sure if he was serious or just being his usual obtuse self. Sensing her confusion, he explained, 'Did I mention it was an experimental piece?'

'Yes, Maurice. You mentioned that.'

He chuckled. 'Mind you, I think they might be

looking for someone with their own set of bazoo-kas . . .' He cast a leery eye towards Cash's less than ample chest. 'If you get my drift.' He laughed uproariously at his joke. Cash gave a polite but rather strained smile. Maurice's sense of humour was difficult to take at the best of times. When he had recovered sufficiently, he wiped his eyes and added, 'Of course, the ocular contrusion's just the thing to swing it, girly. Very warrior-like. Get along with you. It won't take long.'

Desperate, Cash whined, 'Isn't there anything else on the go?'

Maurice leaned back in his chair, lacing his hands behind his head. 'There's a detergent ad. They're looking for a young housewife type.'

'That'll do.'

'They're looking for a *young* housewife type, girly. Not a *battered* housewife type. Get along to Andrew's Lane. It's your best bet till your wounds heal. And think of the money you'll save them on the old slap.'

Aware that in her present state her options were limited to say the least, Cash grudgingly gave in.

Gary Hindley, a Scot, was a serious and earnest chap. All thirty-something angst, ratty clothes and woolly hair, he was explaining his concept of the production to a jaded-looking Jimmy Hatton. Jimmy raised an eyebrow in greeting as she walked in.

Cash stood by and eavesdropped. Jimmy kept throwing her the odd look over Hindley's shoulder.

'. . . and I see Lady M.'s dagger scene as the shower scene in *Psycho*, a sort of homage—' he pronounced the word *omh-aajh* '—to Hitchcock, except instead of water we'll have blood, of course. Very symbolic, don't you think?'

'Very,' Jimmy agreed.

Cash coughed to attract Hindley's attention, and they both turned to face her.

'Good God! What happened to your face?' Jimmy said.

'I had an accident,' Cash explained. She held out her hand to Hindley. 'Cash Ryan. Maurice Foley sent me along to audition.' Hindley, who looked slightly startled by her appearance, nodded a greeting.

Jimmy said, 'Cash and I were in *Liffey Town* together. I played her pimp.'

At this Hindley nodded enthusiastically and pumped her hand. 'Good to meet you, Cash. Maurice tells me you're deffo going places.'

'That sounds like Maurice.'

He went on to explain his broader concept which sounded completely dotty to Cash, but she oohed and aahed in admiration anyway, though she did think that perhaps it was just dotty enough to get the play noticed. She read for him and he made the usual promise about letting her know. Jimmy, who had already been contracted to play Macbeth, gave her a broad wink as she left.

Feeling peckish, she headed for Templebar for a bite to eat, and whilst crossing Dame Street at the lights she saw Joanne just ahead of her. She hurried to catch up and touched her on the arm to catch her attention. Joanne's face registered horror as she recognised her sister.

'Good grief! What happened to your eye?'

'I was in an accident.' She was beginning to feel as if she should hang a card around her neck to save herself the bother of explanations.

'An accident. My God! Are you okay?'

'I was just goin' to get something to eat. Have you time?'

Joanne, who was weighed down with shopping bags, readily agreed to a pit stop so they headed together towards Crown Alley. Cash ordered a bowl of soup and a hot chocolate. Joanne chose a large slice of chocolate fudge cake and a pot of tea.

As soon as they were settled Joanne said, 'So tell me about this accident.'

Cash hesitated, not sure whether to tell her, then thought, What the hell. 'You remember I told you at Eileen Porter's funeral how Mort was looking for Daisy because Eileen thought that she'd run away with a cult?' Joanne nodded, mouth full of cake. 'Well . . .' Cash collected her thoughts, then told the full story from the beginning.

By the time she had finished, Joanne was staring at her, staggered. 'And you think someone deliberately tried to run you down?'

Cash nodded. In doing so she realised that her head was no longer as sore as it had been. 'Absolutely. I'm convinced. But all Doyle can say is that I'm stressed out, that I was imagining it. I'm not altogether sure who it was yet. Dr Keogh has a Toyota Land Cruiser, but I've no proof he's involved, or really any reason to think he could be, but I don't know . . .'

'And were they out there? Did Eileen Porter go to this Better Way place?'

'Doyle maintains that they say no. Neither she nor Mort were there that day.'

'Who says?'

'The Better Way people or the nursing home people. I'm not sure.'

'Aren't they one and the same?'

'I suppose so. Yes.'

'So what does Daisy say?'

'Daisy?'

Joanne shrugged. 'Well, she seems like the logical one to ask, as far as I can see. If her mother was there, she'd know, surely.'

It hit Cash then that they had never actually asked. When Holly had talked with her on the phone at the time of their mother's death she would have had no reason to ask. And when she had asked Holly if Eileen had visited Daisy, Holly had taken it for granted that Eileen couldn't have found Daisy at the nursing home or she would have told their father and there would have been no need for the whole charade to continue. 'I never asked her.'

Joanne scraped the remains of the chocolate fudge fondant from her plate and licked it off her fork. Cash reached over and wiped a stray bit from her chin with her paper napkin. 'Can I borrow your car?'

Chapter Twenty-Seven

It was cold in the lock-up. Sister Jude rubbed her hands together to get the circulation moving, then bent down to light the paraffin heater. At least her feet were warm. The heavy leather biker's boots were fleece-lined and she always wore them with at least two pairs of thick socks. She had learned to live with cold hands. It was a legacy from the bombing and to do with her arm injury, but she had never quite grasped the details.

On the way over to the lock-up early that morning she had been waylaid by Mrs McKenna, who was having problems with Social Welfare. Someone had reported that her husband was working and they'd stopped payments. She was in a terrible state, so Sister Jude had stayed with her for a couple of hours, talking the problem through and advising her on her best course of action.

'But he only does the odd bleedin' day,' Mrs McKenna had wailed. 'It's not flamin' well worth signin' off for that. We'd lose more 'n he'd bleedin' well earn.'

Sister Jude had understood the woman's dilemma, and had advised her to appeal, scribbling down a couple of phone numbers. She'd further promised to get her help from the Vincent de Paul Society for the poor. The rest of the time she had sat and listened while the harassed woman had spilled out her troubles.

Through the years on the sprawling estate Sister Jude had learned to become a good listener. At first she had listened because she'd had no idea what advice to give and certainly had had no constructive help to offer, but she'd later realised that a friendly ear was far more use to many of the women than well-meaning, and probably useless, advice. Mrs McKenna had insisted on another cup of tea just as she had been preparing to leave, so it was going on eleven-thirty before she finally made it to the row of lock-ups at the back of the shops.

Once the heater was well alight, she closed it up and held her hands close to the rising warmth. She could hear music drifting in from Spike's garage, but it wasn't loud so she assumed that he, too, must have the door closed against the cold. She cocked her ear and caught enough notes to recognise 'Stairway to Heaven'. She was surprised. She hadn't been aware that Spike was a Led Zeppelin fan.

Her hands were warming up now. She picked up her gloves and laid them on top of the heater. Already the elderly contraption was getting the better of the cold in her small space. She breathed in the fumes. She'd always enjoyed the smell of paraffin. It reminded her of days watching Uncle Joe fiddling with his Triumph in the old shed at the bottom of the garden.

She sat on the edge of the trunk to remove her boots, then struggled into her leathers. It occurred to her that they had become tighter in the last couple of months. She resolved to cut down on the fat. It wouldn't do Sandra any harm either, she decided, at once feeling guilty that she had encouraged the child to eat at Burger King that night.

Leaving the top button undone, she bent down and pulled on the boots again, fastening the buckles firmly at the sides. As she stood, she caught sight of her reflection in the dusty mirror that some previous tenant had left aeons ago. It was an incongruous vision. Like one of those children's books constructed in sections where the child can randomly choose various heads, torsos and legs. Here was a weird creature with the head and torso of a nun, navy polo-neck and heavy silver cross, and the lower body and legs of a Hell's Angel.

After folding her navy pleated skirt, she bent down and opened the lid of the trunk, then placed the skirt inside. The trunk held what was left of her past. She wasn't sure why she had held on to the random bits and pieces. There was no logic to any of it. There was little enough in there, small bits of personal stuff she had gathered in a panic from the deserted safe house not long after she had been released from the hospital. A few photos and bits and bobs, amongst them her first holy communion wreath, still with the veil attached.

The nun leaned into the trunk and picked it out. It was yellowed and tatty now. She remembered with fondness the day her mother had bought it for her, along with the flocked nylon communion dress. She recalled that it had had a hoop in the skirt which had caused her no end of difficulty. The sacrament had left little impression, but that day she had felt like a princess.

It was rare for Sister Jude to have any thoughts of her family, though on the odd occasion when they came to mind she still felt an empty ache. Years back, in the early eighties, she had returned to Derry. She'd had an overwhelming need to see them again. After the long bus journey from Dublin, she had taken a taxi from the coach station to the house and had made the driver wait at the end of the road in the hope of catching a glimpse of her mother. The house had looked different – new double-glazed windows and the front garden had been paved over with crazy paving. No one had come in or out, and after twenty minutes the taxi driver had got jumpy.

'The meter's tickin', missus.' That had been his excuse, but the nun had suspected his agitation had been more to do with a fear that she might be eyeing the place up with a view to some sectarian atrocity. Perhaps he'd thought the short veil on the headband had been some sort of cunning disguise.

A woman came out of number seven and she recognised her as Mrs Malone. She walked right past the taxi and Sister Jude was tempted to wind down the window and ask after her mother, but her courage left her. Mrs Malone thought, like the rest, that she was dead and, apart from anything else, she didn't want to risk the neighbour's dicky ticker. As the taxi was pulling away, a young woman opened the front door and put milk bottles on the step. She was a stranger.

On her way back to the coach station she had detoured to the cemetery but the driver refused to wait and she paid him off without protest, then searched for the gravestone bearing her name. She half hoped to see her mother there. As if. The simple tablet bore only her name and the date of the bombing. There were no flowers, but the plot was neat and tidy. She wondered if her mother tended it or were the clipped grass and evenly raked marble chippings the work of the parish council? She regretted that she had brought no flowers to lay down for Alice. It pained her that she had no idea how her mother felt about her, though in the light of the general media outrage at the time perhaps she would have been dead to her mother anyway even if she had been aware that her daughter was still alive.

Replacing the headdress and veil, she took out the box. At the sight of it she vividly recalled hacking at the floorboards with the claw hammer to get at it, terrified that the security forces or, worse, Rory would walk in on her. After the event she wasn't even sure why she had felt it so important that she get the gun. As far as the world was concerned, Helen Mulloy, IRA terrorist, along with Brenden O'Flannery, had died when a car bomb had exploded prematurely. And good enough for them.

Afterwards the Uzi had proved only to be a nuisance. In her experience, nuns had little need of semi-automatic machine pistols. She could hardly throw it on a dump, and if she had handed it in to a police station there would have been too many questions. In the end she stashed it in her trunk at the convent, then in the lock-up, and tried to forget about it.

Now she was glad of it. It gave her the courage to face Rory. It bothered her, though. At first, when she had seen him in the flesh from her vantage point in the shop doorway in Marlborough Street, she had wanted to kill him. Literally kill him. The anger had boiled in the pit of her stomach. Now the anger had died down, but what if, gun in hand, it erupted again and she blew him away?

No, it wasn't in her nature. She knew that deep down. The gun was only a precautionary measure. The means by which to make him tell her the truth.

She lifted the Uzi out of the box and cradled it in her hands. Although this was the mini-version of the firearm – it was neater than the conventional Uzi, measuring not more than fourteen inches overall – it had the same lethal fire power of its big brother on automatic, a cyclic rate of 950 rounds per minute from a 32-round magazine. She'd seen its power on the covert firing ranges in the depths of County Monaghan, but that had been back in the days when it had still all been a game to her. She hadn't equated shooting at bags filled with straw and cardboard targets with the killing of human beings. Youthful naïvety or crass stupidity? The jury had been out for too long on that one. The gun was heavy and cold to the touch. 'Means to an end,' she murmured.

At that, the door swung open and Spike stepped inside. Sister Jude froze, gun in hand.

'What the fuck?' He blushed. 'Sorry, Sister . . . I mean . . .'

It was too late to hide the cursed thing. He'd seen her. Seen the gun. Sister Jude, ever the pragmatist, decided to come clean. 'It's all right, Spike. I can explain.'

He was still standing in the open doorway, mouth agape at the sight of the nun with the gun. And not any prissy little gun, a fucking Uzi. Now that was a serious gun. And Spike knew all about guns. He and his mates from the chapter ran a lucrative illegal rent-a-gun business – Guns 'R' Us – along with their other nefarious activities. Sawn-offs, 38's, the odd AK47 and half a dozen Kalashnikovs – very popular for bank robberies and security van heists these days. So much for the nun's belief that he and his chapter were harmless wannabes.

Spike shoved the door shut behind him. His eyes never left the Uzi. 'That yours?'

Sister Jude nodded. 'In a manner of speaking. I suppose it's been mine longer than it's been anyone else's.'

He edged over and dropped the lid of the trunk, then sat down. 'You really a nun?'

Sister Jude sat down beside him, resting the gun on her lap. 'Yes. I'm really a nun. This . . .' she raised the butt of the weapon ' . . . is from a long time ago, in another life.'

He folded his arms, with some difficulty as they were

short in comparison to his barrel chest. 'I'm goin'
nowhere. So talk t' me.'

Joanne drove. She didn't trust Cash with her car and,
anyway, Rodney would go mad if he found a scratch on
it. Cash was glad of the company. At the back of her
mind it made her feel safer.

Joanne, however, still had a problem getting her head
around Cash's story. 'So what do these people *do*
exactly?'

'Dr Keogh runs these self-improvement courses. Billie
did a couple, she said they were pretty good. And he's
involved in the nursing home and treatment centre, too.
Daisy once had a drug habit, you see. She did rehab with
him and he cleaned her up.'

'Daisy gets around,' Joanne murmured. 'This Dr
Keogh doesn't sound very sinister to me.'

'No. Particularly as he looks after homeless pregnant
teenagers for free, too. He's a regular saint.'

'So what on earth makes you think he tried to kill
you, for heaven's sake?'

'I don't know that he did. He just has the right sort of
vehicle.'

Joanne frowned. 'So why are we going out to the
nursing home, then? Aren't you afraid?'

The truth was that Cash didn't know. She gave up
trying to explain what she didn't herself understand.
'Yes . . . No . . . It's very complicated. If I really
thought it was him I suppose I wouldn't be coming out
here, would I?'

Joanne sighed. 'I certainly hope not.'

They drove for a while in silence. Cash was annoyed
with herself for not having asked Daisy about her
mother on her last visit. It would have been easy enough
to ask without upsetting her.

As they stopped at a red light Joanne said, 'I bought baby clothes this morning. I couldn't resist them . . . Have a look, they're in the back.'

The last thing Cash felt like doing was rooting through baby clothes, but she humoured her sister and leaned over the seat to retrieve the shopping bags. 'Oh. By the way, yesterday at the nursing home I saw your friend – you know, that woman from the agency?'

'Mrs Haffner?'

'That's the one.'

'At the nursing home? What was she doing there?'

Cash thought it was obvious. 'She runs an adoption agency. The nursing home looks after homeless pregnant girls. I suppose some of them want to have their babies adopted.'

'Good heavens. I wonder . . .'

'What?'

'Nothing.' Joanne stared straight ahead at the traffic, but a tiny smile played on her lips.

The traffic was lighter than the day before. When the turning came up, Cash directed her sister to turn right, and a few minutes later they turned into the driveway of the Glencullen Nursing Home and Treatment Centre. There were more cars parked in front of the building than on the previous day. As they drove to the end of the line, Cash counted no fewer than three off-road vehicles – a Range Rover Discovery, a smaller Suzuki Rhino and a Cherokee Jeep. In a strange way it made her feel calmer and less paranoid. Joanne, too, had noticed the plethora of four-wheel drives littering the car park. 'You have to admit there are a lot of them about.'

Cash was all for tiptoeing past Reception straight up to the day room, but Joanne held her back.

'Hang on a minute. I want to check on something.'

'What?'

Joanne didn't reply because at that moment Nurse Slimm walked into the hall. 'How can I help you?' Then she recognised Cash. 'Oh, hello. Back again?'

'Back again.'

Joanne cleared her throat. 'I wonder if you could help me?'

Nurse Slimm shrugged and smiled. 'Tell me the problem and I'll see what I can do.'

'I'm looking for a young girl. She was admitted yesterday evening. Mrs Haffner would have brought her in. She came from Morocco.'

'Mrs Haffner? I don't think so. We'd no admissions last night at all. I'm sorry. Are you sure you have the right nursing home?'

Joanne looked disappointed. 'Well, no, actually. Thanks anyway. She must be somewhere else.'

'Sorry, I can't help. But why don't you ask Mrs Haffner? I think she's around somewhere.'

Joanne blushed like a naughty schoolgirl. 'Oh, no . . . um . . . No need, thanks.' She turned and fled towards the stairs. Cash hurried after her.

'What the hell was that about?'

Joanne was still flustered. 'I've just done a terrible thing.'

'What are you talking about?'

They were at the top of the stairs now. Joanne stopped. 'Yesterday afternoon Mrs Haffner phoned to tell me that the girl – you know, the mother of our baby – had just flown in from Morocco. Did I mention she had a bit of a problem there and she was in jail and we paid a fine and then they let her go?'

Cash shook her head. Joanne was babbling and it was hard to keep track of her story.

'Anyway, the fine was paid and Mrs Haffner met her plane yesterday at ten past four and she said she was taking her to a nursing home, and when you said you saw her here I thought this might be the place.'

'You weren't going to try and see her, surely?'

Joanne blushed scarlet. 'I know I shouldn't have, but I was curious.' She looked totally mortified.

Cash stifled a snigger. She didn't think her sister's actions so terrible, but she couldn't resist the temptation to wind her strait-laced older sibling up. It wasn't often she got the opportunity. 'You'd better be careful. If Mrs Haffner finds out she'll give you a detention.' Then, without waiting for a reaction, she hurried on towards the glass doors.

Daisy wasn't in the day room. It hadn't occurred to Cash that she might not still be sitting in the same chair. Tiffany, however, and another young girl were sitting together at a table, playing Monopoly. She was counting the spaces as she moved her counter around the board. 'Euston Station. I'll buy it.'

'Yeh can't. I already got it. Yeh owe me rent.'

Tiffany peered at the girl's cards. 'Oh, yeah.' She counted out the rent and handed it over. Her companion smiled smugly and picked up the dice. She appeared to be having more success than Tiffany at this point in the game as Tiffany had only three cards in front of her and she had at least ten.

'Excuse me?'

Tiffany looked round. She stared for a moment, then said, 'You lookin' for Daisy?'

Cash nodded. 'Yes. Do you know where she is?'

Tiffany heaved herself out of her chair. 'I'll go get her if yeh like. She's prob'ly in her room.'

'Are you sure it wouldn't be any trouble?'

Tiffany gave a half-smile and indicated the Monopoly board with a flick of her head. 'I'm fed up playing bleedin' *Monotony* anyway.'

'Only cause yer feckin' losin',' her companion muttered.

Tiffany held up her middle finger to the disgruntled girl and waddled from the room.

Cash wandered over to the window and looked out. The weather was duller than on her previous visit and the garden looked grey and damp. Behind the house she could see a substantial two-storey brick outbuilding, possibly at one time a stable block but now there were curtains on the windows and it looked inhabited. Then she noticed another of the small hand-shaped signs. It read ADDICTION TREATMENT CENTRE and the index finger was pointing towards the building. A couple of cars were parked outside, amongst them Keogh's Land Cruiser. All of a sudden the world seemed to be teeming with large off-road vehicles. Cash wondered if it was the same phenomenon that littered the city with pregnant women when someone you knew was pregnant, or brides when a friend was getting married.

She heard the creak of plastic as Joanne sat down, then heard her sister hiss, 'Do you think that could be her?' As Cash turned she saw Joanne's head twitching in the direction of the Monopoly champion.

'Who?'

'You know! Her. The mother . . . our baby,' she said irritatedly.

'Hardly. The nurse said she isn't here,' Cash hissed back.

A look of disappointment crossed Joanne's face. She'd forgotten. 'Oh, yes.'

Suddenly a thought crossed Cash's mind. 'Jo?'

Joanne looked up at her, eyebrows raised. 'Yes.'

'What time did you say that Mrs Haffner was at the airport yesterday?'

'She met the plane at four-ten. Why?'

'She couldn't have. I saw her at around half-four in the cafeteria, so she couldn't possibly have been out at the airport. Are you sure she met the plane herself?'

Joanne's brow was furrowed now. 'Yes. Certain. She said the mother was fine, a bit on the thin side but fine. Are you sure *you're* not mistaken?'

Before she could reply Daisy wandered in alone, Tiffany having obviously decided that she'd better things to do than play 'Monotony'. Daisy had the rolling gait of the very pregnant, and walked with her hand pushed into the small of her back for support. She was wearing a pair of shapeless black leggings stretched over her belly and an outsized lime green T-shirt over the top. The outfit only served to make her swollen abdomen look even larger and her limbs even thinner. The words 'all the king's horses and all the king's men' flashed through Cash's mind. Daisy stopped in the middle of the room, caught sight of Cash and looked around.

'I thought Holly was here.'

Cash stepped forward to help the girl towards a chair, but Daisy shook her arm away and lowered herself into the plastic seat unaided. 'No, but this is my sister, Joanne. She was at school with Hazel.'

Joanne stood and offered her hand. Daisy gave her a limp handshake. 'Hello.' She turned to Cash. 'Where's Holly?'

Cash sat herself sideways on the edge of the chair next to Daisy's. 'At work, I expect. So how are you today?'

'Same as I was yesterday. Holly was giving out about me again, I suppose?'

Cash felt herself blush. 'Maybe just a bit. But it's only because she worries about you.'

Daisy knew when she was being patronised. 'Sure. So

what are you doing here? Did they send you along to try and make me change my mind about the baby?'

'No. No, not at all. Holly doesn't even know I'm here.'

Daisy frowned.

'I'm not making a very good job of this,' Cash said, almost to herself. 'Look, Daisy. The reason I'm here is because I need to ask you a question.'

Daisy shrugged. 'Ask away.'

Cash had thought carefully about how to phrase the question on the drive out to Enniskerry. She looked over at Joanne, then took a deep breath. 'Okay. How did your mother seem to you when she visited you here last week?' Out of the corner of her eye she noticed Joanne's eyebrows taking a hike towards her hairline.

Daisy also looked startled for a moment and Cash was afraid that she'd blown it. Then she slumped a little in the chair and said, 'How did you know she was here?'

'It's a long story. Never mind about that now. How was she, Daisy? How did she seem to you?'

'Why? What has it to do with anything? It's not my fault she had her accident. I'm not to blame.' She wasn't upset, more on the defensive.

Cash wasn't sure how much Daisy had been told about the accident so she trod carefully, not wanting to upset the girl if she could help it. 'No one's saying you are, Daisy. I just need to know what time she came in, and if she said anything to you.'

Daisy stared at her for a good twenty seconds. Cash held her breath. Then Daisy sighed. 'She turned up in the morning, about ten. There I was reading a book and the next minute she was standing right where you are now.' She looked over at Joanne. 'I got the shock of my life. At first I thought Hazel or Holly had told her, but she was going on about cults and brainwashing and, oh, garbled rubbish about a cult making me pregnant.'

'Did she make a scene?'

'Mummy? No. Mummy isn't into making scenes. She sat down and held on to my arm and muttered on about all the stuff I said before. She wouldn't let me get a word in edgewise. Anyway, I was so shocked to see her there I didn't know what to say.'

'So what happened?'

Daisy shrugged. 'Well, eventually, when she'd run out of steam . . .' She inclined her head to one side to make the point. 'I've always found it's easier all round to let her say what she has to say before even trying to explain anything to her. Anyway, eventually, I put her straight and told her that I was here voluntarily, and that Dr Keogh didn't run a cult and had no hand in making me pregnant. I suppose I shouldn't have laughed when I said that, but to tell you the truth it was all so ridiculous I couldn't help it.'

'You laughed? How did she react to that?'

Daisy smiled. 'Actually, it did the trick. It brought her back down to planet earth. I think she felt a bit silly, to tell you the truth.'

It didn't make sense. Eileen Porter must have phoned her *after* speaking to Daisy, and she had been anything but calm. 'So that was it? She wasn't upset about anything when she left you?'

Daisy clapped her hands in her lap and cast her eyes down. 'I didn't say that.'

'So she *was* upset.'

Daisy nodded. 'About as upset as Holly was when I said I was going to keep the baby, except Mummy was upset because I told her I was going to have the baby put up for adoption.' She looked up. 'Honestly! There's no pleasing anyone. First Mummy was at me because I was going to . . .' Daisy's face crumpled and she wept '. . . going to give up my baby, now Holly's . . .' She couldn't finish the sentence. Cash jumped up and put a comforting arm around her.

'Holly's fine. Whatever you want to do, she'll back you up, honestly. We were talking about it on the way home, and she's fine about it.' Daisy was still weeping. Cash rooted in her pocket and handed her a small packet of tissues. 'Look, I'm sorry. I didn't mean to upset you.'

Cash felt awful. Daisy dabbed her eyes and blew her nose, then waved her apology away. 'It's not you,' she said. 'You're not upsetting me. It's just that it reminded me that that was the last time I saw her, and she was angry with me.'

'I don't think she was angry exactly. Just worried. Afraid that you probably hadn't thought things through, maybe.'

Daisy sniffed. 'That sounds like Mummy all right.' She inhaled and then gave a deep long sigh. 'Anyway, it made me think, and that's why I changed my mind about the baby. She was right. I'd regret it one day if I gave him up. I know that now. I suppose I was just scared that I wouldn't be able to cope. Of course, Mummy still couldn't get the notion out of her head that Dr Keogh had brainwashed me into giving up my baby.' She shook her head and looked down at the floor. 'Like I'm not capable of making my own decisions.'

There was an awkward silence, then Joanne coughed nervously. 'Em . . . Did you say there was a cafeteria? Why don't we go down and get a cup of tea? I could really do with one – I don't know about you.'

Daisy smiled a sad smile. 'That was always Mummy's answer. Have a cup of tea.' She heaved herself out of the chair. 'Who's buying?'

Cash picked up her bag. 'Why don't you two go down there and I'll join you in a couple of minutes? I have to make a phone call.'

Joanne hesitated for a moment, giving Cash a questioning look, but then she gave her a curt nod of understanding and linked Daisy's arm in hers. 'Lead the way, Daisy. I'm parched.'

Cash waited until they were well ahead of her, then headed for a fire escape door at the end of the corridor which she had noticed on her way in. The air had grown colder and she shivered a little as she stood out on the metal stairway that looked down over the treatment centre at the back of the house. She dialled Dan Doyle's number.

He answered on the eighth ring just as she was about to hang up.

'Doyle.'

'Sergeant? It's Cash Ryan.'

'Cash. What can I do for you?' He sounded quite chirpy.

She didn't bother with any niceties. 'I'm out at Glencullen House.'

She heard him sigh impatiently at the other end of the line. She thrashed on, not giving him the opportunity to talk her down. 'I talked to Daisy Porter, and she told me her mother *was* out here the day she died. She visited Daisy in the morning, and she was very agitated when she left.' Doyle was silent for so long that Cash thought that they'd been cut off. 'Are you still there?'

'Yes, yes. I'm still here, Cash. What else did she say?'

'How do you mean, what else?'

'Just that. What else? Did she say that her mother was meeting Mort? Did she give you any indication of why her mother would have been in Bath Avenue that night and why her car was at the RDS?'

'Well, no. I didn't ask her. She's eight and a half months pregnant, for God's sake. And I don't know how much her sister told her about the accident. I don't want to traumatise her.'

Doyle sighed again, though this time the sigh bore no sign of impatience. After a further pause he said, 'Okay. Look. Can you stay there with Daisy? I'm in the middle of interviewing a suspect right now. I'll be out there in about an hour and a half. Is that okay? Can you manage that?'

'Me? Why me?'

'I'd like to have a woman there when I'm talking to her, given her present condition.'

'Can't you bring out a Ban Garda?'

He was impatient again now. 'We don't have Ban Gardai any more. Cash, the Garda Siochana is an equal opportunity employer.'

Irritated by his splitting of hairs, Cash snapped, 'You know what I mean. You must have a female officer rattling around there someplace.'

'Not at the minute, I'm afraid. Please, Cash. The girl knows you. Stay with her. I'll be out there as soon as I can to take a statement. Okay?'

What could she say? She pulled the fire door open again and headed for the cafeteria.

As she was halfway down the stairs, the vestibule door swung open and a tall, grey-haired woman in biker's leathers walked in. As she unzipped and took off her jacket Cash could clearly see that around her neck hung a heavy silver cross on a long chain. She was carrying her crash helmet over her arm and in the other hand she carried a small black Nike sports bag.

Good grief, she thought. A sporty biker nun. Now I've seen everything.

Chapter Twenty-Eight

Sister Jude headed straight for the door marked RECEP-TION and walked in. Cora was standing behind a desk, staring at a computer screen and tapping the keys with one finger. Next to her, a tiny middle-aged woman in a nurse's whites was talking to someone on the phone. Her name tag announced to all those who might be interested that her name was Nurse Edna Large. It struck Sister Jude, who had encountered Staff Nurse Slimm on her previous visit, as rather Pythonesque. With that in mind, when Cora looked up as she entered and instantly smiled her usual dazzling smile, it prompted the nun to wonder if Cora's name could be Cora Glumm.

'Sister Jude. How lovely to see you again.' She shot out her hand. Sister Jude put down her bag and took it.

'Nice to see you, too, Cora. Is Dr Keogh in?'

Cora strode out from behind the desk. 'Of course, of course. And he's very much looking forward to meeting you.' She caught Nurse Large's eye, and the woman put her hand over the receiver. 'Could you give Dr Rory a call? Tell him we're on our way over?'

The diminutive Nurse Large nodded compliance.

Cora gestured towards the door. 'This way, Sister. It's quite a hike, I'm afraid. Dr Rory's office is in the clinic annexe.'

Sister Jude picked up the sports bag. The weight

inside it gave her some assurance, but her stomach was churning. Cora was at the door now and she looked back. The nun hesitated for a moment but, conscious of the fact that if a speedy retreat proved necessary, at least her bike was at hand where she had parked it in front of the clinic annexe as there had been no spaces left in front of the main house, she took a deep breath to boost her confidence, then followed.

Cash found Joanne sitting with Daisy at a table by the window. Each had a cup of coffee, but Joanne also had the remains of a large slice of coffee cake. They seemed to be chatting away quite happily. Cash went over to the counter and ordered herself a pot of tea and picked up a small pack of chocolate wafers.

By the time she joined them at the table Joanne had polished off the remainder of the cake. 'Can I get either of you anything?' Cash asked as she unloaded her tray.

Joanne's eye fell on the packet of biscuits. 'Is that a chocolate wafer?'

'Have you got a worm or something?' Cash asked. She had never seen her sister consume so much sugar in so short a time. Joanne was generally very particular about what she ate.

Joanne looked appalled. 'What a thing to say!'

'Sorry.' She slid the pink packet across the table.

Daisy watched the exchange with much amusement. 'I'm glad to see we aren't the only ones who bicker amongst ourselves. Holly and Hazel are always at it.'

'Has Hazel visited you?' Cash asked, making conversation. Daisy shook her head, then gave a good-humoured, if ironic chuckle. 'Derrick doesn't approve. He thinks I'm a lost cause.'

But he's paying your expenses anyway, Cash thought, though she was glad that Daisy seemed to be so laid back at the moment. It would make things easier when Doyle came to take her statement. She poured out a cup of tea and took a sip. It was way ahead of the coffee. After a pause she said, 'Daisy? Em, before when I said I had to make a phone call . . .'

Daisy nodded.

'Well, actually, I was phoning a policeman. Sergeant Doyle. He's the man looking into your mother's . . .' She faltered. 'Your mother's accident.'

Daisy was staring at her, waiting for her to get to the point.

'Anyway, he wants to come out here and take a statement from you. Is that okay?'

Daisy's brow crinkled. 'But what can I tell him? I wasn't even there.'

'Just what you told me. That she was out here with you that morning.'

'But how can that help? Holly said the accident didn't happen until late that night.'

Cash made light of it and shrugged. 'I don't know. It's just the way the Gardai do things. Anyway, I said I'd stay here with you to keep you company if you like. He should be here in just over an hour.'

'An hour?' From her tone it was obvious that Joanne wasn't happy about hanging around for another hour.

'You don't have to wait. I can get a lift back with Doyle if it doesn't suit you,' Cash snapped.

Martyrdom settled on Joanne. She shook her head. 'There's no need. I'll stay and drive you back.'

Irritated, Daisy cut across them both. 'There's no need for either of you to stay. I think I can manage to talk to the policeman without you holding my hand, for God's sake. I'm not a child.'

Cash shot a warning look at Joanne. 'Not at all, Daisy. We'd love to stay and chat.'

Daisy wasn't convinced. She pushed her chair back and struggled to her feet. 'Whatever. I have to pee.' They watched her trundle off towards the toilets.

'Why did you have to say we'd stay?' Joanne hissed as soon as she was out of earshot.

'Because Doyle asked me to. How do you know she won't get upset when he's asking her about her mother?'

'She didn't seem that upset when you were talking to her about it.'

'I know, but he'll ask her other things like what her mother was doing in Bath Avenue and stuff.'

A strained silence followed. Cash stared out of the window, avoiding eye contact with her sister. She found Joanne as difficult to deal with as Yvonne when she slid into martyr mode. It usually meant long icy silences so surprisingly it was Joanne who spoke first.

'You know what we were saying before, about Mrs Haffner being here when she told me she was at the airport?'

Cash turned her head back from the window. 'Yes?'

'Why would she lie?'

'What's the story there?' Cash refilled her cup from the pot. 'You say this girl, the one having the baby for you, was in Morocco?'

'That's right. She's an Irish girl. That's the thing, you see. We wanted an Irish baby and this girl wanted Irish parents for her child.'

'And what about this fine?'

Joanne closed her eyes and rubbed the sockets with the heels of her hands. She gave a wretched sigh. 'It was terrible. The poor girl was thrown into this filthy Moroccan jail. And her pregnant. So obviously our first concern was for the child, so we paid the fine and her air fare home and, of course, her expenses.'

'And the agency fee, I suppose.'

'Of course.'

'So how much did you pay them altogether?'

Joanne did a quick calculation. 'Just over eight thousand. Why?'

Cash wasn't quite sure how to put it. She took a sip of her tea. It was stewed now. She pushed the cup away. 'What do you know about Mrs Haffner's agency, Jo? Are you sure it's all above board?'

Joanne gave a nervous giggle. 'Above board? What are you talking about?'

'Look, you and Rodney checked into this adoption business and you were under the impression that adoption was going to take a good two years at the least, right?'

Joanne nodded. 'But Mrs Haffner said if we had the home study done privately . . .'

Cash cut her off. 'I know what Mrs Haffner said, but don't you think it's a bit . . . well . . . iffy that within two days of seeing her for the first time she offers you an Irish baby, and within the next couple of months?'

'What are you getting at?'

'Come on, Jo! You met her less than two weeks ago and already you've handed over eight grand. Then she lies to you about meeting this girl at the airport.'

'But she said there's a baby . . .'

'I don't doubt it.' She looked around the cafeteria. Two teen mothers-to-be were sitting together at a table, drinking from cans of Fanta. 'How do you know she's not just building up a story for a couple she knows are desperate to have a child? A story to get the maximum amount of cash? You said yourself that Chinese adoptions can cost up to ten grand between one thing and another.'

'So you *do* think there is a baby, then?'

'Jo. Aren't you listening to me? This woman's probably ripping you off.'

'Yes, but you do think there's definitely a baby?' She was leaning across the table towards Cash now, a look of pleading on her face.

Cash snapped her out of it. 'Jo! Get a grip. You have to talk to this woman. Confront her. Demand to see proof that what she's told you so far is true. Are you listening to me?' Over Joanne's shoulder Cash saw Daisy making her way across the cafeteria. 'That nurse said Mrs Haffner's here. Why don't you go down and ask her to page Mrs Haffner for you?'

Joanne looked unsure. Deep down she didn't really want to know as long as there was a baby at the end of it all. But, then, what if there wasn't? Suddenly she felt nauseous again. She jumped up from the table. She knew Cash was waiting for her to say something. 'I have to go to the loo,' she muttered as she pushed past Daisy and fled across the cafeteria.

'I dare say we could get another fifteen hundred out of them, but I don't want to push it.'

'Why? Do you think there's a problem?'

'No, no. They're terribly keen, but at the same time I still feel we should take it easy. It's too soon now. Maybe nearer the time.'

Rory Keogh nodded. He trusted Selina's judgement. She could read people better than he, despite his psychology doctorate.

'How about the O'Gormans?'

Selina Haffner shook her head. 'No. No way. I don't think they've got it. They already took out a second mortgage on the house.'

'Fine, whatever you think. How did you get on with Daisy Porter?'

275

She smiled. 'It's only a blip. You know her mother died?' Keogh nodded again. 'The sudden change of mind's down to that, I think. She doesn't really want to keep the child. She's not the type. A little gentle persuasion and she'll change her mind again, mark my words.'

'You're sure?'

Selina Haffner nodded confidently, though, in fact, she was anything but confident that the stupid girl could be talked round, but she didn't want Keogh to lose faith in her.

He smiled. 'Good, good. I'll have a word, then.'

'How's Tiffany doing?'

'Tiffany's doing fine. No problems there.'

She gathered her papers together and slipped them into the briefcase. 'Good. But keep up the counselling. We wouldn't want any change of mind there, not with only six weeks to go. The McAndrews are expecting a baby boy in six weeks or so.'

'They'll get their baby.'

There was a tap on the door and Cora poked her head in. 'Sister Jude to see you, Rory.'

Rory Keogh walked Selina Haffner to the door and opened it wide. He had been expecting navy polyester, so was surprised when he was faced with Sister Jude. Selina Haffner nodded hello, then hurried off down the corridor.

Cora swept her hand towards her boss. 'Sister Jude, I'd like you to meet Dr Rory Keogh.'

Sister Jude took Rory's hand and shook it firmly. 'Nice to meet you, Doctor. Cora's been telling me all about your institute.'

Close up he looked older than the photograph, but he was still wearing well. Better than her.

Rory smiled. 'The pleasure's mine.' He ushered her

towards a chair by his desk. The accent was mid-Atlantic now, with just a hint of Donegal. Derry softened to Donegal after twenty-odd years in California or wherever. 'What can I do for you, Sister?' He made his way behind the desk and sat down.

Cora said, 'I'll leave you to it, then.' And she melted from the room.

'I don't know if Cora told you, but I look after disturbed teenagers, and I'd like you to tell me about your courses and what you do here in case any of it could be useful to them.'

'Is that a Derry accent?'

'It surely is. But I've been away from there a long time. How about yourself? Cora tells me you're one of our own.'

Keogh's eyes crinkled at the corners as he grinned at her. 'I hail from Donegal myself.'

'Is that so?'

Liar.

'For my sins.' He sat back in his chair and steepled his fingers. 'Saint Jude. The patron saint of hopeless cases. Rather appropriate under the circumstances.'

'In more ways than you can imagine.' She was surprised that he hadn't recognised her. Surely she hadn't changed that much.

'So tell me about your charges. What kind of problems do they present?' He was staring at her intently now, swinging slightly from side to side in his chair.

The nun leaned over and placed her helmet on the floor with her jacket by the chair, though she still kept the sports bag on her lap.

'What do you *really* do here?'

He cocked his head to one side and his eyes narrowed. 'Excuse me?'

'Don't try and bullshit a bullshitter, Rory. What kind of scam are you running?'

Keogh stared at her for a long time. Sister Jude held her nerve and stared right back. After what seemed like an eternity, he clasped his hands in front of him on the desk. 'Who are you? What gives you the right to come in here and make assumptions about the valuable work we do here?' His voice was steady if teetering on the verge of anger.

The nun sat quite still for a further ten seconds, then slowly rolled up the sleeve of her polo-neck, revealing the knobbly, shiny white scar tissue that covered most of her arm below and above the elbow. He still hadn't copped on. He shook his head. 'I don't understand.'

'You don't understand.' She nodded. 'Okay, let me tell you a story.' She crossed her legs and sat back in her chair, conscious of the need to appear comfortable and unafraid. 'Once upon a time long, long ago, a young Irish girl, full of silly misplaced ideals, met a dashing prince at a rock concert in Hyde Park. They had a good time together, and some time later the young girl met the dashing prince again in her home town. He told her that he was going to win back their kingdom from the oppressors. He dazzled her and pretty soon she was hanging on his every word.'

Keogh sat expressionless.

'Anyway, it turned out that this dashing prince wasn't a prince at all. In fact, he was a frog in prince's clothing. A very dangerous frog. And soon the young girl discovered that he was causing horror and mayhem wherever he went. Anyway, the young girl told the evil frog that she didn't agree with his ways and means of winning the kingdom. She told him that she was leaving. He listened sympathetically, but he had other ideas and devised a cunning plan.'

Rory Keogh shifted in his seat. 'What is this rubbish? What are you talking about?'

'Please . . . bear with me. I've just got to the cunning plan part. You see, he found a way to kill two birds with one stone. He . . .'

Keogh stood up abruptly. 'I don't have time for this . . .'

Sister Jude stayed where she was. 'You don't have time? But you haven't heard the best bit. He blew the girl to pieces in a car bomb, along with half a busy street. Don't you think that's clever?' She was shaking inside now, but it didn't show. As Keogh looked down at her she smiled up at him. She didn't trust herself to stand in case her legs went from under her.

He rubbed his mouth with his hand, betraying uneasiness for the first time. 'Who are you?'

'Don't you recognise me, Rory?'

Like a bulb suddenly clicking on, realisation dawned on his face. He mouthed the word 'Helen', then shook his head. 'No, you can't be. You're dead.'

'Blown up in the car bomb? No, Rory. I got out to buy cigarettes. I wasn't in the car.'

'But they found the body. It was identified.' He was still relatively calm and he was talking about it as if it were nothing.

'They found *a* body. Alice Flynn. You didn't know her. She stopped us for a lift. She was Brenden's next-door neighbour.'

Keogh's colour had drained now. He leaned back against the desk for support. She saw him swallow, then he muttered, 'Jesus.' He cleared his throat and pulled himself together. 'What do you want?'

Chapter Twenty-Nine

Selina Haffner's beeper alerted her to a message just as she reached her Range Rover. Impatiently she checked it, only to be told that she was needed at Reception. Annoyed, because she was hoping to get home early, she carried on towards the main house, wondering what on earth was so serious that it couldn't wait until tomorrow. She was extremely surprised to see Joanne McAndrew standing in the hall, waiting for her.

'Joanne! Good heavens, what brings you all the way out here? How did you know I was here?' For no explicable reason she got a bad feeling in the pit of her stomach, but she smiled warmly anyway.

'Mrs Haffner. I need to ask you a few questions.'

'Couldn't it wait, dear? I do have a rather pressing appointment.'

Joanne McAndrew looked very tense. Close to tears almost. 'No, Mrs Haffner, it can't wait. I *really* need to talk to you. Is there somewhere we could go?'

Selina Haffner had a terrible sense of foreboding now. There was something almost accusing, almost hostile, in the younger woman's tone. She calmed herself. 'Well . . . if it's that important, I can spare you a few minutes. There's an office down here.' She walked ahead and Joanne followed. Her mind was racing, trying to think of a reason for Joanne McAndrew's sudden change of attitude. She reached the door and swung it open, standing back to let Joanne pass, then she closed the door behind them.

'Now, what's the problem, my dear?'

Joanne was wringing her hands. She looked tense enough to snap. 'It's about your call from the airport yesterday.'

Mrs Haffner stayed silent, waiting to see what was coming.

'It's just that you said you were there around four and my sister was here visiting someone and she said she saw you here at half past four, so I was confused. How could you have been at the airport at four and here by half past?'

This wasn't how Joanne had planned to handle the situation. While she had been waiting for Mrs Haffner to arrive at Reception she had been forming questions in her mind. Tell me about the mother of our child. What time did you say her plane arrived? Do you have proof that the fine was paid? Do you have any receipts or documents? Where's the girl now? But the moment she started, the words just started to tumble out willy-nilly.

Selina Haffner did a hasty rewind on her memory. She smiled and crinkled her brow. 'The airport? You misunderstood, my dear. *I* wasn't at the airport. I said an *associate* met our mother at the airport and she was taking her to a nursing home. How on earth could I have been at the airport when I was here? I had a meeting with Dr Keogh.'

Joanne was confused. She was certain that Mrs Haffner had said, '*I'm* at the airport.' She rummaged in her memory, trying to remember the conversation word for word. Seeing her doubtful expression, Mrs Haffner put a reassuring arm around Joanne.

'Are you all right? You look very stressed out. You really need to relax a little. You'll need to be rested and relaxed when you get your little one home, you know. Only six or seven weeks now.'

'There *is* a baby, then?'

'Of course there's a baby. I told you. Our mother and baby are doing fine. Now, why don't you go home and get an early night? All the stress has worn you out.' She moved towards the door, ushering Joanne along with her. 'Go home and have a relaxing bath and tuck yourself up in bed. You've had far too much anxiety these past few days.'

Talk of the baby calmed Joanne somewhat. Sensing this, Mrs Haffner led her down the hall. 'Your baby's perfectly fine, and you mustn't compromise your health by getting yourself so upset.'

They were almost at the stairs now and Mrs Haffner was encouraging Joanne towards the vestibule exit. Joanne stopped at the foot of the stairs. 'Maybe you're right. But I'll have to go and tell my sister. She's in the cafeteria.'

'Your sister?'

Joanne nodded. 'We were visiting a friend.'

'Oh. Right. I see. I'll leave you to it, then.' As Joanne walked back towards the cafeteria Mrs Haffner called after her, 'Remember now, Joanne. Rest yourself. You'll need all your energy for when the baby comes.'

Joanne gave her a shaky smile. 'I'll do that.' She hurried off.

Selina Haffner watched her go. Even though she felt that she had allayed Joanne McAndrew's fears, she still felt uneasy about the situation. This sort of hiccup was the last thing she needed right now. She decided it was time to take advice, so she turned on her heel and headed towards the vestibule.

'So what did she say?'

'Where's Daisy?'

'Don't change the subject. She's gone for another pee. What did your Mrs Haffner say?' Cash could be very bolshy when she wanted to be.

Joanne pulled out a chair and sat down. 'She said I was mistaken, that a colleague picked the girl up from the airport.'

'What about the money? Did she have any proof or receipts or anything? Where's the girl?'

Joanne said, 'She assured me the baby's all right. Seven weeks, she said. Only seven weeks.' She was staring down at the tabletop, tracing a path through some spilt sugar with her finger.

Cash was exasperated. 'You didn't ask her, did you? All you can think about is the bloody baby. Can't you see that she's probably ripping you off, for God's sake?'

Joanne looked up. 'I'm sure she isn't.'

Out of the corner of her eye, through the window, Cash caught sight of Mrs Haffner hurrying towards the treatment centre. 'Well, if you won't ask her I will.' She jumped up and hurried towards the exit. Joanne tried to grab her arm but Cash shook her off.

'Please don't annoy her, Cash. She explained about the airport. I took her up wrong, that's all. I'm sure it's all above board.'

Cash looked back. 'Well, she won't mind me asking a few pertinent questions, then, will she?'

Joanne followed. 'Please, Cash, leave it.'

Cash tried a different tack. She waited for her sister to catch up. 'Look, Jo. What if there *is* no baby? I don't believe for a minute you just took her up wrong. She lied to you. The woman lied. Who's to say she isn't lying about the baby, too? Who's to say in seven weeks she won't come back with some story about the baby dying

283

or something? Anything to fob you off. This whole thing sounds distinctly dodgy to me.'

Joanne thought about that. The anxiety returned again. What if Cash was right? She didn't want to entertain the idea. No. Mrs Haffner definitely said there was a baby. But, then, she was also sure that the woman had told her that she was phoning from the airport.

'Come on, Jo. It can't do any harm.'

Chapter Thirty

'What do I want?'

He was staring down at her, and she could see fear in his eyes. It surprised her. It hadn't occurred to her that he would be afraid. She had never seen him afraid before. She repeated the words. 'What do I want? I'd like to know why.'

He rubbed his mouth again. His face had gone grey. 'Why what?'

She gave a snort. 'I'd like you to do me the courtesy of telling me why you tried to blow me to kingdom come. I was no threat to you. I had every intention of just walking away.'

Keogh stared at her for what seemed like an age. She couldn't read his expression and she could only imagine what was going on in his mind. Eventually he shook his head and walked behind the desk again where he sat down. 'Get real, Helen. Sorry, *Sister* Jude. Tell me, was it some sort of Damascene conversion?' He was smirking now.

'You could call it that, I suppose,' the nun replied. 'I promised God I'd make it up to him if he let me live.'

He laughed out loud. It was genuine, amused, spontaneous laughter. Not a hint of irony in it. 'You promised *God*?'

Undaunted by his apparent disdain, she nodded. 'Yes, Rory. I promised. What I don't understand is why you had to blow up an entire street of people on a Saturday afternoon. Catholics and Protestants alike. Surely you didn't think that an atrocity like that could possibly do anything for your stupid cause.'

'Stupid cause? You've changed your tune.'

'No, Rory, I grew up and realised that the only cause you've ever truly believed in is yourself. You knew damn well I wouldn't make any trouble for you. More to my shame.'

He leaned his elbow on the arm of his chair and cupped his chin, regarding her through half-closed eyes. Thinking. After another protracted silence he shook his head and said, 'Why are you really here? Why now?'

Mid-Atlantic with a touch of Donegal had hardened to broad Derry. She noticed it particularly in the way he pronounced the word 'now', making it rhyme with 'spy'. Echoes of the kids' playground chant after Donal Moran, a rumoured RUC informer, disappeared drifted across her consciousness. 'Donal Moran was a spy. Where is Donal Moran now?'

She didn't reply. He shook his head again. 'Don't try and tell me you were – *are* – so naïve that you don't know the score. You don't walk away from the Movement. No one walks away from the Movement. You're either with them or against them.' He was angry now. He stood up abruptly and placed his hands, palms down, on the desk, leaning over towards her. 'I was the one who brought you in, so I had to take you out. Simple as that.'

Sister Jude nodded. 'I see. Simple as that. So what about all those people? What had they done to offend you? Why did they have to be blown to bits?'

'Casualties of war.' He spat the words at her. 'Freedom doesn't come cheap.'

She had heard him use those phrases before, many

times. The passage of time only served to make her see how gullible and impressionable she had been back then. She was disgusted to think that puerile clichés like these could have driven her to get involved in such unspeakable actions.

He sat down again in his seat and clasped his hands together on the desk. She had no idea what to say, what to do, so she just continued to stare right at him. After a couple of seconds he looked away.

'I'm sorry,' he said. 'If I had my time over . . .'

It was the nun's turn to laugh out loud. 'You're sorry? Is that it?'

Keogh shrugged. 'I thought your religion was supposed to be all about forgiveness.'

'*Touché*. But you still haven't answered my first question. What do you really do here? What crowd are you mixed up with these days?'

Keogh sighed. 'I left all that behind me long ago, Helen – sorry, Sister Jude.' The corner of his mouth twitched in a half-grin. 'I can't get used to you being a nun. Anyway, look. I know the bomb was a mistake. The eejitt that made it up hadn't worked with Nitrotex before. It wasn't meant to be that big.'

'Oh, I see. It was only meant to be a *small* car bomb. How many did you intend to kill? Five? Ten? Fifteen?'

'Don't be like that. I did a lot of things I wish I hadn't, but times were different then. You know how it was. You were in it, too.' He pushed his chair back and stood up again, walking over to the window. Even though he had his back to her it was clear he was very agitated.

'That bomb finished me. I couldn't hack it after that. I went to the States. You weren't the only one to go through the Damascene thing. It knocked me for six.'

She wondered if that was true. It didn't sound like the ruthless Rory Keogh of her memory. But, then, who would recognise *her* now? It was true, a lot of water had flowed under the bridge. He turned to face her. 'I do a lot of good work here, Helen. I'm doing my penance in my own way. I care for homeless kids. I take them in and help them get their lives together. You're not the only one making up for past sins.'

'So you're not involved with Republicanism any more?'

He shook his head emphatically. 'Not for years. Not since then. I was too hot. I had to disappear. I did a psychology doctorate at Stanford, then went on to work with underprivileged kids. Much like yourself.'

'So much for no one walking away from the Movement.'

'That was different. I didn't turn.'

The nun acknowledged the point with a shrug. 'So how did you end up back here?'

He walked around the desk and leaned his back against it, folding his arms across his chest. He looked more relaxed now. 'How long have you got?' He smiled his charming smile.

The door flew open and Selina Haffner burst into the room. 'We have a problem, Dr Keogh. A big problem.' So focused was she on her anxiety, it took her a moment to notice that Keogh had company.

'Can't it wait, Mrs Haffner?' The Derry accent at once disappeared as completely and suddenly as Donal Moran.

Selina Haffner stood in the middle of the room, arms flapping by her sides in a state of complete agitation. 'No. I have to talk to you now.' She acknowledged Sister Jude with a curt nod. 'Excuse me, Sister.'

The nun got to her feet. 'I could wait outside . . .'

Keogh gave her a strained smile. 'If you wouldn't mind. We seem to have a crisis.'

She picked up her jacket and helmet and made for the door.

'Please don't go anywhere, will you? I'll only be a minute,' Keogh called after her.

'I'll wait outside.'

She walked out into the corridor and closed the door. A sign on a door opposite read, COUNSELLING ROOM 1. A smaller notice below said, DO NOT ENTER WHEN THE RED LIGHT IS ON. There was no red light. Two chairs stood against the wall so the nun dumped her jacket and helmet on one and sat on the other.

The meeting with Rory hadn't gone at all as she had anticipated. But, then, she'd really had no conception of what might take place. It surprised her that he appeared to have taken hold of his life and turned it around. She was tempted to leave right there and then. To walk away and let him get on with his life. But something stopped her. Maybe it was a subconscious need to hear the whole story from him.

Cash and Joanne turned the corner, expecting to see Mrs Haffner ahead of them. Silly expectation. She was nowhere in sight. Only the biker nun was seated in the corridor, her helmet and jacket on a chair beside her, the sports bag at her feet.

'Where is she? Where did she go?'

Joanne tugged at her arm. 'Leave it, Cash.'

Cash shrugged her off and headed towards the nun. 'Excuse me. Did you see Mrs Haffner?'

Sister Jude, deep in her own thoughts, was taken by surprise, and looked up at her blankly. 'Sorry?'

'Beige trouser suit, blonde short hair? Did you see where she went?'

The nun pulled herself together. 'Oh. Right. Yes . . . Mrs Haffner. She's in there with Dr Keogh. Some kind of crisis, I think.' She indicated the closed door of Keogh's office.

Cash looked back to where Joanne was hovering uncertainly. 'There, you see. She is rattled. There is something up.'

Joanne had a look of utter panic on her face. She refused to entertain the notion that Mrs Haffner could be anything other than honest and above board, even though Cash's assertions had seriously worried her. She was also anxious, as she believed that Mrs Haffner's assessment of her suitability for adoption would be seriously compromised if Cash didn't get a grip.

'Leave it, Cash, *please.*'

Cash grabbed her sister's arm. 'Joanne. Stop it! Face facts, this Mrs Haffner's definitely on the iffy side.' She cocked her head at the office door. 'She's obviously worried now because you confronted her before about the airport. Can't you see? She's already conned you out of almost eight grand.'

'You don't know that.'

Cash threw her hands up in frustration. 'She lied to you, for God's sake. She said she was picking the girl up at the airport when I saw her here. They lied to the cops about Eileen Porter being here. For all you know, that kid Tiffany could be the mother, or any of the others. God knows, there are enough to chose from.'

'So you do think there *is* a baby?'

Cash was stunned into silence. It was clear that Joanne could only focus on whether there was a baby in the equation or not.

At the mention of the name Tiffany Sister Jude's ears pricked up. 'Excuse me.'

Cash looked round.

The nun stood up. 'Did I hear you say Tiffany?'

Cash nodded. 'Yes, why?'

'Would she be about fourteen and heavily pregnant?'

Cash nodded again. 'Do you know her?'

Sister Jude's heart sank. Cora had lied to her. Blatantly lied. But, then again, who was to say it was *her* Tiffany? Even though common sense told her that the probability of there being two fourteen-year-old heavily pregnant girls called Tiffany in the general vicinity of Rory Keogh was slight, she felt she had to ask.

Cash had turned back to Joanne, waiting for her to say something. The nun reached out and touched Cash's arm. 'Em . . . Does she have dark shoulder-length hair?'

Cash turned around, impatient with the nun for diverting her. 'Yes, she does.'

'And she's here?'

Very impatient now. 'Yes!'

Joanne coughed. 'Cash. We should go.'

That was when Cash lost it. 'How can you say that? Surely you can see that if they're conning you, you won't be the only one. What they're doing is tantamount to selling babies, for fuck's sake.' She flipped her head towards the nun. 'Sorry, Sister.'

'Selling babies?'

'We don't know that,' Joanne cut in, casting a panic-stricken look in the nun's direction. 'My sister's just jumping to conclusions.'

'I'm doing no such thing! Look at the wider picture here, Joanne. How do you know Mort's death isn't tied up with this?'

'Selling babies?' Sister Jude again. 'You're saying that Rory Keogh and this Mrs Haffner are selling babies?'

'That's what I want to clear up,' Cash said. 'But it looks that way to me.'

So much for the new whiter-than-white, reformed, saintly Rory Keogh. Like Joanne, Sister Jude could only focus on one thing – in her case, Tiffany and the fact that Cora had lied when she had claimed not to have seen her. Why would she do that?

She looked over at the two women. The older one, Joanne, was arguing with her sister, trying to get her to leave, but the younger woman was having none of it.

'Don't be such a spa, Joanne. I'm going in there now whether you want to or not,' she hissed. 'We have to find out one way or the other.'

With that she yanked her arm free of her sister and made a lunge for the door, bursting it open.

Chapter Thirty-One

Rory Keogh was on the phone when Cash exploded into the room. He was startled but not entirely surprised. Despite Selina Haffner's agitated assertion that she thought she had contained the situation, he had a gut feeling that the prospective parent, Joanne McAndrew, wouldn't let it lie there. He knew that, faced with the same set of circumstances, he certainly wouldn't.

Cash made a beeline for Mrs Haffner. 'Mrs Haffner, I need to ask you some questions.' She had the urgency and apparent authority of an investigative reporter about her. This was no accident. Cash was drawing on her experience here, having once had a small part in a film as a hot-shot TV reporter.

Unlike Rory Keogh, Selina Haffner *was* taken completely by surprise, especially as she was utterly taken in by Cash's adopted persona. She gave a little gasp and shrank away. She could see Joanne McAndrew reluctantly hovering in the doorway. She couldn't fathom how the woman had so quickly involved the press when the first inkling she'd had that Joanne wasn't altogether happy had been less than fifteen minutes before. She had completely forgotten that the younger woman was Joanne's sister.

'I'll call you back,' Keogh said into the phone, then hung up.

Cash had advanced on Mrs Haffner now and had her hemmed in against the desk.

The woman cleared her throat and gave her most confident smile. 'Certainly. Ask away. If you've any concerns, ask away. We've nothing to hide.' She cast a hasty look over her shoulder at Rory Keogh.

He looked perplexed. 'Is there a problem?'

Cash glanced at him. 'You could say that. My sister . . .'

'And you are?' he asked, making Cash feel small.

She ignored the ploy and assumed Cash Ryan, Ace Reporter mode. 'I'm Joanne McAndrew's sister.' She indicated Joanne with a twitch of her head. 'We have a few questions to ask Mrs Haffner about some irregularities concerning an adoption she's handling.'

Joanne visibly winced. 'I'm sure Mrs Haffner can explain,' she said lamely.

'Shut up, Joanne,' Cash said, without looking round.

Rory Keogh walked around the desk and spread his arms in an expansive gesture. 'Why don't we all sit down and discuss this in a non-confrontational manner?' he said, sweeping Cash and Mrs Haffner towards a three-seater sofa. He cast a glance in Sister Jude's direction. 'Perhaps we could talk another time, Sister?'

Sister Jude stood her ground. 'I think I'll hang around, actually. I have a few questions to ask myself.'

Keogh frowned. 'Can't that wait, Sister?' He was now right in front of Cash who was also standing her ground, refusing to be whooshed towards any sofa.

Ignoring Keogh, she was making unrelenting eye contact with Mrs Haffner. 'Why did you lie about meeting the pregnant girl at the airport?'

Mrs Haffner broke out in a sweat, prompting Keogh to realise that she was going to be a liability. Then she gave a silly laugh. 'I explained that. Your sister was mistaken.' She looked over at Joanne. 'I explained that, didn't I, Joanne? You misheard me. I said the girl had *arrived* at the airport. I never said I met her myself.'

Joanne looked uncertain. 'Well . . .'

Cash pressed on. 'So what about the money? Eight thousand. Do you have any receipts or documentation to prove where it's gone?'

Keogh gave a conciliatory smile, which Cash found particularly patronising, and strode across the room to Joanne, ushering her into the room proper. 'Please, ladies. What's the problem here? You only paid normal expenses, didn't you?' He turned on the charm. 'It was all explained to you, wasn't it, Mrs McAndrew? May I call you Joanne?'

Joanne smiled at him and nodded. 'Well, yes. I was trying to explain that to Cash . . .'

'Shut up, Joanne,' Cash repeated. 'We have to get to the bottom of this.'

'Your sister seems perfectly happy,' Keogh said. 'What has this to do with you? We are registered professionals. Just what do you think's going on here?'

Cash turned to face him. 'Well, as you ask, I think you're taking in homeless pregnant girls in the guise of looking after them, then conning large amounts of money from women, like my sister, desperate to have a child. I think you're selling babies.'

Keogh's face flushed with anger, but his voice was even. 'I'd be very careful, Miss Ryan. Those are very serious allegations. Slanderous allegations. We do good work here.'

Cash was seriously intimidated by him but hid her fear behind her Ace Reporter character. 'So why did Mrs Haffner lie, then? There was no girl in Morocco, was there?'

'Mrs Haffner didn't lie. It was a misunderstanding. We are professionals. We do not lie.'

'Then why did you lie about Tiffany?' Sister Jude cut in.

Rory Keogh had temporarily forgotten about Sister Jude, so her interruption took him unawares. 'Excuse me?'

'Tiffany Ring. The young pregnant girl I was fostering for the Eastern Health Board. Your associate Cora swore to me that she hadn't seen her, when all the time she was here. What are you doing with her? Why didn't you tell me she was here?'

Mrs Haffner gasped again. Her face was as white as a sheet, telling Cash more than words could. 'Why did you lie to the police about Eileen Porter visiting Daisy?'

Keogh looked stunned. It was all unravelling.

Cash was carried away now, reckless almost. 'Did you kill Eileen Porter? Did she find out about what you really do here? Did you kill Mort Higgins?'

Keogh shook his head. 'Young lady, you are seriously deluded. I have never seen you before in my life, yet here you are spouting ever more preposterous allegations . . .'

Then it hit her. 'So if you've never seen me before, how did you know my name? You called me by my name just now.' She turned to Sister Jude for confirmation. 'He did, didn't he? He called me Miss Ryan.'

Sister Jude nodded. 'Yes, he did.' Her heart sank. Not only because she was disappointed – she had almost believed Rory's story about him having turned his life around – but also because she knew only too well how he was capable of reacting when faced with a dangerous situation.

Rory gave a strained laugh. 'You need professional help, Miss Ryan. Serious professional help. You told me your name yourself.'

'I did not! I introduced myself as Joanne's sister. I never gave you my name.'

Keogh glared at her, frustrated that she was making such a big deal out of it and not sure how to react. He chose attack. He looked around the room. 'This woman is insane, sick. She needs treatment.'

'Really? So why did you try to kill me the other night?'

Sister Jude was appalled. 'He tried to kill you?'

Cash nodded frantically. 'Too right. Just like he ran Eileen Porter down. He came at me in his Land Cruiser and tried to kill me.' Her voice was rising now in conjunction with her adrenaline levels.

Rory laughed dismissively. 'Now I know you're delusional.'

Mrs Haffner gave a little squeak of terror. 'You killed Eileen Porter?'

Sister Jude said, 'Who's Eileen Porter?'

'The mother of one of the patients, Daisy Porter. She was killed in a hit-and-run the same day as my boss, Mort Higgins.'

'Who's Mort Higgins?' Sister Jude.

'Why did you kill Mrs Porter?' Selina Haffner.

'*Please*, Cash!' Joanne.

Everyone was talking at once.

'Ladies!' Keogh bellowed, catching their collective attention. 'This is preposterous. No one was killed. We're not selling babies. Miss Ryan is obviously a very disturbed young woman.' He smiled engagingly at Joanne. 'Mrs McAndrew – Joanne – you must help your sister. She's displaying all the classic signs of paranoia. Has she been this way long?'

Sister Jude shook her head. 'Stop it, Rory! Stop it and tell me what's going on here.'

'I told you what's bloody going on,' Cash snarled. 'But no one's listening to me. These people killed my boss. They're selling babies.' She turned and sneered at Keogh. 'Anyway, the cops are on the way here as we speak. That should put a halt to your gallop.'

'I don't think so.'

They all spun around. Cora was standing in the open doorway, holding a gun on them.

'Cora!' Keogh snapped. 'What the hell are you doing? I have the situation under control.'

'You heard what she said, Rory. She called the cops,' Cora shrieked.

Keogh walked over to Cora and gently took the gun from her hands. 'Relax, Cora. It's okay.'

'You haven't changed, have you, Rory?' Sister Jude said wearily. 'It was all a sham.'

Rory Keogh faltered for a second, then firmly nudged Cora behind him and levelled the gun at the other women in the room. He cast a withering glare in Selina Haffner's direction. 'You stupid cow. I told you you were making the story too complicated.'

Mrs Haffner was almost hyperventilating now. She grabbed Keogh's arm. 'Is it true? Did you kill Mrs Porter? Did you? Did you?'

Keogh shook her off. 'Shut up, you stupid moron.' The Derry accent had returned in spades. He jabbed the gun in the general direction of the women who, apart from Mrs Haffner and Cora, were now grouped together in a huddle by the desk. 'Get over there with them and shut the fuck up.' He gave Mrs Haffner a shove and she stumbled over towards Cash, who caught her by the arm, preventing her from falling.

'You killed Mort, too, didn't you?' Cash didn't realise

it, but she was still in character. Courage didn't play any part in her bravado. 'He found out what you're up to and you killed them both.'

Keogh burst out laughing. 'You stupid woman. You've no idea.'

Cora said, 'What about Tully?'

'I called him,' Keogh said, without looking round. Still training the gun on the women, he walked towards a door to the left-hand side of the desk and opened it. 'In there, all of you.' He waved the gun in the general direction of the door. No one moved. 'In there!' he yelled, making them wince.

Sister Jude was the first to move. 'Come on,' she said, leading the way.

'No way!' the ace reporter snapped.

Keogh reached forward and yanked her by the shoulder. 'Do as you're told!' he barked, cuffing her across the back of the head, then pushing her towards the nun. The cuff across the head set Cash's ears ringing and brought her back to reality. She stumbled, but caught her balance by hanging on to the nun's arm.

Joanne, now as white as a sheet and feeling faint, mutely followed her sister and Mrs Haffner through the door.

Chapter Thirty-Two

'How much do they know?'

'Nothing,' Keogh said. 'They're just speculating.'

Tully was a small man. Small and wiry. But what he lacked in size he more than made up for in psychotic tendencies. The media had collectively labelled him 'Mad Dog' in acknowledgement of this. This suited Tully. Criminal dynasties were founded on such reputations.

'They know enough,' Cora said, and Keogh glared at her.

'The situation's under control,' he insisted. 'I'll deal with it.'

Tully nodded. 'Whatever. Just see to it.'

'But there are four of them,' Cora pointed out. 'You can't kill all four of them.'

Tully stretched his legs, intending to put his feet up on the desk, but he was too short and had to propel the chair forward a little. 'I don't see we've any choice.'

Keogh shot a look at Cora. 'It wouldn't have come to this if you hadn't tried to run the Ryan woman down the other night. She'd have let it be.'

'I thought I was doing the right thing.' She addressed her remark to Tully.

He nodded. He had a soft spot for the American girl. 'It doesn't matter.' He looked directly at Keogh. 'You have the situation under control, haven't you, Rory?'

*

'Who's Tully?'

All ears were tuned to Mrs Haffner.

'He's Rory Keogh's partner. He's not very nice,' she hissed.

The space was cramped – a stationery cupboard really, about seven feet square, shelved on three sides. This meant that there was only a very small space in the centre of the room, about four feet square, for the women to stand. It was intimate to say the least. In the fifteen minutes they had been in there, the air had grown hot and humid. The only light filtered under the crack at the bottom of the door, through which they could only hear muffled conversation.

'What do you think they'll do to us?' Joanne whispered. She sounded terrified. 'Did they really kill Eileen Porter?'

'If they killed Mrs Porter, who's to say they won't kill us?' Mrs Haffner whispered back – unhelpfully, to Cash's mind.

'Shut up, both of you.' Cash fumbled in her bag and took out her phone. 'Sergeant Doyle's on his way out here.' She punched in his number.

'So you really did call the police?' Sister Jude said in a hushed voice. 'I thought you were bluffing.'

Doyle answered almost straight away. 'Doyle.'

'Sergeant Doyle. It's Cash Ryan.'

'Sorry, can you speak up? I can barely hear you.'

'I can't,' she hissed. 'Dr Keogh has us locked in a cupboard. He has a gun. He killed Eileen Porter and Mort. You have to call back-up. We're in the treatment centre at the back of the main house.'

There was silence at the other end of the line and she was afraid that the signal had been lost.

'Sergeant?'

'Okay. Got you. I'll be there a.s.a.p.' The line went dead.

Cash heaved a sigh of relief. 'He's bringing back-up.' She put her arm around Joanne. 'Have courage, Jo-Jo. We'll be okay.'

Sister Jude wasn't so sure. Her chief worry after Keogh was the man Tully. She touched Mrs Haffner on the arm. 'Tell me more about this man, Tully. Who is he?'

'He's an old friend of Dr Keogh's. The doctor launders money through the clinic for him. He's very shady.' Her voice was shaky now. 'Of course, that's nothing to do with me. I never knew anything about Mrs Porter being killed either. I swear.'

Sister Jude put a comforting hand on her arm, though the news that Tully was an old friend of Rory's was no comfort. 'Old friend' suggested that he was probably involved with the paramilitaries. However, she placated Mrs Haffner anyway. 'I know. I'm sure you didn't. Is he involved in this baby-selling racket?'

'You make it sound so terrible,' Mrs Haffner said. 'We were helping people. Ask Joanne. She was prepared to pay a lot more and wait years for a foreign baby, weren't you, Joanne?'

'Is there *really* a baby?' Joanne pleaded predictably. 'You wouldn't say there was if there wasn't, would you?'

Mrs Haffner groped in the dark to find Joanne's hand. She gripped it. 'Of course there's a baby. You're going to get young Tiffany's baby. I swear there *is* a baby for you.'

Cash considered, under the present circumstances, that this was an over-optimistic view.

The situation didn't make sense to Sister Jude. A baby-selling racket didn't, if Cash Ryan was to be believed, warrant murder. There had to be more to it. Something more sinister. Something too big to risk letting this Mrs Porter and Mort Higgins talk to the police. However she looked at it, her mind kept coming back to the IRA connection. And if that was the case, she didn't give much for their chances if the cops didn't get a move on. She decided it was time to take matters into their own hands.

Without taking a vote, she shoved her way to the door and started banging. 'Let me out. Let me out. I can't stand it in here. I'm claustrophobic.'

Cash grabbed her arm and tried to stop her. 'Shut up! Keep quiet. The cops'll be here any time.'

'Maybe not soon enough,' Sister Jude hissed. 'Trust me.'

Something about the nun's manner made Cash stop. The nun continued banging on the door. Cash joined in.

'Help. Help. She's suffocating.'

The muffled conversation ceased and they heard footsteps. A moment later the door opened and Keogh was standing there. Behind him, with his feet up on the desk, Cash could see a small middle-aged man. He was cleaning his fingernails with a letter-opener and appeared unconcerned. Cora was standing near the window, looking out.

Sister Jude was panting, apparently distressed. Cash had her arm around the older woman. 'She had a panic attack. She can't stand small spaces.'

Keogh, who had the gun held loosely in his hand, dithered for a minute, then waved the women out of the cupboard. Cash, supporting Sister Jude, moved out into the room. Keogh pushed the door closed on Mrs Haffner and Joanne. 'Not you,' he said. 'Just these two.'

Cash heard Joanne let out a small squeak of terror. She looked over at the desk. 'I suppose you're Tully.'

Tully eyes her contemptuously. '*Mister* Tully to you, and I'm your worst nightmare,' he snarled melodramatically, then smiled.

Cash was surprised that neither Keogh nor Tully seemed particularly worried about the fact that the cavalry was on its way. Sister Jude was mopping her brow with her sleeve. Keogh looked at her. 'Are you okay?' he asked. It struck Cash as a tad bizarre, considering that he was probably contemplating blowing them all away in the not too distant future.

'So what are you going to do now, Rory?' Tully asked, almost amused.

Rory glanced over at him. 'I'm considering the possibilities,' he replied ambiguously. He was holding the gun down by his side now. 'I think probably the best thing would be to dump them at sea.'

Cash was appalled. He was talking about it as if it were nothing. The nun was breathing normally now and Cash noticed that she was opening her sports bag and rummaging inside. Keogh took no notice. Cash wondered what was keeping Doyle. He was cutting it fine. She craned her neck to look out of the window and along the drive, searching for any sign of a police car or a flashing blue light.

'Why don't you put the gun down, Rory?' she heard the nun say. A rather naïve hope in Cash's estimation. She looked at the nun, then froze as she saw that the woman had a heavy machine pistol in her hands. Keogh saw it at the same moment. He hesitated and Cash heard the rasp of metal against metal as the nun slid the bolt to engage the first round of the magazine. 'Sorry, Rory, but my gun's bigger than your gun.'

Suddenly Cash had an amazing sense of déjà vu, until she realised that she'd heard almost the same line in the movie *Divorcing Jack*. She didn't have time to wonder if the nun was aware of the fact. As Keogh brought his gun up a millimetre, the nun yelled, 'I mean it, Rory!'

Tully froze. Cora spun around from the window. Keogh hesitated for a beat, then dropped the gun on the carpet. As Cash snatched it up and pointed it unsteadily at Tully, she backed up and opened the cupboard door to let Joanne and Mrs Haffner out.

'Oh, my God!' OhmyGod! *OhmyGod!*' Joanne shrieked as she tumbled out of the closet. 'What's going on?'

'I'm sorry, but I think you'd better stand over there for the moment, Mrs Haffner.' Selina Haffner, as pale as a ghost, mouthed an objection, so the nun added gently, 'Just for the moment, anyway.'

Cash caught the nun's eye. 'Who *are* you?'

The nun smiled at her. 'Sister Jude. How do you do?'

'But who *are* you?' Cash persisted. 'What the hell are you doing with that gun?'

'Not now, dear,' the nun replied. 'Let's just wait for the Gardai, shall we? Then we can talk about that.'

Just then they heard the sound of a car engine and a moment later Cash, with relief, saw Doyle's car pull up just in front of the window. 'Thank God. Here's Sergeant Doyle.' She strained her ears but couldn't hear any sirens.

'Joanne, go out and show Sergeant Doyle where we are, would you?' Sister Jude asked. Joanne faltered for a second. Her brain was on overload and it took a moment for her to compute the request. As the cogs clicked into motion she abruptly turned and hurried from the room.

'Where's the back-up?' Cash whispered to the nun.

The nun shrugged. 'Probably on the way.'

A couple of moments later they heard Joanne's near-hysterical voice jabbering to Doyle as they raced along the corridor. He burst into the room, a small pistol in his hand.

He looked at Cash, then at the nun. 'Who's this?'

Cash smiled. 'One of the good guys, Sergeant,' she said. 'What kept you? Where's your back-up?'

'On the way,' Doyle said. 'Here, Sister, let me take that from you.'

Sister Jude gratefully handed the Uzi over to the garda. 'Careful, the safety's off and there's one up the spout,' she warned.

'Fine,' he said, taking the firearm from her.

Cash pointed at Cora as she handed him the gun she had retrieved from Keogh. 'She's the one who tried to kill me the other night.'

Doyle said, 'Is that so? And how do you know that?'

Something about his tone of voice set alarm bells ringing in Cash's head. Joanne, calmer now but still only a micro-tad away from hysteria, gabbled, 'I told you already. It was Dr Keogh. He said it! He said it!'

Doyle looked over in Keogh's direction. 'For fuck's sake, Rory. What did you have to do that for?' As he was speaking Doyle placed his hand on Joanne's shoulder, then gave her a hefty shove towards Sister Jude and Cash. 'Now we'll have to get rid of them, too.'

Joanne yelped. Sister Jude gasped. Mrs Haffner gave a strangled cry but Cash just groaned inwardly. 'Not you, too,' she said.

'Shut up,' Doyle snapped. 'Shut the fuck up and get over there.' He walked over to the desk and slid the Uzi across it to Tully, who was still sitting with his feet up, apparently unconcerned. In fact, he hadn't moved a muscle, except to register mild surprise when Sister Jude had produced the Uzi. Slowly the reason for his relaxed state dawned on Cash. He'd known Doyle was on the way so there had been nothing to worry about.

Suddenly her anger outweighed her fear. 'Why did you kill Mort? Why did you have to do that?' She spat the question at Doyle. 'Surely you didn't do it just to get inside Janet's knickers?'

Doyle looked her in the eye and smirked. 'Don't be so bloody stupid. It was his own fault, like always. I didn't have a choice. He was snooping around and saw Tully here doing a bit of business with me. What the hell else could I do, for fuck's sake? He saw us. He knows Tully. Work it out for yourself.'

'But what about that man you arrested? He had Mort's passport and stuff.'

Doyle grinned smugly. 'I took them from the office that day when I was looking through the files.'

Cash groaned. She'd helped him. Helped him to get away with it. 'So why Eileen Porter? Why did you kill her?'

'Same reason, except it was an accident,' Keogh cut in. 'She legged it and Cora went after her in the Jeep. She didn't see her in the dark and hit her a wallop. It was an accident.'

'So why did you dump her on Bath Avenue? Why leave the car at the RDS?'

'That wasn't the plan. The car got a flat so I had to leave it. It was supposed to be . . .'

'Shut up, Rory,' Doyle snapped. 'Enough.'

Cash was appalled. Slowly the elaborate charade of Mort's suicide made a macabre sort of sense. Doyle knew that if Mort was found in his office he could make sure it would be put down to suicide as he'd be first on the scene. She wondered who'd put the IV line in his arm. Doyle knew Mort's history so it had probably been his sick idea.

Sister Jude said, 'I thought you said you'd finished with that crowd, Rory?'

'What crowd?' Then he understood. 'The Provos? I have. Mr Tully's nothing to do with the IRA.'

Tully's eyebrows knitted together in a frown. 'You know her? Who the fuck is she?'

Rory Keogh shook his head. 'She's no one. I knew her a long time ago.'

Tully laughed. 'I didn't think you kept company with her sort.'

'I wasn't always a nun,' Sister Jude said. Then to Keogh, 'If you didn't mean to kill Mrs Porter, what else were you going to do with her?' It was a valid question.

Keogh looked uncomfortable but didn't reply.

Tully slid his feet off the desk then and stood up. 'Okay. So what's the game plan?' He sounded impatient now. 'It's time to tie up the loose ends.'

Cash took exception to being referred to as a loose end. 'You won't get away with this, you bastard. Janet knows I'm here. So does Holly. When I'm found they'll . . .'

'I'll assure them that I'm pulling out all the stops to bring the killers to justice,' Doyle said, then burst out laughing. He turned to Keogh, who was also enjoying the joke. 'Isn't that so, Rory?'

Keogh smiled and nodded. At that instant Doyle raised his arm and shot Rory Keogh in the head.

Chapter Thirty-Three

Their ears were still ringing from the shot, but the room was silent and the unmistakable odour of cordite reminded Sister Jude of a time she would sooner forget.

Rory Keogh was lying on the floor by the desk. His eyes were open and he looked dead. There was a neat hole in his forehead, but no exit wound. Cash wondered if Doyle's gun was a .22, as he had used in Mort's case.

Tully was the first to move. He walked over and poked Keogh's body with the toe of his shoe, then knelt down and felt for a pulse. 'Why the fuck did you do that?' he asked, his tone mildly inquisitive.

Cash, Joanne and Mrs Haffner were in shock, Sister Jude less so. She was quick to notice that Tully had laid the Uzi down on the desktop. Doyle was holding the pistol in his hand, though his attention was focused on Tully.

'After receiving a call for assistance from Miss Ryan, with no regard for my personal safety,' he said gravely, 'I burst in and shot Dr Keogh, but sadly not before he had callously killed these four.' He gestured towards the women with the gun. 'I should get a bravery medal out of it if I play my cards right.'

Tully looked up at him. 'You're a smart bastard, Doyle, I'll say that for you.'

Cash was frozen with fear. She heard Mrs Haffner sob a couple of coughing gasps. She glanced over at

Joanne. She was so white her skin was tinged with green. Without warning her hand shot up to her throat and she vomited on to the carpet, splashing Tully who cursed and leapt up out of the way.

Cash grabbed her sister and supported her as she retched violently. 'It's okay, Jo-Jo.' Stupid remark. Things were far from okay. In fact, on a scale of one to ten they couldn't be worse.

Suddenly they all became aware of a rumbling sound which steadily grew louder and louder. Doyle's eyes shot towards the window. Tully's head snapped around, as did Cora's.

Snatching the opportunity, Sister Jude made a lunge for the Uzi. Tully reacted a micro-second too late. He grabbed at the barrel, but the nun was quicker. In the ensuing struggle half a dozen shots raked the ceiling and plaster rained down on them. Doyle was standing, mesmerised, staring out of the window as what appeared to be hordes of Hell's Angels roared up to the treatment centre.

'Drop the gun, Sergeant! Drop it or I'll kill you.' Her voice was hard and full of conviction. She was standing with her feet planted apart and her arms extended, holding the Uzi in both hands. She was a fearsome sight. A moment later Spike smashed the window with the butt of an AK47. That was when Doyle, weighing up the odds, cut his losses and dropped the gun. Cash leapt forward, picked it up and pointed it at Tully and Cora.

'And the other one!'

Doyle fished Cora's gun out of his pocket and dropped it on the floor.

Selina Haffner had passed clean out on the carpet. Joanne was still dry-retching, and Cora was screaming hysterically.

'Y'okay, Sister? Spike yelled.

'I'm fine, thanks, Spike.' Her eyes never left Tully and Doyle. She looked at Doyle and twitched the barrel of the Uzi towards the fireplace. 'Get over there with Tully. Put your hands on your head.' Her heart was pounding. Although grateful for the timely intervention of Spike and his chapter friends, it dawned on her that perhaps they weren't quite the wannabes she had thought them to be. The AK47 was a surprise to say the least. It was certainly not a thing easily come by.

Doyle was in a state of shock now, but all Tully seemed bothered about was the fact that he had Joanne's vomit on his Italian shoes. The man had the emotions of a lizard.

Spike had climbed through the shattered window, followed by his four fellow Angels. 'Thought yeh migh' need a bitta help.' He grinned his gap-toothed grin. 'So me an' the lads got together. Cool, wha'?'

'How did you know I was here and not in the house?'

Spike flicked his head towards the shattered window. 'Hung around in the bushes for a while an' saw the bike. Then we heard the shot.'

Sister Jude couldn't help but smile, despite the grim circumstances. 'Good thinking, Spike.'

Cora had stopped screaming and had her hands clamped over her mouth. Her eyes were huge and terrified. Cash moved back and lowered her sister on to a chair, then bent down and rolled Mrs Haffner into the recovery position in case she choked, all the time keeping a weather eye on Tully and Cora.

She was completely numb.

Someone in the nursing home, on hearing all the commotion, must have called the Garda, because a few minutes later they arrived *en masse*, sirens whooping, lights flashing, and soon the place was swarming with gardai and ambulances.

Before they arrived, Sister Jude took Cash and Joanne to one side and muttered, 'The guns *all* belong to Tully and Doyle, right?'

Cash looked at her blankly for a moment, then caught on. 'Right.' She glanced at Joanne, still pale but not quite so green. 'Got that, Jo-Jo?'

Joanne nodded. 'Whatever.'

'Good, as long as we stick to that, you can tell the cops the rest as it happened.'

Of course, Doyle tried his best to dissociate himself from Tully, who was saying nothing whatsoever.

Cash called Rodney on her mobile and he was instrumental in persuading the Garda that Joanne, Cash and Sister Jude were telling the truth. It wasn't a huge leap of faith on the part of the Garda. Tully was obviously well known to them. Sister Jude vouched for Spike and the rest of the chapter, and the only one who disputed ownership of the assorted firearms, but only because of Tully's silence, was Dan Doyle.

Selina Haffner gladly told the cops all she knew about Tully, Keogh and the baby racket, and confirmed seeing Doyle in the company of Tully.

Cora, following Tully's example, kept her mouth shut.

Chapter Thirty-Four

Mort's funeral was a dismal affair. The day was cold and wintry and it was raining heavily as Cash and Billie made a dash from the taxi to the church. They spied Holly and Niall Donovan sitting five rows from the front, and Maurice sitting a couple of rows behind them, so they slid into the pew with Maurice. He squeezed Cash's hand as she sat down. After a moment he whispered, 'Don't know if this is the time to tell you, but your participation in the Hibernian saga died a death.' Needless to say, Cash wasn't greatly upset.

She looked around the small church. The coffin was lying in front of the altar. Janet had stipulated no flowers, instead asking that donations be made to charity. 'Mort wasn't one for flowers,' she explained. Cash thought that this was sad. The coffin looked so bare, lying there without a wreath of any kind.

She saw Sister Jude genuflect and bless herself at the end of the pew. 'Do you mind if I join you?' she asked. Cash slid along to give her room. She thought it was nice of the nun to attend the funeral, though she was still not sure what to make of her. She hadn't come across that many nuns so adept with an Uzi.

The nun knelt and prayed silently for a while, then sat back on the seat. After a couple of minutes she leaned towards Cash. 'Tiffany decided to come home,' she said. 'I told her what was going on there – you know, the

baby-selling racket – and she decided to come home.'
Her face was beaming.

Cash smiled. 'That's marvellous.'

The organ started to play as Janet arrived, accompanied by Mort's two brothers and his sister. They sat in the front pew. Hot on their heels Joanne and Rodney, Justine and Yvonne filed up the aisle. Cash was surprised and pleased that Yvonne had put in an appearance. She was aware how much her mother hated funerals and she was grateful for her support.

The service was short but nice. Though not an overtly religious man, Cash knew that Mort had believed in God and an afterlife. After the service Janet and the immediate family accompanied the remains to the crematorium. It was only as she watched the cars drive away that Cash felt as if the whole episode was over. It left her feeling empty.

The previous afternoon she had gone to the office to help Janet pack everything away. Janet had been subdued. Cash had felt she was embarrassed and somewhat ashamed that she'd been so taken in by Doyle. Cash hadn't known what to say on the subject so she'd avoided saying anything.

As she'd moved the Norseman Direct box from her desk she'd seen a familiar buff folder sitting underneath. 'Look.' She lifted the file and held it out to Janet. 'Eileen Porter's file.'

Janet shook her head and smiled a sad smile. 'So it wasn't missing after all.' She turned back and continued stacking Mort's files in a cardboard carton.

Cash opened the folder and scanned the solitary page. Mort hadn't added new information. She smiled to herself, conscious that had the file been where it was supposed to have been in the first place, Mort's death would have been put down to suicide, Doyle would probably have succeeded in seducing Janet and Keogh would still be selling babies. The only losers were Joanne and Rodney.

She walked round the desk and placed the file in the carton with the rest.

Epilogue

Two days after the funeral, Maurice informed Cash that she had got the part in *Slappers*. Cash was thrilled, glad to be busy as it took her mind off Mort. (The series proved to be a great success and, unlike Fifi, her character lived on into a second series.) Yvonne eventually, due to the success of *Slappers*, learned to live with the fact that her daughter was now the national face of sanitary protection. Niall Donovan called the same day and asked her out to lunch. Her first thought was to make up some excuse until he mentioned that he wanted to talk to her about donating the use of a property, rent-free, for the Strolling Players, so she could hardly refuse. Surprisingly, she found him to be good company and agreed to meet him again. She never had cause to meet Janet again.

Full of new-found confidence and self-esteem, Billie left for the Caribbean cruise gig and Cash took over the flat.

The following week, Joanne called in a state of euphoria to tell her sister that she was three months pregnant, which explained her constant nausea and sporadic projectile vomiting.

Daisy delivered a healthy baby boy. So far she is coping well. She moved home and helps to keep house for her father.

Tiffany gave birth to a healthy baby boy four weeks

later and Sister Jude and Sandra collected her and her baby from the Rotunda Hospital and took them home. Sister Jude still sees Spike and occasionally she and Sandra ride out with the chapter. She never mentioned the AK47 again or asked any questions concerning Spike's other activities. The dreams stopped, but from time to time she wakes up in a sweat remembering Rory Keogh.

Dan Doyle was convicted, mainly on the evidence given by Cash, Joanne, Sister Jude and Selina Haffner who was offered immunity from prosecution. He is currently serving twenty-five years in Mountjoy. During the trial it came to light that Cora was a nurse, so in all probability it had been she who had put Mort's IV line in and administered the Valium knock-out shot.

The week before the trial, Tully and Cora skipped bail. Their whereabouts are unknown.

If you have enjoyed *First Holy Chameleon*
don't miss Maggie Gibson's first novel

THE FLIGHT OF
LUCY SPOON

Available from Orion
ISBN: 0 57540 331 4
Price: £5.99

Chapter One

Lucy Spoon lay on her back and watched a penguin, wearing a sun hat, marching across the ceiling towards the window. The hat was new. It had appeared after a storm lifted a slate and the rain got in again. She turned on to her side and squinted at the damp patch. He was carrying a suitcase now. Maybe it was a sign.

Her ears were wet. Tears in my ears, she thought, and an ironic snigger escaped. Normal folk had tears in their eyes. Only she cried silently in the dark, lying on her back, staring at the ceiling, dreaming of escape.

A sudden draft flared the curtains and the bedroom door rattled. He stirred next to her, rolled on to his back and, after a certain amount of snuffling, continued to snore. Loud, epiglottal, slobbery, porcine snorts. In the dimness, she watched his chest rise and fall. He stirred again and smacked his lips, then took a rumbling breath and stopped, his chest fully expanded. Lucy waited. Hoped. How long before his brain would be starved of oxygen causing immediate brain damage and ultimately death? After ten seconds or so he exhaled like a Harley Davidson, and yanked the duvet off her as he rolled over on to his side again.

Rain lashed against the window and the wind battered the frame. It was cold. She shivered and tugged at the edge of the bedclothes, trying to reclaim a few inches. More slurping sounds from his side, then the cover slid back over her. She snuggled under it, holding it up around her ears. Her nose was freezing.

Wide awake now, she gave up and slid out of bed, grabbing her dressing-gown from the chair and wrapping it around her against the numbing cold. It felt damp. The mist on the Wicklow mountains left everything damp. At the bottom of the stairs she picked her sheepskin coat off the newel post and put it over the dressing-gown. Cold radiated up from the flagged floor through the soles of her thick woollen socks.

The kitchen was warm, though, and the old iron range still lit. She opened the door, threw on a shovel of fuel. Sparks flew as the coal hit the hot embers. She sat in front of the open door with her feet on the fender and warmed her hands and knees. Fionn, still drowsy, stretched herself and yawned. Lucy leaned over and scratched her behind the ear. The dog licked her hand, wagged her tail and went back to sleep. Too early. Too cold even to think of going outside for a pee.

After a while Lucy stood up and peeled off the sheepskin, dressing-gown, old shrunken cardie and flannel night-dress. The heat from the range hit her skin and she felt a wave of pleasure at the comfort of it. She dressed quickly in the layers of clothing she always wore. Knickers, leggings, two pairs of woollen tights with thick socks over the top, long-sleeved vest, deliciously warm from where she had hung it on the rack above the stove the night before, denim shirt, long heavy cotton skirt, hand-knit thick stripy jumper, ancient Timberland boots and fingerless gloves.

She heard a distant rumble of thunder, then the light dimmed and recovered. She pulled back the curtain and peered out into the darkness, hoping for lightning, but saw only her reflection in the glass. She ran her fingers through her hair, raking out the tangles. Warm now. Time for tea.

She filled the electric kettle and plugged it in.

Zzzapp! Two hundred and fifty volts shot up her arm, throwing her back against the dresser. Wallop! Dishes crashed to the floor and the milk jug shattered, splattering its contents up the walls and everywhere. The kettle bounced across the room. Fionn barked furiously in fright, hackles up.

Lucy sat dazed in a heap. Her left hand was numb and her arm still tingled.

Footsteps from the room above. Thump, thump, thump down the stairs, roaring, 'What the fuckin' hell's happening?' No, 'Are you OK?' No, 'Are you hurt, pet?'

She did hurt. Her back hurt where she'd collided with the sharp corner of the dresser, her ears were ringing and her head ached. She looked up at him. Then at the kettle, then hesitated.

'Em . . . nothing . . . I just slipped,' she said. 'Could you – could you put the kettle on?'

The dog padded over looking concerned. Lucy grabbed her collar.

His eyes were bloodshot from the night before and his hair was standing on end. A vision in off-white saggy long-johns. White flabby flesh. Angry with her for snatching him from sleep. Angry at the world for spoiling his life. Angry about everything.

He scratched his armpit. He scratched his beard and shook his head. 'Dozy stupid bitch,' he muttered as he bent to pick up the kettle and refilled it. Water gushed from the tap and splashed him, soaking the front of his vest.

'Clumsy fucking cretin. Now look what you made me fucking do.'

She flinched back as he reached towards the socket. She closed her eyes as he hit the switch. Then . . . nothing. He clicked the switch on, off. On, off. Nothing. That's when she knew that the bastard was fucking immortal.

At thirty-nine and three-quarters, Lucy Spoon was a little the worse for wear. Hippiedom doesn't sit well on the over thirties. A long road of too many drugs absorbed through the system, too much drink. Somewhere around the middle of the eighties, hippies metamorphosed into new-age travellers, and Lucy didn't travel. That was the trouble. She wanted

3

to get away. She wished with all her heart to be somewhere else, but she didn't know where. She had no idea how. Years of living with Marcus had drained her brain of rational constructive thought. Marcus had been a dreamer once. Now he lived his life in a state of disappointment and he was very, very angry.

They had met when she was nineteen. She was an art student in her second year at Hornsey College. She was good. Had talent. He was Irish. Ten years older. Had dropped out. They had met at the top of Glastonbury Tor. The Spring Solstice. Dawn. The sun rising, crimson and gold behind the ruins of the tower. She had followed him back to Ireland and they moved into a stone cottage an old uncle had left him in the Wicklow Hills. Very romantic. He'd been sexy then. Tall, slim and tanned. Had travelled the world, or so he said. Now she doubted that. Marcus only ever made grand plans. Impossible schemes to make his fortune. Their fortune. The trouble with Marcus was, he never had a realistic, achievable goal. Thus his disappointment.

There had been many projects through the years. There was the great candle scheme, for one. She was quite content making enough coloured carved candles to sell at the local market. But that wouldn't do. Painstakingly, Marcus had worked out how many candles she could produce in a given time, making moulds from her original carvings. He worked out to the penny how much profit they could make per candle. How rich they would be when he got the export market going. What grants they could get from the government. By the end of the day he was close to his second million. That was as far as it went. The plan had become so big and complicated it was impossible for him to settle for less. To do so would mean failure.

Another brainwave was the amazing foolproof individual ready-made trifle plan. One day Marcus found a case of small plastic beakers which had fallen off the back of a lorry (*really* fallen off the back of a lorry) and, for no apparent reason, decided that they should make individual trifles for

4

sale to the catering trade. He dragged Lucy round the Cash & Carry, and they stocked up on jelly and catering tins of custard powder and UHT cream. Marcus was full of enthusiasm as usual, though by this time Lucy, knowing his track record, had her doubts. She tried to reason with him, but he accused her of not having faith in him. Of being disloyal. Consumed with guilt, she helped him. He wasn't too happy when she suggested that maybe he was adding too much water to the jelly, or perhaps they should make smaller batches of custard. This time he played the 'I know what I'm doing, you're always criticising' card. The jelly wouldn't set. The cream wouldn't whip. The custard was lumpy. And she hadn't the heart or the courage to say I told you so. He sank into a deep depression and blamed her for the failure.

If Lucy looked back she would have had to agree that, although all of Marcus's other get-rich-quick schemes had come to nothing, the failure of the great foolproof ready-made individual trifle plan was the turning point. Marcus got angry. With her. With the world. With life in general. After that, everyone was thick/stupid/moronic. The world, including Lucy, was conspiring against him. Trying to ruin his life. He was the only sane and sensible person alive. She was the butt of his frustration. It was left to her to put a crust on the table and this she managed quite well. There were the candles. She sold eggs from her flock of chickens, all of whom had names. She grew organic vegetables on a little plot behind the house, and a small quantity of cannabis for their own consumption in pots on the living-room window-sill. She drew charcoal portraits for tourists in the summer and between times sold the odd canvas. He would sit outside the market and wait for her. He was jealous if she talked to anyone. Watched her like a hawk. Alienated all her friends. He was envious of her talent and belittled her work. Because of that, she lost confidence and stopped painting. He had her total attention. He made himself the centre of her universe, believing that this state of affairs was normal and acceptable.

The truth was that Marcus wasn't the centre of Lucy's

universe, at least not in the way he believed. Lucy was afraid of him. Terrified of his temper and his mood swings. Not that he ever raised a hand against her, but there was always that threat in the black screaming rages that consumed him without warning. They sapped her energy. Drained her emotions. Lucy would have been quite content with her lot if only Marcus had been nice to her. Even though she didn't love him any more; didn't even like him any more. But he couldn't be nice because he depended on her. He needed her to look after him. He required someone around whom he could blame. He couldn't do without her, and he hated and punished her for it.

Maybe it was the electric shock. Perhaps that was the straw that broke the camel's back. But, on Monday, 4 November, at six forty-five a.m., Lucy Spoon knew that she had to get away.

Chapter Two

Jodie McDeal rattled the key in the front door. The lock didn't budge. Puzzled, she checked to make sure she had the right key and tried again. Same result, or rather lack of a result. The door stayed firmly locked. She heard movement inside. The thought crossed her mind briefly that maybe it was a burglar, but she dismissed the idea immediately. No one in their right mind would dare to rob Rogan Hogan's woman. Not if they valued their lives. Not if they wanted to hold on to all their limbs and avoid brain damage. He wasn't called the Grim Reaper for nothing.

She peered at the lock, checking to see if there was an obstruction. Maybe the kids she'd told to sod off on Hallowe'en night had squirted superglue in it to get even. As she was poking at the lock, Gnasher Gill, Hogan's minder, general assassin and handyman opened the door. All six foot odd and twenty-nine million stone of him.

'What the hell are you doing in my house?' she demanded as she tried to push past him.

He stood four-square, filling the doorway. 'Sorry,' he said, sounding far from it. 'More'n my job's worth.'

'Piss off, you pig-thick eejit.' She shoved him in the chest, but he didn't budge. He stood there with his arms folded across his chest. He had a smug smirk on his face, and his lizardy eyes gave him a look of a python who'd just swallowed a goat. Any minute she expected a forked tongue to flick out between his podgy lips.

Two can play at that game, she thought. She delved into

7

her bag and rooted out her phone. But he didn't react. Just stood there sneering at her. Was he tired of living? Had the last atom of grey matter in what passed as his brain given up the ghost? She glared at him, and started to dial Hogan's number.

Gnasher swiped the phone from her hand. 'You don't geddit, do yeh? Yer out.'

'What?' She was angry with him now. You can only make so many excuses for the brain dead. 'Give me back my frigging phone, you moron!' She thumped his chest as hard as she could. He didn't notice. He held the phone up in the air, way out of her reach. She resisted the urge to jump up and down in a vain attempt to grab it.

'Yeh won't be needin' it. Misther Hogan's got a young wan, an' you're history. He's taken her on the holliers.' In the telling she felt he exhibited more glee than was kind in the circumstances.

It stopped her in her tracks.

'What are you talking about? What d'you mean, a young wan – one? What do you mean history?' As she spoke, the truth dawned. If what Rogan's ape was saying was for real, she had just been dumped. Unceremoniously, cruelly, without any warning, dumped. He must have planned it. The locks changed and her only out of the house for an hour? The bastard! The unspeakable bastard.

Realising brute force wouldn't get her past Gnasher, she decided to try charm. 'OK, Gnasher,' she said calmly. 'I get the message. Just let me go inside and pack my things.'

Gnasher looked uncertain. He hadn't expected this. He'd been looking forward to having an excuse to give her a good smack. 'Sorry. No can do,' he said.

'But it's my stuff, Gnasher' – still trying to be reasonable. 'I need my clothes. My bits and pieces.'

He ignored that. 'An' I'll need the keys fer the Merc.'

To hell with charm. She exploded. 'The Merc? Are you out of your tiny mind? I'm not giving you the keys of my fucking car!'

8

'It's Misther Hogan's car, s'not yours.'

'It is mine!' – indignant.

'S'not.'

This was getting her nowhere. She spun on her heel and fled down the path. Possession is nine-tenths of the law, she thought, leaping into her car and speeding away. Gnasher made a token gesture of chasing her, but she saw he was laughing when she looked in the rear-view mirror. He was standing in the road, looking after her, helpless with mirth. Maybe it was all a joke? Naaaah. Not even Gnasher would be that stupid. OK, granted she and Rogan had had a few rows lately, but no more than usual.

As she always did, Jodie rationalised. It was all a big misunderstanding. She would go and see Rogan and sort it out. She might have to humour him, but so be it. If that was what it took, she'd humour him. Even apologise – maybe. A bit of wheedling would bring him round, as it always did. Pander to one of his favourite fantasies. He was putty in her hands when it came to her creative and unusual sex games.

Then she had second thoughts. Perhaps it would be better to talk to him on the phone first. If Gnasher was right, and he did have a young one . . . What did he mean, *Young One*? She was young. She was only twenty-six. That was young – wasn't it? She pulled the car in to the kerb and looked at her reflection in the vanity mirror. I am young, she thought. I am beautiful. Everyone says so. Why would he want someone else? She wanted to cry. *Get a grip*! Rogan was playing games. He didn't have another woman.

She had been Rogan's woman for six years. OK, so he had a wife, but *she* was his woman. *She* was the one he loved, inasmuch as Rogan could love anyone.

Rogan – aka Rogue, tee-hee, his little joke – Hogan was the Godfather of South Dublin crime. Nothing happened that he didn't know about. Apart from his drugs empire, protection racket and prostitution network, all criminals working within his domain paid their dues. Every robbery, burglary, bank or post office job on his turf was within his gift, and heaven help anyone who ignored that not insubstantial fact. There was guarded talk of people being nailed to floors and skinned alive.

They remember the pain.

They had met in one of his clubs. Always a party animal, she knew how to have a good time and wasn't about to let the small detail of no money affect her social life. She had run away from home when she was seventeen after her father caught her in bed with – whatever his name was. She couldn't remember. She never got on with her father. He hated her. She looked too much like her mother. Her mother, who ran off with the neighbour's husband when she was ten.

'Like mother, like daughter,' he had said, as he stood in the doorway of her room. He wasn't even angry. She was mortified. Not because he had caught her *in flagrante*. It was the look of total distaste and disgust on his face. After what's-'is-name had legged it, she packed her things, took her Post Office Savings book and thumbed a lift to Dublin.

She had seen him eyeing her up as she stood at the bar. Her original intention had been to bum a night's drinking out of him and maybe a bite to eat, but he overwhelmed her with his charm and generosity. He was a good fifteen years older than any man she had been involved with previously, and she loved the way he treated her, opening doors, pulling out her chair for her, holding her coat. She wasn't slow to observe the way other people's attitudes changed towards her when it was realised that she was his woman. An apartment, an allowance, credit cards, a decent car soon followed. She had a good idea how he earned a crust but didn't ask questions. She enjoyed the reflected glory and it beat the hell out of life in a small country town. And it was fun. No more Miss Selfridge. No more Penny's. No more Dunnes Stores. He only wanted to see her in designer labels. Brown Thomas charge card. Three holidays a year.

Then he got her to mule for him. She had been afraid at first. Bags of drugs taped to her body. Only three or four times a year, but she always travelled first class. Always with the Louis Vuitton. Flashing the Cartier watch. Sashaying along on the Gucci four-inch heels. And she got away with it. It was exciting. It turned her on. Rogan had the added bonus that she was so turned on by the danger that she was always gagging for sex when she got back from a trip. One time he suggested that she pose as a pregnant mother. She sailed through customs with four kilos of one-hundred-per-cent-pure, best Colombian Smack cunningly concealed in her bump. She felt her masterstroke was packing her case full of Baby Gap and declaring it in the red channel.

Now that really turned her on. Rogan thought all his birthdays had come at once.

Then one very close shave brought her back down to earth with a terrifying thump. It started when a butch-looking female customs officer, who resembled someone who would probably be involved in ethnic cleansing given half the chance, took, in Jodie's view, an irrational dislike to her. OK, so maybe she shouldn't have clicked her heels and given the Nazi salute, and it probably would have been wiser not to have made the comment about superfluous facial hair. Later, Jodie put it down to an adrenalin overload, extreme turbulence over the Atlantic and too much free champagne quaffed on the flight from Acapulco. Only fast talking and a certain amount of humble grovelling prevented a body search and a full rubber gloves job. It took Jodie past the point of turn-on, to cold, spine-numbing, knickers-wetting fear.

When she got through to Arrivals, she raced to the Ladies and threw up. Rogan thought she was over-reacting, but she refused to mule again. He tried to talk her round, but she refused. The honeymoon was over. He gave her a beating. Humiliated and mortified that anyone would see her with a black eye and bruising to the body, she ran away to a luxury health spa, pretending to the other guests that she was recovering from a road traffic accident. He, by this time was missing her, or rather her creative carnal arts. When he tracked her down, he begged her to come home. He promised he'd never touch her again, but something in her had died.

She had grown up, and fast. She had learned what her assets were and how to use them. How to keep him where she wanted him. Or so she had thought until now.

This was a whole new ball game.

She drove on a little way and stopped at a call box. She tried all his numbers but got no reply.

Humph, she thought. So he thinks he can dump me, does he? Wait till he comes crawling back, begging for it. I'll show him.

She put the car in gear and drove to the Shelbourne, where she booked a suite. After a long hot bath and room service she went shopping. Well, all her clothes were being held hostage by Gnasher Gill. What else could she do?

One hour and forty minutes' retail therapy in BT's designer department, trying on Donna Karan and Louise Kennedy, improved her mood no end. She picked out a forest-green Louise Kennedy suit, with trade mark scarf, a bitter-chocolate six-piece capsule wardrobe from DKNY (she felt obliged, what with brown being the new black) a charcoal-grey John Rocha trouser-suit, and a couple of pairs of obscenely expensive Manolo Blahnik shoes, just for spite. She had the saleslady bring up four sets of her favourite La Perla undies and half a dozen pairs of tights at twenty-five quid a shot. That'll show the bastard not to mess with me.

She handed over the BT Privileged Customer card. Better than sex, she thought. Well, better than sex with Rogan Hogan anyway!

That was when she discovered that she was in trouble. Real trouble.

'I'm sorry, madam,' the saleslady said, with a certain amount of embarrassment. 'But I'm afraid this card is no longer valid.'

'What do you mean, no longer valid?'

'Erm . . . It's been cancelled. Look.' The saleslady pointed at the VDU on top of the discreet cash desk. 'Sorry . . .'

Jodie didn't need to look. It was obvious what had happened. Rogan bloody Hogan had cancelled her Privileged

Customer card. Her stomach tied itself into a knot. She feigned surprise.

'I'm sure it's just an oversight,' the saleslady fluttered. 'How about a credit card?'

Jodie didn't want to chance having her gold card confiscated. She rummaged in her wallet, then shook her head. 'Don't seem to have it with me. Tell you what, you keep my parcels here at the till, and I'll pop home and get it.' She was burning with embarrassment. How could he?

It was a sure bet that if the rat had cancelled one card, he'd have cancelled them all. She ran up Grafton Street to the nearest ATM and stuffed her bank card in the slot. Her worst fears were realised. Her account held the princely sum of three pounds fifty. He'd stopped her allowance too.

She retrieved her bank card, stuffed her gold card into the wall and punched in her pin number. Maybe she'd be lucky and the machine would spit out some cash. No such luck. It swallowed the plastic whole and refused to give it back.

Jodie McDeal retreated to her suite to lick her wounds and draw up a battle plan.

All Orion/Phoenix titles are available at your local bookshop or from the following address:

Mail Order Department
Littlehampton Book Services
FREEPOST BR535
Worthing, West Sussex, BN13 3BR
telephone 01903 828503, *facsimile* 01903 828802
e-mail MailOrders@lbsltd.co.uk
(Please ensure that you include full postal address details)

Payment can be made either by credit/debit card (Visa, Mastercard, Access and Switch accepted) or by sending a £ Sterling cheque or postal order made payable to *Littlehampton Book Services*.
DO NOT SEND CASH OR CURRENCY.

Please add the following to cover postage and packing

UK and BFPO:
£1.50 for the first book, and 50p for each additional book to a maximum of £3.50

Overseas and Eire:
£2.50 for the first book plus £1.00 for the second book and 50p for each additional book ordered

---

BLOCK CAPITALS PLEASE

name of cardholder ....

address of cardholder ....

....

....

....

postcode ....

delivery address
(if different from cardholder)

....

....

....

....

postcode ....

☐ I enclose my remittance for £..

☐ please debit my Mastercard/Visa/Access/Switch (delete as appropriate)

card number ⬜⬜⬜⬜⬜⬜⬜⬜⬜⬜⬜⬜⬜⬜⬜⬜

expiry date ⬜⬜⬜⬜   Switch issue no. ⬜⬜

signature ....

prices and availability are subject to change without notice